When Blood Meets Earth

E.A Noble

For permissions, inquiries, or other requests, please contact:

E.A. Noble @ theeajournal.me

Cover Design by Miblart

Formatting by AB Book Services

Editor: Sylas Seabrook

Proofreading by Priscillah Bancy

Music produced by Matt Welchaus

Art by Nick Dunlap

ISBN: 979-8-9887908-2-2 (eBook Edition)

ISBN: 979-8-9887908-1-5 (Paperback Edition)

ISBN: 979-8-9887908-0-8 (Hardback Edition)

DRI

SUN

KI

Cheers to a great read!

To my readers: Y'all are amazing, and I mean that from the bottom of my heart. You've kept me going, stuck with me through all the changes, and continue to inspire me.

To Chloe Pacifico: Your belief in me kept me from giving up. I truly appreciate you! You deserve all the flowers.

To Tonja K. Johnson: Thank you for studying with me, teaching me, and helping me strengthen my pen. In the words of one of my favorites, "I was not born with a whole lot of natural talent, but I work hard, and I never give up! That is my gift. That is my Ninja way!" -Rock Lee.

To Mo Flames and K. McCoy: For those late nights in the writing studio, falling asleep at the keyboard, and still pushing through—thank you for being there at the start, let's get to the end...together.

To all of you: Thank you for sticking beside me and loving my debut novel. When I no longer have the strength to carry myself, it is my community who gathers around me and carries me toward the finish line.

This is only the beginning.

Pronunciation Guide

Agrim Tagore – ah·grim tah·gore

Attali Benideeve – ah·tah·lee ben·ee·deev

Axiom – ax·ee·om

Bellamy – bell·ah·mee

BOOM – boom

Bunko – bun·ko

Candia Dricon – can·dee·ah dri·con

Data – day·tah

Diyo – dye·yo

David Dricon – da·vid dri·con

Everest Tagore Abiola – ev·er·est tah·gore ah·bee·o·lah

Evna – ev·nah

Fia – fee·ah

Glaydecee – glay·dee·cee

Julian – ju·lee·en

Keon Thakur – key·on thah·koor

Whynonna Benideeve – why·no·nah ben·ee·deev

Malakey – mal·ah·key

Mesala – mee·sah·lah

Minks – mee·nks

Oneo – o·neigh·o

Oyame Abiola – o·yah·mee ah·bee·o·lah

Quande – kwun·day

Rico – ree·ko

Rwju – roo·ju

Sarue – sah·roo

Silvia – sill·vee·ah

Teka – tee·kah

Theolo Thakur – thee·o·lo thah·koor

Twoa – tway (too·way, one syllable)

Venus – veen·nus

Wallay Davient – wall·aye day·vee·ent

Yemi the Horse – yee·mee

Zef Coe – zef ko

Glossary

Amplifier – A device used to amplify voices. It can be placed on the throat or in front of the mouth.

Bartees – Some say the original meaning comes from a combination of *bartender* and *tease*. Bartees work at taphouses and are responsible for serving drinks and providing entertainment.

Blood Elite – A small division of the Shadow Army under the direct control of Agrim Tagore.

Blood Wine – A common alcoholic beverage in the Reaper Kingdom.

Blood-Control – A rare ability used to control others through their blood. Typically stems from Reaperborns.

Booster – A red liquid designed to magnify a user's gifts.

Council of Amalgamation (C.O.A.) – A council that unites the Seven Kingdoms to form a unified government.

Doyen – A term for grandparents. Variations include:

- *Doyen-ma* (grandmother)
- *Doyen-pa* (grandfather)
- *Doyen mama* (great-grandmother)
- *Doyen papa* (great-grandfather)

Drisunki – A bar drinking game. The term can also be used to mean "cheers!"

Erba – The selected one; the inherited one.

Extinguisher – A blue liquid used to extinguish manifestations.

Fer l'amor – A protected mate. This title is used by the upper class as a formal acknowledgment and protection for a lover. It is an honorable title, and the titleholder often works closely with the spouse to navigate their relationship. Once the *fer l'amor* title is given, the holder cannot take another title or have another lover. This specialized title can only be given to one person by the title giver. *Fer l'amors* must be cared for by the title giver for the rest of their lives. (Typically used among the highly upper class.)

Gifted/Ungifted – *Gifted*: A person born with manifestations. / *Ungifted*: A person born without manifestations.

Griffes – Giant birds with curved black beaks and massive red talons. Commonly found in the Reaper Kingdom, they can also be trained to work with the Reaper Army.

Intertwined – When two manifestations (usually of the same gift) combine to create a greater manifestation.

Redux – A sect of Fireborns who have renounced King David Dricon and vowed never to take up arms in war against other kingdoms.

Shadow Assassin – A division of the Reaper Army specializing in stealth and eliminating assigned targets. Typically works directly under the Reaper Queen.

Shadow Kiss – A common gesture among Reaper families where their shadows lightly tap each cheek.

Taphouse – A more upscale version of a tavern. Some taphouses also offer lodging.

Uma – Paid staff who work in palaces, castles, or private homes.

Wessie – A derogatory term for Fireborns. The origin of the term is unknown.

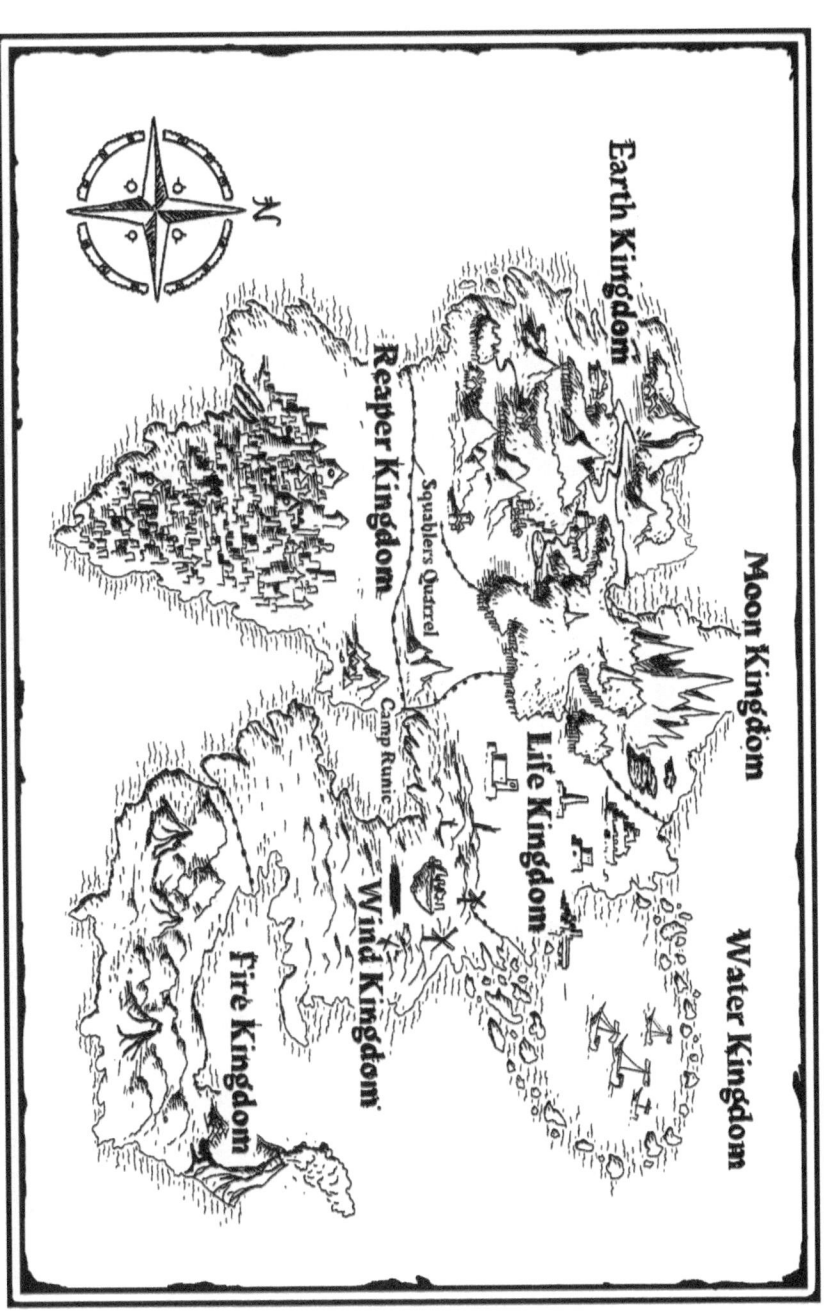

Contents

Act I

I

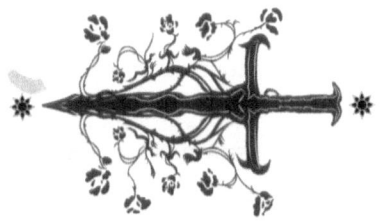

"If curiosity killed the cat, then ambition brought it back."
Proverb 7:02 from the Book of Face, Mortem Era

IT'S NOT A MATTER OF IF, BUT WHEN...

My gifts will manifest. This meant I could open my Mother's earthbox with a simple flick of my wrist and rip away the vines, roots, and branches that protected the secret buried inside.

That day was not today. Standing over my father's desk in his office, I held the box in my hand and shook it. Was I not my mother's daughter? Her emerald-green eyes matched mine. The mark of an Earthborn with immense power. Yet, I didn't feel powerful. I was ungifted, and many people viewed the ungifted as weak. I was far from weak.

Clutching the earthbox, I bit down on my bottom lip and dug my nails in between the taproots. I yanked on one branch. "Open, you stupid box!"

"You're going to break it," Everest said, scanning Father's bookshelves.

I glared at her, trying my damndest to figure out why my eighteen-year-old baby sister could manifest and I couldn't at twenty!

"How is it possible to break an earthbox? This thing is double fortified by heart roots from the oldest white oak tree in all the Seven Kingdoms." I pushed the chair out from underneath the desk and flopped into it.

"Did you know roots are so strong that they can grow through rocks?" Everest pulled a book from the shelf and opened it. "Trees can also communicate by exchanging chemicals." She glanced up from the book and turned to me. "See, underground, there's this entire root system where they speak through fungi and when a tree recognizes its family, it can offer things like nutrients and sometimes even warnings for what's to come." She snapped the book shut and placed it back on the shelf.

I stared at her. She looked like every bit of our Earthborn Mother. Golden brown skin like sandy soil with hair like red clay. Today, she had chosen tiny featherfews to decorate her rounded afro. Like Mother, she wore traditional Earthborn clothing, which was the same as saying she wore little to nothing at all. The thin yellow cotton skirt split into two slits on the sides that came up to her waist. To match it, she wore a tiny cotton bandeau that complimented her petite figure.

"And what does any of that information have to do with me getting into this earthbox?" I punched the box to the edge of the desk.

"Everything." She strutted my way and scooped up the earthbox. "As Earthborns, that's how we communicate to the living earth around us."

"By fungi?" I was unimpressed.

"No, dummy. By an exchange of chemicals." Everest placed the earthbox on the mahogany glass surface. "Maybe if you spent more time studying instead of sneaking off to fight, then you would have manifested already."

"And this is coming from the princess who spends her time on her knees, licking boots and kissing the noble's asses?"

Everest shrugged. "I would rather be that than the princess with the reputation of spending her time on her back."

"Are you calling me a whore?" I leaned in.

Everest adjusted her featherfews. "All I'm saying is, most problems should be figured out by intellect and not physicality, big sister." She stroked a finger on a vine alongside the box. The vine shuddered, almost unfolding at her touch.

If I were an honest woman, I would admit that she might be right. I would also admit that I couldn't care less about Earthborn gifts. I hated my emerald-green eyes and what they represented for my future. A future that was already planned out since I was spat out of my Mother's womb. I was half Reaperborn. Daughter of the greatest general known to the Seven Kingdoms. Yet, here I was, giftless, weak, and a disappointment to both lineages of my family.

"Well," I said, rising from the chair. "Tell that to all the kids I had to beat up on your behalf since physicality is never an answer to a problem." My arm itched, and I instinctively scratched it.

Everest clicked her tongue, slapping at my hands. "Did you not put on your cream today? You've been scratching like crazy lately. It's making me itch," she said, brushing her painted nails on her skin.

"Of course I did. I put it on daily. It's just been getting worse." I rolled up a black sleeve to monitor the skin underneath. The skin was cracked and scaly; the ash lines showed up even whiter on my rich ebony skin.

I yanked my sleeve down. *Shit.* "Anyway, are you going to help me open this box or stand there and continue to be a thorn in my side, Eve?"

Everest sat on the edge of the desk, stroking the earthbox. "And what's in it for me?" Her lashes batted like hummingbird wings.

I tucked my arm underneath my breast. "Why does everything have to be give and take? Why can't you just help me without an outstretched palm?"

"Because that's how the courts work, Bellamy! And if you spent more time doing the duties of the eldest daughter rather than spending all your time with Quande, then you would know that, Bee!"

I huffed. *And the truth comes out.* "Are you jealous because I spend more time with Quande than you?"

"No." She poked out her bottom lip.

I smirked. "You are, aren't you?"

"I'm not." She quickly stood, avoiding eye contact.

"Just admit it, Eve. You want me around more."

"I don't. Never did. You'd just get in the way, as usual." She glided over to the map of the Seven Kingdoms. Her foot tapped on the hardwood as she pretended to study the synthetic paper.

"Okay, fine," I said, slowly walking behind her. My five-foot-eight frame standing over her five-foot-five one. "What is it you want from me?"

"Tonight, at the Reaper Festival," she began without the slightest hesitation, "allow me to stand beside Mother and take over the duties of the next crowned queen of the Earth Kingdom."

I studied the map of the Seven Kingdoms, wishing I could travel to see the world. But I was never permitted to. The Reaper Kingdom was all I knew. To be the next queen of the Earth Kingdom and rule over a place I'd never seen or been to was the opposite of what I wanted for my life. I was Reaper-born, through and through. If anything, tonight's festival was a celebration of my people, our customs, and traditions. There was no place I would rather be.

"Bellamy." Everest turned to me, her dark brown eyes meeting mine. "I'm asking for just one thing."

I let out a sigh. "Even if I could, I can't *not* show up. Mother would murder me. This is the only year the Reaper Queen allowed her to host the festival for the court. We all have to be on our best behavior."

"I know that." Everest pouted. "I'm not saying don't show up completely. What I'm proposing is to show your face, mingle with the crowd, and then, when no one is looking, wander off to the great abyss or to the Moon Kingdom for all I care. The point is, if Mother isn't able to find you, she chooses me, Bee. Please."

I hate it when she uses big brown puppy eyes on me. I fold like a lawn chair every single time.

"You know," I said, walking to the desk. "You should have been the firstborn." I picked up the earthbox.

"Being the firstborn is pointless if the Earth Spirit still doesn't gift me with emerald-greens."

I nodded, knowing my eyes were the only thing that kept

7

me in good graces with my Mother. "Not having emerald-greens doesn't make you any less powerful or any less Earth-born." I handed the box over to her.

"And yet, your eyes alone are the only thing that qualifies you for the throne."

"Ouch."

"It's true." She shook the box to her ear. "What's in this box, anyway?"

"A gun."

Everest dropped her shoulders. "We have been in here this entire time to look at some ancient relic? Are you serious, Bee?"

"Deadly so." I gave her puppy eyes this time.

"For the sake of the Spirits, the old world is dead."

"I disagree." I scratched. "People still sing songs about guns, wars, and a time before the Mortem Era when the world was split into seven continents." I rushed to the map, tracing lines in between sections of the Seven Kingdoms. "Can you believe that? The world was spread out into seven pieces, and they had things like flying metal birds to take people from one place to another."

"Those are myths and folklore. It isn't true, Bee."

"It is, Eve. They say if one looked closely, one could see the dancing of the old world within the threads of a woman's skirt."

"Who's they?"

"Philosophers, Moonreaders, theorists. I don't know. You're the smart one, remember. Me dumb one, me get things done by brute force." I beat my chest.

Everest rolled her eyes. "And the next thing you'll try and convince me is that Fireborns are favored by the Spirits."

"Maybe they are. Maybe times are changing." I dropped my smile.

"Blasphemy." Everest laughed and sauntered away.

"Open the box. If I'm wrong, I will do as you want me to.

Show my face at the Reaper Festival. Say my hellos, steal a couple of rolls from the dinner table, and vanish into the night." I dusted my hand clean.

"You added a few things, but fine. Deal." Everest held out her palm.

I shook it.

She placed the earthbox on the desk. "Mother created this. She's one of the most powerful Earthborns I know. Just give me a moment." Everest cracked her knuckles and licked her bottom lip. She inhaled, then slowly exhaled, waving her fingers over the earthbox.

The sunbeams from the window cascaded over the desk, highlighting the chestnut of the roots and branches and the forest green of the vines and leaves. I observed a faint flickering of light from Everest's fingertips as the shimmering particles dusted over the earthbox. The roots and branches bent and shivered like a dog shaking itself from water. She was communicating, and the branches were speaking in return. The last of the roots stretched out and laid gently on the mahogany desk.

At the center lay something wrapped in cloth. I slowly undid the pieces, my heart leaping in anticipation. As I unwrapped the last fold, I stopped. My nose scrunched and my eyes narrowed. "What the fuck is that?"

Everest snickered. "What? You're not happy?" She laughed, looking from me to the object in the center.

I dug my fist into my eyes to make sure I was seeing this right. Double checking—no, triple checking—the anticlimactic display, I curled my fist. All this sneaking around in Father's office to see a real gun from Mortem Era, the death age, only to be met with an earthbox enclosed with tubes of red and blue liquids?

I picked one up, a red tube with liquid that bubbled when flipped upside down. "Seriously, what the fuck is this?"

"Don't shake it. If it's in the earthbox, that means whatever it is shouldn't be trifled with," Everest said through laughter.

"This isn't funny."

"Oh, but it is. You should see your face right now. Wait a minute, let me just..." Everest leaped from the chair, grabbed a fist full of air, and raised it to my chin. "There, your jaw is reconnected." She giggled.

I was pissed, and if Everest didn't stop cackling like a screaming cat, I was going to punch her square in the nose. *Would it solve the problem? No. Would it make me feel better? Considerably.*

Wiping tears from her eyes, Everest leaned against the desk. "I guess this means no Reaper Festival for you then?" She giggled.

I glared. Before I could send her a wave of curses that would shame the vulgarest of women, a loud stomp followed by incoherent muttering echoed from the end of the hallway.

My sister and I both froze, knowing those mad protests only came from one individual. In unison, we blurted out, "Glaydecee."

Glaydecee was the oldest uma in the palace and was known to whoop my Father's butt when he was a kid. A hit from that eighty-year-old hand would bring the strongest Blood Elite to their knees.

"Hurry. Put it back together!" I shouted in a hushed tone, gathering the tubes of liquid and wrapping them in their case.

"I'm trying," Everest said, already forcing the roots to weave in place. It was sloppy, but it would have to do.

"You're breaking it." One root popped. "Don't shatter the tubes," I commanded.

"Shut up! Let me work." Everest had her tongue popped out as she made the earthbox whole.

I snatched the earthbox from the desk and tucked it into the safe behind the portrait of the Seven Kingdoms.

Everest whined. "She can't catch us here. My ass still hurts from two years ago when she popped me."

Tears welled in her eyes. She bounced on her tiptoes, looking every bit of my baby sister. I searched the room and spotted the window. I ran to it, unlocked the hatch, and threw open the shutters.

Down we go then.

Glaydecee's muttering grew closer.

"Like old times, sister?" I said, pointing out the window.

"Like old times." She rushed across the office.

There're seven vines along this side of the palace. "Tangle them together and bring them to us. Make it fast!" I commanded.

Everest went to work. Watching her gather the vines to create a large one almost made me long for my manifestation. Despite not having the emerald-greens, my baby sister was a force to be reckoned with.

"Done," she said, right as the office door burst open.

"Who's in here?" Glaydecee's voice sounded like crumpling paper. She was partially blind in both eyes, but there was no doubt she could see us from a mile away.

"After you, Eve."

Everest didn't wait two seconds before she was out the window, sliding down the vines.

Glaydecee turned the office corner, her dress hiked in her fist. "Come here, you sneaky brat!"

I smiled, already grabbing hold of the vine. The adrenaline pumped through my veins.

Glaydecee clapped her hand, and black smoke shot out like a lasso. I loosened my grip on the vines, allowing my weight and gravity to pull me down quickly before her shadow could reach me. When I hit the ground, Glaydecee's body was half out the window, her shadow drawing back into her palms.

"You don't think she will take the vine, do you?" Everest asked, new leaves clinging to her afro.

"Just in case she does, we better get to running," I said, waving at Glaydecee.

The uma pumped her fist. "Your Father will hear of this!" she said, screaming from the fourth floor of the palace.

We took off running. The squealing of the old uma was drowned out by our laughter.

II

"Who is born wise? Let them speak."
Proverb 96:08 from the Book of Face, Mortem Era.

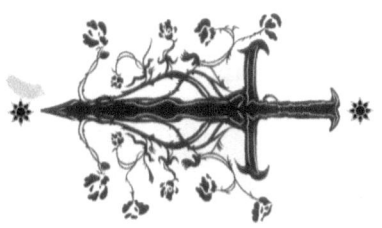

WE TURNED THE CORNER to the west side of the palace. Everest's giggles were like wind chimes to my ears. I closed my eyes and listened to the quiet laughter of my sister's voice. When I opened my eyes, she was ten again, and I was twelve. Transported back to a time when we could let down our

13

hair and soar under the wings of doves. We imagined fighting dragons and becoming a part of our father's army. I, a Blood Elite, and Everest, a shadow assassin. We would take over the world together. Rule the kingdoms in peace by defeating the Fire Kingdom once and for all.

I blinked and my vision returned to the present as we collided with the prince of the Reaper Kingdom.

"Princess Everest," he said, holding her in his arms, like she was a celestial being that had fallen from the sky.

May the Spirits rest.

I dug my nails into my itchy palm, attempting to catch my breath.

"Prince Theolo." She beamed, making herself far too comfortable in his grasp. "When did you arrive?" Everest, leaning dramatically, reached out her hand to him. He took it, bending to kiss it, before finally releasing her to stand.

Prince Theolo tucked a purple umbrella under his arm, which matched his bright purple shirt with ruffles. Tight black dress pants and bright purple shoes completed the outfit. His wardrobe was further enhanced with his signature hairstyle, a sleek swirl of black hair plastered to his forehead. I wanted to throw water on him. But I must admit, the shoes were nice, and they didn't deserve such hostility.

"I arrived just now. Your queen is being escorted to her quarters as we speak."

Queen Keon Thakur, Theolo's mother, The Reaper Queen. The scariest bitch walking in all the kingdoms.

Theolo, as if just realizing my presence, side-eyed me. "Bellamy," he said, as if my name was a wad of spit in his mouth.

"Theolo."

"It's Prince Theolo."

"And it's Princess Bellamy."

He looked at me head-on, moving his umbrella to the opposite side.

"You look..." His eyes trailed my body.

I wanted to close myself off, but I refused to bend under his scrutiny.

"You look as you usually look. All black and drab."

"Why, thank you." I mockingly curtsied. "And you look..." I took my time appraising the height of his long skeletal frame. The perfect picture of casket ready. "Like you're late for a funeral."

"I am," he said matter-of-factly. "The laying to rest of your ungodly resolutions to what you call a fashion sense."

I laughed, letting his insult roll off my shoulder and onto the ground.

"And that," I gestured to him, "was what you decided to wear? You might as well take the shovel out back and bury yourself."

Theolo smiled, but it was the type of smile that was somewhere in between smelling someone's stank breath and holding back a fart. That made me laugh more. Theolo dropped his umbrella and took a step forward. My sister jumped in between us.

"I love your choice of fashion," she said, rubbing his shoulder. Theolo paused, glancing at Everest. His face eased into the porcelain mask of pride and dignity, his chin pointing toward the sky.

"Of course, you do, Princess Everest. At least one sister was born with decorum. It doesn't surprise me it was the better-looking one of the two." He winked at her.

My laughter stopped.

No, this goat-fucking corpse didn't just go there.

His thin red lips curled as if he knew he had ruffled me.

"Prince," my sister interrupted before I could retort, "I

would love to show you some new installments we have made in preparation for tonight's Reaper Festival. That's if you have time," Everest said, bowing slightly.

"I have all the time for you, my sweet."

"Okay." I cut in. "My breakfast is about to make an entrance any moment now."

"Good, then maybe you can make an out-trance as it takes your place." Prince Theolo popped open his umbrella, blocking out the hot reaper sun.

Everest cut me off with a wave of her finger.

"One moment, Prince Theolo." Everest reached back and yanked my forearm. "May I have a quick word with you, sister?" she said, not waiting for my response. She dragged me behind her, and I almost forgot how strong she was. We were a good distance away from Theolo before we stopped.

"Must you show your backside every time the prince arrives?" Everest chastised.

"He started it."

"Let me guess, you must finish it?"

"Umm, yea. That's how that typically works."

"No. No, it doesn't. You forget, Bee, that you are not a commoner, a peasant, an uma, or some village dweller. You are the next Queen of the Earth Kingdom, and you must present yourself as such."

"Why are you getting on me? Are you going to have the same talk with him?"

Everest folded her arms. Her head jerked as if I just hit her with information she didn't anticipate.

"It's not my job to correct him."

"But somehow you think it's your job to put me in my place?" I sucked my teeth.

"Yes, you are my sister. It is my duty to remind you that the bonds we make today will mean everything for the future of our people."

"And what bonds do I need to make with the prince of all things piss and horse shit?"

"One day, he will be the Reaper King. That means he will have the power of the greatest army under his belt. That includes Father."

I flinched at the mention of my father.

"You need to stop with these childish games and start thinking more long-term. Make peace with the prince."

"What would you suggest I do, Eve? Stroke his ego and eat his ass for dinner?"

"If that would solidify the bond, then yes."

"May the Spirits rest. Are you serious right now?"

"Deadly so." Everest reached out and pinched the side of my belly.

I swiped her hand away. "What was that for?"

"To remind you that while you're alive, you must be wise, Bee."

"Oh," I mocked. "Look at the baby sister teaching the big sister."

"Bee, I am serious."

"I don't like the way he looks at you." I changed the subject. I wanted to get what really made me sick off my chest.

"How does he look at me?" Everest reached one finger to the back of her hair and started twirling a curl around her finger.

"He looks at you like he wants to devour you or something. Like you're his juicy strawberry, ripe for plucking. I hate it."

Everest abandoned twirling her hair. Instead, she took one finger and tapped it on her bottom lip. "You think he desires me?" Her eyelashes fluttered.

I stepped back to look at her, my mouth gaped slightly. "You like his flirtations?"

"Well..." she sang.

"Well, what? What about the importer's son? What's his name, Kash? Kash Porter?" I raised my voice so it would echo against the steel towers.

Everest grabbed my arms, looking backward towards Theolo. He stood, umbrella over his head. With a handkerchief in hand, he dusted off the garden bench before sitting down.

Everest turned, her voice low. "Shut up!" she said.

"What? Afraid he will hear me? I thought you liked the importer's son."

Everest pulled me farther down the path of the steel towers. "I like him as in, he's here for now, but not here for later. For goodness' sake, Bee. He is the importer's son. Do you think I, a princess, will spend the rest of my days with a man who deals in bringing services and goods across the kingdom's line?"

"Yea, if you love him."

"Love?" Everest laughed. "You really do live in the realm of the Spirits. Do you think we are afforded love?"

"Father and Mother—"

Everest cut me off. "Father and Mother are a great example of what not to do. Mother was all but kicked out of her kingdom for choosing Father. The only title she has to her name is High Priestess of the Earth Temple. Ruler over a bunch of religious Earth worshiping nuts."

"Religious Earth-worshiping nuts that you and I will pledge to at the age of twenty-one," I added. "Or have you forgotten, in order to take the throne, you must be pledged to the Earth Temple?"

Everest sighed. "That's not the point I'm trying to make."

"Then what is your point? Make it quick because I'm bored."

Everest glanced over her shoulder, then back to me. "We already have a mark on our records. We are mixed-bloods. How many ruling monarchs do you know that are mixed-blood?" She crossed her arms, waiting for my answer.

I didn't have one.

"Exactly, and there's a reason for that. Could you imagine if you received the Reaperborn gifts instead of Earthborn gifts?"

Of course, I could. I had imagined being Reaperborn all my life — to adorn the battle black of the Reaper Kingdom's military uniform, to stand with the army whose very name sent fear down an enemy's spine. But how could I tell my sister that's all I ever imagined? Instead, I shook my head.

"Exactly. It would be a disaster if a Reaperborn sat on an Earthborn throne. Loyalty, Bellamy. Stay close to our kingdom. Earth is rooted in soul." She gave the Earth Kingdom pledge.

I narrowed my eyes. "Do you mean *my* kingdom?" I tested her.

Everest straightened her shoulders, looking every bit like our Mother. "Of course, sister. Your kingdom, to which I will help rule. Or do you really think you could do it alone?"

My sister was the brains, born with wisdom I couldn't even begin to possess. I was born with the strength and the ability to fight toe to toe with anyone bold enough to test me.

"Of course not, sister." I licked my lips.

"Good," she said, reaching up to smooth out my hair. "You look too Reaperborn as is." She stroked my wavy black strands. "You should braid this. Give it some tighter curls."

I grabbed my hair out of her grasp. "Listen," I said, gently touching her shoulder. "Promise me you won't take heed of that selfish creep's request to court you."

"You have my word, sister. I wouldn't marry Theolo if he

were the last man on Earth. My loyalty is to our throne." I released her, satisfied with her proclamation.

Everest slapped my hand. "Stop scratching. You're making it worse. Go and put on your cream."

I hadn't known I was scratching.

Everest continued. "And unlike you, sister, I will show our guest the utmost hospitality. For this, I bid you adieu." Everest gave me a little shoulder bump and strolled away. She paused, then turned. "Bee, I hope you didn't forget your final dress fitting for tonight. I had mine earlier."

My head went backward. "Fuck."

III

"Better than covert devotion is an open reproach."
Proverb 63:18 from the Book of Face, Mortem Era.

IT WAS OFFICIAL. I'd had enough running. The climb up the winding east palace stairwell sent my breasts bouncing. If they kept moving like this, they might bounce too hard, fly up, and render me unconscious on these granite steps.

When I finally reached the top of the stairs, family

portraits, maps of historical conquest, and a hallway of greenery greeted me. Turning left, I marched to my bedroom door. The itchiness of my skin would not leave me be. I dug my nails into it, relieving some built-up anxiety before I greeted my Mother on the other side.

As soon as I cracked open the door, a wisteria vine wrapped around my wrist and dragged me in.

"Where have you been? Your fitting started an hour ago!" The wisteria released its hold and snaked toward my Mother, wrapping itself around her waist, shoulder, and right arm. Her shaved head was glistening from slight sweat. She took a cloth and patted the top of her forehead. She was careful not to smudge the forest green painted line on her face, which extended from her forehead down to the middle of her emerald-greens. She had another green line going from her chin to the V-cut of her breast. Her sheer dress revealed smooth brown skin. Even on the day of the Reaper Festival, she wore the marks of the High Priestess of the Earth Temple.

"I was—"

She cut me off. "May the Spirits rest, Bellamy. You smell like an army camp." She sniffed.

"Some say that smell is an aphrodisiac." I noticed Silvia standing at the foot of my bed, stifling a smile.

"Watch your mouth." The purple wisteria petals appeared to be hissing at me. "One hour ago!" Mother pointed a single finger between my eyes. "Do you understand how important tonight is? Do you understand all the things I must do to prepare for the guests that have been arriving since daybreak?" She clicked her tongue, and the wisteria shifted around her waist. "And do I get a thank you, Mother? Do you need help, Mother?" she said, placing her hands on her hips.

I shifted. "Do you need any help, Mother?"

"No." The wisteria shot from her arm like a whip and

stopped a few inches from my face. "Why would I need anyone's help when I would have to clean up after them, anyway?"

"You just said—" I stepped out of the wisteria's way to plop on my bed. It curled back to her like a snake around her figure.

"I know what I said. If your head weren't attached to your shoulders, I would have to spend half the day looking for that too."

I kicked off my black boots. "So, what would you have me do, Mother?"

"Help!" She threw up her hand.

"You said you didn't need help."

"Showing up on time for your fitting is the least you can do, Bellamy." Mother grabbed a sheet of paper from the collection of documents sprawled on my desk. "And what is this? Huh? Your Earth Temple written test? Why does it say fail?"

I bit my lower lip, glancing at Silvia, who kept her head down, smoothing out the front of her skirt.

"What have you been doing that is more important than your studies? Do you not plan on pledging on your twenty-first birthday? Do you plan on not taking your place on your throne? Do you plan on making me look like a fool?" She slammed the paper on the desk.

"Speak!"

"I—"

She snapped her fingers, cutting me off. "Uma, ensure she's fitted correctly. I have far too many things to do than to oversee this spoiled brat. Are you able to handle that?"

"Yes, High Priestess." Silvia nodded.

Mother glanced at my room, as if seeing it for the first time. "And clean up in here. The pigs are neater than this." She fanned her fingers at me instead of my room. With a sigh, she lightly strolled out. The wisteria unwrapped from her wrist, tightened its grip around the doorknob, and slammed it shut behind her.

"Well, that went better than I expected," I said, turning to Silvia. Her lips sucked into her mouth, revealing deep dimples in her cheeks. "Are you going to stand there all day?"

A slight glimmer twinkled in her eyes. She jumped on the bed, crawling like a prowling tiger before landing directly on top of me.

Her lips tasted like brown sugar.

"First," she said, nibbling on my ear.

For the love of all things beautiful, that turned me on.

"I need you to get undressed." She unbuttoned the back of my dress.

"For a fitting? Do you really need to see me in my unders?" I licked her neck.

"If I'm to do as your mother commands, I need to do it correctly," she said, pulling me out of the fabric.

Silvia wore her hair wrapped today, but she allowed her curls to do a slight peekaboo at the top. I wanted to twist my fingers through her strands.

Silvia stopped. Her eyebrows bunched together.

"What?" I ran a thumb over her chin. "Are you thinking about telling Mother that I've been doing you?" I smiled. "You know, that's probably why my studies have sucked over the past year."

Silvia grunted. "Who are you kidding? Your studies sucked way before you started sucking these." She pinched her hard nipple through the fabric of her clothes. "Bee, you might need to go to the Life Doctor."

"Why?" I followed her gaze to my arm. The scales grew up my forearm to the top of my shoulder. "Don't worry about it. Usually after I soak in water and reapply the cream, my skin is smooth again. It's no big deal."

"Hmmm..." Silvia un-straddled me.

"Where are you going?" I pulled at her dress.

"To run you some bathwater for your soak. Your Mother's right. You do kind of smell like an army camp." Her words were laced with playful sarcasm as she twirled to the bathroom door. I slid out of the bed and chased her.

"YOUR BATH IS READY." Silvia sat at the edge of the tub, resembling an oil painting of a graceful village girl. I slid off my robe and eased into the hot water, dosed with the relaxing herbs of chamomile and comfrey. As I settled in, Silvia beckoned an elderflower to come. It rose off the bench and floated over. The flower hung above the tub, waiting for the next command. Silvia shook her finger, and the elderflower sprinkled its tiny white blooms like snow.

"How does it feel?" I asked when the last of the blooms fell. Silvia laid the branch to the side and picked up an exfoliating net.

"What?"

"Having an earth manifestation?" I submerged everything from the neck down into the steamy water.

"It's like breathing." She dipped the net into the water. "You just do it. Instinctively. It feels natural."

"You've never told me about the first time you manifested. What was it like?"

Silvia searched for my arm. She gently pressed the net on my skin and scrubbed. "I was twelve, in my Mother's garden, crying," she said, chuckling. "And I felt a little tap on my leg. When I opened my eyes, the sage leaned into me as if to comfort me." She paused, washing my arm, her deep brown eyes distant. "My body didn't feel any different. There weren't any tingles. I didn't grow extra hair in places—no. If anything, I

25

felt comforted. Whole." She went back to gently scrubbing alongside my arm.

"What were you crying about in the garden?" I shifted, lifting myself to a seating position. My breasts bobbed on the surface of the water.

"I was upset because my older sisters were chosen by the Earth Temple to serve alongside the priestess, and I wanted to go too. But the Earth Spirit didn't gift me with the emerald-greens. So, I wasn't qualified." She dragged the cloth along my shoulders in circular motions.

"Did you ever feel powerless?"

"You're asking someone with earth gifts that aren't strong? I can barely grow a sapling. Of course, I feel powerless compared to the chosen." She leaned in close, planting a kiss on my forehead. "I learned that day, in my Mother's garden, surrounded by sage, that one doesn't need external power to be considered powerful. True power always dwells within. You just have to tap into it." Silvia tapped my nose. "Plus, I'm glad I wasn't chosen, because if I were, I would have to spend all my days in some old stuffy temple, and I would've never met you."

I caught her by her wrist. "Are you sure? To live a life watching me with others publicly while you wait in secret?"

Silvia's lips disappeared into her mouth, popping out her dimples. "Oh, the tragic life of a *fer l'amor*. The lover, the secret keeper, but never the chosen." Her breath danced on my cheeks.

"I choose you." I loosened my grip.

"At this time, in this moment..." Silvia freed her wrist, dropping the net in the water. She reached deep in between my legs, searching. Soon I felt her fingers splitting me open. "At this very second, you choose me." Her kiss was soft as she gently stroked my clit. "But we both know, the moment the right one comes along, you will choose them." She slid two fingers inside.

I leaned back, letting out a gasp. "Does this bother you?" I asked, my breath heavy.

"What makes you think you're my only lover?" she said, spreading my legs wider.

"You have others?" A ping of jealousy lingered in each word.

"A fer l'amor would never tell." She took her empty hand and zipped her lips.

"Are they better than me?" I tried not to moan as her two fingers rubbed my spot.

She shook her head, a smile playing on her lips.

"Do I know them?"

"Shhh," she said. "You'll spoil the moment. Relax and let me please you, princess."

"You'll please me if you join." The water splashed as I reached out a hand to rub her soft brown legs.

"What if someone walks in?"

"Let them." My blood pumped.

"Your mother would kill me."

"She would have to kill me first."

"Then we die together?"

"Yes, but we will live through every love song, every gentle poem, and every stolen kiss."

Silvia grinned. "You know, you're only romantic when you're horny." She slipped her fingers out of me and walked to the bathroom door. I clung to the side of the tub, my mouth hungry and longing. Silvia locked the knob. She then unbuttoned the front of her dress and let it fall to her feet. She was completely nude. My eyes wandered to her heavy breasts, then trailed down to her pussy, which was the perfect size to sit on my face.

"Come," I said.

"Is that a command, princess?"

"I can make it one. Come quickly," I said in a breathy whisper. I made room for her in the tub. She eased in and straddled me. I wrapped my arms around her waist. The water sloshed over the edges as our bodies swayed.

"We have to make this fast. You still must be fitted for your dress," she said in between moans.

I grabbed her ass, positioning her clit against mine. "I do nothing fast," I said, scooping her nipple into my mouth with my tongue.

IV

"There are plenty of stars. There is no need to wish upon
someone else's."
Proverb 4:17 from the Book of Face, Mortem Era.

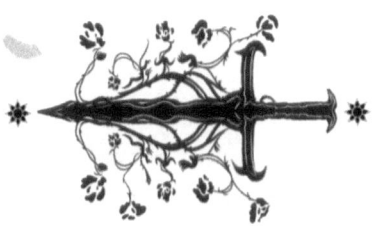

THE NIGHT HAD FALLEN, and the griffes, giant birds
with curved black beaks and giant red talons, batted their
massive wings against a full worm moon. A sign that the winter
was over, and spring had arrived. I pulled my reaper hood over

my cascading waist-length curls to conceal my face. Rushing in between steel towers, I dodged the palace guests by cutting through the maze garden. This was the shortest route connected to the mini bridge; the Reaper Festival was just beyond it.

Emerging past the thick trees, I was met with yellow lights that flooded the gardens like fireflies. A statue of the Reaper Spirit, a tall, dark hooded figure, stood defiantly in the center, surrounded by a swirling cloud of shadow that leaked from its hand. Even though the traditional reaper clothing for this celebration was an oversized black hood and fitted black clothing, more and more people had branched out to colors of red, navy, and even fuchsia. As people gathered, their laughter and chit-chat were evidently louder than the hum of music playing. Mother had outdone herself. She should be proud.

"How did I sense that my eldest daughter would be making her grand entrance covertly, like a shadow assassin?"

I clenched my jaw and turned around slowly. "Clearly, I'm not as gifted as a shadow assassin. If I were, you wouldn't have sensed me at all, Father."

My Father, General Agrim Tagore, donned a traditional black suit. His face, slightly hidden by his reaper hood, was like a polished moonstone. As he drew closer, his steel medal of accomplishments clinked against velvet fabric.

"Then why is it that my beautiful daughter insists on sneaking around and sticking her little nose in places they don't belong?"

I took a page out of Everest's book and batted my lashes. "Whatever do you mean?"

Father glanced at me; his dark pupils showed little to no whites. I overheard one soldier call his stare the death gaze. As he turned those eyes on me, they couldn't be more right.

"Fine. It was Glaydecee, wasn't it? She's such an old

snitch." My skin itched. I dug my nails into my forearm. "I was looking for the gun in the earthbox, but I found these weird tubes of blue and red liquid instead. Completely irrelevant, so I had Everest wrap the box back up, and I put it away. Sorry for snooping," I added, as his gaze fixed upon me.

"How many times have I warned you not to go snooping through other people's things?"

"All the time."

"And when will you start listening?"

"Tomorrow?" I gave a cheesy grin.

Father let out a small smile. He extended a hand to my hood to straighten it. "One day, you'll find something you wish you never started looking for."

"But if I was looking for it, why would I regret finding it?"

Father bent and kissed me on the center of my forehead. "Beta," he said. "Some things are better off not knowing. You have always been the curious one." He let go of my hood and placed his hand tightly behind his back. "Let's just hope your curiosity doesn't get you into too much trouble."

I nodded. "So, does this mean you will not tell me what those tubes were?"

"I will not. But for your transgressions, I assigned you the duty of showing the queen the grounds tomorrow morning."

"Come on! Anything but that. I would literally clean the bathroom floor before dealing with her. What if I spoke with Mother and apologized?" I whined.

Father froze, his hood slipped away from his face, and I saw his dark eyes turn to slits.

"You haven't told Mother, have you?"

"I have not."

"Why?" I wasn't curious before, but now I was intrigued.

"Should I? Would you like to get in trouble twice?"

"No, but—"

"No buts. Your duty is set."

"But—"

"Tomorrow morning," he said, walking past me and into the festival.

Maybe Everest was right. Walking into the abyss *does* sound like a perfect plan. I rather that than spend the morning with the Reaper Queen.

BEFORE I ENTERED the festival, I took a deep breath. Large gatherings were never my thing. If it were up to me, I would avoid them at all costs. I spotted Everest on the far side of the crowd. She wore a reaper dress made from blue royal roses with the upper back cut out. Her reaper hood was pulled halfway and pinned with a mixture of gold and blue roses—a perfect mixture of her heritage, reaper and earth. I scanned for Mother, but I didn't see her. At least I wouldn't have to worry about that. I rolled my sleeve to gauge my skin. It was smooth for now. I pulled the sleeve back down, exhaled, and forced a grin as I entered the festival.

Five minutes. That's all it took before a lady in a gaudy pink dress with a reaper hood covered in fur introduced herself as Lady Wynonna Benideeve of the Eighth Reaper Ward.

"Princess Bellamy, you have grown into such a spectacular sight to gaze upon." She raised her palm and a small shadow formed from her hand. The black smoke darted like a little arrow to both of my cheeks, a shadow kiss. A common gesture amongst reaper families.

"Thank you." I smiled out of politeness.

"When will you be preparing for marriage?" She raised a glass to her lips, blood wine. I didn't understand how anyone could drink that stuff. The smell was extremely bitter.

"Soon." I was careful to choose my words wisely. In my experience, the fewer words used, the less incriminating.

"Does this mean you have potentials?"

"Not quite."

"Such a shame. A beautiful princess like you should be already courted and claimed."

Courted and claimed? I almost snarled. I forced my face into neutrality.

"If you are seeking," she leaned in, "I have a son. He is twenty-six years old. A good boy who just received the title of Congruent, the youngest seated at the Council of Amalgamation." Lady Wynonna beamed.

Congruent? As if I would date a politician.

"That is a significant accomplishment," I said.

"Here he is now, Congruent Attali Benideeve." She waved her son over. Luckily, he looked nothing like the orange-faced woman. Where she was short and stout, he was tall and lean. He had an olive tint to his skin, but with reddish hair.

"Princess Bellamy, my son I was telling you about."

Congruent Attali took my hand and kissed the back of it. "Princess Bellamy, it is an honor."

"Pleasure is all mine, especially since I hear I'm in the presence of lived history. Congratulations on your call," I said with a forced smile. My stomach growled, which reminded me I hadn't eaten since this morning. The smell of honey butter rolls from the far table was calling my name.

"Thank you." Attali kissed his mother on the forehead. "I hope she wasn't bothering you."

"Oh, of course not. She's been a gentle breeze thus far." What I really wanted to say was that she was annoying the shit out of me. Not because she was annoying or because her voice sounded like two coins rubbing together, but because she was the one thing that prevented me from getting to that damn bread table I spotted. I could imagine the taste of freshly whipped butter on my tongue.

Lady Wynonna shoved her son closer. "I will let you two get more acquainted. Let me know if you need me," she said, her smile spread from ear to ear, revealing one missing tooth. She called out to another woman in the crowd and disappeared after her.

"Excuse my mother." Congruent Attali held out the side of his arm.

I looped my arm within it. "She *is* expressive."

"Overly dramatic and presumptions, to say the least." He grinned.

Blunt. I like.

He escorted me through the crowd and right to the bread table. He released my arm and bowed to the assortment of loaves.

"Was I that obvious?" I nervously giggled, digging my nails into my skin.

"I didn't catch on until the third glance over my shoulder. Or maybe it was the sixth?" He raised an eyebrow.

"I'm embarrassed."

"Don't be. I would choose bread and butter over me anytime." He picked up a roll and cut it in half with a knife. With the same knife, he gathered an unhealthy amount of butter and slabbed the inside of the bread.

My mouth watered. I peeked over my shoulder at the nosy eyes watching before looking away, aloof. I grabbed a small saucer and placed my warm roll on top.

Congruent Attali's eyebrows knitted together, watching me closely.

Using a butter knife, I sliced a tiny piece of the roll and placed a small amount of butter on top before popping it into my mouth. *Etiquette 101.*

Congruent Attali stopped mid-chew. He placed his roll down and picked up a second roll. He slathered it with tons of butter, then stood in front of me, blocking the people's view.

"Here," he said, holding the roll to my mouth. "Big bite."

Hesitantly, I sniffed the roll, making sure the viewing party did not see me. I opened my mouth wide, and he stuffed the roll inside.

"See, tastes better this way."

"Yes." My cheeks ballooned out. "Thank you." I swallowed the last bite.

"It was my pleasure, Princess." He bowed. "If ever you need someone to"—he cleared his throat— "be your food guard, then you know where to find me." He reached into his jacket and pulled out a card. I took it, tucking it into my dress pocket.

"The two people I've been wanting to see." A rat-faced man with a pipe in his mouth and a beard that reached his belly strolled over.

Great, more politicians.

He lifted his palm to send a shadow kiss to both of us.

"Congruent Armstrong," Attali said, towering over the man.

"I wanted to come over and congratulate you for getting your proposal on the voting bill. Even though we all know it won't be passed." Armstrong removed his pipe and patted Attali's shoulder with a hardy laugh.

"And why would you believe a bill affecting thousands of people wouldn't pass?"

"Because who the bill is affecting isn't worth the resources spent."

I cleared my throat. "What is the bill you speak of?"

Attali, whose olive skin was blushed red, spoke. "The legalization of Fireborns within the Six Kingdoms."

"It's a bill"—Congruent Armstrong lit his pipe— "that

grants legal citizenship to all Fireborns who have forfeited their birthright and their heritage to merge into another kingdom."

I thought for a moment before speaking. "Isn't there a bill already passed that states that any Fireborn seeking refuge amongst their neighbor shall be protected under that kingdom's law?"

Armstrong puffed his pipe. "Yes, but you see where that got us. A bunch of ungifted half-breeds with sullied bloodlines."

I swallowed hard. Seeing that I had yet to manifest, I couldn't help but take that comment personally. "Forgive me, Congruent Armstrong. I didn't realize you felt this strongly about the Fireborns and the ungifted. Should I be under the impression that you would like to reform the Fireborn Protection Act, which will deny any Fireborns and their descendants refuge?"

"Oh, no, Princess. I'm just saying that the resources divided amongst the kingdoms should be for taking care of our own."

Congruent Attali folded his arms. "And under the protection act, all fleeing Fireborns are our own; therefore, they should have the right to our resources and to the citizenship of whichever kingdom they choose."

Armstrong puffed his pipe and blew white smoke directly in Attali's direction. "The problem with youth is they often forget history." Congruent Armstrong turned his beady eyes to me. "The Fire Kingdom has the largest population outside of the Earth Kingdom. And as the next Earth Queen, it is wise to do as your ancestors have done in the past and draw the line in the soil. The Earth Kingdom has not allowed a Fireborn or anyone who isn't pure Earth-aligned in their borders since the start of the New World. Even when one had gotten close..." Armstrong turned to the side. I followed his gaze. There stood my parents, raising their glasses amongst the nobility. "Earth chose Earth and stripped titles of all others who went against their kingdom." Armstrong took a puff out of his pipe. "Trust and believe that the elders have not forgotten. We are gathered here today at the great Reaper Festival to celebrate the end of a war that lasted a century." Armstrong crossed himself. "May the Spirits rest."

"Well," I said, biting back the need to dig my nails into my itchy skin. "I'm Earthborn and Reaperborn, and yet my doyens, my mother's parents, have decided that the next concession to rule would be me, a mix-breed." I raised my chin, staring into those beady little black eyes. "Maybe it's not that the youth has forgotten the past but understand that as long as our kingdoms continue to be divided, that history will, in fact, repeat." I studied Congruent Attali and watched him lick his full pink lips with a faint smile. "And it is up to us to prevent that, don't you agree, Congruent Attali?"

"Of course, princess. May the Spirits bless your reign."

Armstrong placed his pipe into his mouth as he straightened his reaper hood. "I guess we shall see what the future holds for us all, princess. May the Spirits bless your reign." He bowed and walked away.

I leaned into Congruent Attali. "Can you believe that fucking guy?"

"Princess?" He teased me.

Black smoke filled the night sky, cutting our laughter short.

My Father took his place on the stage, followed by the Blood Elite, a small sector of the Shadow Army strictly under his control. "My family." Father's voice rose and the music and chatter died out.

"I would like to recognize our Reaper Queen, Keon Thakur, and our Prince, Theolo, for giving us this opportunity to host this monumental celebration. May the Spirits bless their reign in power, glory, and blood."

The crowd raised their glasses.

"Most importantly, we're gathered here today to give honor to the Reaper Spirit who gave their gifts upon our people after the Mortem Era, the death age. The Reaper chose our ancestors as the protectors of the kingdoms, should any evil reveal themselves again, bringing terror to this world."

"Here, here!" voices shouted from the crowd.

"May we all remember the blood that was shed in this world due to the greed of those who are fire aligned. Those who called upon the Fire Spirit in order to rise to power and beat the rest of the world into submission. May they burn in the seven realms of outer darkness!" Whistles and claps broke out in fierce roars.

"May we never fall or bend the knee to anyone! We are Reaperborn! We have prevailed from the ashes of those who have come before us. Our ancestors' blood runs through our veins. It is what binds us, what gives us our strength, what allows us to heal from the brink of death. We live, we live. We die, we die. We fight, we fight until the last drop of reaper blood turns black!" Father chanted, calling his Blood Elite to center stage.

Fia, his second in command, led his companions dressed in a black skirted cloak and reaper hood. Their bodies were covered in tattoos that told the story of their ancestors, their battles, and their awards. They beat their chests, twisting their faces to call forth the Reaper Spirit within them. As Fia called out, "We live, we live. We die, we die," black smoke poured from their eyes, nose, and mouth.

Their red tongues matched their red fingertips as they flicked and fluttered them. Fia shouted, "We fight, we fight until the last drop of reaper blood turns black!" The soldiers released a war cry that sent a wave of black shadow over the crowd. The griffes, giant red-clawed birds, dove from the sky as if to partake in the reaper chant. In sync with the griffes, the Blood Elite leaped off the stage and onto the birds' backs.

I swelled with pride and honor. My heartbeat pounded against my chest as the drums sounded. The Blood Elite flew to the Reaper Spirit statue and rotated around it, as their shadows brought the statue to life. It seemed to dance in the shroud of smoke, until the griffes shot into the air, their silhouettes outlined by the worm moon. I could almost imagine the ancestors of my Father's lineage twinkling amongst the stars, and I wished that the Reaper Spirit found favor and shined their light on me.

My voice lifted with the chorus of others. "We fight, we fight until the last drop of reaper blood turns black!"

V

*"We'll always choose knowledge; we'll hurt ourselves in its
pursuit, and if need be, we'll put our hands in the fire for it."*
Proverb 83:72 from the Book of Face, Mortem Era.

AFTER THE SHOW, I did what I promised Everest. I disappeared. And I knew exactly where I was going. Umas, the palace staff, rarely attended the nobility version of the Reaper Festival. Instead, they had their own. I checked the time on the silver tower that rose above the buildings. It read thirty minutes past the twentieth hour. Silvia would be in the uma's corridors on the west side of the palace. Maybe I could steal her away, just this once.

I was rounding the corner of the west side wall when my eyes caught a shadow of movement scaling downwards from a fourth-floor window. *Father's office.* I searched for guards or soldiers, but I knew both would be protecting the nobility at the Reaper Festival. There was a slight groove in the wall, and I tucked myself into it while watching the shadow figure jump the remaining distance to the ground. The figure landed like a stealthy cat before rising to stand. A reaper cloak covered much of their body. When the figure turned to survey the surroundings, their face was hidden behind a black mask.

Some people wore masks to the Reaper Festival, so this wasn't an uncommon look for attendees. But crawling out of a window from Father's office? Not so common.

Seeing the way was clear, the figure walked briskly between the silver towers toward the south end of the palace. I followed, tugging my reaper hood lower over my face.

There was an on-campus training ground for the Blood Elite on the far south side of the palace grounds, but the figure made a sharp turn and headed to the east wing instead. Their movements were fluid, their steps barely making a sound. Transfixed, I watched them weave in between the towers as if they knew the palace grounds like the back of their hands.

Before I knew it, I heard my heavy breathing along with rapid beating in my chest. The shadow figure stopped. I flattened myself against a tower. A foot sliding on rocks echoed before the figure took off in a full-blown sprint.

I jumped from behind the tower to see a fluttering cloak make a right. I pursued, knowing these grounds better than anyone, but no matter how quickly I ran behind them, I only caught glimpses of the tail end of their cloak. Soon, I hit a dead end. *Fuck.* My head was spinning. Just that quick, not only did I get turned around, but I didn't know where the dark cloak went next.

Backing out of the dead end, I retraced my steps as the sound of silver unsheathed at my back. The pointed end grazed my spine.

"I'm unarmed." I raised my hand, feeling the cold daggers securely wrapped around my thighs. I never left home without them.

I felt a poke at my back, and I shuffled forward, closer to the dead-end wall.

"Listen, you don't want to hurt me." My palms were begging to reach into the slit of my dress for the dagger handle.

Another poke. *So annoying.*

"What is it you want, huh? Just name it. It's yours. Just stop poking me with that sword."

The sword withdrew. I whipped around, pulling my reaper hood down.

"You really don't want to harm me." I said, lowering my hands. "My father has soldiers under his command that can track you down to the end of the world. They're twins. They're annoying as shit, but they will get the job done."

The shadow of the hood hid the figure's face. The mask covered their eyes, but revealed a bearded chin. I couldn't make out the color or shade. There was barely any light where we stood, and the towers blocked the moon. Everything looked black.

The figure had their sword raised but suspended as if they were still contemplating their next action. I didn't need to think. I needed to do. Quickly, I ripped daggers from my thighs and threw them at the figure. The blades left my hand in one fluid motion, as a decade of practice had taught me.

The figure used their sword to dodge, knocking my daggers to the ground. I reached for two more, this time holding my ground and assessing the hooded figure. They hadn't used their manifestation on me. That could've meant one of three things.

One: They were waiting for the right moment to strike.

Two: Their manifestation was low or depleted; therefore, they had to use weapons to make up for it.

Three: They could've been like me and had no manifestation.

Which one was more likely at this moment?

I assumed the worst, never underestimate the enemy. I launched a blade while running and pulling another. As the figure blocked one attack, I had already set in motion the second blow. My legs were more powerful than my fists. I round kicked the figure in their gut while launching another round kick to knock the sword from their hand.

Adrenaline pumped, sending way too many endorphins to my head. The figure recovered quickly, throwing a punch. All it connected to was cool air. I countered, grabbing the length of their outstretched hand and using their own body weight to drive them down to my raised knee. A second direct hit to their gut, their root center, which destabilizes their manifestation. One more blow and I wouldn't have to worry about their gifts.

The figure doubled over with a gruff shout followed by coughing. "I don't want to hurt you," he, *it was definitely a he*, said as he stumbled backwards.

"It looks like you're the only one hurting."

I bounced on the balls of my toes, in four-inch heels, by the way.

"Why were you sneaking into the palace?" I used this opportunity to reach for the rest of my blades on my thigh.

The man straightened, placing his hands on his waist. He

let out a long breath and then spoke. "What are your legs made of, reaper steel? Shit," he wheezed.

I smiled, pride expanding my ego. *Try not to get distracted, Bellamy.* I attempted to tell myself, but I had already dropped my guard.

The man was on his toes, flying across the concrete as a series of combinations of fist and feet swung. I dodged, ducked, and protected my vital organs as best as I could.

Was he Windborn?

My heel caught in a crack of concrete, and I lost my balance, causing me to drop my guard. His fist connected with my jaw, which sent me spinning to my ass.

I hit the ground hard, the air completely knocked out of my lungs. My fist clenched my daggers. He sprinted toward me so fast that I could only think about defense.

He stood over me, his hood covering his face in a mysterious shadow. "I don't want to hurt you."

"Then what do you want?" I wiped the blood from my lips. I cracked open my jaw, moving it around to make sure it wasn't broken.

The man went over to his sword, flicked his cloak to the side, and sheathed it. Attached to his hip was my Mother's earthbox.

"Put your blades away. No one has to die tonight." His cloak settled back over his waist, covering the earthbox.

"What do you want with those tubes?" I stumbled to my feet. My ankles crumpled under the weight of my body and I lost my balance again. The man grabbed me at my waist, pulling me into him for stabilization.

"You good?" I asked, hyper aware that he stood a tad bit taller than my five-foot-eight-inch frame.

"Are you good with your weak ankles?" He smirked. His mask rose slightly on sharp cheekbones.

"My weak ankles? The same weak ankles that almost round kicked your ass to the spirit realm? Must I remind you?"

He laughed. "No, may the Spirits rest. Never again."

"Then let go of me before I change my mind."

He let me go, throwing his hands in the air. "Sorry, princess."

"You knew who I was?"

He shrugged.

"Then who are you and what are those tubes?" I asked as he stepped backwards.

"If I tell you who I am, that defeats the purpose of this," he pointed to his mask. "And these are top secret. You shouldn't even know they exist."

"Yeah, but now I know, and I demand you tell me what they are!"

"Demand?" He laughed, bringing his sleeve to wipe a drop of blood from his nose. "Neither Earth nor Reaper has jurisdiction over me."

"So, you're Windborn?"

"Do yourself a favor, princess, and pretend you never saw me."

He turned his back to walk away. I kicked off my heels and ran to him, daggers in hand. He whipped around, dodging my steel. He knocked a dagger out of my right hand, and I punched him square in the nose with my empty fist. The mask cracked, and my knuckles throbbed. I might have broken a few finger bones. The pain shot up my arm and I dropped the dagger in my left hand to clasp my fingers.

"Are you happy now?" he shouted, removing the cracked mask.

His nose, mouth, and beard were covered with blood.

"Actually, yes. You punched me in the jaw."

"So, you break my nose!"

"Don't blame me for your weak nose. If it were stronger, it wouldn't be bleeding all over the place!"

"Damn it, woman!" His reaper hood slipped back just enough for a touch of light to highlight his face. Blue eyes as rich as hydrangea planted in acidic soil stared back at me. He shifted his hood, casting his face in shadow.

I swallowed the pain, reaching for the earthbox stowed away at his hip. His bloody hand grabbed at my bloody palm and electricity shot through my entire frame. A loud buzzing filled my ears as my body trembled under the electric pressure. This feeling—this feeling felt better than sex. My body exploded with a surge of energy that switched a button on in my mind and I could taste the universe. Oddly enough, it tasted of raspberries and sweet rum.

The man grabbed the back of my neck; his hood fell to his shoulders. Dirty blonde curly hair spilled out around a handsomely strong face. His body vibrated. His eyes exploded with want.

I attempted to let go, even though I didn't want this feeling to end.

I moaned, "Please."

He groaned.

Our foreheads touched as we both forced our hands to open. When our fingers untangled, a blinding white light grew in between us, knocking us off our feet, and blowing us back onto the concrete. I hit my head with a smack, and my eyelids slowly blinked shut.

VI

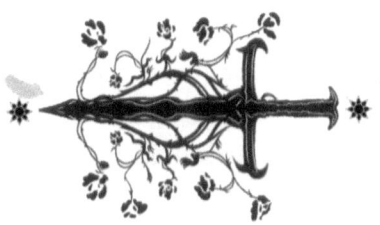

"Anatomize the value of what is spoken, not the speaker."
Proverb 51:01 from the Book of Face, Mortem Era

WHEN I AWOKE, my mind was in a haze. The man was gone, and the clock tower read fifteen past the twenty-third hour. I stumbled into the palace, up the flight of stairs, and into my room. My dress was blood-stained and burned. I took it off and threw it into the trash. For the next hour, I ran bath water, soaked, bandaged myself together, and laid in bed recounting the events that happened. I needed to know who that man was and, most importantly, what were those liquids and why were they so important?

My bedroom door opened.

"I don't want to see anyone," I said, rolling over toward the wall.

"Don't care. I'm not going anywhere," Everest said, plopping at the edge of my bed.

"Shouldn't you be at the Festival? Don't tell me it's over already."

"Quite the opposite. The party is just getting started. I thought you would be somewhere in somebody's bed by now." She tapped my thigh.

"Thank you for thinking so highly of me," I said, putting the pillow over my head. "Is there something I can help you with?"

The bed shook as Everest rose, her footsteps trailing away. There was a slight rummaging as if she was going through papers and then I realized what she was looking at.

"What happened to your dress?" she said, holding it up.

I threw the pillow off my head, marched over to where Everest stood and snatched the dress from her hand. "Can you not go through my things?"

"What happened to your chin?"

I clicked my teeth. "I fell."

I balled the dress into the tightest knot possible and slid it under my bed.

I'll dispose of it properly tomorrow.

Everest leaned on my dresser. "Your hand is wrapped. Did you spend your entire night fighting?"

I froze. "No."

My eyes darted from side to side, telling her everything she needed to know.

"Who was it?"

"Why does it matter? You wouldn't approve, anyway."

"Bee, when are you going to put away these foolish fighting lessons and cleave to the Earth way?" Everest pushed off the dresser.

"And what? Become some Earth pacifist and spend my time within the border, closed to the rest of the world, daydreaming in my own little perfect bubble?" I faced her. She had her arms crossed, judging me with those same almond eyes as Mother's.

"Fine. I was fighting with Quande. You happy?"

"You lie! Quande was on the west side of the palace most of the night, celebrating with *his* type of people. I saw him."

"So, what do you want from me then?"

"The truth, Bellamy. I want the truth."

"The truth about what?" I almost screamed. The itch intensified. I remembered I hadn't applied my skin cream after I bathed. I went over to the desk and grabbed the cream from the shelf. My head was pounding.

Everest stuck her bony finger into my side. I gasped, not realizing how sore I was.

"For starters, when were you going to tell me you were pledging to become High Priestess in the Earth Temple?"

My mouth dropped. "What the hell are you talking about, Eve?"

"Mother announced to everyone tonight that you'll train under her as High Priestess as you prepare to take your throne."

My eyes narrowed. "I never said I was pledging to become High Priestess. I don't even want to pledge to the Earth Temple!"

Everest cocked her head. "You really didn't know?"

"No. I had no clue. I haven't manifested yet. There's no guarantee that I'm Earthborn."

"You were born with the sign of the great Earth Spirit." Everest pointed at my eyes. "Don't be daft."

"I'm not trying to be daft, Eve."

I moved to the bed. I needed to sit down; the bedroom was spinning. The waves of electricity still lingered underneath my skin, causing me to shiver. "I don't want this. I didn't ask to be High Priestess."

"So, what now? You're going to confront Mother and tell her to take the announcement back?"

"That's exactly what I'm going to do."

"And you think she will listen?"

She never listens.

"If this is what Mother plans for you, then you have no choice." Everest turned her back on me. Her foot tapped on the floor.

"Don't you think that's fucked up, Eve?"

"Language, Bee."

"Why? It's just the two of us. Why can't I ever be myself around you?"

"Because just being yourself isn't good enough!" Everest spun around.

My anger flared as the itch jumped from my forearm to my neck. I dug my nails into the base of my neck until the pain hurt so bad it became sweet. "I must be better than you. No matter how much you pretend to be the *good daughter*, you will never be an Earth Queen, High Priestess, or praised. You're just my annoying shadow that can only be seen when the sun shines on me!" I rose from the bed. "Maybe, instead of worrying about what I'm doing, you should probably worry about your damn self."

Fuck! I bit my tongue, unscrewing the lid on the cream and slathering a huge chunk of the white stuff on my arms.

Everest's face was as even as a summer day. She blinked a few times as if coming out of a daydream. "Is that really how you feel?" she whispered.

Of course, it wasn't how I felt. But I said it. Regardless of how sorry I was, wasn't there a bit of truth buried inside?

"No," I finally said to her. "I don't feel that way. Forgive me."

Everest laughed a soft, cracked chuckle. "Do you know what I overheard Glaydecee telling the umas tonight as they sat around the campfire?"

I shook my head.

Everest's eyes watered. "Glaydecee said, I was born first to my Mother. That when she gazed upon me, I was nearly perfect, everything she ever wanted. Golden skin kissed by the sun. Hair that grew to the sky to give thanks to the Earth Spirit. Red-brown hair to show I was made by the clay of the Earth. But there was one catch. I didn't have the eyes. Seeing the disappointment on my Mother's face, I decided to try again, to be reborn, but I was too late. Mother had a new daughter, skin black as the ebony tree, hair waved like the ocean, and eyes emerald green, just like the ancestors of old. Even though my eyes were brown like the oak tree, the Earth Spirit didn't bestow their gift onto me." Everest hung her head.

Silence dangled in the air, and I didn't know what to say next. I had heard stories about a baby lost before I was born, but no one ever spoke of it. It was common law in the palace that instead of speaking about hard things, one must bury them deep inside and continue moving.

"Eve–" I said gently.

Everest held up a finger to me, shaking her head. "Don't," she said. "You are the eldest, Bellamy. The Spirits willed it so.

And for that, I hope you understand the privilege that you hold." Everest turned and walked to the door.

"Eve, don't go."

Everest side-eyed me with watery pupils. "You are right about one thing," she said. "It's time for me to worry about myself." She flung open the door and left.

I grabbed the back of my neck, cursing myself out. My nails touched something wet. I drew my fingers back and looked at the tips.

Blood.

Act II

VII

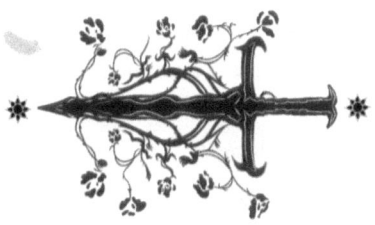

"Who holds the power, the stubborn mule or the man forcing it to drink?"
Proverb 11:23 from the Book of Face, Mortem Era.

I'M LATE. I'M ALWAYS FUCKING LATE! My bra-strap dug into my shoulders something fierce. I swiped my hair out of my face as I made my way to the dining hall.

I hate mornings. I hate waking up, and I fucking hate that I have to sit through breakfast with fake smiles and submissive head nods.

My heels caught in the hem of my dress. *I should have worn my boots!* I wiggled my heels free when I heard a slight rip in the fabric.

"Fuck!" I screamed.

"Not having a good morning?" Silvia said, leaning against a wall right in front of the dining hall.

"I didn't get enough sleep last night." I ran my fingers through my hair, shutting my eyes for a moment of rest.

"How come? You weren't with me last night. You should have slept fine."

I opened my eyes, taking a long look at Silvia. Her hair was wrapped in a purple scarf that matched her cotton gown. Her jaw was set and her lips almost seemed to disappear into her mouth, which indicated that she had something to say, but she was holding back.

"Silvia, come on. Are you mad at me too?"

"Depends. Who else is mad at you?" She pushed herself off of the wall.

"Eve."

Silvia waved her hand nonchalantly. "She's always mad at something."

"So, what's your problem then?"

"I don't have a problem."

I sucked my teeth. "Cut the shit. Obviously, you do. Is it because I didn't come to see you last night?"

Silvia raised a brow.

"That's it, isn't it?"

A group of umas rounded the corner. Silvia stood straight as the umas bowed in passing. One of the older umas glanced at us with pursed lips but hurried along down the corridor without a word.

When they were out of sight, I stepped closer. "Listen, I was coming. I swear. I just got caught up."

"With what?"

"Just with things."

"What things?"

"Why does it matter, Silvia?"

"It doesn't," she shrugged.

"Okay. Then why the pout?" I grabbed her by her cheeks, pushing her against the wall. She tried shoving my hands away, but I held firm.

"People will see," she said, scanning the hall behind me.

"And you don't think every uma in the palace knows about us already? It's been over a year. Let's stop pretending."

"The queen and the prince are literally in the next room."

"So what?" I said, planting soft kisses on her lips. "Isn't this what you wanted last night?" I wrapped my arms around her waist.

"Your hair"—she said, in between kisses— "is everywhere. Did you even comb it this morning? And your chin looks a bit swollen." She slid a finger on the puffy side. It stung slightly, but not enough to wince.

I sighed and planted one last kiss on her forehead.

"I fell."

"Sure," she said, reaching into her pockets and pulling out a four-tooth wooden hair pick. Turning me around, she combed through my tangles and then braided it into a bun while securing the bun with the wooden hair pick. She then fixed my dress and loosen my bra strap for comfort.

"Thank you." I turned to face her.

She pulled out a few strands of my hair and curled it around her fingers. "What type of uma would I be if I allowed you to face the queen looking that way?"

"You'll still be the best," I said, staring into her beautiful brown eyes.

She reached into her pocket and pulled out an herb. "Rosemary," she said, pinning the herb onto my hair. "There. You look presentable, a proper Earth Princess." She pulled away, tucking her bottom lip underneath her teeth.

"Tonight," I said, walking to the dining doors. "I will see you tonight. I promise."

Silvia smiled, revealing deep dimples. She bowed. "I'll hold you to it, princess."

"BETA, SO HAPPY you could join us," Father said, sitting at the round table. Mother sat to the left of him, followed by Everest. Prince Theolo to the right, followed by the queen. There was another familiar face sitting at the table, which I was surprised to see, Congruent Attali. Haloed in the morning light, his deep bronze skin almost shimmered as his luscious black hair glowed. He appeared to be bathing in sunlight.

A looker indeed.

"Sorry I'm late," I said, kissing Father on the cheek, then taking my place in between Attali and Everest.

"Excuse my daughter's lateness, Your Highness. Time is but a nuisance to the youth," Mother grinned.

"That is why I teach my son this saying: a blink is a thousand years to a turtle," The queen said.

I bunched my nose. "A blink is a thousand years to a turtle? Spirits forbid if I ever move that slow," I blurted out. Everest slammed her thigh into mine, causing my knee to hit the table.

The queen brought a napkin to her mouth and dabbed the corners. "Oh, Princess Bellamy. The one thing I love about you is your gratuitous probity."

"Thanks?" I glanced at Everest, who was holding back a smug snicker.

Mother gave me the eye which read, *"Don't make me look like a damn fool at this table."*

I sat back in my chair as Father snapped his fingers. In perfect harmony, the umas poured out of the kitchens with piping hot entrees in hand. The table was decorated in the typical reaper black, but Mother had added green vines and dark flowers to brighten the space.

The umas whirled around the table as if performing ballet. Their shadows trailed behind them like a third hand, laying out French toast, bacon, eggs, fruits, vegetables, and bread. So much mouth-watering bread with freshly whipped white butter. My stomach rumbled at the sight.

Is it possible for food to sexually turn someone on? If so, that is me right now.

"My lovely wife, will you do us the honor?" Father extended his palms in prayer. We bowed our heads. Mother's sing-song voice rose like she was preaching from the highest altar.

"To the Spirits. We thank you for this meal created by loving hands. Let it refresh us as the rain refreshes the soil. Let it strengthen our bones and prepare us for a harsh winter. To the most Divine, please send your guided light of wisdom..."

And that was when I tuned out. After what felt like an eternity, Mother finally completed the prayer.

Forks clinked against plates. The sound of knives cutting through food, the sipping of lemonade, and gentle chit-chat soon filled the room.

Everest folded her cloth napkin in her lap. "Your Highness, I pray you're enjoying your stay," she said, cutting tiny bites of food.

"Princess Everest, you are always the most upstanding host. Your palace makes my castle pale in comparison."

"Your Grace," Everest cooed. "I highly doubt that. I could only tour half of your castle grounds on my last visit." She smiled.

Ass-kisser.

"Then we should invite you back to tour the second half, my child."

Prince Theolo cut in. "I think that would be a great idea. I would be your guide."

I sipped loudly on my cup of lemonade. Congruent Attali popped a grape into his mouth as he continued to watch in silence.

"I would love nothing more," Everest agreed. Mother tapped the back of Everest's hand in approval.

"How does that sound, Bellamy? A tour of the reaper castle?" Everest smirked.

Was she fucking with me?

Before I could speak, Theolo blurted, "I'm sure your sister has plenty of work to do here. Especially with the construction of the Earth Temple. As well as her training to become the next High Priestess."

I opened my mouth to speak, but Mother cut me off. "Yes. She must prepare not only for her pledge, but for her trial. It's not every day one is chosen for a higher calling."

I fixed my tongue to speak again but was interrupted by the queen.

"The next Earth Queen, half Reaperborn and half Earthborn, a sight that has never been seen since the creation of the kingdoms," she said, sipping her lemonade. "And she hasn't manifested? What a peculiar predicament to be in. I'm still shocked that her *kind* will be allowed to touch the throne."

My kind?

The silverware halted.

Father rested his fork on the edge of his plate. "With all due respect, my Grace. Do you think my daughter is incapable of ruling due to her mixed nationality?"

The queen surveyed Father. "Do you not have any doubt? Correct me if I'm wrong, but neither of your daughters were raised in the Earth Kingdom's way. As far as I can tell, they are Reaperborn. And let's just say Princess Bellamy pledges to the Earth Temple, takes her vows, and her throne. How could she rule with no power? How would she successfully protect her people?"

The bread on my tongue turned to ash, and I had to fight not to choke on it. Weak. Powerless. Ungifted. Those were words that had haunted me since puberty, and here they were again, being spat into my face as if I weren't sitting here? I balled my fist underneath the table, my nails digging into my itchy palm. Heat rose to my cheeks, and the ache from yesterday's fight became dull to my growing anger. I spoke, but once again, I was cut off by Mother.

"I assure you my daughter is completely Earthborn without a doubt. She will manifest, and if she doesn't, we have already prepared her to marry."

"To marry?" I said, searching the side of my Mother's face. I glanced at my father, who poked at his plate.

Bastard!

The air became thick as bodies shifted at the table.

"Bellamy, married? What poor sap would take that responsibility?" Prince Theolo laughed.

Mother chimed in. "We know she can be somewhat difficult. But her father and I will make sure we choose the best suitor for this duty." Mother clasped Father's hand.

My skin was inflamed. The itch crept up my arm, engulfing me with tiny pricks that felt like wasps stings. I couldn't breathe. My words caught in my throat. I sank into my chair. The voices that erupted in laughter faded away as I tried to wrap my mind around why everything that happened in my life was never my choice.

I am not weak! Yet, at this moment, I was helpless. Feeble, pathetic, and ungifted. Maybe if I had manifested, I would be strong enough to silence their voices forever!

"How do you feel about this, Princess Bellamy?" A calm tenor whispered in my ear, cutting through the haze of my thoughts. I turned to my left to see Congruent Attali staring at me with obsidian eyes.

The table was silent, all watching me. The room split in and out of focus, but I straightened my shoulders and lifted my chin. *I am not weak.*

I cleared my throat to speak. "My kind—"

Mother cut me off.

Congruent Attali interjected. "Princess, I would love to hear from you and you alone."

Mother coughed, her bald head shining underneath fluorescent lights.

I nodded to Attali and then to the queen. "To address your concern, Your Highness. I am a daughter of Reaper and Earth. Born from the soil and raised in the shadow of death. I do not fear you or your courts. I will pledge to the Earth Temple and elevate my throne. My enemies will fear me, gifted or ungifted. I will protect my people. And if anyone"—my eyes bounced from Prince Theolo, to Mother, and back to the queen— "or anything stands in my way, they all will return to the dust from which they came. Never question my loyalty or my power, with all due respect, My queen." I forced my snarl into a smile.

Prince Theolo's pink cheeks were quickly turning into a chrysanthemum red. "You dare speak to your queen in this manner?" he said as a slight spill of black smoke rose from his palm.

"Now dear." The queen patted a wrinkled hand on top of his, causing his black smoke to vanish. "Princess Bellamy has every right to express her concern. We are not the Fire Kingdom; we pride ourselves on freedom of speech and democracy like our ancestors of old."

Everest shifted next to me, scooting closer to Mother.

"That being said," the queen continued. "I respect your stance and look forward to creating and strengthening our bonds in the near future." She raised her glass. Her stained red lips looked like two parallel lines sitting on top of a crumbling porcelain doll.

A hand slipped underneath the table, applying pressure on top of my bouncing leg, halting it. Congruent Attali raised his glass to me. With shaky fingers, I lifted my glass in return before setting it back down.

"See, Your Highness, we are not each other's enemies, but allies." My Mother reached across the table. The queen placed her frail fingers into Mother's palm. They squeezed each other's hands, sipped their drink, then let go, returning their glasses to the table.

"Exactly," Prince Theolo took a gulp of his lemonade. "The real enemies are the Fire Kingdom," he said, slamming his glass down onto the table, almost shattering the fragile crystal. "The ungifted, the cursed. Not one ounce of the Spirit's manifestations flows through their malignant bones. If it were up to me, I would rid all ungifted from existence. Isn't that right, Mother?"

The queen agreed with a gentle smile.

"Not all ungifted are Fireborns and not all Fireborns are inherently evil," Congruent Attali spoke. "To say you wish death upon all the ungifted also means wishing death upon our own people."

"And what of it?" Theolo narrowed his eyes. "The ungifted are cancerous. They need to be cut out from the source or else they affect us all. And to say Fireborns aren't all evil is to turn a blind eye to the thousands of innocent people they kill, steal, and enslave to this day," he scoffed.

"Can you not see it's the Fire King, David Dricon, that's the source of the poison of the Fire Kingdom and not the people?" Attali countered.

"And can you not see, Congruent Attali, that once the cancer has infected the brain, the only fix is the death of the entire body? There's no need to waste precious resources to make their end comfortable. Just pull the plug."

"And what of the Redux? The sect of Fireborns who are denouncing the king, fleeing the kingdom, and vowing never to take up arms for war? And what of our honor that states we, the reapers, will shelter and protect anyone who stands for peace?"

"What of the cowards!" Spit flung from the prince's lips.

The room was silent. Everest was tucked into Mother's arm, as Mother patted her gently. Father stroked his beard, his eyes bouncing from Attali to Theolo. The queen shifted the black pearls on her wrist as if she hadn't a care in the world.

"This is mad," my voice cracked. "We are talking about genocide over breakfast."

Theolo clicked his teeth. "Get over it, princess. You'll speak of worse things once crowned queen."

"Worse than genocide?" I looked at my parents. Their faces were unreadable.

Father cleared his throat to speak. "In the old world, those with Fireborn blood ruled in tyranny. They enslaved millions for centuries while destroying the ecosystem, stirring up blood lust, and going to war with other nations and kingdoms at the drop of a hat. Their greed, in fact, ended the First World. If it weren't for the Six Spirits that stepped in to save humanity, the world would have been destroyed by fire." Father leaned in, placing his elbow on the table. "That being said, the Spirits entrusted us with their gifts while cursing the Fireborns to damnation. Full or half-blooded, they bear no gifts, no manifestation, no power. And if ever the Fire Kingdom is restored to their fire alignment, it could mean the death of us all," Father said as he leaned back into his chair. There was a slight pop in the seat as he stroked his beard.

Theolo stabbed a fat piece of bacon and shoved it into his mouth before speaking. "Reaper above all else," he said, nodding to Father. "That's something worth toasting." He raised his glass. The rest of the table joined. Everest, with a stretched grin, raised her glass the highest.

To my surprise, it was Attali, Mother, and I who sat quietly. Mother glanced at me, giving me the weakest of smiles. I gave her one in return.

"Well," the queen announced once the table settled. "All this wessie talk has turned my appetite."

I flinched at the derogatory name for Fireborns.

The queen continued. "I could go for some fresh air now." She fanned herself. "Princess Bellamy, will you?" She folded her napkin onto the table.

I turned to Father. He pointed his head to the door, nudging me to go.

"Of course, my queen."

I bit back the disgust crawling out of my throat. As I removed myself from the table, Congruent Attali also dismissed himself. He reached out an arm to the queen, and she grabbed hold with a pointed smirk.

"Father," Everest spoke as I headed toward the dining hall exit. "I have something to discuss with you and Mother, if you don't mind," she said as the dining hall doors closed behind me.

VIII

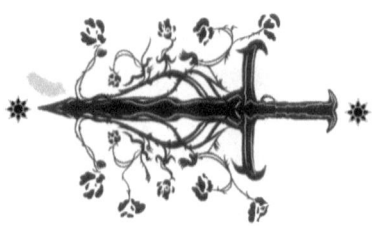

WE ROUNDED THE SOUTH side of the palace as the Blood Elite were doing their morning runs. The queen was engulfed in conversation with Congruent Attali, and I was relieved that he was doing all the conversational heavy lifting. As the Blood Elite passed by, they paused, saluting the queen.

66

"Reaper above all else!" they shouted, bringing their fists over their hearts. First lieutenant Quande, followed by second lieutenant Fia, ran over and bowed. The queen raised the back of her hand to Quande, who was sporting black joggers and hard muscles slick with sweat. His hair was in medium-sized individual plaits with the sides shaved to reveal a black reaper dagger.

"My queen," he said, kissing her rings.

I pretended not to notice the queen's lips twitch as if she was holding in a girlish grin.

I had to interrupt. "Shall we stroll through the garden maze?" I asked her.

The queen rolled her shoulders. The tip of her fingers lingered in Quande's hand. Finally, Quande released her fully, dropping his hand to his side.

Am I the only one in this place that refuses to kiss the queen's ass?

"I have a better idea," the queen said. "Today is such a beautiful day and I would hate for it to go to waste. Quande, won't you be a dear and fetch my carriage?"

"Right away." He bowed again before heading towards the palace's parking lot. Fia, a tall man with biceps larger than my face, shouted to the Blood Elite to continue their jog down the pathway.

"This is where I will take my leave, Your Highness," Congruent Attali bowed. "Princess," he said, turning to me. "I hope we can see more of each other. Maybe even share some bread with fresh whipped butter." He raised a brow.

"That sounds perfect." I nodded, trying my hardest not to trace his full lips and long neck. He bowed again, then left, headed toward the palace as the queen and I continued our stroll.

"This Earth Temple being built on Reaper soil is another

historic first. Many people are against this idea. They say two spirit temples in one kingdom are bound for trouble." The queen contemplated, peering off into the distance. "What is your opinion, my child?" There was a slight influx to her tone.

I knew I needed to tread lightly, especially because of my speech at breakfast.

I can do this. Don't piss off the queen. How hard could that be?

"Respectfully, I have little of an opinion because there are still some factors that I must take into consideration in order to produce an accurate statement."

The queen huffed, "Oh, please. Enough with politics. Tell me the truth, child." She turned to me; her amber eyes stared daggers into mine. "What are your real thoughts?"

I swallowed my spit, not knowing how to give a sugar-coated answer. I attempted to muster the deepest Everest in me, but came up short. I closed my hands into fist, making sure my nails were digging deep into my itchy palm. "I don't see the point of building an Earth temple in the Reaper Kingdom. Especially since I'll take my throne. Supposedly, all the Earthborns that have migrated into the city will follow me back to the Earth Kingdom. Unless..." I pondered for a moment. "...they don't plan to. Many Earthborns still see Mother as the rightful queen. As you pointed out at breakfast earlier, many Earthborns are purist and don't believe a mixed breed could success-fully rule the throne." I paused, looking at the sky.

It was a clear day. The sun barely peeked over the steel towers. I laughed for a second.

"What's so funny?" The queen halted.

"It's just. I had this idea pop into my mind that when I take my throne, the Earthborns will flee to the Reaper Kingdom and join with Mother. Maybe even try to overthrow me." I studied the queen, whose pursed pink lips had gone white as she pressed the fine lines harder together. "But that would never happen," I said, the itch-like little bites crawling up my forearm.

"And how sure are you of that last statement?"

This was my mother we were speaking of. Do I believe she loves Everest more than me? Yes. That was no secret, but would she hate me enough to overthrow me, her own daughter? No, I couldn't believe that.

"I'm sure, Your Grace."

The queen's lips relaxed; her black dress made her pale skin appear powder-like. "We parents hold many secrets from our children. Most of those secrets are from our past. Throughout my life, I have seen brother rise against brother and mother against daughter. For a piece of privilege, people will do and believe the unimaginable."

"Excuse me, Your Highness. What are you suggesting?" My mind drifted to the red and blue tubes in Mother's earthbox and the unknown stranger.

"Absolutely nothing, my child. We're just having a light conversation." The queen tilted her head as she scanned my body. "If you keep scratching like that, you will cause yourself harm," she said, raising a brow and walking away.

I rip my nails out of my skin. What was she implying? Every word that came out of her mouth was for a reason. So what was the reason for those?

"You know," I called from behind her.

"If Mother plans to flood the Reaper Kingdom with Earthborns, it'll make more sense to overthrow your throne and demolish your courts instead. I mean, why would mother go against daughter when we could work together?"

The queen's shoulders stiffened. The shouts from the Blood Elite carried on the wind.

"And what are you suggesting, Princess Bellamy?" The queen didn't bother turning around.

I walked up behind her, my chest puffed in satisfaction. "Nothing, *my* queen. I was just making light conversation." The queen's carriage pulled up and parked at the end of the pathway. It was painted in a traditional matte black with wheels that were retractable for the glide mode. Attached were black chrome horses with a silver shimmer that reflected in the sunlight. These mechanical beasts needed no rest, sleep, or food.

Talk about horsepower.

I stood next to the queen as Quande jumped out of the carriage. "Here you go. Sorry for taking so long," he said, still shirtless. "I didn't intend to keep two beautiful women waiting."

The queen's cheeks turned bright pink. "Thank you, first lieutenant Quande. I'm very appreciative of your service to the throne." She glided a finger over his chest before placing her hand in his as he helped lift her into the carriage. In front, manning the horses, were queen's guards. Their reaper hoods cast their faces in shadow.

Quande held out his hand to me and I took it, silently mocking him behind the queen's back.

He pulled me in and whispered. "Meet me at 1500 hours in the Wooden Leaf," he said. His breath smelled of blackberries.

I nodded and climbed into the carriage.

"Have a wonderful day." Quande gave a thumbs up to the guards.

"What a gentleman, that one." The queen folded her hand into her lap.

I scoffed.

"You don't think so?"

"He's okay."

"Interesting," she hummed. "He would make a great fer l'amor."

My head snapped to the queen, who was gazing out of the window. The carriage rocked as we took off, but she stayed in perfect stillness.

Quande my fer l'amor? My lover?

The fact that the queen could present that idea made me ask.

"How many fer l'amors have you had?"

"Many," she said coolly.

I knew I was pushing it, but I asked anyway, "Before or after your king?"

I braced myself for the push back, but she simply chuckled. She turned to face me; her smile a direct reflection of Prince Theolo's. A sort of twisted grin that didn't make it to her eyes. When most people smile, something in their eyes lights up, but not hers. The piercing dark amber irises made shivers run down my spine.

"When I married the king, I was fourteen."

"You were a baby!"

"Hmm. The world that raised me differs from the world that is raising you now. By your age, I was well into my queendom."

"But why did he choose you rather than someone that was an older high noble?"

"Power, my dear. Never be mistaken. At the end of each day, power is all any man ever wants." She straightened her shoulders, pointing her chin. "At eight, I manifested. By ten, I had my gifts under complete control. By twelve, I could command a person by calling to their blood."

Blood-control. My Father was also a blood-controller. That rare ability meant someone could call to the blood and control them from the inside out.

The closest I've ever witnessed Father's gift was when I was seven. Father came home and went directly to his office. Excited, I raced to him, ready to throw my body into his. I wanted him to swoop me into his hands and spin me around like he always did. But that night, as I walked into his office, Father was bent over on his knees. Blood soaked the carpet; his clothes and hands were drenched in crimson.

I rushed over, tears in my eyes, praying to the Spirits that my father was alright. I pulled at his arm, shaking him as hard as I could. But Father was distant, as if his mind had flown away and left his body behind. When he came to, he grabbed me so tight that I screamed for him to let me go.

He kept repeating. "I did it to protect you. To protect you." He continued to squeeze me until Mother rushed in, quickly separating me from him. Later, when I asked Mother what he had meant, she simply tucked me into bed, flicked off the light, and warned me never to mention it again.

A year later, after that night, Father formed the Blood Elite, and the king had died.

As the queen sat across from me, staring out of the window, a tinge of guilt swept over my countenance.

"If I overstepped earlier, I apologize."

"Do you?" She glanced over.

"Yes."

The puff in my chest deflated.

The queen returned to gazing out of the window. "The first thing I learned as a young queen was once you make a decision, stick to it, and never apologize."

"What if it was a mistake?" I rubbed my nails along my skin, cooling the itch.

"You're the queen, my child. Write it in law. Let your

mistake be an innovation for tomorrow. Show no weakness. Show no mercy."

CONSTRUCTION ON THE temple grounds was a nightmare. The temple was half-erected, its pillars competing with the highest trees. The construction workers used their manifestations to levitate wood, steel, and iron from the grounds to lock them in the proper places. There were loud machines digging holes and cutting material in rectangular shapes. The temple would be small, unlike the gigantic Reaper Temple that resided close to the queen's castle.

The queen was right: this was historic. And now the question mocked me in my mind.

Why?

I could guess the queen's reasoning for allowing the temple to be built. The Earth Kingdom's resources. Whether the queen wanted to admit it, without the Water Kingdom and the Earth Kingdom, the Reaper Kingdom's army would be nothing. Sure, they could fight, but could they fight on an empty stomach while being dehydrated?

The queen and I strolled the length of the temple grounds before crossing over to the opposite street to take a break at the park. We sat on a bench in front of a beautiful lake. The sun's rays peeked over the steel towers, highlighting the lush, green grass. Children's jovial screams rang in the distance. Pedestrians moseyed by, ecstatic to get glances at the queen.

"I like you, Princess Bellamy. I believe with the right guidance, you will make an excellent queen," she said, crossing her legs.

"Do you think my doyens aren't suitable teachers?"

"I'm sure your mother's parents have good intentions, but it doesn't take a blind man to see that you are not Earthborn."

"Is that the reason you questioned my loyalty?"

A mother duck quacked at her babies waddling behind her. As the duck settled into the lake, her babies followed suit, all except for one. It stayed back on the edge of the land, quacking at its family swimming away.

"Loyalty is a fickle thing. Easy to come by, hard to keep. From one queen to another in waiting, question everything and everyone."

"That seems exhausting. Always having to watch over your shoulders. Who do you trust?"

The queen inhaled, and then slowly released her breath. "I trust people to be exactly who they are."

"How do you know who a person truly is?"

"By watching what they do, my child."

I hummed and nodded in understanding. "My sister says I'm gullible and don't understand the way of the noble courts. She says without her help, it would be like a sheep walking into a wolf's den."

"Do you think she's right?"

I thought for a moment.

The baby duck that was left behind sat at the shore, quacking to its family that were farther into the lake.

"I think I'm different, sure. But I also think, fuck the courts." I cringed, almost slapping myself across the forehead.

A slip of the tongue.

The queen let out a laugh. I had to do a double take to make sure I was hearing correctly.

"Reaper through and through," she said. "Can I tell you a secret?" She leaned in.

I couldn't help but close the gap between us.

"I agree, fuck the courts," she giggled.

I eyed her warily. Her smile crinkled the skin of her porcelain doll visage. Then her face went completely cold. The switch was so sudden that goosebumps formed on the surface of my skin. I tried to move my legs, but I couldn't. It was as if concrete weighed them down. My heart thudded against my chest and sweat prickled at my forehead. I tried to speak, but my mouth clamped shut.

My head twisted forward without my permission, looking out at the lake. The baby duck called out to its family, but they had drifted farther away. At the corner of my eye, a black figure with long wings swooped down and snatched up the lone baby duck from the edge. My heart dropped as the small duck cried out one last time, then went silent.

"Take this as a lesson, Princess Bellamy. The moment you let your guard down is the moment you allow someone else to take complete control."

My body grew tighter, as if it were crumpling onto itself. In my head, I was screaming to be released.

The queen continued. "Those in power must remain in power. We have spent centuries putting systems in place to maintain said power. It is not only for our protection, but also for protecting all those who come after us. There will always be those with no power. This is how the system works. Everyone must know their place."

My back cracked as my body involuntarily slumped forward. The queen scooted closer, placing her hand around my neck.

"To them"—she breathed before continuing— "the queen and the princess are sitting here enjoying a beautiful day at the lake. Perception is a part of upholding power over their sheepish minds."

The queen gently stroked my hair.

I strained to break free of her grasp, but I could not move. I wanted to call for my father, my mother, my family, but I knew they were far away. My body prickled as if someone was pinching my entire skin.

Anybody, please help me!

The queen spoke softly into my ear. Her breath smelled of fresh cut onions. "You, my dear, were born in a place of power and with unimaginable privilege comes responsibility and duty. When you disregard the courts, you disregard everything we fight so hard to protect." She patted my thigh. "In another life, I would have been proud to call you my daughter. That being said, I will let you go with a warning. Never"—she hissed through her teeth, her grip tightening around my lungs, snatching the oxygen away— "disrespect our kingdom again. Reaper above all else." She smoothed my hair back into its pin. "Now, be a good little girl and straighten your face." She smiled, her eyes blank and pupils round.

My body released from its torment, my lungs expanding as air returned. Blood rushed through my veins, causing me to become lightheaded. I wanted to shout. I wanted to make a scene and rush home. But I was too scared to move.

Weak. Pathetic. Ungifted. A disappointment to my bloodline.

Words that haunted me at night, robbed me of my sleep, echoed in my mind once more. I was living my worst nightmare at this very moment.

When the queen rose, I did not follow her. I sat on the bench, too paralyzed to even make the slightest sound. Just like that, the queen showed me what I was.

Weak. Pathetic. Ungifted.

Unable to defend myself or my people.

The laughter of children grew louder behind me as the world continued to move without pause. And the family of ducks quietly glided on the surface of the water, not giving a second glance to the baby duck that went missing.

IX

"How do you assess the depths of a river? 'With both feet,' said the fool."
Proverb 68:91 from the Book of Face, Mortem Era.

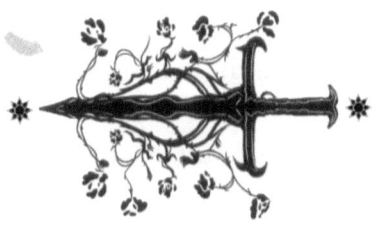

I KICKED A PILE of leaves as I entered the clearing of Wooden Leaf. The familiar smell of old wood and oak trees relaxed my shoulders instantly. Birds cawed within the canopies, followed by the heavy flapping of wings.

Quande stood in the center of the clearing.

Does this fool ever wear a shirt?

His caramel skin glistened under the rays filtering through the trees. There were daggers laid in a strategic circle on top of a wide tree stump. He ran his fingers across each handle until he found the perfect one. He plucked it up, balanced it on the back of his hand, and then, with one swift motion, he sent the blade flying. It whistled sixteen feet within a second, only stopping when the blade found the circular red target painted on an oak tree.

Quande grabbed another dagger. With the same intense concentration, he released it through the air. "You're late," he said. He was about to throw another dagger until he did a double take, looking my way.

"Uh-oh, what's wrong?" He tucked one of his plaits behind his ear.

"I don't know what you mean?"

He pointed the sharp end of the dagger at the box in my hand. "You're carrying a case of cinnamon rolls." He sniffed the air again. "With cream cheese and maple pecan toppings." Quande placed his dagger amongst the others on the tree stump. Adjusting, then readjusting the blades carefully, lining them with exact precision.

"You know, you could just let the daggers be," I said, crunching through the leaves.

"Shhh..." He slid the last one into place.

Ever since I could remember, Quande had been extremely tedious over the care of his blades.

"There," he said, licking his lips. "Now." He clapped his hands. "What do we have here?" He grabbed the cinnamon roll case before I could flop to the ground. "Where's the rest of them?" Quande plucked the last sweet, delicious roll out of a case of twelve.

I patted my belly. "Lost in transit, I would guess," I said, falling onto the soft grass.

Quande stared at me, then stuffed the last cinnamon roll into his mouth as if it would disappear the moment I looked at it. "May the Spirits rest, Bee. What has ruined your day?"

"Nothing." I shifted in the leaves.

"You come to our training session late. You're pouting as if piss poured from the clouds instead of rain, and you're gonna sit here and tell me nothing is wrong?"

I sighed. The truth was, I had sat on that bench for hours before I could finally rise. Even then, I spent another hour or so pacing the Second Reaper Ward, trying to pull myself together. Just thinking of the queen, the way she could have done anything she wanted to me without breaking a sweat, chilled me to my bones. I simply wanted to shove the memory into a sealed vault in my brain and never open it again.

I laid back on the grass, redirecting the conversation. "When I was at the bakery, I saw your fer l'amor. What's her name? Dahlia?"

"I don't have a fer l'amor," he said, walking to the stump.

"Then who's the strawberry blonde you're bumping private parts with?"

"You mean Jenka?"

"Ah, yes. Jenka," I said, rolling the name on my tongue.

"She's half wessie," he said.

"What?" I faked a look of shock. "The first lieutenant of the Blood Elite army is having relations with a half-Fireborn? Scandalous."

Quande's face twisted in disgust. He lifted a water jug from beside a log, turned it over, and allowed the water to wash away the sticky toppings from his fingertips.

I propped myself on my elbows. "Let me guess. They are

good enough to release your cum into but not good enough to be seen in public with?"

Quande scoffed. "Whatever is wrong with you, you don't have to take it out on me."

Shrugging, I said, "I'm not taking out anything on you. I just want to know why Fireborns are so hated, but *prestigious* men like yourself always find your way into their bedrooms. Breeding more ungifted half-breeds that everyone despises."

"For me, it's complicated. I can't speak for those other *prestigious* men," he mumbled. He ran his fingers over the daggers, picked one, scanned it, and then placed it back down.

"It doesn't seem too complicated to me. If I hated someone, for example, Prince Theolo, I wouldn't dare let his shit-stained underwear, limp, lifeless dick, get anywhere near me."

"And how do you know his unders are shit-stained?"

"Aren't all boys?"

"Nah," he laughed.

"I'm just saying I wouldn't do it." I tried to use the word wessie, but I could not pull it from my lips. "That woman really likes you, and you're toying with her. That's not okay."

Quande let a dagger fly.

I heard a thud as the blade connected with its target.

Before he went for another, he turned to me. "You know, I don't understand why I am getting all this flak from you. I didn't wake up in your bed this morning, or is that the problem?"

"What?" I sat up straight.

"Admit it. You want me to be your fer l'amor?"

"Absolutely not." I said flatly.

"Well, somebody ain't fucking you right. You know I would." He winked.

"Don't make me fucking gag," I said. "You're like a brother to me. I'll never see you that way."

Quande paused, his hand hovered over his daggers. "You wanna fight me?" he said, his voice low, almost threatening.

"Maybe I do."

I rose from the ground, dusting the leaves off my dress.

Quande backed away from the tree stump, his muscles taunt, revealing a hard-earned sculpted six-pack. I walked to the stump, studying the daggers before reaching underneath the slit of my dress and grabbing the one strapped to my thigh.

Quande stopped when his back hit a nearby tree. "What's up, princess? Show me what you got."

I launched the dagger directly at the center of his forehead.

He didn't flinch as the blade hurled his way. Black smoke shot from behind him in one blink of an eye, stopping the dagger an inch from his temple.

"Again," he said, his muscles flexed in his jaw.

My heart pumped as the need to satisfy my anger exploded from the pit of my belly. I yanked the daggers laid out on the tree stump and hurled them at Quande. His shadow stopped each blade before they could come close to him.

My skin itched, and I wanted to rip my flesh off my bones. *Fuck the queen!* I launched another dagger at Quande. It stopped two inches from his penis.

I am not weak! I gritted my teeth, picking up the last blade and rushing toward him. His black smoke broke out into eight extended arms as he braced for impact.

It wasn't fair that he gets to have this power and I don't. That he was the son that I could never be. The prodigy, the trusted, the one that Father spent countless hours training with when it should've been me. It wasn't fair that I was ungifted. If I only had a taste of his power, I would have been able to fight the queen. I wouldn't be scared shitless like some six-year-old too frightened to turn off the lights because of the big bad monster that lurked under the bed.

I sliced at Quande, my limbs shaking in anticipation. Quande blocked my blows, dipping in and out of my arm's length.

"Who are you fighting?" Quande shouted.

I bit down on my bottom lip, faking a punch only to do a round kick. He blocked, snatched my leg, and pulled me off balance. I allowed my weight to guide me forward as the dagger in my hand sliced at his torso. The blade connected, tearing a thin layer of flesh that quickly filled with blood.

Quande tossed me to the ground. His eight shadow arms balled into fists as he aimed them at me. I rolled to my feet just in time as the first punch hit the ground. I kicked off my heels, burying my toes into the soil for a better grip. The next shadow fist came quicker, followed by the third and fourth, each blow in rapid concession.

"You're sloppy, Bee!" Quande spat as a shadow punched me in the gut. "You're slow." Another black shadow slapped me across the face. "You're wild and uncontrolled. Where is your focus?"

Another black shadow wrapped around my legs and pulled me off my feet.

"This is unlike you." Quande strolled closer, his shadows releasing me, and drew back to him. The eight inky black shades looked like spider arms encapsulating his person.

The dagger was still in my grasp. I attempted to catch my breath, but instead, tears ran down the corner of my eyes, all the way to my ears.

"You are fighting with emotions, not with mind, not with skill. You will never win like this," he said, bending over me. His torso had already healed from the earlier wound. Only a fine vertical layer of dried blood was left. Quande's shadows quickly disappeared. When the last shadow vanished, with all my strength, I launched the blade at his heart.

I screamed with all my might, allowing my frustration to be released in this one deadly blow. Quande's face morphed into the smirking queen that I could never touch. I wanted to kill the queen, not Quande. Panicked, I glanced at the dagger. The blade had stopped a few inches from his chest. One shadow acted as a protective layer and another shadow wrapped around my wrist. Shocked that I would ever get this angry. The wound from the queen was too raw and too deep to properly process.

"I'm sorry." My voice cracked, avoiding eye contact. The dagger slipped from my hand to the ground.

Quande pulled me into his arms. "I know you're hurting right now. When I heard the news, I didn't like it either. But you must allow her to make her own choices and be her own person."

I pushed away from Quande, looking into his eyes. "What?" I said.

"Everest." He tilted his head. "Isn't this what you're fighting about? I know you don't like Prince Theolo. None of us do, but he's to be our next king. I think it's an honor that he chose your sister to be our next queen."

My body slacked, my head spinning. "What?" I rapidly blinked my lashes.

"You haven't heard? They announced their engagement when the queen returned to the palace. It's all everyone has been talking about."

I wanted to vomit. The inside of my belly was doing somersaults. This blow hit harder than any of Quande's shadow punches.

My legs almost gave out as I wobbled on my heels.

"Where is she?" I mustered to speak.

"Bee. Calm down."

"Where is she?" I ripped myself out of his grasp.

Quande swallowed, his Adam's apple bobbing. "She's hosting an outing by the garden maze."

I turned to walk away.

"Bee, please. I think you should cool off first. Breathe," he said.

My mouth dropped. Pressure built in my chest.

Quande stepped toward me. "Bee, it's no big deal."

"No big deal!" I screamed. "How could she? She promised me!" I reached for the dagger off the ground while my mind processed. How could this be? Everest just said she wouldn't take any of his advances seriously. "She fucking lied to me!"

Quande's shadow grabbed the dagger before I could reach it and held it in the air.

"Bee. I know this is a lot to take in. But it's her life and honestly, it's a great strategic move for her."

"What?" I paused. "Strategic move?"

"Yea, I mean... She's half Reaperborn. If she marries a full Reaperborn, there's a good chance their seeds will be Reaper-born. She will literally birth the next Reaper heir. Don't you want that?"

"Are you asking me if I want my future niece/nephew to be raised by a self-important, egotistical, bastard prince and the evil queen? Do you know what she did to me today?" I dug my nails into my itchy skin.

Quande shook his head.

"Blood-control," was the only thing I had to say before Quande's mouth turned into a surprised O.

"Bee. I didn't–"

"And now you want me to remain calm when my sister has announced she will get married to monster number two?"

"Bee, I'm sorry that happened to you. That was not okay. It's just, I don't think it's the right time to talk to her."

"Then when will be the right time? When she's walking

down the aisle, or would it be when she's pregnant with his seed?"

Quande was speechless. He ran his tongue over his bottom lip, searching for the right words to say. "Just wait until tomorrow when you're levelheaded."

I clicked my tongue. I didn't want to hear that shit.

"Bee!" Quande shouted.

But it was too late. It was like I took my ears off and placed them in my pocket. As I stormed off, the only voice I wanted to hear next was Everest's.

MY SKIN WAS ON FIRE. No matter how much I scratched, I couldn't shake the prickling needles running rampant all over me. The hot sun beamed on my neck as I hiked the hill to the east side of the palace, where the maze garden stood. Any uma in my way quickly made themselves disappear the moment they caught the wave of my wrath.

As I rounded the last corner, I immediately spotted Everest sitting facing her friends. Mesala, one of Everest's childhood friends, reached out and pulled Everest's ring finger. They all squealed and gushed at the new diamond placed upon it.

One lady looked past Everest and spotted me. She then leaned in and whispered something into Everest's ear. I couldn't see my sister's face, but her shoulders immediately stiffened.

Breathing heavily, I finally reached my target. I patted as hard as I could, one finger on Everest's shoulder. The other women muttered words to each other that I didn't care to hear.

"May I help you, sister?" Everest sipped from her teacup, rolling her shoulders as if I hadn't just stabbed a hole in them.

"May I borrow you for a moment?" I said through clenched teeth.

"Whatever for?" She smiled at her so-called friends, not bothering to look at me.

The ladies snickered underneath their breath, which pissed me off more. One of the bougie socialites pointed at my muddy bare feet. I didn't care to cover them up. As a matter of fact, I placed a muddy foot on one of the empty chairs for them to see. They went silent, eyes wide, as if they were watching a crash in slow motion. I plucked a cookie from a plate with my thumb and forefinger, holding my pinky high. I bit into it, then took the rest of the cookie and crumbled it into my palm. The ladies gasped, clutching their pearls.

"Sister!" Everest yelled, slamming her teacup on the table. She grabbed my arm, tugging me away from her friends. A coy smirk played on my lips as I blew kisses at the ladies. Mesala hid a smile underneath a raised teacup.

Everest dragged me several feet away from the nosy tea party.

"What is your problem?" she said, straightening her sheer dress.

"My problem?"

"Yes, your problem. You're acting like an uncivilized wessie."

"When did you start using terms like that?"

"And when did you care, Bellamy?" My sister crossed her arms. "What is the meaning of you interrupting my gathering?"

The way she stood in front of me, as if she didn't just announce the very thing I begged her not to do, was astounding.

Is the universe playing bloody tricks on me?

"When were you going to tell me about you and Theolo?"

Everest sucked her teeth. "May the Spirits rest, Bee. Is this what your tactless display is all about?"

"Tactless? Are you really going to insult me as if you're not engaged to the prince of tacky and tasteless?"

"Don't talk about him in that way," she commanded.

"Since when do you stand up for him?"

"Since I decided to marry him."

"So now, fuck me, huh?"

"Why do you make everything about you?" Everest shoved my shoulder.

"I'm not making this about me. The prince, the queen... they're all mountains of horseshit and you're trying to spend a lifetime with them? Have his seed?"

"You're jealous!" Everest said, followed by a loud, "Ha!"

"Jealous of what?" I threw up my arms.

"That you won't be the only queen in the family."

"For the love of all things gifted, Eve. I don't care about titles. This isn't a competition. We are not in a race of who can finish with the highest nobility!"

"Are we not?" Everest's voice lowered. "I can't go a day without Mother grooming me to be your advisor to the throne. Every waking moment all I hear is 'what's best for Bellamy', 'be a dutiful sister for Bellamy', 'watch Bellamy', 'Bellamy this', 'Bellamy that'. It's like I was only born to be of service to you!"

I ran my palms down the length of my face, sucking in my breath.

"You're blaming me for Mother's actions?"

"I'm blaming you for ever being born!"

I stumbled backwards. "You don't mean that, Eve," I said, shaking my head, biting my bottom lip. "We are both angry right now—"

Eve cut me off.

"That's it. Right there." Everest poked me. "I have the right to be angry. My feelings matter!"

"Of course they do, Eve."

"You were the one that said, and I quote, 'Maybe, instead of worrying about what I am doing, you should probably worry about your damn self'." She placed her hands on her hip, cocking her head to the side.

"I didn't say that to mean get engaged to the fucking prince!" I hissed.

"Well, what's done is done." She wiped her hands together and shrugged.

"Listen," I pushed down the rage building inside of me. "Today on the outing with the queen, she..." I bit my lip. "She used her gifts to threaten me." My eyes watered. The panic that I felt during that moment flooded my mind.

Everest blinked rapidly. Her jaw shifted. She looked down at her feet, then back up. "If the queen did something unbefitting, then it was with reason."

I was stunned. "Eve," I whispered.

"It could very well be something you did or said, and maybe you should examine yourself instead of shifting blame to the queen."

"Sister. You can't possibly mean that."

"I mean every word." Everest glanced behind her. The ladies at the table stood up, holding on to one another. They set their sights in our direction with concerned looks plastered on their faces.

"Eve." I reached for my sister's arm, and she pulled away.

"Can you even imagine how it feels to do everything right and still be considered a disappointment?"

My mouth opened to speak, but she cut me off with a finger.

"I will never be you, Bee. But I can be me. I can make a way for myself and for my future generation. Unlike you, I can smile, and pretend, and play my role just like the best of the court's nobility."

"But you're saying this like you're a disappointment and you're not," my voice cracked.

"I know I'm not. The disappointment is you." Her golden skin blotched red.

My heart sank, and my knees almost gave out. I stepped back, ripping my eyes away from her face.

"The emerald-green eyed daughter blessed by the Earth Spirit to continue the Abiola name." Everest shook her head. "Look at you. You can't survive a day at court and now, the fate of an entire kingdom rests on your shoulders?"

"Stop." My voice sounded foreign to my own ears. It was like a twelve-inch nail was being hammered into my chest with each word she spoke. I clenched the side of my ribs, the itching spreading like wildfire.

"Why should I stop?" Everest said. "I will be a better queen than you can ever be, sister."

The fiery flickers of my anger blew out like a candle wick without wax.

Everest opened her mouth.

Please take it back. Take it all back.

Everest clamped her mouth closed, raising her chin and squaring her shoulders.

"Pathetic," she said, while strutting away.

I dug my nails into my arms, the physical pain taking away the emotional blow to my heart. My skin wouldn't stop itching, and I dug deeper, unintentionally drawing blood.

Everest regrouped with her friends. They hugged her, patting and comforting her in their embrace.

I stumbled, allowing my feet to take me as far away as they could.

X

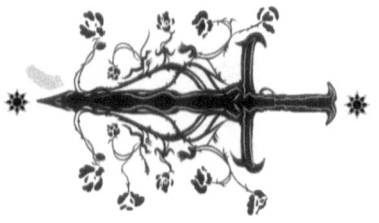

"A drunk man knows no secrets or regrets."
Proverb 5:05 from the Book of Face, Mortem Era.

THE SECOND REAPER WARD came alive at night. Dim lights, flashy business signs, and buildings suspended in the air. I stood in front of the taphouse, a place that allows anyone to legally indulge in their satisfactions without judgement. Music, shouts, and howls blasted from within. A patron stumbled out into the night, clothes slipping off his slim frame. He sang loudly as he wobbled into an alleyway. A few moments later, the poor guy fell face-first into some trash. He laughed, hiccupping between drunken murmuring and a state of stupor. He eventually passed out, making one of the trash bags a pillow.

There was a sign on the taphouse door that read, "A Reaper never sleeps, nor do I. Welcome." I pulled my reaper hood forward, casting my face in shadow. Underneath, I had on my father's button-down white-collar shirt and black jeans. I laced my favorite pair of black boots that held a dagger snuggly inside. Now, I didn't know if I was standing in water or piss, but I shook my boots before climbing the steps to the entrance door.

Inside, the place was packed. I immediately crashed into a man that smelled like he had gone weeks without a bath. The front of his chest was wet, his thin hair plastered to his forehead. His belly bounced as he spoke, "Excuse me, er..." He looked closely, his hand reaching for my hood. I jerked away, pushing myself through the crowd until I spotted a corner seat at the bar.

Crossing the room was no easy feat. I rubbed against enough people that starving for physical touch would no longer be a problem. Beer splashed on me when I navigated past a topless bartees that held six beers high above her head on a platter. Reaching the corner seat, I perched on the edge. I tugged my oversized hood over my brow. I didn't want anyone to recognize me, even though I disguised my emerald-green eyes using dark brown lenses.

Tonight, I didn't want to be Earthborn, Reaperborn... hell, I didn't want to be born. I wanted to be nothing. A penny forgotten in the streets of an abandoned village. I wanted to dull the lingering heartache that pinched and rubbed like a too-tight bra. I placed my head on the counter and allowed my thoughts to be drowned out by the musical instruments played by a live band in the opposite corner.

"Whatcha drinkin' t'night?" The accent was thick, like a wad of spit being held in her mouth. I popped my head up to see a woman with dark, straight hair, almond eyes, and full red lips, cleaning out a glass.

"Blood wine, please."

The attendee moved in closer. "How old is you?" She scanned me.

I reached into my pockets and pulled out twenty coins. "Is this old enough?" I plopped the coins in her hand.

"Honey, with this amount of mon'y, you damn near bo'ght the bar!" She quickly put the coins in her purse. She disappeared and reappeared with a swirling thick red liquid.

"Now, dis ret here is our strongest batch! Le' me know if ya need another."

I nodded as she walked away. I hated the scent of blood wine. It smelled like acid and gas. I knew not what this stuff consisted of, but what I did know was that drinking too much of it would cause me to forget. And forgetting was what I needed the most right now.

A bald man sat next to me, watching. I nodded my head to him and he nodded back, tipping his beer to me.

The music went silent, and a man called out, "Drisunki!"

"Drisunki!" Everyone shouted in return. They hit the nearest thing around them with one thud, then picked up their drinks, swallowing them whole. The man that watched me slammed his empty cup back onto the table. A different topless bartees, a male with blue hair, went to work filling the stranger's cup. Before the music started again, the bald man cried out, "Drisunki!" over the crowd.

The crowd shouted back, "Drisunki," and slammed their fist on the table and downed their drinks. The bald man gave me a nod to take part. He slammed his hand down, I slammed my hand down; he brought his beer to his lips, and I brought my wine to my lips. He tossed his head back, his Adam's apple bobbing with each gulp. I bit back a gag and drank as fast as I could.

A minute later, I slammed my empty glass back on the counter; the music started. The jovial crowd, bouncing out of their seats with slurred voices, sang.

The room was spinning. I understood why people spent their lives chasing the bottom of a cup. It wasn't the taste, but the feeling once the intoxicating liquid got to work. My cheeks heated, and I smiled at the man across the room. He nodded back, holding his mug to me. The bartees filled my glass, and I allowed myself to be taken away by the drunken harmony of the song.

Love affair with War

"Drisunki!" Someone shouted after the song ended.

I shouted along with the crowd, "Drisunki!" I slammed my fist on the countertop and downed another blood wine. When I was done, the bald man appeared ten years younger. Something about the unibrow and unwashed look had a peculiar sex appeal. I burped, watching the blue-haired bartees pour me another. I tossed what must have been my fourth glass of wine down my throat as if I had waited my entire life for this liquid slice of heaven. Everything from this dreadful day melted away the quicker I found my reflection at the bottom of the glass.

"Another!" I called to the bartees, who immediately poured.

How dare the queen attempt to threaten me by using her gifts?

Who does she think she is? I laughed into my cup.

She's the fucking queen, stupid. The queen can do anything to anyone. And her pathetic excuse of a son thinks he can waltz in and take my baby sister away from me too? I will rip every single hair follicle one by one out of their heads! Do they not realize that I will be queen one day? That I will have the power to cease trading with them? Not only letting her and her son slowly starve, but all her people as well. I will do it. I swear I will do it.

"Another!" I yelled, licking the sweet tasting wine from my lips. Before I knew it, I had slipped off my stool and onto the floor. My hood fell onto my shoulder.

Why was everything so funny? I pulled myself from the floor and the bald man had disappeared. There was a large gathering in the middle of the room, and I wobbled to my feet and shoved my way through the packed crowd to catch a glimpse. In the middle of the circle, a redheaded bartees danced in front of a mechanical bull. She then climbed on top; her hardened nipples pointed at everyone with a watering mouth.

There was a written law about those who work as a professional bartees. To keep the safety and protection of topless and nude workers, each business must abide by the rules: Barteeses cannot be touched, groped, or take money for sex or sexual favors without written consent by the attendee, the bartees themselves, and the participant. If someone infringes upon the bartees, the establishment may punish the offender as they see fit. There was a rule in bold hanging behind the bar that read:

YOU TOUCH OUR BARTEES WITHOUT THEIR

CONSENT, THE ENTIRE BAR WILL TOUCH YOU WITHOUT YOURS.

I watched the redhead climb on top of the bull with shorts so small that her ass hung out of the bottom. The only other form of clothing was brown boots and beads wrapped around her waist. The bull flipped on. She grabbed the reins tight and rode. Fucking the bull while she moaned to the beat of the music playing in the background. The crowd howled, drumming on whatever surface they could find. I moved in closer, caught in the unchecked sensual energy that surged through the room. As the bull rocked its way toward me, the redhead's eyes locked on mine. She pointed out her finger, beckoning me to come forth. Heavy hands slapped my shoulder and pushed me into the center of the crowd. The blue-haired bartees, who was completely nude, walked over with papers in his hand.

"Consent," he said, grabbing my hand and guiding me to sign the papers. I scribbled something unintelligible on the dotted line. Afterwards, he handed the paper off to the attendee and guided me to the bull.

"Up you go." He lifted me off my feet and onto the bull. It surprised me how strong he was, especially since he looked so delicate and dainty. I straddled the mechanical beast facing the redheaded woman as she wrapped her long-tanned legs around me. She grabbed my arms and secured them around her waist. The bull kicked on. I grabbed hold of her tighter to keep my balance. The room was already tilting to the side. As the bull spun, the world went with it.

"Focus on me," she said, clapping her hand on my cheek.

"I've never seen you in here before." She sniffed me. "You smell like soap with a hint of fresh fruits." She leaned in and licked my neck. Cheers sounded around me, and I let out a little moan into her ear. She pressed her waist against mine. The redhead grinded on my lap. All my senses were dull and the only thing I could feel at this moment was the dam leaking between my legs.

Her lips brushed against the base of my collarbone as she undid the buttons of my white collared shirt. "Look around. Which one of these men do you want as tonight's main course?"

The music changed its tune to a slow, rhythmic, intimate beat. I pressed my cheek against her cheek as she guided my gaze to the howling men in the room. Most of them had stripped down to their unders. I wanted to see if I could have the blue-haired bartees until my eyes settled on a dirty blonde with long eyelashes in the room's corner.

The stranger.

He was easily the finest man here. My heart leaped and a ping of electricity shot from my mind to between my legs. Seeing him clearly, it was no mistake. It was him.

The bartees followed my gaze. "Ooh, you know how to pick them," she said, rubbing her breasts against mine. The bartees pointed to the man in the crowd. Another naked bartees ran out with papers. The blonde-haired man signed them without looking. He pushed himself off the wall, striding towards us. The bull stopped, and the bartees slid down, taking my hand and guiding me off the bull. When the man reached us, he automatically pulled the bartees in his arms while his deep blue eyes pierced mine. The bartees grabbed both of our chins. She pulled my face closer to his until our lips eventually met. The crowd cheered. A tiny jolt of white light flicked when our lips separated. That feeling of perfect bliss like a tidal wave, coursed through me.

I didn't want to stop kissing. I tasted his lips as if I wanted to eat him whole. He matched my energy by ripping open my shirt, exposing one breast.

He tasted of mint and herbs freshly plucked from the garden. I slipped my hand underneath his shirt and ran my fingers across lean muscles and a strong back. The bartees shouted, "Drisunki!" The crowd shouted back, "Drisunki!" and we all knew what came next.

The curly-haired, blonde separated from me, and I thought I was going to suffocate without his air. If he wanted to, he could take me right here in front of everyone and I would ride him like this bull until the sun came up.

The bartees leaned in and kissed me on the lips, then kissed him. She then bowed to the crowd, which had stripped. Many had already found partners to fuck. One man had another bent over at the bar, pulling his hair as he screamed with pleasure. Another man had two women, one already riding his dick and the other smashing her brown breasts into his face. I wanted to stay in this moment forever and forget everything outside of it. Forget about the palace, the queen, the prince and my fucking sister, who I hate and love with all my heart. I pushed those thoughts deep and smashed my lips into the mouth of the blonde-haired man. He welcomed me.

He unbuttoned his shirt, pushing me against the bull. With a swift movement, he gathered my legs, making sure he secured them around his waist. He then bit my neck, which made me jump with pleasure. He did it again, but harder.

Don't be a fucking bitch about it. Hurt me good.

I leaned back so he could get a better view. My skin was hot and only his touch could cool it. The passion, the carelessness, the destruction—I wanted all of it. Yet tears fell from my eyes as crippling thoughts invaded my mind.

Don't do it, Bellamy. What of your mother?

I'm not trying to fuck my mother. I'm trying to fuck him.

You will bring disgrace to the Abiola name.

Then so be it.

Your sister was right. You are a disappointment. A spoiled, pathetic brat that thinks of no one else but herself. You're the greatest disappointment to your family and to your people. You were better off never being born.

I stopped and placed my hand on his chest.

"I was hoping to see you again," he whispered.

I had so many questions about last night. Who was he, why was he stealing, what was he going to do with those tubes, and what were those red and blue fluids? And most importantly, why was it when he ran his fingers over my skin, the itch disappeared and all that was left was a slight electric buzz?

I swayed, but he held me strong.

"What's your name?" I slurred.

"Why? Do you plan to call upon me?"

"Maybe. Why are you here?"

He sighed, pulling me in closer. "You're asking all the wrong questions, princess."

His beard brushed against my cheek. "Then what should I be asking?"

He threaded his fingers through my hair. "For starters, what secrets are your parents hiding from you?" He kissed my collarbone.

I hiccupped, unwrapped my legs from around his waist and gently placed my feet on the ground. My body magnetically clung to him like I was a positive to his negative charge.

Don't let go of me. I wanted to scream. As if reading my thoughts, his chest smashed into mine, and his right leg split open my thighs.

"Why..." I shook. Knowing I should ask a follow-up question about my parents and how he knew them, but instead, I asked. "Why do I feel power between us?"

He smiled. "You're my intertwined."

My mouth gaped open. "That's impossible. I haven't manifested yet. To be intertwined means both parties have manifested and are capable of creating new energy or power through an exchange of gifts."

"Will you doubt what your body feels?" he said, running his fingers across my bare skin. I glanced down at the small light shooting from his fingertips and dancing across my chest. The buzz of power within craving for his touch. My eyes rolled back, giving in to his connection. Then suddenly, it was gone. I ripped my eyes open just in time to see him being thrown backwards.

The bald man stood over me with a different type of lust in his eyes. He wrapped his fingers around my neck, freezing me in place.

My head spun. The only music playing was from the loud groans of meat slapping against meat and moans in the background. My eyes darted widely, my skin itching for that touch of power. It took every inch of me to focus. The bald man reached into my pockets. His unibrow formed a single line across his forehead as his hazel eyes filled with greed. When he found what he was searching for, he pulled out my bag of coins. His long tongue licked his entire mouth as drool ran down his chin.

The blonde, combing his hair back with his fingers, cracked his neck. "You interrupted us," he growled.

The bald man turned to him. "Piss off, you wessie scum."

Wessie? I looked toward the blonde. Fireborn? He couldn't have possibly been Fireborn. They have no manifestations, no gifts, no power and yet, this was the second time I felt the growing need of electricity bloom within me.

The Fireborn narrowed his eyes. Blood lust oozed from his

pores. The bald man let go of my throat. I gasped for air, leaning over my knees, and catching my breath.

"You don't want to fuck with me." The bald man pursed his wet lips together and whistled.

I looked to see a group of men surrounding us. The Fireborn laughed. Faster than lightning, he snatched the coin purse from the man's fist and then threw it back at me. I barely caught it.

The bald man turned to his men. "Watch her," he commanded, then stepped toward the Fireborn.

The blonde did not back down. The smile that stretched across the Fireborn's face was one that I recognized. It read, *"You done fucked around, now you're about to find out."*

The bald man threw the first punch. The Fireborn dodged easily.

He threw a second punch. The Fireborn batted it away as if he was batting away an annoying kid who thought he was stronger than he actually was.

The bald man reached back for the third punch, but before he could launch, the Fireborn hit him square in the nose, sending the man flying back into the circle of his shady friends.

I thought Fireborns didn't have gifts. So, how the fuck did he punch this man so hard that he flew out of his shoes? Literally. One shoe rocked, then stopped where the bald man once stood.

"You should get out of here," he said as he turned to me, combing his fingers through his hair.

I shook my head. "And miss this fun? The party's just getting started." I tucked my coin purse securely in my pocket.

He tilted his head slightly. I didn't miss his eyes scanning me over before an inviting wink.

Then a white fist went across his jaw. The Fireborn stumbled back, blood prickled at the corner of his mouth. He swiped the blood with the back of his hand, smearing it across his chin.

This was the best intoxication of them all, adrenaline.

A hand clamped on my shoulder, and my vision became clearer than the sun on a cloudless day. My body did what I regularly trained it to do. Fight.

My fist automatically connected with this stranger's jaw. The man wasn't expecting the punch. He shook his head hard as if bells floated around him. I threw another punch while he was dazed, knocking him onto his ass.

I quickly assessed the situation. There were five men, correction, there were now four men standing, the fifth lay unconscious at my feet. The moaning from the room stopped as the patrons looked on with a new type of hunger in their eyes.

One man inserted his large dick into the ass of another man and yelled, "Fight! Fight! Fight!" Then he pumped quickly, slapping the bottom's ass until it turned bright red.

"You want to fight?" The Fireborn bounced on his toes.

I thought of Quande and the fight from earlier. "I don't think I'm in control," I said, eyeing the four men who had their fist up, ready to go.

"Fuck control!" The Fireborn growled. "Show these fuckers who you are." He shot a mischievous grin my way and I couldn't help but shoot him one in return.

"To make it fair, you take the big one and this smaller one here. And I'll take this big one and that smaller one," the Fireborn said, dividing the four men apart.

"That's not fair. Your big man is bigger than my big man." I cracked my neck.

"Maybe next time, princess."

The remaining men rushed us. One grabbed at my shoulder. I gripped his arm, swinging myself underneath it, causing his arm to twist. If I wanted to, I could pull once more and cause it to snap in two. Instead, I kicked him in the ass. He stumbled headfirst into an overturned table.

My fist flew wildly.

Music cranked on in the background, and an upbeat tune flooded the room. The crowd cheered on, taking up bottles, mugs, and soon fighting broke out all around us. Titties bouncing, dicks jumping, the bartees were on the counter dancing to the music. The attendee had pulled a metal door down around the bar to protect the merchandise.

I think I liked this more than the fuck feast. Every face became the queen and Prince Theolo.

A fist connected with my jaw, which shocked me back to the present. I stumbled but did not fall.

"Harder," I said, spitting out a mouth full of blood. "Harder, you little bitch!"

The man was shook. He frantically looked around, but it was too late. The side of my face was already swelling, and he had to pay.

"Hit me harder!" I screamed, marching toward him.

He stumbled, hesitant. Then resolve washed over him as anger set in his brows. He threw another punch. The wind whooshing past my cheek.

He's Windborn.

Got to be careful with Windborns. They can throw a punch without connecting to skin. The Windborn tried again, and I dodged. His face morphed into the Reaper Queen, and I snarled.

You're trying to use your gifts on me. You think I am weak! I'll show you.

I snatched the man. He was sweating profusely. Exerting his gifts must have taken a lot out of him. That was his fatal mistake. My fist revved back to punch him repeatedly until his body sagged to the floor. I climbed on top of him, his face switching from the Reaper Queen to the Reaper Prince with each blink. Blood squirted on my face and white shirt as I hit him harder. I kept punching until my fist cracked bone.

A bottle slammed against the side of my head. It knocked me onto my back. I lay there on the floor, staring up at the bigger man, his face bloodied and looming as he stood over me.

I laughed. A deep, gut-wrenching laugh. Before the big guy could reach out to grab me, a chair slammed into the side of his face. It sent him soaring into a crowd of people that I couldn't tell if they were fighting or fucking.

The Fireborn rushed to my side. He lifted me from the ground, brushing off shattered glass and dirt from the floor. His blonde hair pooled into his face, his mouth full of blood.

"Don't tell me that's all you got, Earthborn," he said, spitting out liquid crimson.

"Me?" I let out a loud, "Ha!" before stating, "You look like you've been losing the fight."

"I'm just playing around." He shrugged. "You know, trying to keep the morale up for the other guys. Make it look like they have a fighting chance."

"Oh, so that's what you're doing? Well, keep up the excellent work." I patted his shoulders.

"I always aim to please." He winked.

Fast movement caught my eye, and I ducked as a chair went flying over my head. The five men, broken and bruised, limped towards us.

"Grab my hand." The Fireborn held out his palm. I didn't question him. It was like my body knew instinctively what to do. I grabbed on tight, feeling the surge of lightning collide within me as my body burst with energy. I let go of his hands, and sparks of light flicked around my fist.

The Fireborn and I placed our backs to one another. The

connection of his body to mine sent a wave of fire into my chest.

A man charged at me. I cranked my fist back and struck. My knuckles connected directly to his nose as he blew backwards across the room.

Power.

I craved more power. I was salivating from blood lust.

Destroy them all. A faint whisper budded in the darkest corners of my mind. And I was elated to oblige.

Act III

XI

"Your rage won't be able to cook yams, no matter how hot it is."
Proverb 33:42 from the Book of Face, Mortem Era.

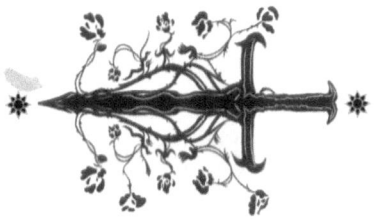

A MARE WITH AN IMPECCABLY BRUSHED MANE on black chrome peeked over the stall. I recognized that horse. I groaned. It was my horse. Her ocular lenses zoomed in and out as she silently judged me. My head thrummed like a drilling machine.

"Oh, shit." My stomach flipped as I rolled over to spill out my guts. Using my shirt as a napkin, I wiped the corners of my mouth. I almost hurled again because it smelled like pig shit. I leaned into the hay, examining the dried blood splatter on my clothing and stains from Spirits knew what. I had spent the night in the stables. The black mare neighed, lowering her snout to nudge me.

"Hey." I swiped her nose. "You're too loud." I shooed her away. I could almost hear ants eating a leaf twelve blocks north of here. I tried to stand. But my legs weren't ready. I rolled off the hay, barely missing my vomit.

Yemi, the judgmental mare, neighed harder, as if she was laughing.

"You're enjoying this?" I rasped. "Just wait. I won't be riding you for two months. See how you like that." Yemi's head bobbed as if she's shrugging. She then threw her head back over to her stall, ignoring me.

"Yeah, that's what I thought." I pointed. "And you better keep this between you and me!"

Yemi flicked her tail, neighing grouchily.

I used the stall door to climb to my feet. Slipped, caught myself, then tried again. Quande made hangovers appear so easy. This wasn't easy at all. My body ached something fierce, and I swear it felt like my kneecaps were removed. Every bone in my body screamed for a hot bath or maybe a tub filled with ice.

I cracked my back, finally able to stand on my own. The barn leaned. No, wait a minute, I was leaning, almost diving headfirst into Yemi's stall. I held onto the gate until my stomach settled. Yemi neighed, nudging my shoulder.

"I'm fine, girl. Trust me. I'll be okay."

The truth was, I was far from okay. The night was a painful

blur. How did I get home? The Spirit's guess was better than mine. I assessed a shaky step, then another, then another.

Okay, I can do this. I just need to sneak back into the palace without the ground hands, umas, parents, sister, and the entire reaper army seeing me. Oh, and yes, all the guests that haven't gone home from the Reaper Festival.

"She's in here." I heard someone say from the entrance of the barn door.

Shit. Shit. Shit. But before I could react, a ground hand, followed by my mother and sister, rushed in. Yemi pushed me with her snout as if to hide me.

"Too late, Yemi. I'll catch you in another life," I said, patting the mare's nose.

"What is the meaning of this!" Mother yelled with white-hot fury. Her wisteria coiled around her right leg, wrapping itself around her torso as it headed towards her shoulders.

"Hey, Mother. Fine morning," I slurred, trying to look as normal as I possibly could. Mother's clean-shaven scalp had smoke rising from the center. She crossed her arms; Everest mimicked her stance. Then Mother went silent, her chest rising and deflating with each breath.

This was worse than anger. Shouting and screaming, I could manage. But silence? Just axe me where I stood.

"Who has seen her like this?" Mother asked the ground-hand,

"Only me. I came to you right away, High Priestess."

Snitch. I made a mental note.

"You did well. You're dismissed."

The ground hand bowed, then ran out of the barn.

I turned to my sister, whose lips were tightly pursed.

Help me! I sent a wave of mental messages. She shifted in her heels as if to stomp on the messages received.

Mother's voice revealed no emotions. "What happened?" The lavender blooms on the wisteria trembled.

"Nothing."

Mother's fist clenched her skirt; the wisteria whipped the tip of its vine toward me like a purple snake head.

I almost jumped away but held my place. Then Mother's shoulders relaxed and the wisteria snuggled its vines on her shoulders.

"My daughter has been missing all night, then shows up this morning, in men's clothing, face bruised, smelling like vomit and you"—she flexed her jaw— "sit here and look me dead in the eye and tell me nothing happened?"

"I-I," I stuttered.

"Do I look like Boah, the fool?"

"No."

"So, why are you playing me for one?"

I swayed a little, balancing myself on the stall door. "I'll ask you again. This time, I better hear the right answer."

I nodded.

"What happened?"

I didn't tell her everything, just the parts that made sense. I needed to leave the palace, went to a taphouse in disguise, drank, and got into a little tiny fistfight. That's it. When I was done, Everest's mouth gaped open and Mother... well, let's just say I didn't think brown skin could turn red.

"Go directly to your room, get cleaned up, and do not leave until I send for you."

"But Mother—"

She cut me off with a finger. "No buts, you're out of buts, and if you open your mouth again, I will tape it shut myself," she growled.

I nodded and stumbled past her. She didn't reach out to slap my face, but what she said next slapped me, nonetheless.

"You are a great disappointment, Bellamy." Her voice was barely above a whisper. Her wisteria hissed.

I bit my tongue.

I know.

GLAYDECEE KNOCKED ON my bedroom door and commanded me to follow her. If mother wanted this to remain a private matter, then she should have chosen another uma. Glaydecee couldn't hold a cup of tea without spilling it.

It was almost evening, and dark gray clouds loomed thick in the sky behind steel towers. Fitting, really, that the day matched my mood. Let me guess, it'll probably start raining soon.

The uma led me to the south side of the palace, where the Blood Elite trained, to a section that was far away from prying eyes.

Glaydecee nagged every step of the way. "Your Father is furious, Beta. You've really done it now. About time you get punished correctly. If they left it to me, I would have bent you over my knee and taken a shoe to that round tail of yours."

I ignored her. Instead, I kicked rocks and dragged my feet.

"Pick it up! You're walking slower than snail snot," she yelled a few feet in front. "I'm three times older than you and can run circles around yo' fast behind."

I rolled my neck but picked up the pace. When we made it to the training grounds, Everest's afro was filled with feather-fews. She was dressed in reaper black, unlike her typical wardrobe. She stood next to Mother, along with a few soldiers.

Glaydecee led me to a spot between sister and Mother. "Here she is, wit' her hard-headed self. In my day, hardheads made for soft behinds!" She wagged a wrinkled finger in my face.

"When was that, exactly? Two centuries ago?" My voice was flat.

Glaydecee gasped. Everest slapped my hand, and Mother pinched the fatty part of the back of my arm. I flinched as she twisted my flesh.

"Thank you, Glaydecee. We will handle it from here." Mother twisted harder, then let go. I grabbed onto the back of my arm, attempting to soothe the sting.

Moments later, Father rounded the corner. The steel towers amplified his long strides. Within seconds, he stood before me in reaper black and leather, his fist positioned behind his back. He seemed to have grown gray hairs in his beard overnight.

He examined me, then grabbed my chin. I bunched my nose as he turned my face from side to side. He lifted the nape of my hair. There was fresh blood from a cut on my neck. It was probably created when someone hit me with a glass bottle. But I would not tell him that.

Father released me.

I knew it was pointless to explain, especially if he heard the story from my mother. I was positive that she blew everything I said out of proportion while adding her own flavor to the mix. Plus, if Father didn't ask a person to speak, then it wasn't wise to do so.

Quande whipped around the corner and ran to Father's side. He had his hair in a unique style today. The braids mended together like a scorpion. He whispered into Father's ear, then stepped back. Quande did not look at me. He stood at attention, waiting for Father's orders.

"Bring me the men who did this," he commanded.

Quande took off without wasting seconds.

A good little soldier, like always.

We waited in silence, which made the mood thicker. Guilt,

shame, self-loathing, and disappointment impregnated the surrounding air, and I could not breathe.

My skin itched from my arms to the right side above my upper thigh.

Be mad, throw something, hit something, don't just stand there and say nothing.

It was the silence that kept ripping my heart out. I dug my nails into my forearm, wishing I didn't forget to put on my skin cream. Underneath the epidermis, a million tiny needles prodded and poked, and I wished the Fireborn was here to cool my skin. The moment my thoughts fluttered to his bloody smile and blue eyes, my chest burned, and my body craved him.

A gentle tug at my dress made me glance down. My sister held out her hand. I stopped scratching and placed my palm in hers. She squeezed, sending some sorely needed comfort to remind me I wasn't here alone.

My eyes immediately watered. I squeezed her hand in return, sending the mental message of, "I'm sorry."

Soldiers marched in with men covered in black sacks. Along with Quande stood the Moonborn twins, the best trackers in the army. Father turned to face the men as the soldiers kicked the back of their knees sending them to the ground. There were five of them. One by one, the soldiers lifted the black bags from over their heads.

The heel of Father's boots dug into the gravel. The rocks shifted as he lined up with man number one.

Man number one had two busted eyes with a busted lip that hung. The second man had a broken arm with a matching broken nose. The third man had a cut going across his face all the way to his neck. He had a white bandage wrapped around his shoulder that was soaked through with blood.

I realized my dagger was missing from my boot.

The fourth man also had a broken nose that was hooked to

the left, with dried blood clogging one of his nostrils. The fifth man was worse than all of them. I remembered him. He was the man who punched me. His entire face was black and blue. Fresh blood dripped from his ears onto his shoulder. The top of his head looked cracked like a hard-boiled egg. The bandages were barely holding the pieces of his skull together. His right arm was in a sling and his fingers were broken. Father halted, inspecting the man.

"Who did this to you?" he asked.

The man did not answer.

"I will not ask again."

All five men looked directly at me, their eyes flashing with anger.

"Do you mean to tell me one woman did this to you?" My father shifted for a better view behind him.

The third man dared to speak. "By all respect, General. That ain't no one woman," he said.

Father turned to me, the rocks grinding under his shoe.

"Take them away," he signaled to Quande. "You know what to do with them." Quande clasped his fist over his heart and snapped into motion, directing the soldiers to remove the five men from the grounds.

What fate would they have? Only the Spirits knew.

Father took his time marching toward me. When he stopped, he re-examined my face. This time, he kept his fist behind his back.

"Follow me."

"Father, I–"

"That did not require a response." I shut my mouth and followed.

XII

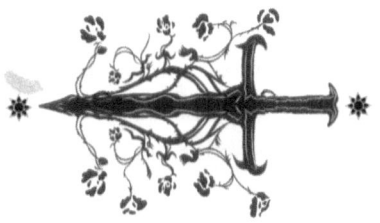

"Fathers, do you not see yourselves in your daughters?"
Proverb 3:01 from the Book of Face, Mortem Era.

I ENTERED MY FATHER'S OFFICE. The scent of leather and sandalwood immediately hit my nose. The walls were a deep shade of blue. Upon them hung paintings depicting the stories of my ancestors and the battles they fought throughout time. A portrait of my doyen-ma dressed in reaper battle black, a sword high above her head, an army at her back as she went against the Fire Kingdom in battle, hung above the fireplace. Medals, awards, and certificates of honor covered the wall behind Father's desk.

Father stripped himself from his jacket and neatly folded it on the back of a black leather chair. Naturally, my eyes fluttered to the map of the Seven Kingdoms and the stolen earthbox that was no longer hidden behind the frame.

The embers of a low fire cracked and popped from wood burning in the fireplace. Father took a poker, shifted the ash, then placed another log on top. The office was nice and cozy. I could melt into the couch and fall asleep for weeks.

Father patted the top of a chair positioned in front of his desk. "Sit," he commanded.

I did what I was told with haste, and my feet thanked me for the relief. Father stroked his beard once before heading to a brown shelf beside his desk. He pulled out a chestnut case, sat it on the edge of his desk, and unlocked the hatch.

At this angle, Father looked like he had aged. I kept asking myself, when did I miss the subtle signs of his youth leaving his features? To me, Father never appeared to grow old, but with the gray hair peeking from his beard, I had to acknowledge the creeping wrinkles etched into his moonstone skin.

He opened the box. Inside were four compartments, each one filled with medical supplies. He reached out his hand to me, palm up. I placed my fist with the cut knuckles into his calloused palm, then he went to work. He flipped the alcohol into a cotton swab and dabbed it on my knuckles. I flinched at the bubbling sizzle, not expecting the burn to be that strong. Afterwards, he fanned it dry. Then he took an adhesive patch and laid it over my tiny lacerations which sealed the skin shut seamlessly.

The minor bruising reminded me of the time Quande hit

me so hard, he knocked me out. When I came to, he was a mess. All snot mixed with tears. I asked him what he was crying about, and he threw his arms around me so fast and said, "You're not dead, I'm not dead. Next time, duck quicker!" Ever since that day, I learned to duck to reduce physical damage. I also learned how to use the weight of my body to hit as hard as I could before my opponent got the best of me. So, it's not surprising that my fist had the worst of my injuries.

Father wrapped my hand carefully, his eyebrows raised thoughtfully. His face relaxed, but his eyes had hints of red at the corners. When he was done, he stood.

He returned to the medical case and plucked out a small hairbrush and another adhesive patch, then made his way to my neck. He cleaned the cut and sealed it closed. My hair was sloppily done up in a bun which he undid.

When I was a young girl, maybe around the age of four, I hated getting my hair combed. Mother, always clean headed, left the hair duties to the umas. I would claw the umas until they released me. One day, my father called me into his office and told me to sit. He took out a water bottle and a brush, much like the one he was using now. He wet my hair first, untangling my knotted ends with his fingers. Then, he brushed my hair while he sang to me. When Father was home, he became my primary head comber. While he sang, I would fall asleep in his lap and he would hold me until I woke again. When I was old enough to comb my hair, I yearned for those sweet memories.

Now I had it again. As he brushed my hair, he hummed. The tune was the Blood Elite 'Home' song. The soldiers sung it when returning from battle. Before realizing it, I sang along. My father's cello base intertwined with my alto as he shifted through the strands of my hair.

Come Home

When the song ended, Father was on his knee. My face cupped in the palm of his hand. His eyes were red, and I was on the verge of tears. He scooped me into his arms and hugged me tight, as if I would float away the moment he released me.

"You reckless daughter of mine. What shall I do with you?" he asked, his voice trembling.

"Not too hard, Daddy. My body still aches pretty badly," I grunted. He quickly let go. When he pulled back, a wide grin spread across his face.

"That's what you get. Who told you to fight five grown men?" His voice rose like a little kid in a candy shop surrounded by all his favorite things.

"Well, I wasn't going to fight them. But they practically asked for it," I shrugged.

Father rose to his feet to take a seat on the edge of his desk. "So, tell me. What happened?"

"Well," I said, adjusting in my chair. "It went something like this." I told him what happened at the taphouse, omitting the parts about the red-head girl, the Fireborn, and the weird and yet exhilarating fuck feast, of course. Father's eyes lit up like he was gazing upon stars. He laughed, shouted, and wooted. I stood up, throwing punches completely engulfed in the story. Father clapped and insisted that I continue.

"Wait. Wait. Your stance is good, but punch like this, watch my feet. Make sure you're firm, and then hit them with the one-two," Father said, rushing to my side. I mimicked his stance, practicing with him a few times as we threw punches. When the stories and impromptu training were over, he belly laughed like I'd never heard him before.

"So," I picked at the ends of my hair. "You're not mad at me?"

"Of course, I'm mad at you. You could have gotten hurt, or worse." He tried to force the smile from his face, but it just grew wider. "It's just hard to be upset when I'm so damn proud." Father looked at me, and for the first time, it was like he saw me. The real me, not the one that I try to pretend to be to make Mother happy.

"I know it was Quande who taught you how to fight." He eyed me, one eyebrow raised.

"How did you know?" I jumped into the leather chair in front of his desk.

"With moves like that? It has Quande written all over them. Plus, you don't think I know what happens when my daughter and my first lieutenant disappear into the woods for hours on end?"

My eyes widened. "How long did you know?"

Father went behind his desk. He rolled up his sleeves to his elbow. "For about two years."

"Huh," I said, unimpressed.

"Has it been longer?" He paused, opening his desk compartment.

"It's been about four, going on five years now. And that's if you don't count us fighting as kids because then it would be a good ten."

Father paused.

I quickly explained. "I begged you to teach me to fight. But you wouldn't allow it. So, I would pick fights with Quande. At first, it was a wrestling move here, a punch there, but then we made a mistake and started fighting for real. After that, it just became our thing, fighting each other. Are you going to kill him?" I said, teeth clenching together.

Father snorted. "Quande is like a son to me. I would never harm him. But if you had gotten seriously injured, well... I would probably harm him a little."

"What?" I said, scrunching my face at the contradictions.

"I will have to scold him in front of your Mother, but he

will be alright." Father continued to open the top compartment of his desk and pulled out a tiny silver box. There was some dust on top, which he blew off. He took a few strides and was back in front of me, sitting on the corner of his desk. He passed me the box with all thirty-two teeth showing.

"What is this?"

"Open it and find out." He raised his eyebrows.

I don't know why I attempted to smell it first, but I did. Father chuckled. I cracked open the box. The inside was laced with red velvet. There was a pendant shaped like a red-tipped dagger hanging from a reaper steel chain.

"I got this created when your Mother was pregnant the first time. It was supposed to be for..." He shrugged. "Well," he sighed deeply, "this pendant is what I give to the soldiers I trust. This model was the first. I kept it because I wanted to give it to my first son." Father crossed his arms. He contemplated before returning his gaze to the tiny silver box. "I made this with my own hand," he said.

My countenance fell. I rubbed my thumb across the pendant before shutting the box and holding it out for my father to take back. "I am a daughter," I whispered.

"Yes, but you're *my* daughter. You carry the heart of a warrior. Brave just like your doyen-ma. You remind me of her." Father turned to the portrait hanging over the fireplace.

"Do you miss her?"

Father reached out, pushing the silver box to my chest, making sure I held it firm. I watched his eyes water. "She lives on in you," he said, letting his hand fall into his lap.

I tried to bite back my own tears, but I could not. I cried like a big baby, and my father held me in his arms like a fragile piece of precious art. We sat in this position for a long while before he released me again.

Father dried my tears with his thumb. "Now, what should

be done about your mother? She believes I enable you too much."

I gripped the silver box tightly. "She might be right," I giggled through sniffles.

He nodded. "Well, we need to come up with a believable punishment." He cocked his head. "Do you know how to fake cry?" He grinned.

I nodded, taking this moment in. "Daddy?" I paused, unsure if this was the appropriate time to ask, but I did anyway.

"Yes, Beta?"

"Mother's earthbox. What were those liquids inside?"

"Haven't we been through this, Beta? It's none of your concern." He leaned over and kissed my forehead before packing up the medical supplies.

"Is the box still here?" My fingers clenched around the pendant inside the silver carrier.

Father froze. "Why do you ask?"

I shook my head. "Curious, I guess."

Father continued packing the supplies. "Of course, you are. No. We had the earthbox shipped away this morning."

I bit my bottom lip. "You wouldn't hide anything from me if I asked, would you?"

Father eased into his chair behind his desk. "Would you?" He narrowed his dark eyes.

I LEFT FATHER'S office, holding the silver box close to my chest. I walked past Fia, the second lieutenant, in the hallway.

"Hey," he called out. "I saw your work, good job, badass," he saluted me, a fist across his heart.

My cheeks burned at his compliments, knowing that Fia was one of the fiercest soldiers in the Blood Elite.

"Thank you." I stood taller, straighter, and walked away

with a new purpose. As I turned the corner, that purpose flew out of the window when I caught sight of Mother. I hid the box and swallowed everything down like hard liquid and conjured sadness.

She stopped me, holding on to my shoulder, investigating for any signs of discrepancy.

"I'm sorry, Mother," I hung my head.

Her shoulders straightened. "And what did your father tell you?" Her wisteria was wrapped tightly around the length of her arm.

I sucked in my breath. "He said, not to leave the palace unless escorted. My location must be reported at all times, and I must attend every social event and not disappear." This one hurt the most. "And I begin my training to pledge to the Earth Temple." I forced myself not to roll my eyes. "He said he also had another punishment for me, but he had to talk to you about it and wait for further instructions."

If Mother had flowing hair, I was positive that she would flip it right about now.

"Hmmm." She studied me.

Why was she so damn intimidating?

Her presence filled the entire hallway, which made me feel small. A few heartbeats passed, then she released me from her claws. "Very well," she said, heading toward Father's office.

I released a slow exhale, my heart thumping within my chest.

I was convinced that woman must be a secret blood-controller. The way my body stayed frozen until the click of her heels faded from earshot reignited the paralyzing fear of the queen's grasp.

My palms itched, and I dug my nails into them to ease the irritation.

XIII

"What motivates someone if not their needs, wants, and desires?"
Proverb 70:15 from the Book of Face, Mortem Era.

"THE PRINCE HAS FORMALLY INVITED you to an intimate afternoon nosh. Come in your best reaper black." Silvia folded the paper in half and laid it on my bed. "Are you going?" she said, taking a comb and sectioning my hair for braiding. "Bellamy, are you listening?"

I couldn't help thinking about the Fireborn. Intertwined? That couldn't be possible. Since last week, after I had left Father's office, I'd tried to manifest. To move vines and roots like Mother, grow flowers like Everest, and even checked to see if I specialized in herbs like Silvia, but nothing. I couldn't even make a fucking leaf bend. Even so, to be intertwined with a person, it was often with someone of the same spirit alignment. I'm Earth, but he's Fire. The shit made little sense. Unless he was really Earth and just pledged to the Fire Temple. Cross pledges happened daily, but who in their right mind would willingly pledge to the Fire Temple?

"Princess Bellamy?"

And why did Father lie? I know the Fireborn took the earthbox. I saw it. So why say it was removed that following morning? The Fireborn said my parents were keeping secrets from me. But why? And why would I believe him over my parents? I didn't even know his name. Yet, I couldn't deny the effect his touch had on me.

"Bellamy."

How I no longer itched under his hold. How my body buzzed with electricity, how my chest burned in his presence, how I didn't want to let go.

"Bee. Would you like a red-orange shoe stained blue with hair glue?"

"Yeah, sure," I mumbled. How many intertwined people did I know? There were the Moonborn twins, but they're twins. Would their intertwining be any different from strangers, friends, or lovers? Regardless, most intertwined bonds were eternal. They live together, die together; they're fated.

"Bee!"

But why would the Spirits fate me with him?

"There's a fresh loaf of bread with butter here."

"Where?" My mind snapped from my thoughts. I gazed out to what I called my organized, messy room to search for the basket of bread. "Is there cheese too?" I asked.

"No, there's no cheese, no butter, and no bread!" Silvia pushed my head away and jumped off the bed. She circled in front of me, her hair wrapped and arms crossed. I sat on a pile of pillows that lifted me up so she could better braid my hair.

"Sorry, I thought I heard you say bread was here," I shifted.

"But did you also hear me say anything else for the past four hours?"

I glanced at the clock. It read 1100 hours. Damn, where did the morning go? I checked my individual braids; they were completed and styled to hang down my back.

"I have a lot on my mind. My apologies for my lack of listening."

"Do you mean that?" Silvia's feet tapped against the floor.

"Yeah. You think I'm disingenuous?"

"I think you're quick to say sorry, thinking that'll solve all problems and move on."

"Yeah, well...that's how apologies work, right? Say sorry and move on." I rose from the pillows, stacking them back onto the bed.

"Sorry is meaningless without changed behavior."

I faced her. "What *changed* behavior do you want? I'll listen more. Got it. Speak. Say whatever it is you have to say." I plopped on the bed.

Silvia's lips disappeared into her mouth as she stood, silent, her heels tap-tap-tapping against the hardwood.

"I don't have time for this. Are we done here?" I pulled loose some of the tighter braids that were causing a slight ache at my edges.

Silvia's mouth dropped open. She rushed over to the bed, packing up her belongings. "I guess we are, *master*."

"Master? Hold on, wait."

She brushed past me, and I grabbed her arm.

"May the Spirits rest, Silvia. Talk to me. I'm listening, deadly so."

Her lips disappeared.

"I don't know what to fix if you don't communicate with me."

"You—u," she stuttered. "You promised you would be with me that night. I waited for you. It's been a week and I'm still waiting for you."

I let go of her arm and sighed. "I have a lot going on. I keep getting caught up, Silvia."

"With what? Alcohol? That night, was it your plan to get pissy drunk then come stumbling into my bed?"

"No, not at all."

"They say they found you in the stables. That's not too far from the uma's plot. Maybe you couldn't make it before passing out."

"That's not the case," I groaned.

"What happened to telling me everything? Good and bad? I feel like I don't even exist to you sometimes." Silvia took two steps toward me. "We would lie in this bed until the sun rose, talking, and now I can't seem to get close to you without you rushing off to be somewhere else."

"What do you expect, Silvia? You, better than anyone, understand the amount of pressure I'm under. The duties I must complete and the image I'm already struggling to uphold. I will not keep every promise I make."

"Then why make them at all?" she shouted. "Don't say you're going to choose me when you know you're not."

"That's rich coming from you." I stepped toward her. "You

sleep with other people, and I say nothing. Anything you asked for, I supply to you and ask for nothing in return. Even before we started sneaking around, I was ready to give you a noble title, elevate you, make you more than just an uma, to which you declined. I've always chosen you. I've been with no other, even though it's my right to do so. You aren't even my public fer l'amor and yet everyone in this palace knows you belong to me." I licked my lips and stepped away. "I don't know what you want from me sometimes, Silvia. I feel like I do my best and it's never good enough. Not to you, my family, or the courts." I pointed to the letter on the bed, then dropped my hand. "Just tell me what it is you want and I'll do it. Anything you want, it's yours."

Silvia parted her lips, full, plump, and glossy. *Just like I like them.*

"I want you to choose me next time before you choose the bar. I want you to come to me before chasing your next bad decision. I want you to talk to me instead of holding everything in your head." Silvia strutted over, placing her fist over my heart. "I know one day you won't be mine. And a part of me is scared to lose you sooner than I had expected."

"You're not losing me." I pulled her into my arms.

"It feels like it. I'm not ready for it."

I rested my forehead on hers, breathing her in. She smelled like brown sugar and oatmeal.

"Bee, tell me what's really going on. What are you hiding?"

I thought for a moment. It should've been easy to tell her about the queen, family secrets, and the Fireborn; however, there was a grinding doubt in me not to do so. What could she do? My sister dismissed me and Quande, the first lieutenant and the closest thing I have to a brother, even his loyalty lies with Reaper. What was the point of talking about it? To gain sympathy?

I didn't need sympathy. And I didn't want her to worry about something she couldn't fix. I kissed her forehead.

"It's nothing of concern." I sounded just like Father.

Silvia's shoulders deflated as she pushed away. "Go to the nosh," she said dryly. "It's a part of your punishment to attend all gatherings without disappearing."

I clicked my tongue. "I'm not going."

"This is a perfect opportunity to not only show up to support your sister but also plant seeds for future relationships between the Earth and Reaper Kingdoms. And again, you have no choice. Both your Mother and Father signed off on it according to your schedule."

"You know, the older I got, the more I thought the leash around my neck would loosen, but every day it seems to get tighter to where I sometimes physically can't breathe."

"Maybe," Silvia said, walking towards the door. "If you start being a sweet and obedient puppy, then your parents will let you off the leash." There was slight playfulness in her tone. "Regardless, princess. You must go."

"Then come with me," I said, watching her hand grip the doorknob.

"As your uma?" She kept her back turned to me.

"As my plus one. My date."

"You know what *that* type of move would mean, don't you?"

"Of course, I do. We'll be confirming what everyone already knows," I said, stepping towards her. "You'll be my public fer l'amor. Meaning, you'll no longer be known as an uma, but my protected companion that goes where I go." I tilted her head to the side to kiss the crease of her neck. "Be mine, officially."

"Princess," she moaned in that sensual tone that I craved. My grip tightened around her wrist. A pulse of energy ran through me as I heard her heartbeat thump from the vein in her neck.

"Be mine."

Her body heat rose as her warmth called out. Sweat bubbled on her skin. I licked it, tasting the salt and smelling the aroma of brown sugar that bathed her. Her temperature rose again, and my grip tightened, flattening her to the door.

"Be mine," I growled.

"Bellamy," she squeaked.

The heat, I needed the heat. My skin rippled and my bones cracked. An insatiable hunger clawed its way up my throat. My nails dug into Silvia's skin. I wanted to eat her, consume her, lay her out on the bed like my own personal buffet. My grip tightened, pinning her in place. My mind became lost in the aroma of heat wafting off her skin in waves. My heart pounded as the itch pricked the surface of my skin.

You're mine. A faint whisper in the back of my mind sent electricity down my spine. An overwhelming sensation of ripping a body to shreds consumed me.

"You're hurting me!" Silvia pushed me, her elbow catching me in the chest, snapping me back to the present.

"I'm sorry, I'm sorry. I don't know what came over me. I'm sorry." I made a large gap between us. My skin flared into a batch of itching. I dug my nails into my skin, scratching my arms, undoing my dress, attempting to remove the fabric from my flesh. Silvia rushed to my dresser and pulled out my skin cream.

"Stop scratching. It only makes it worse." She grabbed my hands, attempting to secure them. But the itch was too power-ful. It was like I was being burned alive, slowly and painfully.

Silvia helped me out of my clothes and laid me on the bed.

"It hurts!" I screamed, unable to hold back tears with every stab of itchiness.

Silvia quickly unscrewed the cream lid and slathered it over my arms. The itch died down with a satisfying sizzle. Silvia then went to work on my legs and the relief almost made me close my eyes and sleep. Exhaustion overwhelmed me. The energy zapped from my body.

"Is that better?"

I nodded, pushing myself up on the bed.

"Your condition is getting worse. I think you should see a Life Doctor. I should let your Mother know—"

"No." I yelled. "No, I'm fine. I just forgot to put the cream on after the bath this morning, that's all. I'm fine."

Silvia studied me silently.

"I'm fine, Silvia."

She helped me back into my clothes. "Your Father is expecting you in twenty minutes, according to your schedule."

"Where?" My voice was harsh, my throat dry.

"South side of the palace, training grounds."

"Got it." I placed my hand on Silvia's wrist, and she jumped, pulling away. "I'm sorry, I'm sorry. I'm truly sorry. I..." I didn't know what to say. "I won't do it again. I promise."

Her lips disappeared into her mouth. Her brown eyes darted from me to the door.

"Will you come with me? To the nosh?" I dared not move, too scared that she would flinch.

"Yes," she eventually said. "But as your uma."

"Okay. That's enough. More than enough."

She rushed toward the door. "You should really see a Life Doctor. Your skin, it..." She swallowed, her grip firm around the knob. "Just promise you'll go."

"Tomorrow. I'll go tomorrow."

Silvia sighed as she threw the door open and left.

. . .

I ROUNDED THE SOUTH SIDE OF THE PALACE CORNER. Three figures stood under the vine-covered veranda. I noticed the vines shift as Mother spoke to Father. The leaves leaned in as if they wanted to comfort her or choke Father. Hard to tell.

I flattened myself to the wall and listened closely.

"You spoil her, Agrim."

"And what would you have me do, Oyame? Lock her away? Force her into submission?"

"That would be better than what you're proposing," Mother barked.

Father gripped the bridge of his nose. "She's young, exploring—"

Mother cut him off. Her wisteria coiled around her right arm. "She's immature, bratty, and needs discipline."

"And that's the reason this decision will be good for her."

"Agrim, darling. You're just giving her what she wants."

"Maybe giving her what she wants will allow some closure. If not get it out of her system completely."

I gripped the wall, my shoulder tensed as the dispute continued.

The third figure spoke. "I think this will be good for Bellamy. I have enlisted to watch her, help her through manifesting, keep her on the path toward the Earth Kingdom," he said.

The gears clicked in my brain. The third figure was Zef Coe. When Everest manifested, Mother called Zef to the palace. He's an Earthborn preceptor who specializes in guiding people through Earth manifestations. He had arrived with my doyen-ma, my mother's mother. I remember what doyen-ma said as Zef coached Everest into controlling her gift.

"She should have been his."

I had always known that my doyen-ma didn't approve of

my father. She had blamed him for the reason I hadn't mani-fested yet, saying his blood tainted our family line.

Watching Zef stand next to my father, in appearance, he was the exact opposite of him. Zef had long black hair that sat past his shoulders, a long thin nose between a pair of down-turned emerald-green eyes, and milk-white skin. His beard was thin and gave an angular cut to his jawline. His eyebrows made him appear to be always in deep thought, as if he was reading the person he spoke to.

The spit turned sour in my mouth at the very thought that my doyens wanted him to be our father.

"Zef." Mother placed a hand on his shoulder. "Thank you for being here. I know the Earth Temple will miss your pres-ence." Mother turned to Father. "This is it, Agrim. No more cradling her. She has a duty and this October, she will pledge on her birthday to the Earth Temple and begin the rite of passage. We are out of options. We cannot let—"

Father placed a hand on Mother's shoulder and responded, "The Spirits will guide her. Just like they promised."

The wisteria trembled.

Father stroked the purple blooms like a pet, and Mother's body eased. Father swooped her into his arms, kissing her on the top of her head. Zef turned away as if to give them their privacy.

"Don't worry, my love. This will work. She's our daughter, and as you witnessed she's already a formidable force," he said.

Mother patted his chest. "I trust you." She returned a kiss to Father's lips. Zef did an awkward shuffle out of my view.

My parents separated. Father stood, his hands behind his back, as Mother escorted Zef to another section of the palace. When they had disappeared, Father said, "Are you going to hide behind that corner all day?"

XIV

"How do you begin? By beginning."
Proverb 37:10 from the Book of Face, Mortem Era.

I WINCED. HOW'D HE KNOW? I stepped out from around the corner, brushing the leaves off my dress. I tossed the tail end of my braids backwards and squared my shoulders.

"Father." I bowed.

"So formal," he said, bowing in return.

"I'm trying to be on my best behavior."

Father raised his eyebrow. "Good. Follow me." He strode forward.

I studied his posture and placed my hands behind my back in a fist.

Shoulder to shoulder, we walked onto the path, heading toward the training grounds.

"So, are you going to tell me what that meeting was about?" I asked.

"Did you not hear?"

"I mean, yes. But I don't want to assume. I'd like to know instead of guessing."

"Wise words."

"I'm smart sometimes. It's not all air up there." I tapped the side of my temples.

Father knocked a knuckle on the top of my head. I faked an ouch.

"Just all rocks," he laughed.

"Which only means I'm solid." I pushed his hand away.

We entered the training grounds. The sun's rays beamed off the still towers, creating a zigzag of rainbow lines through the camp. The Blood Elite were dressed in black tactical pants, boots, and most of them wore no shirts. They were in couples, sparring with one another.

A Windborn woman paired with a Reaperborn man caught my attention as they fought enclosed in a wire cage with padding. She raised her arms above her head. Her hands moved in circles as if she was gathering an invisible ball. When the Reaperborn charged, with one release, she sent a large gust of wind that collided with his chest.

He was lifted off his feet and thrown into the side of the cage. His body hung suspended in the corner until the wind surged past him. With a grunt, the Reaperborn tumbled to the mat, landing on his knees. The Windborn took a towel and tapped her sweating forehead before smugly exiting the cage.

Father led me farther into the grounds. In the distance, a loud crack ripped through the air, followed by a flash of light. I jumped, unprepared to see a portion of gray clouds descending gradually to the Earth. When we finally arrived where the cloud settled, there was a Waterborn man standing underneath it. The inside of the cloud roared with thunder and lightning.

Next to him stood a man holding a timer. The watch clicked on as the cloud swelled. Another crack, followed by flashes of light, went off inside the cloud. It appeared as if it was about to burst. The Waterborn shook as the cloud released rainfall onto his head.

This was mind-blowing. I bounced on my heels, my body buzzing with excitement. I knew exactly who this Waterborn was, Rwju! I've only heard stories about his greatness. They say he could call a tsunami with a clap of his hands!

Rwju smoothed his long hair back from his face, revealing his famous scar running down the right of his eye that stretched from his forehead to mid-cheek. They say he got it from a Fireborn raid. Some say he got it from fighting a Skully, a beast with razor-sharp claws that dwelt in the shattered lands. I'd always wanted to ask him, but never had the chance.

The cloud above him dissipated, his knees buckled, and he dropped to the concrete. As soon as the cloud disappeared, the man holding the watch called, "Six minutes. You held it for six minutes, Rwju!" He patted the visibly tired Rwju on his back.

Father leaned into my ear. "He developed this new skill last week. He has been improving it ever since."

My mouth fell open. "You can develop new skill sets? I thought we all get what we are born with and that's just it."

"Developing new ways to use your manifestation is like learning any physical skill. It takes arduous work, practice, dedication, and concentration." Father pointed to another duo. Two women, both Reaperborn. Their shadows leaked from their palms. Black whisks like smoke spilled to the ground. The ladies never took their eyes off each other. The shadow wrapped around their ankles as it encircled their figures. A hurricane of black shadow rose to their hips, then breasts, before going all the way until it covered their heads. When the smoke broke, the two Reaperborn women had vanished.

I never took my eyes off them. I stepped forward, wanting to investigate, but Father held me back.

"Intertwined," he said. "Alone, their gifts are nothing special, but together, they create a more powerful manifestation that allows them to teleport." Father continued walking along the path.

I chewed the inside of my cheek. "Can two different alignments be intertwined?" I asked, clinging to every word he would say next.

"Why do you ask?"

"No reason." I paused, rubbing my nails on my skin. "It's just I've been reading lately about manifestations and how they work and it seems there's nothing more on why two people can intertwine and create new gifts and skill sets. I mean, there are hypotheses, speculations, a ton of medical journals, but nothing concrete."

"I would suppose it's because it's a fairly new discovery, Beta. As humans evolve, so do our abilities, minds, and bodies. Our very cells morph into genetic codes, spurring new life and resulting in creations better suited for the survival of the species." Father fanned out his hand to the Blood Elite.

My eyes followed with insatiable hunger.

"When the Six Spirits gave us the gift to manifest, they shifted the very DNA of humanity. We are all human, but not like our predecessors. Mortem Era, the end of the death age and the old world, ushered in a new world, a better world, fit for our abilities and who we are now as genetically modified humans." Father glanced at the ground, then at me. "Six hundred years is still young compared to how long the Earth stood beforehand. We are continuously learning how our bodies work. That includes how far we can push our manifestations before our body breaks. New medicines, along with new diseases, develop because of our gifts. Unfortunately, the Six Spirits didn't think to give us a manual before they went into slumber." Father smiled. "We are figuring things out as we go, Beta."

His shoulder lightly tapped mine as we continued our stroll. I mulled over what Father told me, flexing my hand, attempting to move every flower, every blade of grass, and every leaf we passed.

"I don't understand why I haven't manifested yet."

Father stopped walking. I almost ran into the back of him.

"I mean, Mother is powerful, Eve can create plant life out of thin air, and I..." I swallowed, the spit went down like a hard lump. "I have nothing. Am I cursed like the Fireborns?" I balled my fingers into a fist before dropping them to my side.

"Beta," Father swiveled to face me. "Your bloodline is pure. It can be traced to your first Earthborn Mother."

"But what of your side?"

The side of Father's lip twitched. "As far as I know, our family have all been Reaperborns, through and through."

"And Eve and I are the first generations to be born by both families as mixed breeds?"

Father nodded.

"Are you the first blood controller of your family?"

"I don't believe so. But we have no documentation stating otherwise."

"Why would someone not document a rare gift like blood control?"

Father walked, guiding me to follow. "There are people that exist, that have always existed, that are led by greed and power. This means they will stop at nothing to obtain that power, even if it hurts the innocent."

"Is that what the king did to you?"

Father's shoulders stiffened. He opened his mouth to say something, but no words came.

"That was crossing a boundary. I'm sorry. I—"

Father stopped. He released a hand from behind his back and brought it to my shoulders and squeezed.

"Beta..." His dark eyes searched mine. "History and the future live in the present. Be mindful of the choices you make today for it can alter both."

I nodded, my mouth dry. As Father continued to stroll, I stared at the back of his head. I realized I didn't know as much as I thought I knew about him. On Father Appreciation Day, I would create a thank-you card, buy some clothing, or make sure all his favorite foods were cooked, but I didn't actually know him as in, was he happy? What were his fears, regrets, his secrets? What happened that night when I saw him covered in blood on the floor of his office? Who was my Father outside of a dad and husband? Why did men cower when they came face to face with the Reaper General?

When we made it to the next location, the Reaperborn women, who disappeared in a puff of black smoke, were sitting on the bench, guzzling water.

Father cut into my thoughts. "I haven't seen you this engaged since I took you to your first bread shop when you were five," he said.

"Because this is far better than a bread shop," I said, forcing myself not to stare at the Reaperborn women. One was dressed in all black leather, whips, chains, swords, and daggers and the other had green locs and wore a loose-fitted tank top and pants. Both of them caught me with my mouth gaped and waved.

I blushed, pretending I wasn't completely enamored. "I would trade all the bread in the world for this moment." I thought for a second. "Maybe not all the bread, but most of the bread."

Father huffed. "Would raisin bread be a part of the trade?"

"Absolutely it would."

"I like raisin bread; it's nice and sweet."

"Why eat raisin bread when cinnamon bread exists?"

"Why not both?"

I playfully shoved him.

"Beta, look. Quande is up." He pointed with his chin.

Quande, dressed in all black, his hair braided into a fresh style with shaved sides revealing the dagger tattoo inked into his scalp, stepped into the ring. There was no cage, just lush green grass underneath his boots. He took his position, and six Blood Elite soldiers formed a circle around him. The soldiers carried long wooden sticks, whereas Quande held no weapon. The men taunted him, whistling, calling him weak, saying that today would be the day he went down.

Quande was silent, eyes closed, hand tucked behind his back. It was like those men didn't exist. Two out of the six men spun wooden sticks until the sticks disappeared from human eyesight. I was positive that those two men were Windborn. Each man went counterclockwise around Quande. With great swiftness, only attributed to Windborns, they attacked. Quande's eyes remained shut, as if the men aiming for his head did not bother him.

A Windborn leaped into the air, letting out a war cry before connecting with Quande. A crack rang out as the dust settled to the ground. The wooden stick slammed on Quande's forearm.

His arm had to have snapped into two.

But it didn't. Instead, the wooden stick broke. Chunks of lumber littered the ground at his feet. The next Windborn didn't waste the opportunity created by his companion and jumped in. His sticks whirled quickly in his palms until it picked up dirt, creating a swirl of wind. Every part of me wanted to jump in and help, but I remained by my Father's side, biting down hard on my bottom lip.

Seamlessly, one foot after the other, in tune with the beat of the fight, Quande struck. His movements were quick, precise, and calculated.

The Windborns disappeared and reappeared in front of my eyes like ghosts. I couldn't keep up; my senses were overwhelmed. My heart pounded. My fingers twitched. I bounced on my toes as if I were in the middle of the ring. In a flash, the Windborns flew out of the circle. Black smoke stretched outwards like arms swinging the two men like dolls.

The remaining four men sent their shadows at full speed toward Quande. Their black mist wove together like a bamboo basket, covering him. While maintaining the cover they entered fist-to-fist combat. Even the Reaperborns were no match for him. More shadow arms launched from Quande's side.

The basket of smoke attempting to crush Quande was failing.

The Reapers were struggling to hold their black shadows in place. Wooden sticks cracked and snapped, and pieces flew into the gathering crowd.

I clung to Father, my eyes bouncing from one man to the next. The fight I had at the taphouse was child's play compared to the battle unfolding before me. After all those years of

Quande teaching me how to fight, I wondered if it was painstakingly slow and tedious for him.

More arms shot from Quande's side, yanking the men by their ankles. The soldiers tried combating Quande's strength and raw power by teaming up and combining their force, but it was already too late. Quande smashed them apart like a fresh bread loaf ripped in half. The men shot into the air, falling into the crowd. Some landed face-first in the gravel.

There was one soldier left. Before Quande's shadow could get ahold of him, he rolled out of the circle and threw his hands up in surrender. The black smoke loomed over the man as if processing the gesture. Then it snapped back to Quande.

The last man defeated, the arms of Quande's shadow absorbed back into himself. That was when Quande opened his eyes and stared directly at me. A thin smile played on his lips.

I noticed I was clinging on to my father like I was ten years old. I quickly released myself from his arm and straightened out my clothes, as if it didn't happen.

The rest of the soldiers patted Quande on the back of his head, shoulders, and arms. Ignoring them, he beamed at me, his smile growing wider.

And to think I was concerned about his cocky ass.

I flipped him off, and he blurted out in laughter.

Father cleared his throat.

I tucked my middle finger away. "Sorry."

Father wrapped his hands around my shoulder and led me away from the cheering crowd.

WE RETURNED TO THE PALACE.

"Do you know why I allowed you to come to the training grounds today?"

"Yes," I said, taking a seat on a garden bench next to the maze. "You want me to train to manifest my gift?"

"Not quite." Father sat next to me. "I want you to realize your full potential."

I shook my head. After what I saw today, there was no way I could ever fill the shoes my parents wanted me to step in. Mother and Eve were right; I was a disappointment.

In the back of my mind, I thought that if I could be trained to fight, I could show them I'm worth something of value. That I'm actually strong enough, powerful enough to be the daughter they always wanted. I guess deep down inside, I've always wanted to make my family proud.

I bent to pluck a single blade of grass from the ground. I focused all the energy I could into it and commanded it to grow, stretch, bend, move! Do something, anything. Father placed his large hands over mine, causing me to curl the blade of grass into my fist.

"I don't think I can do it..." My voice caught in my throat. "I'm not Eve or Quande; I'm just me, Daddy. And *me* isn't good enough." I snapped my eyelids shut, refusing to let a tear escape.

"That's the thing, Beta. You are good enough. But it doesn't matter how much I try to convince you, you won't believe it until you convince yourself."

I leaned on my father's shoulder.

"How do I even begin?"

"By beginning." Father tightened his grip on my hand. "I have convinced your Mother that part of your punishment is taking you to our private training camp on the far reaches of the reaper border. You will train with us and learn the ways of the Blood Elite."

I popped my head up from Father's shoulder. "Are you serious?"

145

"Deadly so," he said.

"But... I–" My mouth was open, but the words seemed to be trapped.

"This would mean you'll be away from the palace, your noble duties..." Father tilted closer. "... your Mother..." he whispered.

I giggled. "Well, I'm sold."

"See, I knew that would do it." He patted me on the leg. "Beta, when you train with us, you will not receive special treatment." He bumped my shoulder. "I'm doing this hoping to prepare you for the decision you will eventually have to make."

"And what decision will that be?"

"You'll know when you face it."

"What if I make the wrong choice?"

"What if you don't?"

"Daddy, you make it seem easy."

"Is it not?" He turned to me.

"No," I said anxiously.

"Hmmm... I'll tell you something my father once told me. When faced with two paths, it's okay to choose one and see where it goes. If you don't like it, come back and take the second path. If you don't like that one, then cut through the middle and forge your own. Regardless of the choice you make, standing still gets you nowhere."

I unclenched my fist and examined the single blade of grass inside.

"The question is, Beta, when the time comes to manifest, how will you wield that power, and who will you become despite it?"

XV

"If you take away a leopard's spots, is it no longer a leopard?"
Proverb 82:17 from the Book of Face, Mortem Era.

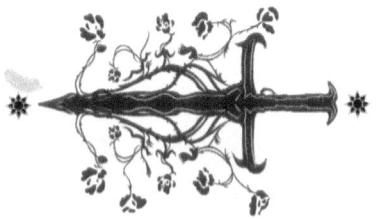

"YOU'RE WEARING THAT OUTFIT I LIKE. Does this mean you forgive me from earlier?"

Silvia sauntered past me.

"Maybe."

She had changed into a beautiful black cotton skirt with

sage leaves etched into it. The skirt had two long slits on each side, revealing full brown thighs and a little curve of her booty. Her top was strapless and barely covered her breasts. Her hair was tucked in a matching head wrap, and golden jewelry completed her outfit and complemented her honey-brown skin. I thanked the Spirits for Earth Kingdom's damn near-naked fashion choices. That's the one thing they got right.

"What do you mean, maybe? Come," I said, wrapping her in my arms.

She chuckled, and I loved the sound her laugh made. "I forgive you, but you're on very, very thin ice."

I rubbed my thumb across her chin. "Maybe I could make it up by throwing a little nosh of our own?"

Silvia bit her lip, then pushed me away. "You sure can, but not today."

I smirked. "Really?"

"Deadly so. Let's go, we're already late."

"Come on, Silvia! Just this once."

"No!" she said sharply, walking into the entrance of the maze. I ran behind her, my heels digging into the grass. I almost slipped, but I caught myself.

"Silvia, wait!" I yelled.

She led the way into the maze until she realized she didn't know how to navigate the tricky passages. I strolled past her, taking my sweet time while soaking in all the sunshine. Silvia smacked my butt. We playfully chased each other until we entered the middle of the maze where the nosh was being held.

As we broke through the clearing, the umas greeted us, then escorted us to a long narrow table covered in white cotton fabric. Assortments of roses, fruits, and vegetables laid on top. Prince Theolo sat across from Everest. Quande sat next to the prince with Mesala, my sister's best friend, in front of him. Congruent Attali was with an empty seat in front of him.

I allowed Silvia to take it as I called for another empty chair to be placed beside her. The umas moved with haste and soon, I took my place at the table.

Quande sent me a glance, his eyes flickering from me to Silvia.

"Hello, everyone." I looked from Quande, to the sour-faced prince, and then to Everest. I honestly thought she had forgiven me by now, but apparently not.

Fine. If it's going to be like that, then so be it.

"My apologies for my tardiness. I have invited my personal uma, Silvia. Please treat her kindly."

Quande reached over to kiss the back of Silvia's hand. "Nice to see you again. Your outfit is lovely, as always."

Mesala cleared her throat. "Princess Bellamy, it's a pleasure to see you. We missed you at the formal dance last night."

"Oh, I hate that I missed it. I would have loved to attend, even if it was only to see you."

Mesala blushed. "I bet you say that to every girl."

Prince Theolo muttered. "And every guy."

Strike one. I squared my shoulders and ignored it.

"Princess Bellamy." Congruent Attali sent a shadow kiss across the table. Much preferred than a back of the hand kiss, I side-eyed Quande.

"Congruent Attali. I'm surprised to see you still here," I said.

"I'm leaving tonight, heading back to the Eighth Reaper Ward."

"Then we need to schedule that bread-and-butter date soon, yes?"

"We have plenty of time. I'm not worried."

Silvia slid a hand over my thigh under the table. I paused, my flesh automatically reacting to her soft touch.

"And excuse me, who are you again?" Prince Theolo pointed a fork at Silvia.

"I'm Silvia, Bellamy's personal uma."

"Well..." Everest took a napkin, patting at the corners of her mouth. "If we were inviting our personal umas to this get-together, I would have certainly brought mine."

Prince Theolo reached across the table to grab Everest's hand. "I thought the charity dinner wasn't until mid-year, sweety?"

"My Prince," Everest cooed. "You know how my sister is. Falls in love with every stray she meets."

I interjected. "Silvia isn't a stray, nor is she a charity case. Therefore, do not treat her as such. Unlike you, I prefer to get to know people based on their character, not their pockets."

Theolo plucked cheese from a platter and popped it in his mouth. "I choose to get to know someone for both merits. Let's not pretend they don't matter in high society, or do you not plan on participating, *Princess* Bellamy?"

"My plans, with all due respect, are my business. Do you ever think to keep yours to yourself?"

Quande slurped his water, his eyes flickering across the table. After he was done, he whispered to the uma behind him. "Do we have something stronger?"

Prince Theolo glared. That idiotic swirl of hair pasted to his forehead didn't move as his eyebrows bunched. Everest reached out her hand to embrace the prince, but he pulled away, taking a sip from his glass. Everest withdrew and instead picked up her lemonade.

I would have felt sorry for her, but I scanned her clothing. She was sitting there in full reaper dress, not a piece of skin showing. Just that quick, she's already conforming. I couldn't muster an ounce of pity.

Mesala shifted in her seat. "Well, I, for one, am happy to be here. Thank you again for the invite, my prince, and my future queen," she said as she squeezed Everest's hand.

The prince straightened his shoulders and stood. He wore a black turtleneck with long sleeves and glossy dark blue animal-printed pants. "You are more than welcome, Mesala." The prince then addressed the table. "Before we get started, I first would like to thank everyone that *was invited* for being present and on time. My fiancé and I appreciate you. I would also like to thank the umas who have *slaved* over preparing this meal for us to enjoy this afternoon." Theolo raised his glass to the umas that lined the maze hedge and then tilted his glass to Silvia.

Strike two.

My legs bounced underneath the table. Silvia squeezed my thigh; her lips disappeared into her mouth.

Theolo continued, "And to my beautiful fiancé, thank you for being my sun in the sky to which I rise every morning and the moon and the stars that guide my way through the darkness." He sent a shadow kiss that fluttered like a black butterfly to Everest's lips, then he took his seat. He clapped twice, and the umas jumped to action.

On trays, they rolled over our main course. Underneath the lids were heirloom tomato sandwiches, avocado, lettuce, and hummus topped on toasted wheat bread. On the side were fresh spring rolls and a watermelon salad with feta.

"This is such a lovely meal on a beautiful day, your grace." Mesala bowed to the prince.

"Not as lovely as my dove but thank you." The prince plucked another cube of cheese and tossed it in his mouth. As it looked to me, he was too busy eyeing the cheese than gazing lovingly at my sister, who sat with a pinched smile on her face.

The nosh descended into an awkward quiet.

Quande cleared his throat to speak. "Bee, I bet you're excited about our trip."

"Yeah, I can't believe Father is letting me go," I said.

"Quande, what trip do you speak of?" Everest said, cutting into her sandwich.

Who the fuck cuts into their sandwich?

"Bee is joining the Blood Elite at our private training camp. She's finally fighting with the best of the best."

Everest's fork screeched across her plate.

"Do you plan on implementing your fighting skills or experiences once you become queen?" Attali asked.

I thought for a moment before speaking. "Earth is a neutral kingdom that doesn't believe in fighting. I think that's a big mistake and that every kingdom should have its own form of protection."

Prince Theolo leaned in. "Do you not believe that the Reapers are sufficient to protect the kingdoms?"

I took a deep breath, careful to answer.

"I believe the Shadow Army, as well as the Blood Elite Army are sufficient in protecting the kingdoms. However, I see nothing wrong with the kingdoms having an internal unit in the event of pressing issues."

"Issues like what?" The prince popped another cheese ball into his mouth.

"Well, like the Fireborn raids. Two weeks ago, a small town on the outskirts of the Moon Kingdom was set on fire. The residents were captured, if not killed, and the youth were sold into servitude to the Fire Kingdom. If the Moon Kingdom had an internal army or a protection division, then maybe they would have been able to save that town without being solely reliant on the Reapers."

Congruent Attali jumped in. "I get your point. The Reaper Kingdom is the third largest kingdom. It is true that a part of our gifts is the ability to heal ourselves and fight, but lately, with the kingdoms expanding, the Reaper Army is spread thin."

"We have a member of the Blood Elite here. Let's hear what he has to say." Theolo turned to Quande. "Do you think our great army is getting weak?"

Quande took a second to chew his food before speaking. "Weak? No, quite the opposite. See, the Shadow Army comprises only Reapers but the Blood Elite Army comprises all talented alignments. Being that this is the first special unit of its kind, I believe the kingdoms are stronger together."

"But we are together," The prince said. "The Six Spirits made sure that each kingdom does their part. The Water Kingdom provides us with fresh drinking water. They keep our oceans clean and regulate sea life and travel. The Wind Kingdom keeps our air pollution free, the Earth Kingdom..." The prince pointed to me. "They supply eighty percent of our vegetables, protect wildlife, and create sustainable products like cotton and bamboo. Us Reapers are the protectors. We are the army, the law. That is how the Spirits made it."

Attali interjected. "We all respect the law and appreciate the Reapers for their service to the kingdoms. I don't think anyone at this table believes the Reaper Army to be weak. But I do believe there is validity in at least training the kingdoms to have a community watch with the basic skills of offense and defense to protect small towns that are being raided in a timely manner."

"I agree. Spread thin isn't saying the Reapers are weak, but statistically speaking," I said to the prince. "The Fire Kingdom is the biggest kingdom. Followed by Earth, then Reaper. There're just not enough protectors to protect the entire world. And let's not even talk about the Shattered Lands. A place so broken that the sun doesn't waste time shining there. I see nothing wrong with the kingdoms creating their own reinforcement squads."

Prince Theolo tapped his nails on the table. "Because that's not how the Spirits made it to be. We were all assigned our duty and we all must stick to that said duty. Reapers have been the law for 600 years."

"And they can still be the law. Nobody is trying to take that away. But much like the Counsel of Amalgamation, to which Congruent Attali serves, they focus on the bigger problems that affect us all while each kingdom has smaller ward counsels to take care of the little things. Why can't the Shadow Army adopt a similar system?" I said, not understanding why this concept seemed so foreign to him.

Prince Theolo shifted in his chair as if he no longer wanted to sit. "Because we have established a system that has been upheld and enforced for 600 years and has been proven to work."

"Then that's where we disagree. It might have worked in the past, but as the world continues to grow and change, I think we should change with it. I'm afraid that if you continue to uphold your Mother's outdated beliefs, it will leave us all exposed to potential threats." I laid my fork on my plate. "I don't know if you know, prince, but the Fire Kingdom isn't the only bad apple we need to worry about," I said, picking up a watermelon slice.

Everest spoke, "Can we just—"

"Shut your mouth." The prince shot a stern finger at her. Everest melted back into her seat, head down, poking at her plate.

Strike three.

"Don't talk to my fucking sister like that. Like she's some dog. She doesn't have to listen to your command." Just like that, my rage exploded. I damn near shook the table. I don't care if Everest never speaks to me again, but I'll never let anybody bully her. Not in my face.

"Unlike you, your sister knows her place. Your Mother has failed to teach you yours."

"And I guess your Mother has failed you entirely. Or was raising a dickless son a part of her grand legacy?"

"You disrespect your queen?"

"I'm disrespecting you and your Mother is no queen of mine."

Silvia squeezed my thigh, her touch begging me to calm down.

"That's treasonous," The prince spat.

"Treasonous! Let me guess, you don't know what that word means, do you? Then let me break it down: Treasonous, betraying one's own kingdom. I'm Earthborn. Fuck. Your. Courts."

The prince and I locked eyes, and I dared him to speak, dared him to act.

Mesala's voice cut through the thick tension in the air. "I think both opinions are valid, and I honestly think, as nobility, we can have civilized conversations without the extras. We aren't wessies," she chuckled.

The prince laughed. "Speaking of wessies, my sources say our dear princess has made friends with one." The entire table turned to me.

"Who, me?" My gaze flickered to each person at the table. Attali stared with mild curiosity. Quande froze all-together. Everest had her eyes fixed on the prince who had a cocky smile on his asinine face. Mesala's eyes were wide and Silvia stopped stroking my thigh.

"Is it not true that you got into a fight not too long ago, princess? The entire palace has been talking about it. They also say that before the fight broke loose, you were unleashing full tongue on a wessie scum." The prince popped another cheese into his mouth and chewed like a horse-eating hay.

155

"Your sources should check again," I said, avoiding eye contact with Silvia. She withdrew her hand from my thigh and I wanted to reach out and stop her, but I didn't.

"My sources are pretty legit," the prince continued, leaning back into his chair. "I mean, how bad does it look that the future Earth Queen is fucking a filthy wessie."

My jaw tightened. "I'm not fucking anyone. So, I suggest that you and your sources go and fuck each other. Then maybe you won't be such a tight ass."

The prince leaned in on the table. "Most of everyone here has been affected by the hands of a Fireborn." He pointed to each person. "Everest, your doyens on your Reaper side were murdered in battle by Fireborns. Mesala, your mother was brutalized and beaten to death by a group of rogue wessies."

Mesala's brown face flushed red. She shrunk into her chair, head down, fumbling with her dress. My palms itched, and I dug my nails into them.

"Congruent Attali. What of your father? You preach of protecting the cowardly wessies that are fleeing from their king-doms to ours, but who protected your father from being stabbed in the heart by one?"

My mouth dropped. Attali appeared to be ready to jump out of his seat and pounce at the prince's head like a jaguar onto prey.

This was the reason the prince threw this nosh. It wasn't about building bridges. It was about reminding us that if it weren't for him, there wouldn't be a bridge in the first place. Heat rose from the bottom of my feet to the top of my head. The itch stabbed throughout my skin.

The prince continued. "And Quande..."

"Stop." I clenched my teeth.

The prince ignored me. "Your parents' murder right in front of you. Then at the tender age of six, you were sold into

Fireborn slavery. If it weren't for the queen executing a hunt order, our Quande would have been lost to the wessies forever." The prince rubbed Quande's shoulders. Quande was as stiff as a board. "And the princess is publicly having relations with a wessie, in the middle of a taphouse no less." He shook his head.

I pushed my plate back, threw my napkin on the table, and stood. I would no longer sit here and listen to this piece of shit. "Come, Silvia." As I rounded the table to leave, I paused and turned to Everest. "And this is who you plan to marry?"

Everest stared at her untouched food; her face hidden by her afro.

"Don't speak to her," The prince commanded.

"You don't control me," I hissed, clenching my fist.

"No, but my mother did." He grinned.

I launched across the table, my fist connecting with his jaw. His chair blew backwards, slamming into the grass. His shadow spilled from his palms, and he gripped it like a whip and released it toward my face. I dodged, rolling off the table and onto the ground.

The prince scrambled to his feet. "You rabid fucking dog!" he shouted. "It's about time for someone to put you down!" The prince shot another whip of inky shadow my way. I zigzagged until I was right in front of him.

Do it. A voice trickled into my mind. *Kill him.* It whispered. I snatched the dagger hidden in the compartment of my dress. Rage blindly led me. The prince's shadow cut through the air, but it was too slow.

Years of training with Quande made this interaction child's play.

The dagger left my hand before I could think a second about it. It spun, the aim straight and true towards the middle of the prince's forehead.

A black shadow shot out and stopped the dagger a mere inch from the target.

Then I was overwhelmed by black mist. My arms, legs, and neck were wrapped in shadow. Quande had stopped the killing blow. The umas, along with Attali all had their shadows aimed at me, locking me down until I was on my knees.

"Let me go!" I screamed.

"I'll have your head for this, princess," Theolo shouted.

"Let me go!" I shrugged to unwind myself from the shadows that had me bound.

"See," Prince Theolo laughed. "These aren't your people. This isn't your kingdom. Look at the Earthborns at this table, they do nothing to protect their own princess."

I turned to Everest, who stood frozen, tears streaming down her cheeks. I looked at Silvia, who looked torn, her eyes bounced from Quande, to me. and back to Quande.

My entire body deflated. The prince's high-pitched cackle rang in my ear.

"Your own people don't want you as their queen. You're nothing Bellamy! Nothing!"

"Let her go," Quande commanded Attali and the umas. Their shadows slowly slipped from around my limbs, leaving me numb and limp on the ground. I rose to my feet with shaky legs and pushed past the umas crowding me.

"You're a disappointment to your entire kingdom!" The prince shouted as I stumbled out of the garden maze.

"I DIDN'T START IT," I yelled, sitting in Father's office. Mother paced the length of the carpet as she screamed at me about the nosh.

"What type of daughter have I raised, huh? Do you know

the gravity of your actions?" she said. Her wisteria rose off her shoulders, the blooms shook as if they were about to strike.

"Why is it my fault? Why isn't he being punished? Father, you and the queen interviewed everyone that was there at the nosh. They all said the prince was the aggressor. Why am I being held responsible?"

"Because you threw the first punch! You threw a dagger at his head. If it weren't for Quande, you could have murder—" Mother slapped a hand on her forehead. "Every fight cannot be won by physical violence! If that dagger would have made a connection. We would be having an entirely different conversation right now."

"But it didn't. He's alive and well and still fucking annoying."

In a blink of an eye, Mother's wisteria struck out and slapped me across the face.

"Oyame!" Father shouted.

Mother turned to him. "She is a bullheaded, lazy, quick-tempered brat who needs to learn her place, Agrim. She needs to know that her actions have consequences."

"And hitting her, will do what?"

"We did it your way, Agrim. And look what has come of it, nothing." She pointed to me.

I clenched the side of my face where the wisteria struck. Blood trickled from my cheek and coated my fingertips.

"And what's the point of her having a personal uma if she can't keep her out of trouble?" she said, glaring at Silvia standing by the office door. "She's fired, we will reassign Bellamy another one immediately."

I balled my bloody fingers into a fist. "No, you won't," I said in a quiet fury. "Silvia isn't going anywhere. She will not be reassigned."

Mother turned to me, putting her argument with Father on

hold. "And who do you think you are to fix your mouth like you have a say-so? After all the trouble you have caused? The embarrassment you have shown?" Mother sucked her teeth. "Our ancestors are rolling in their graves watching you make a complete fool of yourself."

"She's not going anywhere." I dug my nails into my skin.

"You think we don't know you're fucking the help?" Mother crossed the office to Silvia. "She is just another body, easily replaceable. You are not. Do you understand this?"

Silvia bit down on her lips, her eyes watering.

"Daddy," I said, trying to bite back the anger building inside. "Please," I pleaded.

Father stroked his beard. "Beta, this one is out of my hands."

Mother crossed her arms. "She's gone."

She grabbed Silvia's wrist. I shot up from the chair, throwing myself in between the two.

"Beta!" Father shouted.

Tears rolled down my cheek. "No!" I screamed, staring daggers into my mother's eyes. "She isn't leaving."

The wisteria unfurled from Mother's arm, the tip of its head snaking into the air. Mother shouted, a thick, pulsating vein popped from her forehead, as the wisteria struck, slapping Silvia to the floor. The time slowed, as the wisteria struck her repeatedly. Silvia cried out as she took every blow made for me.

The room became quiet as a surge of energy built in my chest. My hand gripped the wisteria, choking it as if it were my own Mother's throat.

That's it, a voice said. *Focus!*

My skin coiled, flashes of red blurred my vision. Smoke streamed from my fist that was wrapped around the wisteria and the look in Mother's wide eyes was that of fear.

"Enough." One tap of a finger touched my forehead, and

my entire body froze. I didn't even hear him move. "Let the wisteria go."

My fingers uncurled immediately at the command.

Daddy.

My body trembled, unable to contain whatever I unlocked inside of me. I wanted to see Mother's fear. I wanted to feed on her pain. I craved it.

Mother's wisteria, broken—the blooms crumpling to the floor—limped itself back to her arm.

"Oyame, get it," Father ordered.

Mother couldn't take her eyes off me. And for a moment, I wondered what she saw. Did she feel that I would have crushed her just like I did her wisteria? Did she know that a part of me wanted to rip out her throat and feast on her blood? My body shook at the thought, my lips curled into a smile. My skin shifted under Father's blood-control and I cocked my head to the side, despite his power.

Mother stumbled back as if I leaped on her. She then rushed out of my eyesight and reappeared with a tube of blue liquid. She popped the cork with shaky fingers.

"Open your mouth," Father ordered.

No. A whisper flared in my mind. *You're mine!* It screamed within my head, shattering my eardrums. Despite wanting to shout, my mouth remained shut.

"Open!" Father commanded; his manifestation applied pressure that felt like bricks being stacked in my skull. His finger trembled on my forehead while a force in me played tug-of-war with my will.

Father stepped closer, his hand clenching the back of my neck. He placed his forehead on the side of my temples. His voice was smooth and low compared to the screaming in my head. "Beta."

Tears streamed down my face.

"Listen to Daddy."

An ache swelled in my chest.

"Come back to me."

The force in my mind threw a fit of rage, screaming that I was theirs and only theirs.

"Come home." Father kissed me on my temple, and all that raw energy melted away like snow.

My mouth opened. Mother quickly drained the liquid onto my tongue, and I swallowed.

"What is this?" My voice cracked. "What are you hiding from me, Daddy?"

Time sped up, and my energy depleted, my body was sore, and my eyes closed.

"Agrim," Mother said. "We are running out of time."

I fell into my father's arms as the weight of sleep took me under.

Act IV

XVI

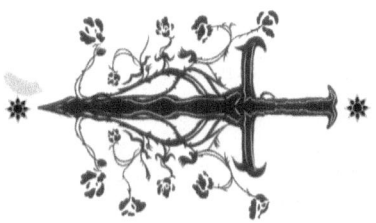

"No matter how long the night—"
Proverb 47:13 from the Book of Face, Mortem Era.

"HOW DID WE GET HERE, AGAIN?" I asked Silvia as I stared at the tall redwood trees stretching toward the star-covered sky.

She placed her hand on my shoulder. "After your meeting

with your parents, you were under so much stress that your condition flared and then you passed out."

The wind gently caressed my cheek, and I shut my eyes to embrace the cool feel of its touch.

"Are you sure?" I said, attempting to recover the last few days.

The images were a mixture of blurred lines and quick flashes with exploding colors and hunting voices. Voices, so many voices. When I focused too much on the jumbled images, my head ached and I found myself bent over, clawing at my skin.

"Princess, you must rest. Come back to bed with me, please." Silvia tugged at my shoulders.

"No." I snatched away. "How did we get here?" I pointed to the moss-covered pathway lined with mushrooms arranged from knee high to standing over six feet tall. They glowed with green, blue, pink and purple luminescence. The forest croaked with noises from wildlife buzzing through the trees and splashing in nearby ponds.

"You're confused right now. It's been a long journey from the palace to the camp. You were out of it for most of the trip due to the Life Doctor giving you a shot to help calm your condition."

"Blue liquid?" Flashes of red and blue tubes flooded my mind, followed by the pressure of my mouth being pried open and the taste of baking soda coating my tongue.

"No, Princess. There weren't any blue liquids. It was a sedative. Your body had a negative reaction, and the doctor said you would be loopy for a few days, but you should come around."

I squatted in the red-bladed grass, dusting my palm over the pointed ends. "This has happened before," I said, plucking a single red blade of grass from the earth.

"What has happened?"

Silvia squatted next to me. She smelled like blackberries.

"Waking up unable to recall events or times or conversations. Feeling like I was missing something, but I just couldn't place my finger on it." I balled the grass into my hand. "What of the prince? What happened?" I turned to her; her brown eyes were glossy under the moon's glow.

"That's why we came to camp early, princess. After the nosh fight, the queen announced she would extend her stay to regulate the courts in the 2nd and 3rd Reaper Wards." Silvia tucked a braid behind my ear. "Your Father thought this would be a good time to remove you from the palace and return when the queen and the prince had taken their leave." She grabbed my hand, lifting me to my feet. My knees cracked along with my back.

"I feel..." I searched for the right words to say but couldn't find any. "Tired," I said, dropping the blade of grass to the ground.

Silvia guided me down the stone path through the redwoods. I stopped, holding her hand tight. "Silvia," I pulled her in close, studying her perfectly arched eyebrows, chubby cheeks, doe-shaped eyes, button nose, and full lips. "You would tell me if something was wrong, right?" Her lips disappeared into her mouth, popping out her deep dimples.

"You wouldn't lie to me, right?"

She shook her head.

The beating of my heart sped as my skin prickled.

Silvia, on her tiptoes, smashed her lips against mine. "I will protect you, no matter what may come. I'll save you." She kissed me again and the prickles under my skin faded away.

"You promise?"

"I do," she said, pulling me along the pathway.

Thick smoke danced in the air above the trees. It came from

a large bonfire that sat in the middle of the camp surrounded by logs. In between the large trees were small cabins made from dark timber and moss. Inside, they were lit by candlelight.

Boots crunched through the grass, and I turned to see Father.

"Glad to see you walking." He watched me. "Have you eaten?"

I glanced at Silvia in confusion. Truth was, I couldn't remember.

"We're headed to the kitchens now, General." Silvia bowed slightly.

"Good, very good. Camp assignments and teams have been established. I'll give you a few more days before your training begins."

"I'm fine, Daddy. I can start tomorrow, tonight even!" I let Silvia's hand loose, standing tall. All my life, training side by side with the Blood Elite has been the only thing I've ever wanted.

"You should take it slow. You've had a rough couple of days." He stepped toward me, placing his thumb on my forehead. I jerked back, a choking panic made my heartbeat skip when flashes of morphed memories forced themselves in my mind. A voice, *the* voice, was muffled and I couldn't tell if it was mine.

"Beta?" Father raised my chin. "Maybe you should take it easy for a few more days." He turned to Silvia. "Take her to her cabin."

I shook my head. "I'm good. I can start tomorrow. It's just..." I glanced from Silvia to Father. Both wore the same worried expressions on their faces, like I was too fragile, weak.

I'm not weak.

"I'm fine. Tomorrow. I'll start."

Silvia glanced at Father; her lips disappeared. He nodded

to her; it was like they were transmitting a conversation on a frequency I couldn't hear.

What was I missing?

"Well," Father said, gathering his hands behind his back. "Tomorrow it is. You will receive no special treatment. You'll be known as a recruit, and you'll call me general. Do you understand?"

"Yes, General." I saluted.

"Alright. Dismissed." He slightly bowed to both of us then Silvia and I took our leave. We went to the kitchens and picked up meat, cheese, bread and butter, then made our way to the cabin.

On the inside, it was extremely spacious and simple in design. There was a full-sized bed on the far wall, with a backsplash of moss. On the other wall was an enclosed toilet, the door ajar. Next to it was an open tub that had two privacy covers around it. There was one window in the middle, with the blinds closed. There was a closet tucked in a far corner and I saw everything was already unpacked and put away.

"You were busy, huh?" I said, running my fingers across the reaper black clothing. I stopped at a full-length ball gown tucked at the end.

"Your Mother made me pack it. She said you never know when the occasion might call for it."

I whipped around with a sudden urgency to defend—no, protect—Silvia. I ran to her, lifting her arms and inspecting them for bruises, scratches, or marks of any kind but only smooth unblemished skin greeted me. My head pounded as I tried to remember, but what exactly?

"What are you doing?" she said.

"You were hurt, right?" I said, puzzled.

Silvia slipped her arm out of my grasp. She sat me down on

the edge of the bed, then hugged me. I rested my head on her breasts, nudging them slightly.

"How did we get here?" I whispered.

Silvia bent down and kissed me gently on the forehead, then my nose, then my lips.

"It doesn't matter how we got here. We're here now, and there's no other place more important." She kissed my neck as she pushed me backwards on the bed. Then she slowly unbuttoned the front of my shirt while kissing my exposed skin.

I closed my eyes, letting the sensation of her touch take me. Her tongue found a nipple, and I moaned as she sucked.

My esophagus went dry. As the seconds passed, my throat became tighter and tighter, as if a noose was being pulled taut around my neck. I couldn't breathe. The pressure grew thicker as my windpipe snapped like it was being crushed.

Flashes. Blurred flashes slashed across my memories. How did I get here! The noose tightened; my eyes rolled back. I clawed at my throat to release a rope I knew wasn't there.

I could almost see it. The images, missing memories, trickling in like a cracked dam. A kid version of me, maybe six, peeked into Father's office. Two deep voices I could barely register were yelling at each other.

"You can't hide her here forever, Agrim. She will manifest."

"We will take care of it."

"How? By locking her away in the bubble of the palace? For how long?"

"As long as humanly possible!" Father shouted.

The blurry memory skewed the second man's face like an oil painting.

"One day, you'll have to tell her who she is and how she came to be." The man stepped toward Father, resting a hand on his cheek.

"The prophecy." Father wrapped his arms around the man.

"It's not a matter of if, but when. We cannot derail fate." The man kissed Father on the lips, then placed his forehead on his.

Father and the man stood silently, wrapped in each other's embrace. I moved, causing the floor to creak. Their heads shot to the door. Father moved so fast that before I could think about running, the door flew open and he was standing over me.

"Beta," Father said, bending to one knee. "What did I tell you about snooping?"

I shrugged, and an awkward giggle slipped from my lips.

Father turned around and shut the office door. He returned his gaze to me; his dark eyes were like two cosmic wormholes sucking me in. He placed a finger on my forehead. "Forget."

The noose crushing my windpipes let go and I shot up from the bed, coughing while trying to catch my breath.

Silvia rushed to get water, and I feverishly drank it down. "You're burning up!"

I dug my nails into my skin. The itch flared, creating black scaly leather patches.

"I need to alert your father."

"No." I clasped Silvia's arm as she was about to run to the door.

She sucked her lips into her mouth.

I searched her face looking for the reasons I trusted her, but found none.

My grip tightened. "How did we get here, Silvia?"

"You're hurting me." Her fingers clawed at my knuckles. I held on a few moments, hoping she would tell the truth before I eventually let her go. She fell to the floor, tears streaming. The itch bit harder into my skin.

"Where's my cream?" I picked at the scaly patches on my arm. The skin flaked away the more I dug my nails into it.

Silvia stood, stumbling over to the closet and pulling out a new container. She handed it to me with the top unscrewed. I dipped my fingers into the creamy white substance that was thicker than before.

"This should help calm the itch much quicker and last longer than the last batch." Silvia's voice trembled.

I nodded, smearing the cream on my arms. I closed the lid and placed the container on the desk, then lay in bed.

"Come." I patted the empty section beside me. I heard Silvia's feet shuffle to the bed, the mattress dipped, and her warm body connected with mine. I pulled her close, rubbing my nose into her hair.

Blackberries, I sniffed.

"No need to tell Father. I'm fine, okay?"

Silvia nodded.

"It's been a long night. I'll be better in the morning," I said, feeling the noose tighten around my neck.

XVII

"—daylight will emerge."
Proverb 47:13 from the Book of Face, Mortem Era.

"PRINCESS BELLAMY?" Silvia's voice trickled through the pillow stacked on my face.

"A few more minutes. I swear I'll get up." I rolled over, pulling the covers over my head.

"Princess, I think you should wake up now."

I pulled the covers tight, shielding the bright light trickling in from the window. The bed dipped as a soft touch caressed my leg, making its way up to my upper thigh.

"Oh," I said under the blankets. "*This* is how you wake me up." The soft touch turned into a hardened grip which tightened around my waist. "A little too tight, Silvia." I reached under the covers to feel...*bark?* Before I could throw the sheets off, I was propelled out of bed and thrown to the ceiling. I screamed, trying to focus my eyes. Below, Silvia stood next to Zef Coe, her hand hiding a smile.

"Mother fuc—" The thick root that held me hostage shook me. My legs and arms were noodles slapping against the air.

"Are you awake now?" Zef flicked his wrist. The root halted on command.

"I'm awake! I swear!" I went limp as the root pinned me against the ceiling.

"You were supposed to be up two hours ago." Zef checked his watch.

"How was I supposed to know that? Did anyone give Silvia my schedule?"

"Is Silvia your keeper?"

I glanced at Silvia, who had her hand on her hip, waiting for my answer.

"No offense, but you are my uma." I shrugged. Her mouth gaped open.

Zef Coe turned to her. "Would you like me to shake her?"

Silvia crossed her arms. "That would be my pleasure."

Zef flicked his wrist, and the root sent me flying. I held on tight as it shook me like a tambourine.

"Okay, okay! I think I'm about to throw up." The contents in my stomach sloshed as they crept up my throat.

The root stopped shaking, and Zef lowered his arm, placing both hands behind his back.

"Must I remind you, recruit, that this isn't the palace. It is your responsibility to follow and keep up with your own schedule. You have fifteen minutes to prepare yourself. Breakfast closes in ten."

The root unwrapped itself from around my waist and I free-fell to the mattress.

"Your time has begun." Zef Coe turned to leave, and the root withdrew out of the cracked door. Silvia followed Zef.

"Wait," I said, rubbing my waist. "Are you not going to help me get ready?"

Silvia paused in the doorframe. "You heard the man, princess. This isn't the palace." She held a cheeky grin.

"Are you serious?"

"Deadly so." She smirked, closing the door behind her.

I ENTERED THE empty kitchen, covered with crumb-filled bowls, platters, and plates on the counters. I saw scraps of bread, eggs, and a few burned pieces of bacon. I picked through the leftovers, biting into a hard, blackened roll.

"Fuck. They couldn't leave me anything! Ugh!" I stomped.

"Nope, not one thing, recruit!" Quande marched in with Fia, who had to duck to get through the kitchen door. After Fia, the Moonborn twins strutted in. Oneo was the eldest, who wore his hair short and cropped above the ears and his identical twin, Twoa, wore his hair down, the ends reaching mid-back. Twoa was the trickster and always had a playful grin on his red-tinted lips.

"That's your punishment for not waking up on time!" Quande said, placing a bowl in the sink.

Fia leaned on the counter. "Take it easy on her. She just got here."

"No one took it easy on us," Twoa said.

"No, no one took it easy on you. I had an amazing first year. *You*, however, couldn't stop getting into trouble." Oneo stuck his hand in a little corner behind one of the empty food trays. When he pulled it out, he held an apple.

"Always got to hide the goods from the ravenous beast of B.E." Oneo held the apple out to me. My stomach rumbled. Oneo threw it and Twoa snatched it out of the air and bit into it with a crisp crunch.

"Gotta be quicker than that, princess." Pieces of apple peeked through Twoa's teeth as he grinned like a laughing monkey.

Quande snickered. I retaliated by throwing the finger at him.

"What did I do?" Quande said, reaching behind yet another corner and pulling out a banana. He peeled it slowly and held it out for me to take. Before I could take a step toward him, he bit into it.

"Seriously?" I shouted.

Quande shrugged.

"Come on guys, stop being dicks." Fia, clearly the eldest at about thirty-eight, walked past me and patted the top of my head. He'd been doing that since I was a kid. He reached into the food warmer and pulled out a covered plate. Underneath the cloth was bacon, sausages, biscuits and gravy.

I clasped my hands together, mouthwatering. "Thank you, Fia. You always look out for me."

Fia dug a fork into the biscuits and gravy and literally gobbled it down in one bite. And he even had the gall to burp afterwards! I watched, mouth agape, as the boys doubled over in laughter.

"See..." I said, coming out of shock. "This is why I thank the Spirits that I don't have brothers. I would have murdered you all!"

"Would that be before or after you had to train on an empty stomach?" Oneo said, pulling out another hidden apple and sinking his teeth into it.

I crossed my arms. "I just find it pathetic that you fools had enough time on your hands to hide food only to fuck with me," I huffed.

Twoa pointed at me. "And that's why you're gonna lose every time. We always have enough time to fuck with you, little sis." He winked.

I narrowed my eyes at the twins. "You're only one year older than me."

"But we are far more experienced than you." Oneo threw an arm over Twoa's shoulder. Quande finished his banana and used his shadow to throw the peel away in the compost in the opposite corner of the room. Fia burped again, throwing his empty plate in the sink.

"Respectfully," I held my hands in a praying gesture to my lips. "Fuck all of you!"

The boys erupted in laughter, but I didn't find one drop of this funny. Well, okay, it was a little funny. I let out a *tiny* smile.

The kitchen door opened and in came a light brown skin woman with green locs and circle glasses.

"Kitchen is officially closed!" she said, clapping her hand. Behind her was a woman taller than me dressed in all black leather decorated with daggers and two crisscrossed swords on her back. Her long thick hair was pinned in a bun.

"You heard the woman. Get out!" The woman in leather pointed a thumb behind her.

I instantly recognized the two. The intertwined couple that could teleport.

The guys groaned but obeyed.

"Hey cousin," the woman in leather said as she fist-bumped Fia.

"General wants to see you in his office." Fia nodded and exited.

"I didn't know Fia had a cousin in the Blood Elite. I mean," I thought about Fia's younger brother, who was tragically murdered and decided not to bring it up. All I knew was that after Fia lost his brother, he refused to allow any of his siblings to join the B.E. or the Reaper Army.

"Yeah, he tried to convince me not to join, but it didn't work. I do what I want." She leaned seductively on the counter while the green loc lady pushed her glasses up the bridge of her nose.

"Stubborn and bossy." Green locs shook her head.

"Sassy and intelligent." Leather lady blew kisses to green locs.

"I'm sorry. Usually, I know everyone in the B.E., but your names escape me."

Green locs straightened, smoothing down her baggy clothes. "I'm Sarue, from the 8th Reaper Ward and this is my partner Venus, from the 5th Reaper Ward."

Venus saluted; the reaper steel on her back glistened.

Them standing next to each other, one in the tightest clothes she could find in the closet and the other in the baggiest, seemed like a very odd pairing. And yet, as they kissed, I couldn't help but feel the genuine love they shared.

"How do you two do it?" I leaned in on the counter, watching them playfully smack each other.

"Sometimes, I use this glass shaft that I strap on, but mostly, I like clit on clit." Venus slapped Sarue's butt.

I damn near rolled off the counter. "I didn't mean that. But glass? Where would one..." I traced my finger on the counter-top. "Never mind, that wasn't what I meant. Intertwined, how do you two pair? How does it work?"

"Oh," Venus plopped down on a stool, rubbing her chin. She looked at Sarue, who took the lead.

"It's energy transfiguration," Sarue said, throwing her arms around Venus from the back. "See, we are all made of energy. Many of us can feel, see, and even taste that energy. For example, have you ever walked into a room and there was a thick tension in the air, and you felt the pressure building even though no one was speaking or moving? What you're feeling is the exchange of energy."

"So, basically, the feeling of bad vibes?" I said.

"Exactly, but people's energy can be good or bad. When you meet someone with bad energy that is a threat to your energy, you might feel tense or on edge. But if you meet someone with positive energy or vibes, you might feel warm, happy, fuzzy inside." Sarue walked over to me and grabbed my hands. She held up my palms to hers. Standing this close, I noticed she had tiny little freckles going across her nose with sharp cat eyes.

"Close your eyes," she whispered.

I hesitated but did as I was told.

"Tell me what you feel."

I waited a few moments. "Nothing." I said.

"Try a little harder. Imagine a door inside your mind that you want to open."

I cocked my head, and to my surprise, it was not a door that I saw, but metal bars expanding in my mind's eye. I felt a slight buzz connected in my palms as heat rushed to my fingertips.

"I want you to open that door and walk in," Sarue's voice cut through my thoughts.

Walking to the metal bars, I found a lock fastened around the metal frame.

"It's locked," I said. "I can't get in."

"Any door in your mind has a key." Sarue hands shifted. "You know what to do. Open the door."

The lock was reaper steel, some of the best and hardest to destroy. I examined the lock, but there wasn't a place to insert a key. *You know what to do. Open the door.* At the bottom of the lock, I smoothed my thumb over the base before my mind drew an eight-pointed star, which glowed red. I studied the symbol as it burned into the lock before disappearing. The lock came undone. I pushed the metal gate open and stepped inside.

"I'm in," I said, looking at my surroundings.

"Good. Now, imagine my energy in your mind. Taste it, feel it, see it. Concentrate on pulling my energy in exchange for yours." Sarue squeezed my hand.

Focusing, I reached for Sarue's energy in the dark space behind the metal gate. A figure formed before me, an outline of a woman. I wanted to imagine Sarue clearer, so I inhaled the scent of maple syrup on her breath and fresh-cut grass from her clothes. I imagined she tasted sweet, not as sweet or as delicate as Silvia, who tasted like brown sugar. I imagined Sarue tasted like lilac with a hint of citrus. I clung to it, my palm getting itchy but instead of wanting to dig my nails into my skin to cool the sensation, I wanted to lean into the itch and dig my claws into Sarue.

The figure standing before wore no green locs, but a pool of red hair covering her like a flowy dress. She stepped closer to me, her face still unclear.

Why was I imagining Sarue this way?

"Can one's energy appear different?" I asked as the figure strolled up to me.

"In some cases, yes," Sarue confirmed.

The red figure stood behind me, her warmth engulfing me. Her touch felt like nothing I've ever felt before. In my mind, another figure appeared before me. This time, I knew instantly that this was Sarue's energy. It burst with blues and purples swirling against each other.

The red-haired woman raised my arm, guiding me on what to do next. "*Call,*" she said.

I called for the energy of Sarue to come to me, pulling at it like a rope. Sarue jumped, a slight moan leaked from her lips.

This wasn't the electric feeling I had with the Fireborn, but something greater, more powerful. I craved for it all. The red woman kissed the side of my cheek, her hand wrapped around my neck.

"*Consume her,*" she spoke.

And so, I did. I didn't know why. I just knew I had to. It was as if not consuming her would be the death of me. I opened my mouth, inhaled deeply, spiraling blue and purple energy. Sarue was fading, her energy flickered in the darkness.

"Princess Bellamy," Sarue whispered as the energy intensified, her glowing aura flooding into my body, giving me a taste of power I had never tasted before.

I need more.

It was the heat of her body that I clung to. I sucked, pulling the source quicker into me. My grip grew tighter, intertwining my hands with hers as she disappeared in my mind.

"Princess—" Sarue words slurred as the temperature of her body declined. Her fingertips were now ice cold.

"*More.*" The red woman spoke. "*You're almost there.*" The woman's voice sounded just like my own, but deeper, darker, more seductive. "*Give me more.*"

I gripped tighter, obeying the voice's command. This power, this energy was better than bread and butter, sweeter than Silvia's touch, more exhilarating than hand-to-hand combat. I wanted more, needed more, and Sarue would give it to me.

The last swirls of energy were about to exit Sarue's lips

when the connection was severed. The sudden change left me dizzy, almost high. My mind disconnected from the red woman, the metal gates, and I was flung back to the kitchen as Sarue's icy fingers were forced away from me.

"What the fuck, recruit?" Venus pushed my shoulder. I reached out to grab her wrist with unhesitant swiftness. Venus' fingers flew to her side, removing a dagger from her thigh.

My type of woman.

She held the dagger to my throat, and I pressed my neck against the blade, allowing it to cut my skin. A trickle of blood dripped, and I wanted to pull her in, touch her, take her, suck every bit of power from her beautiful full lips.

"What the fuck are you?" Venus squinted. "Your eyes—" The kitchen door slammed open.

"Out," Zef commanded.

Venus held still for a moment before sheathing her blade and pulling a dazed Sarue into her arms. When they passed Zef Coe, he stopped Sarue and examined her face, then allowed them to exit the door.

Silvia was right behind Zef. I smiled at her.

"Come," I said, happy to see her. She stepped back, her lips disappearing into her mouth.

Zef stormed across the floor, grabbing my chin. He peered down his emerald greens searching mine.

"Get the General," Zef said, putting me into a chair. He reached into his pockets and pulled out a light, shining it into my eyes. "Bellamy," he said, patting my cheeks. "Come back."

What did he mean? I was right here? I laughed too loud and too high. Heat rose from my skin and I could sense his power rising. His energy was gold, just like the specs shining through his emerald green eyes. I pointed to his eyes. "You're something too." My voice came out in a low growl. "Secrets, secrets, secrets. We're all covered in secrets."

"Now! Go get the General now!" he shouted at Silvia.

Silvia jumped; I could literally hear her heart thump. "You frighten my love?" I said, standing up from the chair. I heard Silvia open the door and rush out. "Big mistake."

"Bellamy, I need you to breathe."

"I am breathing," I said as I stepped closer.

"Bellamy, do you hear me?" Zef did not move. His energy was rooted like a pillar.

I could break him.

"She will find out who she is soon enough, Earthborn," I heard myself speak. *Why would I say that?*

"You will not take her," Zef responded. His emerald greens glowed brighter.

"It's already too late. The seal is broken."

The kitchen door opened, and I fell back onto the stool. I blinked a few times; the heat disappearing from my skin.

The general rushed to the front of me, placing his thumb on my forehead. I jerked away, my heart racing.

"What's happening?" I said. "What are you doing?"

"Bellamy?" Zef said.

I looked at him, then at the general, and then back to Silvia, whose back was against the door.

I couldn't trust any of them.

"Did I do something?" I forced my face into a puzzle. "I don't remember. Where did Sarue and Venus go?"

The general glanced at Zef, who nodded.

And then it hit me. Zef's face unraveled right before me. He was the one that was in the office. His voice, his warning, him in my father's embrace.

"You sure you don't remember?" Zef said, searching for the tiniest lie.

I shook my head. "Maybe I should take a few more days." I

turned to face the general. "Is that okay? I think I'm still feeling a bit wonky from the trip."

General straightened, reaching out his hand again. "Sure, let me just—"

"No! Don't touch me." I knocked over the stool and almost rushed out of the kitchen door. "I just need to lie down. That's all." I glanced at the room. I could see my father's energy surrounding him in a shade of onyx and dark brown. As he stood next to Zef, their energies connected but couldn't intertwine. It was as if a sheer glass was all that stood in the way of combining the two.

Silvia touched my arm. I snatched it away, blinking until the vision of their energies vanished and they were normal again. I had to pretend that I was fine. I knew this now. I leaned in and kissed the top of Silvia's forehead, despite how it looked in front of them. Yet, it took everything I had not to recoil under their watchful gaze. I forced my face to relax and smile. Moving forward, I decided to be the good little recruit and pretend that all was well, until I discovered exactly what everyone was hiding from me.

"I'm okay, Silvia." I rubbed a thumb over her chin. "I promise."

XVIII

"How to move a stubborn tree? By chopping it to pieces."
Proverb 38:14 from the Book of Face, Mortem Era.

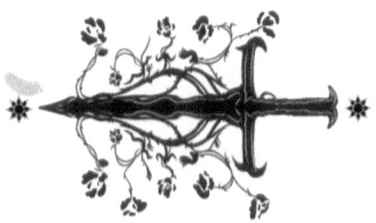

A GIANT SHARP ROOT hung above me. I lay on my back, bathing in dirt as I dodged the root's attempt to smash my face. It's been a week of gruesome training at the hands of Zef Coe, which sent me to the infirmary twice already. It had been two weeks since Camp Runic began.

"Get up! I shouldn't have to tell you to keep up your guard, recruit." The root punched down again, and I barely dodged it this time. Either the root was getting quicker, or I was getting slower.

"I thought Earthborns were a peaceful people. This–I rolled to my feet, catching my breath– "doesn't look peaceful to me." I prepared myself for impact from the giant root that looked like an earthworm but twelve feet tall, when something tight around my ankle pulled. Just like that, I was on my back again, collecting every dirt particle available with my mouth.

"There's always a war happening you need to be prepared for."

I could barely see where Zef stood as the root slung me from off the ground and tossed me into a bush. It knocked the air out of my lungs, and I believe one of my ribs had cracked. "You say that as if another great war is coming our way." I coughed as blood coated my tongue.

"The war, recruit, is the one that rages within."

"The only thing raging within me is the desire to walk away."

Zef flicked his wrist, calling the roots to retreat. I sat up, finally able to catch my breath, but as I breathed in, the upper right side of my torso stung.

"Maybe you're right. This type of training is too hard for you."

"What?" The forest surrounding us briefly stopped all movement. The trees leaned in as if they were spectators watching a show, eager to see what would happen next.

"Maybe you're not worth training at all," Zef said, tucking his hands behind his back.

"Don't you think that's a bit harsh to say?" I stumbled to my feet.

"I'm not saying anything that you didn't say to yourself."

I scrunched my nose and creased my brow.

"You're too slow," Zef leisurely walked in a circle around me. "Ungifted," his emerald greens were calm and focused. "Weak." He stopped directly in front of me.

My chest swelled; the anger burned me from the inside out. If I were gifted, this would be a different story. I could fight him, own him. My palms itched, and I dug my nails into them.

"Are you just going to stand there?" Zef asked, scanning the length of my body.

"You're just trying to rile me up." *And it was working.* I attempted to pull his energy, but ever since that day in the kitchen, I couldn't tap into the power. I finally thought I was manifesting, and yet, whenever I closed my eyes at night, I saw nothing but the backs of my eyelids. No whispers, no voices, no energy, no power. *What is wrong with me? Why can't I get it right?*

"You're not fit to be Earth Queen."

"What?"

"You're not fit to lead anyone. You're stubborn, easily angered, selfish, and powerless when faced with real strength."

I held my tongue. *You weren't saying that in the kitchen! If that was the case, then why have you been watching me like a hawk, having Silvia spy on me and report everything back, and having the Life Doctor monitor my energy frequencies and brain waves regularly? You know something I don't, and if I have to rip it out of your pretty little mouth, I will.*

Taking a deep breath, I closed my eyes and calmed myself, tuning Zef out. I heard the flapping of wings, the sharp nails of squirrels crawling up trees, the rustling of leaves in the wind, and the growth of roots moving through soil.

A root burst from the earth, grabbing at my ankle, but I dodged. Another was already above me. I backflipped out of the way as it buried itself into the ground, bursting out again, behind me this time. I dodged, the side of my ribs aching with each move.

I am not weak.

Another root closed in from the right while another swung in from the left. I calculated the distance between the two and shifted at the precise moment to dodge. Each root split into two, then the two new ones split into two until I was woven into a basket of roots and branches.

"This isn't fair! How am I supposed to beat this? It's impossible!"

"It's impossible because you make it impossible! If you've already told yourself there is no way to win, then you've already lost." Zef aggressively flicked his wrist, the roots sunk into the soil leaving no trace of its presence. "You're simply not ready." He marched past me, headed toward the brick pathway covered in colorful earth-tone moss.

"Ready for what?" I screamed behind him. "To know that you're fucking my dad?" I said, letting the secret slip from my lips. The memory of him and Father replaying again and again in my head with clarity.

Zef halted.

"Yeah, does my mom know about you two?" I wanted to see his face. "You know, it wasn't that hard to figure out. The way you two talk in whispers, you going into his cabin at night when you think everyone is sleeping." I folded my arms across my chest. Just like he was watching me, I was watching him. Trailing him, each night since the kitchen. "Is that what I'm not ready for?"

Turn around, you prick!

"Princess Bellamy," Zef's tone was soft as if all the attitude he just gave me was pulled out of his bones. "There are things I wish I could tell you, but I cannot."

"Why? Tell me now. It's just us. What else are you and my parents hiding from me?"

Zef did not turn around. Pieces of his black strands blew as the gentle breeze went by. "I love your Father," he paused. "Your Mother." His voice cracked ever so slightly. "And you more than you could ever know. But some bonds are unbreakable."

"It's only unbreakable because you already told yourself you can't break them." I spat his words back at him.

His head dipped briefly as if he had smiled, which was the exact opposite reaction I wanted from him.

"I pray to the Spirits that it is your stubbornness that saves you in the end."

"In the end of what? Just fucking tell me!"

"Tomorrow morning, recruit," Zef's voice was again hardened and low. "You'll begin a new training. Hopefully, it will be more fitting for your progression."

Zef continued down the path without looking behind once. I stomped, kicking up dirt and rocks until I twisted too harshly and a piercing, stabbing sensation made my ribs feel like they were splitting in two.

THE BLINDING INFIRMARY light swayed as I lay on the bed.

Doctor Axiom, a Lifeborn, cursed underneath their breath at the end of the medical tent.

"Hold her down, Silvia," they commanded.

A woman, who wasn't Reaperborn, had injured her leg, and the bone was sticking straight out. I watched as Dr. Axiom set the bone with Silvia's assistance. The woman screamed, coughing out the cloth she held in her mouth.

"The hard part is over." Dr. Axiom swept a palm over her

injury, and a shimmering light like sun rays poured out of the Doctor's palm and into the woman's leg. Right before my eyes, her wound healed. The flesh knitted itself back together at a visible rate.

"Rest, now," they said.

The woman slowly relaxed on the table. Silvia quickly went to an herb station, tearing off different plants and leaves and mixing them into liquid-like tea. She then rushed over to the woman and made her drink the entire cup.

"Silvia, you're the best," the woman said before falling asleep.

Dr. Axiom huffed. "I did all the work and do I ever get a thank you? Never." They clicked their teeth and walked away.

Silvia stifled a smile; a bit of a rosy blush bloomed on her rounded cheeks.

She's so fucking cute and sneaky. Cute and fucking sneaky.

A part of me was glad that she found something that made her feel fulfilled, being the assistant to the Life Doctor and putting her herbal knowledge for healing and relaxation to work. I turned slowly and laid back on the bed. The infirmary didn't have many people today. Most of the Reaperborns heal on their own, but since the B.E. was made up of all alignments, Life Doctor Axiom traveled with the camp. As far as I heard, the doctor was top of their class. So, why were they stationed here, setting bones and minor healing?

"You're here again, I see?" The doctor leaned over me with a head full of red curls, sculpted jawline, and long lashes. On their neck was an old scar that was so large it reminded me of a choker.

"What's wrong now?"

I lifted my shirt. "I think it's my ribs. I might have cracked one or a few." I pointed to the area. The doctor pressed down hard and I jumped, almost doubling over.

"Does it hurt?"

"Yeah, did you have to press so hard?"

The doctor reached into their pockets and pulled out a pen, clicking it repeatedly before finally grabbing a click board and scribbling down notes. "Stop getting hurt and maybe I won't have to press at all."

"Zef forgets I'm not Reaperborn, I can't just heal myself. Even if I were Lifeborn, I still wouldn't be able to heal myself."

"No." The pen clicked, and their left hand absentmindedly massaged the scar around their neck. "You're not. And your Father thinks that I have the time to be your personal fixer-upper. You're draining me, kid!"

"More than broken leg lady?" I pointed behind them.

"Unlike her, I have to heal you completely, which requires more effort on my part. I'm not as young as I used to be." They clicked the pen a few more times.

"Well, the faster you heal me, the quicker I can—"

"Hurt yourself and land your behind right back on my table?" Doctor Axiom clicked the pen in three, then placed it back into their pockets.

I rolled my eyes. "I guess the next time I get hurt, I'll just die."

"Sounds good to me, now lie back."

I slammed my back against the pillow, forgetting that my ribs were screaming. I winced at the sudden shock of pain, but focused my attention on the fluorescent light above as it swayed. The glow of golden sun rays brought my eyes back to the doctor's palm. Sweat dotted their brow as their hands went horizontal then vertical along the bruised area.

"Interesting." They cocked their head.

"How many ribs did I damage this time?"

The doctor was silent. There was a warm sensation pene-trating my skin, and I felt something slightly shift, but it was nowhere near as painful as the times the doctor had healed me before.

"Your ribs aren't broken; you just have a bruise."

"That can't be possible. It was hard to breathe, twist, and it felt like something was literally stabbing me from the inside out."

The doctor searched one last time, then shrugged. "Unless you *are* Reaperborn and you have suddenly healed yourself, then all you have here is a really nasty boo-boo. Want a lollipop?" The doctor pulled out a lollipop.

I snatched it from their hands. "No," I said, while unwrapping the candy.

I heard Quande before he even opened the tent door. "Hey Axiom, we need you," he yelled as he dragged in Twoa. Both of their shirts were soaked in blood. "Stab wound," Quande said nonchalantly, handing over Twoa to the doctor. Silvia cleared a table and prepped some supplies on a metal station as the doctor dragged Twoa to the bed.

"That's your girl, huh?" Quande plopped on the stool next to my bed.

"I guess." I laid back on the pillow, hearing Twoa scream like the little bitch that he was. "Shouldn't you get looked at?" Quande raised his shirt. His wound was stitching together as little shadows acted as needle and thread, mending his flesh.

"I'm good, like always." He pulled his shirt down. "You guess? What does that mean? Is she available or not?"

I eyed him. "Why?"

"I'm just asking. You kept this one a secret. I'm usually the first one to know about all your *fer l'amors*. What makes her different?"

"You're far too nosy," I said, trying to come up with a topic that wasn't this one.

"And this is coming from the queen of Snoop? Please, I'm

just trying to look out for you. I mean, she's beautiful. Thick, like damn."

"Hey." I punched him in the shoulder.

"I'm just saying, she looks nice, sweet even. I've spoken with her a few times and I'm just saying, be careful with her."

"Why? Do you have a crush on her?"

Twoa shrieking died down. I turned to look behind me. The pain in my side was completely gone at this point. Twoa sat up in bed as Silvia wrapped herbs around Twoa's freshly healed wound.

"Finish up, Silvia," the doctor said as they washed their hands in a nearby sink.

"This will help with the rest of the healing while also easing the pain. You should be fine." She patted Twoa on the leg. Twoa smiled, a little too playfully, and a tinge of jealousy burned my chest.

"She's mine," I said a little too loudly. I sat up, dangling my legs on the side of the bed.

"Easy." Quande stood. "No need to get possessive."

"I'm not. She can see anyone she wants, just not him or you." I looked from Twoa to Silvia, who glanced over her shoulder at me before walking down to the end of the tent where the doctor had taken their place, flipping through papers.

Twoa strutted over, smoothing his long hair to one shoulder. "What's up, little sis?"

I hit him right in his stab wound; he doubled over. "Fucking hell, Bee!"

Quande laughed.

"Shit's not funny. She's crazy!" Twoa said, trying to catch his breath. "That's okay. I got your ass, Bee."

"You ain't got shit."

"See, that's your problem. You hang around Quande too

much. You're basically a smaller version of him. The both of you, complete psychos!"

Quande and I gave each other knowing glances. Truth was, he was the closest thing I'd ever had to a brother. Before he was promoted to first lieutenant, eighty percent of my trouble-making included him.

"Speaking of, when am I going to train with you?" I asked Quande.

"Sorry, Bee. I'm under strict orders from the general to not train you at all."

"When did that ever stop you?"

"The moment you got caught fighting in a damn bar! You know your Mother was calling for my head, trying to strip me from my titles?"

"What? She thinks of you like her own son. She wouldn't dare."

"Yeah, well. She tried, but eventually settled with yelling at me for three hours straight. So, no. No help from me. Zef is your boss now."

I immediately rolled my eyes.

"You should listen to him, Bee. Other than your mom, Zef is the only one that is really up there when it comes to Earth power. If you're going to manifest with anybody, it would be with him. Stop trying to fight everything all the time, okay?" Quande shoved my shoulder.

I knocked his hand away.

"Seriously, for once in your damn life listen to authority. He's here to help you." Quande leaned down and whispered into my ear. "And don't fuck up your little situationship because I might just be there when you're not."

Before my fist could connect with his jaw, Quande was already at the exit door. "Too slow!" he said, holding the door open for Twoa. "Keep training!" The tent door closed behind him.

I glanced over at Silvia cleaning the medical trays. Truth was, I missed her, but the even bigger truth was, I didn't trust her anymore, not completely.

Sliding off the bed, I made my way over to her. She turned and walked away, getting a fresh pillow, and sliding it under the woman's head with the healing leg.

"Are you going to continue ignoring me?"

Silvia paused, her lips sucking into her mouth. She took the old pillow and moved it to a bin.

"Come on, Silvia. Talk to me?"

"Why should I?"

"Because I miss you."

"Now you miss me?" Silvia pushed past me, heading over to the herbs table lining the tent wall.

I followed her. "Silvia, I honestly don't get you sometimes."

"Where have you been for the last week and a half?"

Like she didn't know, like she wasn't watching me like a good little pet. I pushed the thought out of my head.

"I've been around, you know, doing this and that."

"What I do know is you haven't been back into our cabin since...since..." Silvia looked away.

"Exactly," I said. "How can I be somewhere I'm not wanted?"

"Who said you weren't wanted?"

"You, the way you look at me, like you're scared of me. You continue to give me mixed signs and expect me to figure out which days you're afraid of me and which days you want to fuck me."

"Hey," a groggy voice spoke. The woman sat up a bit on the bed. "Can you take your lover's quarrel somewhere else? I'm trying to rest here."

"I was really into it. The best action I've seen all day," Doctor Axiom said, legs crossed, eating a piece of chocolate.

I rubbed the back of my neck. "Tonight. I'll be there tonight, and we can talk about this, okay?"

Silvia dropped some herbs into some water and sealed the lid.

"Fine."

She walked away into the medical storage room.

"Damn," Doctor Axiom said. "Must be nice."

XIX

"Unspoken words have shattered many happily ever afters."
Proverb 12:12 from the Book of Face, Mortem Era.

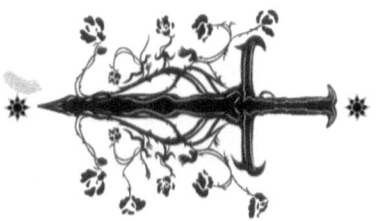

FRESHLY SHOWERED, I HEADED over to Silvia's cabin. The sun was setting, and the luminescent trees and flowers glowed softly, creating a nice low light leading right up to Silvia's door. There were newly planted mint, sage, ginseng, and chamomile in a little garden. Herbs that Silvia couldn't live without. I found it interesting how some Earthborns had the talent to grow whatever vegetation and greenery they specialized in all year around. Silvia was no different, when it came to herbs, they grew wherever she was.

I rubbed my nails over my skin, even though there wasn't any itch present. The familiarity and comfort it brought was enough to bring me the courage to knock.

"Come in," Silvia's silky-smooth voice chimed.

Upon entering, the scent of coconut hit my nose, and my shoulders instantly relaxed. Silvia stood in the mirror, rubbing pieces of the smooth butter on her deep honey skin. Her nightgown was sheer, and she was wearing no unders.

Focus.

"You smell nice." I took off my shoes at the door. The inside of the cabin almost reminded me of Everest's room, but instead of featherfews, white roses, and daisies, there was sage and moss creeping in every cracked corner. "You've been decorating, I see." I flicked a sage pedal.

Silvia checked herself in the mirror before moving to the closet. Some of my clothes were folded neatly. She handed them to me, along with my hygiene supplies.

"What's this for?"

"You can come get the remaining of your things later this week when I'm not here." She crossed her arms underneath her breasts.

"Is this what you want?"

"It's not about what I want," she said.

"I disagree. This is all about what you want." I dropped the bundle onto the floor. "One moment, you look at me like you're lost without me and the next moment, you look at me as if you're terrified to be around me."

Silvia's lips disappeared into her mouth. Her foot tapped against the hardwood.

"This isn't the time to hold back. Just admit it." I stepped closer to her, she stepped backwards. "You're afraid of me."

Silvia moved past me, and I grabbed her upper arm.

"Say it! Now or never." I needed to hear the words and for the life of me, I couldn't bite back the arousal that the anger in her eyes caused. I almost wanted to laugh and smash my lips against hers, but I restrained myself.

"I'm afraid of you." Silvia snatched her arm away.

"And why is that?" My plaits had come undone, and I gathered them together, twisting them into a bun.

"Bellamy—"

"Answer the question! Let's stop with the bullshit and let's be real with each other for once."

Silvia created distance between us. She paced the length of the room, her lips disappearing into her mouth. She froze then turned to me.

"You can be toxic, Bellamy." Her voice was low, but firm. "I'm afraid of you because of the power you hold over me. Over my heart, you cloud my judgments. It's like nothing else matters. All I want is you. Your touch, your kiss, your attention. You're a princess! I will be nothing other than your uma, at the least and at best, a fer l'amor, which is a glorified concubine."

I rolled my eyes. *Bullshit. This is complete bullshit.*

"If you're *so* afraid, then leave! Walk away. Save yourself, since I'm toxic."

"Is that all you've heard?"

"That's all that matters. If it's such a pain to be involved with a princess, then why stick around?"

"It's complicated, Bellamy."

"What's complicated about it?"

"Because I'm in love with you!" Silvia's hardened face unraveled right in front of me. She held her palms over her mouth as if she could recall the words back.

"What's so complicated about loving me?" I didn't realize tears had left my eyes until I wiped the fluid from my cheek. All of my life, people made loving me seem like a hard task to complete. My sister, my mother, and now Silvia? What was so awful about loving me? "I know I've hurt you. I know I've broken my promises as of late, but I've tried my hardest to give you what you need. To be loyal to you, keep you safe. What is this truly about, Silvia?"

"I can't..." Her foot thumped heavily against the wood, creating a sound that annoyed the shit out of me.

I closed the distance between us, throwing my arms around her, applying a small amount of pressure to ease her anxiety. My skin prickled, and the itch ran down the length of my arm.

"If I leave, would you stop me?" She buried her face into my neck.

I breathed in the familiar scent of her hair. "Yes."

"Why?"

I nudged my lips in the crease of her neck. "Because I'm weak." I released her, digging my nails into my forearm. "I know you've been spying on me. Reporting everything I do to Father. Which got me thinking, how long has this been going on for? Did it just start now or has it been going on for longer?" I faced Silvia, her lips gone. "That's it, isn't it? That's why it's so complicated?"

"Bellamy—"

"I'm such an idiot. The thought really didn't occur to me until just now. It was like a missing puzzle piece." The reason she wouldn't accept being my fer l'amor, the reason she tries not to get too close, the reason she will give me her body but not her heart. The itch intensified. "Admit it." My cracked voice turned bitter and cold.

"Yes."

I laughed. "And you have the nerve to stand before me like I'm the fucking problem? How long?"

"How long, what?"

"How long have you been manipulating me, tricking me, whispering lies and then reporting back to my parents? How long?"

"I've never manipulated you or tricked you."

"How long?" I shouted.

"A few years."

"Wow." It's not that I couldn't believe what I was hearing. I simply didn't want to. "Why, Silvia? Tell me the truth."

Silvia shifted on her feet, unable to look me in the eye.

Look at me! Show me the fucking respect to at least look at me!

As if hearing my thoughts, Silvia's eyes locked on mine.

"They promised me my own name. My own title. My own path. The task was simple. Keep the princess out of trouble, report back any suspicious activity, monitor your mood, and your skin condition. I thought it would be easy. But the more I watched you, the fonder my heart grew."

"I could have given you all those things, Silvia." My voice was soft and tired.

"What you offered me was fer l'amor! You didn't care about what I wanted, not really. You wanted to possess me, own me! Can you be accountable for at least that!"

Heat rose to my skin, and I closed the distance between us, anger almost snatching the last little bit of patience I had. "I want to own you!" I said in a low growl. "I want to own your mind, your body, and your fucking soul." I gathered her in my arms, my fist closing around her neck. "You are mine. You are mine. You are fucking mine, and I would rip the world into two for you." My grip tightened, but she did not fight me.

"I've let no one touch me once I committed myself to you," she choked out.

"What?" I loosen my grip.

Silvia quickly placed both hands around my wrist, not allowing me to drop my hand.

"I wanted to tell you, Bellamy. You have to believe me. I was sworn to secrecy. Your Mother placed an earth bond on me and I couldn't say anything even if I wanted to." Her lips did not disappear; her watery eyes were sincere. She was telling the truth.

"So why can you now?" I caressed my thumb on the base of her neck—feeling her windpipe—wanting to crush it and kiss it at the same time.

"It's you. You did something that night in your Father's office." My eyebrows creased.

"After the fight with the prince, you don't remember it because your Father took that memory away."

"Why?"

"Because you were transforming. Like, you weren't human. Your eyes became green slits, your skin darkened, and the power you radiated destroyed your Mother's wisteria. I felt the seal break as soon as you overwhelmed her with your manifestation."

My thumb paused. "Manifestation?"

"Energy, it was like you could control it. But there was something more." Silvia slid shaky hands to my face. "Something or someone was controlling you."

I thought of the red woman in my vision, how she called to me and the power that I felt while draining Sarue's energy.

"What does this mean?" I rocked back on my heels as my head throbbed with blurred memories forcing themselves into my frontal lobe. I sat on the edge of the bed, my head in my palms. The itch on my skin died down to nothing more than a mild annoyance. "What else?"

"I've been trying to figure that out since the office too. Bellamy..." Silvia squatted in front of me. "I'm trying to protect you."

"No." I shook my head, not wanting to hear that. I tried pushing her away, but she clung to me, forcing me back onto the bed. She climbed on top of me, wrapping her arms around me. I cried, unable to hold back years of feeling like shit, never being good enough, not manifesting, only to learn that my parents have been preventing me from doing so this entire time? Why? Why go to these lengths to keep me caged?

Silvia wiped my tears. "You can't let them know."

"Why?" My voice was hoarse to my ears.

"Your parents, your sister, you are all being monitored. And if you start acting unusual or showing signs of manifesting, I think..." Silvia wet her lips. "I think you'll die."

I searched Silvia's face for a lie and only found her tears dripping down onto my cheeks.

XX

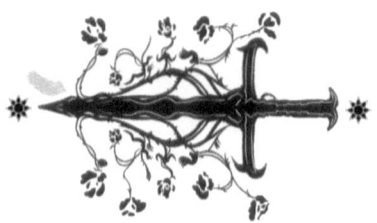

"A mirror only reveals the surface; eyes reveal the depth."
Proverb 21:55 from the Book of Face, Mortem Era.

"ACT NORMAL," I whispered to myself. The breakfast plate shook in my hand as I walked back to the kitchen to deposit my barely touched seasoned eggs, vegetables, and toast into the compost. After last night, processing the new information Silvia told me left me sick. I had fallen asleep in her arms and then awoke screaming, experiencing my first nightmare. I couldn't remember the details, only that I was burning.

Covered in sweat, I pushed Silvia away from me. Her touch was like frostbite on my skin. I was exhausted, but nonetheless, until more intel was gathered, the plan was to act normal.

Like I knew what the fuck normal meant. All I wanted to do was tear up this camp, march into Father's office, and knock over all of his shit. So, instead of being hot-headed, I do the complete opposite. Play it cool. Watch, wait, and listen. Could I trust Silvia? I didn't know, but I needed to find out who I could trust.

Silvia said my entire family was being observed, but she didn't know by whom, only that it was mentioned in the chaos of wiping my memory. My parents argued, then decided to get me far from the Reaper Kingdom until they could find out what to do next.

I emptied my tray into the compost and then sat the empty tray on the rack. I looked out into the camp. Some soldiers saluted me and others didn't exactly meet my eye. Some faces, such as Fia, Quande, and the Moonborn twins, were familiar, and others I needed to get to know more.

If this plan was going to work, it would mean that I must know my surroundings. I'd gone through life far too long, naïve, sheltered, and protected.

On the far side of the camp, the twinkling glimmer of Venus's reaper steel caught my eye. Decked out in her usual skin-tight leather and swords, she walked out of an orange moss-covered cabin and headed towards the training grounds deep into the forest. I hadn't seen Sarue around lately, plus I needed to know how and what she felt that day in the kitchen. As the main camp cleared, I made my way to her cabin. Before I could knock on the door, Sarue spoke.

"Come in, princess."

I bit my bottom lip in confusion. I pushed the door open. The cabin was ice cold. Puffs of white smoke escaped my lips. The only light in the room was from the sunlight creeping in from the open cabin door to which I shut.

"Sarue? I wanted to check in on you." The cabin was set up slightly differently. Immediately in front of me was the sectioned bath area and to my left, in a corner, was the bed. Sarue was tucked underneath a mountain of blankets.

"Sarue, are you sick?"

"Doctor Axiom can't fix me," she said, trying to sit up.

I ran to the bed to help. The moment my fingers touched her skin, I jerked away in pain. *Frostbite.*

"How did this happen?" I searched for her brown face, that had turned a ghostly blue-black with purple lips.

"You know the answer, princess."

I shook my head. "I did this to you?" I pulled a chair to the side of the bed. "How?"

Sarue coughed. "Energy. I barely have any. Once a manifestation is depleted, it usually takes anywhere between three hours to a week to regain full capacity." Sarue shifted, her arm barely able to lift the blankets. "In this case, I can't seem to..." She looked to the ceiling in thought. "In lack of better words, relight the match."

"How can I help?" *If I could do anything.*

"Technically, you're not supposed to be here."

"How did you know I was at the door?"

Sarue's smile was weak. "I felt you, as if you were a part of me."

I leaned in.

"When I left the kitchen, it was like your energy stuck with me. I can feel you as you run throughout camp, but I didn't tell Doctor Axiom or your Father this."

"And Venus?"

Sarue shook her head. "I think you can fix me." Sarue struggled with the blankets. I helped her remove them, careful not to touch her skin. She sat up straight, allowing her feet to dangle off the side of the bed.

"What do I need to do, Sarue?"

"In our connection, you pulled energy out of me. Maybe you can restore it?"

I thought for a moment. Remembering the red woman and the hunger that pulled at my soul to consume more. "What if I can't? What if I..." I examined the fragile Sarue. Her skin was loose as if she had lost weight, her eyes sunken, her green locs matted against her scalp. "...hurt you more?"

"In the kitchen, did you want to hurt me?" Sarue grabbed my hands. They stung my skin, and I tried not to rip my fingers away.

"Yes." I bit my bottom lip to bear her icy touch.

Sarue bent forward until her lips touched my ear. "I saw her too, the woman in red."

My eyes grew wide. Sarue drew back, clutching my hand, her fingers locked into mine.

"Sarue," I said, her palms burning mine.

"Focus."

Chills crawled up to my wrist.

"Breathe, focus your energy on me. Just like in the kitchen."

Veins popped from the back of Sarue's hand as her nails dug into my skin. I knew I deserved this.

"Look at me, Bellamy. Look into my eyes. Tap into the energy within."

I attempted to focus. My eyes went from my hands to her eyes, but the ice that bit at my forearms was worse than the years of itching ever was.

"Connect." Sarue caught my eye. Her eyes glowed a faint blue-ish purple.

I was entranced, her pupils swirling in pools of energy. I could see her life force at the core of her being as I was sucked deeper into the darkest reaches of my mind. I met Sarue, not behind the metal bars like the first time, but in a small cabin. Little brown kids were running around as shouts of adults warned the children to stop. A child gripped my hand. I looked down at Sarue's smiling face.

"Over here," she said, leading me out the small cabin door and into the front yard. Sarue led me to the Great Basin Bristlecone Pine. The brown tree was barren, its roots exposed, white ice-like fine hair wrapped around the roots.

"Up there." Sarue pointed to the highest branch. A single purple blue apple dangled from its dried-out branches. Sarue let go, her small body covered in ice. Thrown off guard, I tripped and fell backwards on my butt.

My heart was pounding fast as the kid version of Sarue slowly froze over. Surveying my surroundings, her siblings stopped mid-chase, her mother coming out of the cabin door and her father chopping wood, all frozen. Icicles grew from every inch of their bodies.

"I have little time." Sarue pointed to the ice crawling up from the root of the tree to the highest branch holding the last of her energy. "You know what to do, Princess Bellamy." Sarue froze into place, her one finger pointing to the tree.

Ice adhered to my clothes, grabbing me like crystal-like fingers. I broke free and scrambled to my feet. I crushed the ice underneath my boot.

The blue sky turned gray. My mouth went dry, and I dug my nails into my skin. The ice decorated the tree branches in sharp icicles.

I closed my eyes, my chest heaving. The red woman flashed in my memory as she directed me to pull Sarue's energy. *I know what to do,* I repeated, opening my eyes. I blew out white puffs of smoke. *I know what to do.* I walked to the tree, crushing the ice underneath my heel. I placed my hand on the base; the ice sent waves of cold pain that shocked my entire system like electricity. I wanted to pull back, but I bit my lip and braced myself. The ice froze over my hand like a glove, locking me into place.

Don't panic. You know what to do. But did I really? I've never heard of anyone having an energy manifestation. There was no teacher for this. The red lady did not come, and yet I was supposed to know exactly how to save Sarue?

The ice encrusted my arm. I placed my other hand on the tree, trying to rip away from the ice, but the ice trapped my other hand too. Whatever needed to happen, needed to happen fast. I calmed my breath, feeling for Sarue's energy.

"Call it forth," I said, embracing the ice, pushing through the pain. "Come." The tree surged like a heartbeat. It was faint at first, but the more I focused, the louder the thumping became.

I can do this. Instead of pulling Sarue's energy, I tapped into my own. Calling forth my heat and redirecting it into the tree. My body warmed as if I was sitting around a campfire.

Swirls of purples and blues ignited the tree's core, and the ice unfroze. Sarue's energy mixed with my blazing red and orange had fused as if intertwining. The ice melted and vaporized as my body grew hotter. I watched red orange swirls wrapped around the tree in a tornado.

The tree burst forth leaves and rapidly growing apples that were vibrant and so huge they hung heavy on the branches.

Once completed, I stepped away. My energy returned to me as the gray skies cleared. The warmth of the sun kissed my face. This power was my power, my manifestation. Restoration felt just as enticing as destruction.

The tree was restored to its former glory. I turned to face

the now-grown Sarue. Her green locs draped down her back, her smile highlighting her cat-like eyes. The children in the background continued to chase as the mother called them in and the father put away his tools to prepare to go inside.

I was pulled away from the scene and opened my eyes. I was back in the chair, sitting in front of a fresh-faced, glowing Sarue. Her hands were warm to the touch. She reached over and kissed me, her black shadow leaking from her palms and wrapping around mine in swirls.

"You did it," she said, her shadow playing along my skin like running kids.

"I don't understand." I rubbed her shadow, and I could swear I could feel the purring vibrations in each strain.

"I've never witnessed a manifestation like yours before, princess. I don't think anyone has."

The cabin door swung open and Venus entered. I pushed back from Sarue, but Venus was quick and her aim true. She pulled the sword from her back before I could stand from the chair. "What the fuck is going on here?" She held the sword to my throat.

In an instant, Sarue's shadow wrapped around the sword, yanking it from Venus's hand and throwing it across the room. Venus' mouth dropped as Sarue rose from the bed, her shadow engulfing her like butterfly wings.

"How?" Venus looked from me to Sarue. Tears formed in her surprised eyes. "How?" she said, running up to Sarue, checking her forehead, her wrist, and her heartbeat.

They hugged each other. Venus' shadow intertwined with Sarue's. I could see their aura glowing the same blueish purple. But faintly, in the wisps of Sarue's shadow, was a fine strain of red orange.

· · ·

SO MUCH FOR LYING LOW. I exited the cabin with the vow that Sarue and Venus would not tell my father or the doctor about me restoring Sarue's manifestation. If they told, they would risk their memories being wiped, if not worse. There was no telling how far Father would go to keep them and me silent.

Silvia was right. This wasn't the time to act strange. I needed to remain focused and move as silently as the shadow assassins. Hiding until the right moment to strike.

I flexed my hand, balling my fingers into a fist, then flattening them back out. The warmth in my palms felt good, and I was ready for my training with Zef Coe.

Marching over to my meeting place, Zef stood with his hands behind his back while his face was soaking up the sun.

"You're late, again," he said, eyes still closed.

"I got caught up. It's only been five to ten minutes."

Zef opened his eyes and faced me. He checked his black watch.

"Forty-five minutes."

Damn.

"Sorry, I won't be late again, I swear."

"Follow me."

I nodded and followed Zef down the path back to the camp. He led me to the community showers. Inside, the air was humid and thick as fog. It made me sweat. The showers were running at full max in the background.

"What are we doing here?" I smelled my pits to see if Zef was trying to tell me I stank.

Zef pulled out the laundry bucket that the soldiers had discarded their nasty training clothes in.

"This is your first chore. You will maintain the cleanliness of the showers and wash and dry the clothing each day, twice a day."

"Excuse me?"

"You heard him, princess."

I looked over my shoulders and Oneo and Twoa entered with wide grins on their faces. Their clothes were covered in mud. How were they getting this dirty already? It was still morning!

The twins stripped, throwing their dirty clothes into the basket. Zef nodded at them.

"It's about time she started pulling her weight around here," Oneo said.

"This is getting fun." Twoa winked.

"Zef, this must be a mistake. Manual labor is something I don't do. Don't we have some umas here to take care of this?"

"Yes, you are the assigned uma," Zef said without flinching.

The twins giggled in the background.

"Did my father sign off on this?"

"Ooh, she's afraid of a little work," one of the dumbass twins said.

"I'm not afraid of anything, but Zef, if this is about being late, I can do better."

"This is about training. Clearly, you need to start from the ground level and work your way back up," Zef said.

"I think this is a waste of my talent."

"What talent?" Zef blinked.

The twins ooed and awed. I bit my lower lip.

"Privilege is given and it can be taken away. After you clean the showers and do the laundry, you will also clean the cabins and help prepare breakfast, lunch, and dinner."

I did quick calculations in my brain. "Wait, if I do breakfast prep that would mean I need to be in the kitchens at..." I subtracted the time.

"No later than 4:30 a.m." Zef finished my sentence.

I've never, in my life, woke up before the sun did. This... this was impossible. It couldn't be done.

"What if I don't?"

The twins' eyes bounced from me to Zef.

"Then let's add wood chopping to your daily chores," Zef replied.

"I said if!"

"Would you like another? There's plenty to do around here. Let's add feeding and taking care of the animals."

"No!" I started to argue when I heard the twins snickering.

"Would you like another chore recruit?"

I dug my nails into my palm. "No."

"No, what?"

"No, sir," I grunted.

"Good. Your training begins now." Zef turned on his heel and walked out of the showers.

"No, sir." Twoa mocked, sliding off his unders. "Chop, *chop*, princess. The real work has begun." Twoa launched his black unders at my face. The fabric smelled of sweaty man balls that consisted of hard work and desperation. Buck naked, the twins headed to the showers, and I had to watch their little pale asses happily prance away.

I balled his unders into a fist.

This is some complete bullshit.

Act V

XXI

"Beware of the day when prey becomes the predators."
Proverb 51:3 from the Book of Face, Mortem Era.

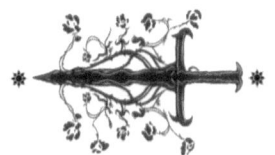

TWO PAINFULLY GRUESOME MONTHS went by. When Father gave me the opportunity to train with the Blood Elite, I didn't think cleaning up after their shit stained unders would be what he meant. And yet, here I was, day in and day out, working my fingers to the bone. At night, before I would pass out, I would stare at a sleeping Silvia with a newfound respect for what she does, always serving others in some capacity.

I wrestled with trusting her completely, but maybe she deserved to be forgiven. She did what she had to do, and if I were born in her circumstances and was given the same proposition, spy on the princess by her own parents, maybe I would have taken it too. A title for her could mean respect from the community, a chance to start her own enterprise, and a prospect at life that she would be able to create for herself. I wanted that for her, and I wanted that for me too.

Even as I gathered the bucket and mop and made my rounds cleaning the cabins, I would sacrifice my soul to never have to mop another room again. Especially the fucking twins' pigsty of a room.

The Moonborns were a pain in my side. They constantly thought of wild food requests, never placed their dirty clothes where I asked them to, and lastly, their cabin was the dirtiest quarters in the camp.

I opened their door, hauling in almost every cleaning tool I could find. The buckets clanked. I dropped them to the floor as my mouth fell open in pure horror.

How did they get mud on the ceiling? My right eye twitched.

Their clothes were scattered on the floor. Beds unmade. Floors dusty. And I didn't want to know what the sticky yellow glue-like substance was on their dresser. There were muddy boot prints on the walls and ceiling. I imagined them leaving for training this morning after stuffing their hands in their boots and pressing them against every wall. The smell was like rotten eggs mixed with the griffes shit.

I scratched my arm, my skin breaking out in hives the longer I stood in the room. I ripped off my gloves. Both arms were on fire. The more stress I was under, the worse the flare grew, and the Moonborn twins knew exactly what buttons to press. I attacked my skin with my sharpest nail until the surface broke.

When scratching insanely didn't calm the itching, I took my frustrations out on the twin's cabin. Blood trickled down my arm.

This is it. I'll teach their asses.

If I could punch something or someone, then maybe I could calm down, but I've been patient with them for months!

My eyes frantically searched the room. In the corner, on top of a dresser, there was a fire stick and matches.

If they won't pick up their clothes, then they don't deserve clothes.

Abandoning my mop and bucket, I gathered the clothes that were thrown about. Hanging from the ceiling fan was a single pair of unders in rotation on one of the blades.

Spirits be an ounce of grace!

I snatched it down, balling it with the rest of the growing wad of clothes in my arms. I grabbed the fire stick and matches and ran out of the cabin door.

My feet led me to the deepest part of the woods, up the mountain's edge, away from prying eyes. I scanned the grounds that were mostly greenery free. I was upset, but I wasn't a complete fool. The only thing I wanted to burn was these stinky-ass clothes, not the entire camp.

I piled the clothes in a large stack, then took out the fire stick and matches. A menacing grin creeped across my face as I lit the fire stick. A tiny flame belly danced in the wind. And I let out a maniacal laugh.

This will show them.

I imagined their clothes in flames and me laughing over them like a madwoman. I also, for the first time in my life, seriously thought about the consequences.

That made me click my teeth and pause. Father would be livid. Zef, disappointed. Then what? Would he make me do another week of grunt work before allowing me to actually train? Why did I care so much about what those liars thought?

Fuck!

I greeted my teeth and blew out the flame. I wasn't above petty revenge, but I concluded my goal to beat Father outweighed this potentially satisfying moment.

I was about to toss the fire stick when low voices engaged in an argument gave me pause. I listened closely, searching to realize the voices came from the other side of the mountain, facing the camp.

They had a slight accent akin to the southern region of the Seven Kingdoms. The arguing voices grew louder as their foot-steps rounded the corner. They were gaining traction at my location. I needed to move. I gathered the musty clothes and spotted a small opening that was covered by boulders. I tucked myself inside, my ass and hips squeezing against the boulder and the surface of the jagged mountain. The opening was extremely tight, but still doable.

I looked through tiny cracks surrounding the boulder and spotted the matchbox I left. Before I could squeeze out of the hole to get it, footsteps fell, then stopped.

Turning my torso, I saw three men but not their full faces. The men's clothes were tattered and boots were beyond worn.

The three men were a few feet away. The closer they came, the clearer their conversation.

"We found dem. But what makes yous think they would help us? Dey Reaperborns; we Fireborns. Huh, Minks?"

I struggled to get a clear view, but the boulder blocked too much.

"Cuz, what choice do we have, Bunko? Starve to death out

in the middle of nowhere." A shoe kicked the side of the mountain, kicking up dirt. "Talk some sense to 'em, Data."

There was a brief silence. The next voice was smooth, almost calming like a lullaby. "Minks is right. We have no choice." Data moved into frame. He had a bald head with dirt stained glasses, which he took off and rubbed on his shirt.

"Not you too, man!" The high pitch voice was Bunko's. He continued, "Dere's always a choice. I say we gather our best men and rob the next carriage we see."

"And den what?" Minks had more of a thicker drawl to his speech. "We keep robbin'? Hidin'? That would work if we didn't have women and children starvin'. Who'll take dem in if we started killin'?"

The men went silent.

I swallowed. My skin flared. I fought the urge to scratch. The sensation stretched from my right arm and inched across my chest to the left side. The more I bit back the urge to scratch, the worse the flare continued.

Please, go, go, go!

My legs wobbled.

Data turned toward the boulder.

I sucked in my breath, fearing it had grown loud from my pumping heart. Scenarios flashed in my mind. *Could I take them?* Judging by their clothes, they looked as if one heavy wind would sweep in and take them away. Of course, I could take all three of them.

Data spoke, "If dey help us, dey help us." He bent over, cocked his head, and picked up the matchbox. His tattered shirt came undone. I saw a burned mark that sat right beneath the collar of his neck bone. It was as if someone purposely took a hot stick and carved a burn mark into his skin. "And if dey don't help us, then we'll find another way. Let's get back to the base before sunset. We got to inform Key what we found." He slid the matchbox into his pockets.

The three men continued their walk around the mountain. Their footsteps disappeared the farther they went. I let out a long exhale.

Shit. That was close.

I squeezed out of the boulder, scratching my skin. I gave chase in the direction they went, rounding the mountain's edge as it opened up to a pathway downhill. I listened closely, the men's voices echoing ahead. I followed them through the clearing. Seeing there wasn't anywhere to hide, I sought cover behind the last of the mountain's edge.

One man had stopped, the bald head man with glasses, Data. He stood there peering back into the mountain as if he could see me. I shifted. My feet slipped on a rock and I lost my balance. I grabbed on to a groove to steady myself, but the shifting of the rocks rang loudly off the mountain's wall.

Data walked back toward the mountain.

"Hey Data! Come on, man!" I recognized the drawl in Mink's yelling. His dark hair was matted to his head.

Data kept staring at the mountain.

There was no way he could have spotted me, right?

"Data. Let's go!" Bunko's high-pitched voice called. His facial features seemed to all be gathering to the middle of his face.

Data hesitated a while longer before turning around to his friends and jogging to catch up. I watched them go until their bodies were tiny dots on the horizon.

QUANDE SAT ON the edge of the general's desk. General Agrim Tagore, stroking his beard, stood in front of me, interrogating me as if I was in front of the Council of Amalgamation. I wanted to jump from my seat, slam my fist on the table, and profess, "It wasn't me!" but I just sat quietly, waiting for the next question to be asked.

"Are you sure that's what you heard?" The general leaned in. My shoulder went stiff.

"Yes, that's all. They were looking for us. It seemed like they needed our help." Sweat bubbled at my nose.

Rwju walked into the cabin, followed by Zef.

"We searched the borders. Their tracks disappeared once they went over the hill. Whoever they are, they are skilled at hiding themselves." Rwju leaned against the wall.

The general sat on the table next to me. Silently, Zef made his way into my eyesight. "Do you think this is the Redux?"

Zef and the general returned intense stares. The presences of both men in the room filled the space with so much energy that the cabin felt as if it were shrinking. They were a force of nature. If the general was steel and iron, then Zef was a forest of redwood trees planted firmly in soil.

The general rolled his neck. "It must be. The only Fireborns that would dare seek reapers must be those who have deserted."

"Then why would they come here?" Zef asked.

"Kingdoms are closing their borders to Fireborns." The general said.

I shifted in my chair. "Why?"

Zef and the general moved at the same time, as if they were somehow synchronized.

The general ran his fingers through his beard. "According to the reports at the Council of Amalgamation, citizens are outraged by the number of resources going towards the relocation of the Fireborns. On top of that, mixed breeding. Judging by the statistics, there were more mixed-breed Fireborns born this year than ever before. Many people see this as a threat to their existence." The general turned to walk back to his desk.

Zef shifted on his feet. "The more Fireborns allowed within the borders, the more they dilute our bloodlines."

Quande took out his blade and twirled it in his hand. "It almost seems strategic," he said.

The general nodded. "That is the rumor. Since Fireborns can't win a fight against those who have gifts, the next best thing would be to send refugees into enemy territory and create more ungifted there. Slowly weakening us as time went by."

"Excuse me," I said, seeing I was the only one that had a billion questions to ask. The general nodded for me to speak. "Just say it was true, the Fireborns want to make the future generations ungifted. Sending out hundreds of their men and women into the Six Kingdoms is a poor plan. We still outnumber them collectively. It just isn't a feasible goal."

The general smirked. "When it comes to mass hysteria, facts are not a sound voice to bias." The general pulled a letter from his desk. "According to this demand, citizens want a law written making mixed breeding illegal. Not only that, but they also want Fireborn and Fireborn sympathizers banned from their kingdoms. Which will overturn the bill passed by the Council of Amalgamation last month that proposed making Fireborns legal as long as they pledge fealty to whatever kingdom they are living in."

So, Congruent Attali was able to pass his bill.

Over my shoulder, Rwju's raspy voice cut through the conversation. "In the Water Kingdom, Fireborn disbandment is already happening. Ripping families apart, excommunicating the ungifted, and pushing sympathizers across the borders. Even if both parents are gifted, if the child has not manifested by twenty-one, age of pledge, the citizens are abandoning them, too."

I cringed, my shoulders rising to my ears, then slumping forward.

"Beta."

That was the first time I heard Father. Not General Agrim Tagore, but Daddy, call me today.

"Beta, you don't have to worry. We won't allow that to happen in our kingdom."

"It's already happening," I mumbled. "Fireborns, mixed-fire breeds are already treated like they have the plague. They are hated, mocked, judged, and receive little to no resources. It makes sense that the next step would be banishing other ungifted children as well. I mean, honestly. What are we good for, if not disappointment and ruin?"

"That's not you." Quande damn near leaped to his feet. "You will manifest."

Little did he know, I'd already begun, and I still had to pretend like I hadn't.

"And how do you know? How do any of you know? Even if I don't manifest, you only care about me as an ungifted because you love me. You're my family and you have status. My privilege protects me, but for how long?" I turned to face Zef, remembering his words. *Privilege is given and it can be taken away.*

Every eye in the room roamed from one face to another. I turned to the general. "What is being done about the unrest happening in the kingdoms?"

"C.O.A. will meet in the coming months. I'm sure I will receive a letter and when I do, I will have to leave camp and attend. Until then, the Water Kingdom along with the Wind Kingdom have both petitioned the Reaper Kingdom for more men to assist with protecting their borders. The queen has granted those requests," the general said.

"So, let me make sure I'm understanding here. Instead of

giving the Redux a place of refuge, they are using the help of our kingdom's army to send them to their deaths?"

"It's complicated, Princess Bellamy," Zef said.

"I just don't understand the complication," I retorted.

Zef continued, "It was the ancestors of the Fire Kingdom who caused the destruction of the old world. We wouldn't be here today picking up the pieces if it weren't for their greed and bloodlust. They're the people who released the Fire Spirit onto the Earth."

"And we are blaming them for their ancestors?"

"We are holding them accountable for the wars they still cause today," Zef said.

"Like what?"

"Like murdering my parents," Quande cut in. I bit my tongue. In the heat of the moment, I completely ignored the fact that a Fireborn raid orphaned Quande when he was young.

"I didn't mean–" I started, but Quande finished.

"The Fireborns are Fireborns. It is in their blood to steal, kill, and destroy everything they touch. Why is it that the rest of the kingdoms can create peace and prosperity, drink water, and mind their own damn business and the Fire Kingdom is possessed to wage war and enslave humans like they're debased animals?" Quande paused, waiting for my answer.

An answer I couldn't give.

He continued. "The Fire Kingdom is the main kingdom that keeps the Reaper Army working. They are an eternal shard of glass embedded in the soles of feet. None of them deserve second chances." Quande turned to the general. "May I be dismissed?"

The general nodded. Quande marched past me and out of the cabin door.

"Rwju," the general sighed heavily. "Retrieve the Moonborn twins. We will need the best trackers to assist you in this mission." Rwju saluted, fist over heart, and left the cabin.

"I think that's enough for now," the general said once the cabin door slammed. "Go ahead, recruit. Call it a night."

I rose from my seat. My skin flared as if a thousand little needles were pricking me.

"Daddy," I said in a tiny voice that I hated. A part of me wanted to face him, look him in the eyes, and see if he would lie to me, even though I knew the answer.

"Yes, Beta?" His gruff voice was comforting and also frightening.

My lips had gone dry. "If I wasn't Earthborn, what would this mean for my future?"

"What makes you think you aren't Earthborn?" General leaned back in his chair. Zef narrowed his eyes at me.

I knew I was pushing it. I had to be careful with each word. "I haven't manifested yet. What if I never do?" The tension in the air eased.

"No matter what happens, I'll protect you. You are my daughter, and nothing will ever change that." The general picked up a pen and began writing. I stood still for a moment, my thoughts racing with questions.

What do you mean no matter what happens? Who's watching us? What am I? What manifestation do I have? Why is everyone hiding things from me? Why wipe my memory for years? I'm twenty years old. Whatever is happening, I am old enough to handle it. I'm not weak, so stop treating me like a child!

My shoulders tensed, but I tried to push my frustration back down. This was not the time to confront them.

Zef stepped in front of the chair in front of the general's desk. "Did you need something else, princess?"

Yes, how long are y'all going to fuck hidden behind glass doors? I wanted to ask.

I shook my head and raced out of the cabin.

Act normal. How in the fuck was I supposed to do that when everyone I love was lying and I was no closer to the reason why?

XXII

*"'What if I fall?' baby bird asked.
'What if you fly?' mother bird replied."
Proverb 85:17 from the Book of Face, Mortem Era.*

THE AXE SWUNG HARD against the timber, splitting it in two. The wood tumbled to the ground. I scooped the pieces and organized them into the wagon. Positioning another log on the chopping block, I flexed my new lean muscles. Chopping wood after breakfast each morning did more for my body than the repetitive drills Quande used to have me do. It's been three whole months, and even though it was a struggle at first, I was able to get into the routine of things.

Even the Moonborn twins had settled down. It could be because they never found their clothes that mysteriously disappeared or because the general had been sending them on missions with Rwju and Quande to search for the Fireborns.

Regardless, my new home smelled of pine and lumber. I relaxed at the sounds of chirping birds echoing through the redwoods. Early mornings were my peace. And for that, I looked forward to completing my task. Anything to keep my mind off the things I didn't know or what I was becoming. My power swelled within me and I could sense people's aura or energy around me. Equal parts wanted to take their energy to myself and the other part wanted to improve upon what they already had. A manifestation with the ability to increase or take away power was dangerous. And with the state of the kingdoms, I could see how my parents wouldn't want this to get out. But that didn't absolve them from keeping me in the dark.

I brought the axe down on the last piece of wood, splitting it clean through. After gathering the wood, I slid my axe into the holder at my waist. I tapped a button on the wagon and it rose off the ground, hovering about two to three inches in the air. From here, all I needed to do was lightly push the wagon smoothly down the path.

No longer did I fight the day begrudgingly. I just did what needed to be done. By the end of each night, with a freshly bathed Silvia cuddled into my arms, I actually felt accomplished.

The voice of Mother's disapproving tone was miles away at the palace and for a moment, as the sun peeked through the trees and the dewdrops coated the grass, everything *was* normal. I was finally good enough, not seen as a disappointment or a mistake. Grunt work or not, manifestation or not, being in the forest, training, working, doing, and being a part of a community that treated me like an equal was all I ever wanted. I fit in here, unlike the suffocating palace walls. And for that, a dangerous thought tumbled around in my head.

Maybe I should never go home. Maybe I should run away.

I gazed at the trees that seemed to stretch towards the welcoming sky. I was but an insect to the giant woods and yet the trees never went out of their way to step on me. They allowed me to exist in their greatness while empowering me to discover my greatness, too.

I entered the main camp.

More Earthborns had arrived to assist Zef with hosting the training for the B.E. Since this was the first time the Earthborns were permitted to train with other alignments, the B.E. had been flexing their muscles and testing their strength against Earthborns. Which was probably a mistake for the B.E. The Earthborns were proven to not be as pacifist as the rumors made them out to be.

I tapped the wagon past the kitchen. Venus, Sarue, and Fia were cooking breakfast.

"Hey!" I shouted. "After I place the wood, I'll be right over."

"You good, recruit!" Fia said, holding a freshly cut fish in the air. "We got it covered."

Venus kissed Sarue. It made me smile at seeing her back on her feet. Sarue pulled away from Venus and winked at me.

She said she could still sense when I was close. They both haven't snitched to my father or the Life Doctor about the sudden change in Sarue's health. But, whenever I was too close to Sarue, I couldn't pretend not to see Venus's grip tighten around the handle of her blade.

Making my way to the woodpile, I unloaded the wagon. I enjoyed this too, stacking the wood like little puzzle pieces.

Now that the Earthborns were here, they could complete this task with a snap of their fingers, but they left a little work for me to complete.

Footsteps gathered behind me. I locked the last wood piece into place and dusted the wood chips off my uniform. The Moonborn twins, with their streaks of white patches on jet-black hair, were grinning from cheek to cheek. I saluted them both, and they returned the salute.

"We have a proposition," Twoa said with a sly smile.

"What the hell do you propose?" I crossed my arms.

"Join our team to conquer the Earthborns," he said.

I looked from Twoa to Oneo, back to Twoa.

"You do realize that I'm Earthborn?"

"Where?" Oneo laughed.

"What you are is one of us. And we," Twoa flicked two fingers between him and I. "Need to work together to defeat them." He tossed a thumb over his shoulder.

"And you approve of this?" I turned to Oneo, the more responsible twin.

He shrugged. "My friend is my adversary's enemy, or what-ever those Mortem Era quotes mean."

My eyebrows bunched together.

"Listen," Twoa said, looking around, then returning his glance to me. "We haven't always seen eye to eye, but with your kick-ass fighting skills we stand a better chance at beating them. We can always use another strong fighter on our team."

I stifled the smile, forcing itself to my lips. "So, you admit it? I'm badass, huh?"

"Oh, piss off!" Twoa said, running his fingers through his long hair.

Oneo chimed in. "You're so fucking cocky." He gently shoved my shoulders.

"Yeah, but you want me on your team, right? Who else is on? What's the plan?"

Twoa looked behind him. Most of the B.E. were lining up for breakfast. Twoa wrapped his arm around my neck, drawing me into a trio circle. "There's a bet we have with the Earths. Today, after lunch, we will enter into somewhat of a friendly tournament. Since the Earth's are the camp's host this year, they can create the terrain and the creatures we need to beat. The B.E. will enter the tournament in groups of seven or less. It's pretty simple really. We defeat them or they defeat us. The team to complete the tournament to the end wins whatever Earth resource we want." Twoa's eyes twinkled.

Oneo grabbed my shoulder. "This includes resources like gold, diamonds, oil, or just fresh food, things the other kingdoms rarely have access to."

Twoa jumped in. "We'll be rich!"

"And if you lose?" I asked.

"We won't," Oneo confirmed. "We're the B.E.. How hard can it be to defeat their little earth monsters?" Oneo smirked.

"We're recruiting Fia, Sarue, and Venus. We already have Rwju," Twoa said.

"The Waterborn? I want to see him in action!" I jumped in excitement. "Wait. Why didn't you ask Quande?" I eyed the twins.

Oneo spoke, "We did, but you know how the first lieutenant gets once he's given orders from the general."

"What orders was he given?" I unwrapped myself out of Twoa's arm.

"You know those Fireborns? We found their camp. Quande has been monitoring their movements and I think"–Oneo leaned in– "the general is going to make a move."

"As in what?" I whispered.

The twins shrugged identically.

Oneo Finished. "We're just the trackers. We hunt the target down and report back."

Twoa added. "Quande is the Finisher. That fucker is more lethal than a shadow assassin. Once it's in his hands, it's officially out of ours." Twoa wiped his palms clean.

"So, are you in or out?" Oneo asked as my mind drifted to the Fireborns.

"You don't think the general would hurt them? Would you?"

"They're Fireborns. Who gives a shit?"

I blinked a few times at Twoa. "They are still people. People who might need our help." Oneo sighed.

"Has Quande ever..." I swallowed hard. "Hurt a Fireborn?"

"Of course he has. I've seen Quande kill a Fireborn for speaking out of turn," Twoa said.

"Are you serious?"

"Deadly so."

Oneo elbowed Twoa in the stomach.

"It wasn't quite like that. The Fireborn in question was the one responsible for the death of his parents," Oneo said.

"So, that makes it okay to have an execution without trial?"

"Listen, princess," Oneo folded his arms. "Risking your life to protect the kingdoms is something you might never understand. And when you're out in the fields, sometimes you have to make a call."

"And revenge is the right call?"

"Revenge is a call. Never said it was the right call." Oneo stuffed his hands in his pocket.

Twoa patted Oneo's chest to leave. "I guess this is a no to joining our team then?"

"Hard pass."

Twoa gave that sly grin. "You know what, *princess*. It's really easy to stand on high moral ground when all you'll be doing for the rest of your life is sitting safe on someone's throne behind palace walls. Don't be so quick to judge. You never know the choice you'll make until you have to make it."

"Yeah. I'll never kill out of revenge."

"Revenge isn't the only thing to kill for. Remember that," Oneo said, walking away, followed by his twin.

AFTER LUNCH, I made my way to the animal section of the camp. This area was mostly flatlands and green hills. The Earthborns brought in living horses, something that was rarely seen in the Reaper Kingdom. Our horses were made of steel and solar power. Yet watching my horse, Yemi—all beautiful black steel—run alongside breathing real horses as they played, made me smile. The other steel horses had their panels out in the middle of the field, soaking in the sun to recharge.

There were griffes perched in branches. These large birds typically followed the B.E. anywhere they went. It was like they were drawn to the B.E. or, more so, the power of the reaper. About ten laid in the shadows of the trees, but hundreds of griffes always flocked to the Reaper Army which marched under the queen.

The queen. A shiver ran down my body just thinking about her. I shook my thoughts away from imagining her face and the Reaper Army at her back with massive black-winged griffes hovering above. It really was an extremely intimidating thought to imagine. And to be honest, I didn't want to think about her, her rosebud asshole son, nor my mother. However, I missed my sister, Everest.

Should I write to her? See how she's doing? Or would she still be mad at me? She always knew how to hold a grudge, but never this long, not toward me, at least.

Fuck it. Maybe we both needed this time apart.

The pigs grunted and squealed, and I made my way to the pin to feed them. One particular pig was on my shit list. I swear, if this pig took human form, it could truly be a worthy advisory. "Missy," I called.

Missy continued to graze.

"Your food is here, *your highness.*"

Missy the pig. Unlike every other normal pig, Missy eats the best foods, and she will only eat it on a silver platter on her own buffet table. It doesn't help that she's also Zef's personal pet pig. I honestly think Zef believes she's human!

Unbelievable!

The giant spotted pink and black pig looked at me once, then looked at her empty table. She grunted, then turned her back to ignore me.

My patience was already thinning. I unloaded her lunch on the table and then whistled. "Your lunch is served."

Missy looked back, her snout poking in the air. She squealed, stomped her foot, and a pile of soil floated in the air.

"Missy, Missy! You better not!"

Missy stomped again. The piece of earth zipped through the air, hurling toward the table, and knocking over the nicely set up display I made.

I grabbed the bridge of my nose. "Fucking Earthborn pigs." Apparently, she was one of a kind.

The pig bounced her head as if she were laughing.

"This isn't funny, Missy! Let's go!" I commanded. She continued to ignore me.

I straightened up the food on the table while mumbling to myself. "You would have to be Zef's pet pig. Both of you are annoying as shit!"

Missy's snout faced me, her black eyes glazed over, her tail sticking straight into the air.

"Yeah, I said it. What are you going to do about it?" Like I'm about to let a pig intimidate me.

Missy's hoofs dug into the soil. Pieces of earth rose, shaping themselves into dirt daggers. One blade of dirt mixed with rocks and grass shot my way, cutting the side of my face. I raised my finger where it burned alongside my cheek. When I pulled my fingers away, fresh blood painted the tips.

"That's it." I threw down her silver platter. "I'm having bacon for dinner tonight!"

Missy squealed, stomping her tiny hooves on the ground. More shards of earth flew. I took off, ducking and running, flipping and tumbling until finally, I found coverage in the thickness of the trees. Catching my breath, I peeked my head to see where Missy stood.

Several cuts ran along my cheek and arms. The dirt daggers tore through pieces of clothing. If someone had told me that today, I would fight a giant earth-aligned pig, I wouldn't have believed them.

"This is some bullshit," I said under my breath.

As if hearing me, Missy squealed out in agreement.

I waited, listening closely. I peeked my head from around the tree and three quick earth daggers zoomed past.

My palms itched. I gently brushed my nails against the inside of them to calm the stress.

"Listen, Missy. I made a mistake. I shouldn't have spoken ill about you or your arrogant owner. I see the error of my ways. Please let me go." There was nothing around me except trees and bushes. I stood and slowly moved from under the tree's protection with my hands up. "See, I surrender."

Missy's earth daggers floated in the air behind her. Every time I shifted, the daggers inched forward.

"I don't want to fight." I scanned the nearby grounds. The other pigs were in their pins, far from our fighting. Their squeals had gone silent as they watched on. Right underneath a tree that was roughly twelve feet away was a rope. A griffe sat on a low bearing branch, its face tucked into its massive wings. Griffes use the day to sleep and the night to explore.

I formed a plan.

Do. Not. Hesitate.

I crab walked to the side, going to her own personalized table. The daggers turned, never faltering. I straightened her table. Each time I placed her food in places she didn't like, the pig hurled an earth dagger at my feet.

Bullied by a bratty pig. Nobody will ever believe this.

Once I completed the job, Missy lowered her daggers and wobbled over. She stuffed her face into her food while her back faced the griffe. I walked backwards toward the tree while I watched the pig demolish the food laid out. I picked up the rope, slipped the rope gently around the griffe's leg, and tied it into a knot. The bird shook, but its head remained in its feathers. I needed to get this rope around the pig's massive body. If the griffes were strong enough to carry members of the B.E. on their backs, then lifting an earthbound pig would be no problem. I snuck up behind Missy while she was distracted, lowered the rope at her feet, and waited until she kicked out her little ankles and slipped the rope right underneath her. This took forever.

I slipped the rope up and around her waist and pulled, tightening the rope.

Missy bucked, kicking over the table.

I yanked the rope, waking the griffe from its slumber. The griffe automatically took to the air, pulling Missy with it.

As Missy was being dragged off, I laughed. "Let's see how you like it in the air for a while! Don't worry, if the griffe never returns with you, I'll make sure to tell your master that you wandered off!"

Missy's front legs clawed the ground. Her hooves were leaving the soil, but she bounced, almost stopping the griffe in its tracks. Missy stomped, allowing her hooves to sink into the earth. An earthlike hand jolted out of the soil and wrapped around the pig's body.

You got to be fucking kidding me.

The griffe cawed, causing more of the griffes to stir. The dirt hand held on to Missy, preventing the pig from flying away, but also holding the griffe hostage in the sky.

This, I didn't see coming.

The waking griffes took off from their branches as the head griffe tied with a pig called for help. I needed to cut the rope fast, or the griffes were going to attack. I snatched the axe from my belt. Pettiness aside, I needed to cut the pig loose before we both became dinner. I ran over, but before I could get close, earth daggers rose to the sky.

"I'm trying to cut the rope!" I yelled at the pig, but she wasn't listening. She let the daggers fly. I ducked, dodging them the best I could, a few nicked my arm, but I kept it moving toward the rope that was now being pulled so tight that the earth hand was shattering. The griffes circled above, clawing at each other as if making a plan to attack to help their friend.

I'm about to die. Either death by earth-gifted pig, or a blanket of shadow griffes. Perfect.

I clutched my axe in my hand.

To my luck, even earthbound pigs suffer from manifestation depletion. Hundreds of the earth daggers were crumbling. The pig was getting tired and could not maintain the daggers and the giant earth hand holding her to the ground.

I needed to survive long enough for her to reach her max. After that, Missy would be a normal, ungifted pig, like me.

An earth dagger zipped past my head.

Just a little longer. She's passing out.

Her eyes rolled back into her sockets. Ten earth daggers shot my way but crumbled before they could reach me.

That's it. She's almost depleted.

The griffes screeched above me. Missy's eyes flew open, but instead of her daggers coming my way, they soared toward the circling birds.

"No," I commanded. I rushed toward the rope to slam down my axe and cut the line, but the griffes dived, blinding me with a fury of black wings and red claws.

"No!" I leaped for the rope, my axe aiming for the cut. My axe came down, but the earth shifted underneath my feet, knocking me to the ground. Wings batted against my back and slapped me across my face. I rolled over, dropping the axe as a griffes claw, attempting to grip my arm. I grabbed onto the rope, using it as a guide to get to Missy. I needed to untie her. The rope loosened as the griffe dived downwards. I reached Missy, quickly unwrapping the knot from around her waist, but it wasn't budging.

I held the rope as the griffe yanked the pig free from the earth hand. Amongst the commotion, somehow the rope wrapped around my arm and as the griffe yanked, it pulled Missy and me off the ground.

Missy, frantic, squealed, still calling to the soil. The earth rose like a hill, attempting to answer her call.

"Stop!" I yelled. "Stop!" Neither animal listened. The blanket of griffes blocked out the sun as they flew around us, creating a black ball of wings. The griffes separated and before I could maneuver, I was slammed into a redwood tree. I felt my shoulder pop as the rope cut off blood circulation to the rest of my body.

Finally, the griffes all separated. Up ahead was a massive earth wall built by the Earthborns to separate sections of the camp from the main camp. We were en route for a head-on collision, going at least 35 mph.

Yep, I was going to die today.

With one loud squeal from Missy, I braced for impact. Lucky for me, Missy had an ounce of strength left. With all her might, she called to the thick earth wall. The squeal was so loud that even the griffe changed directions, but it was already too late. As Missy and I spiraled, the earth wall opened up and swallowed both of us whole.

XXIII

"Every flower must push through soil."
Proverb 62:7 from the Book of Face, Mortem Era.

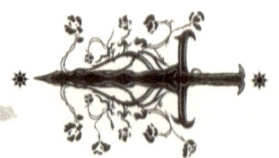

I ATTEMPTED TO RAISE my right arm to block out the sun beaming directly overhead, but I couldn't move. I turned my neck and a jolt of pain shot down my spine. My right shoulder protruded outward as if the bone was completely ripped away from the joint. The rope was wrapped around my forearm, but the end of the rope was frayed. When I inhaled, there was a wheeze in my breath. On the exhale, my ribs stabbed something in me. I couldn't guess what it was.

242

Crumpled, as I laid amongst high golden grass. Cicadas hissed loudly as if I was right in the middle of their den. The sun went from directly above to four degrees lower after I blinked. I blinked again, and the sun was fading beyond the horizon. I blinked again, and a crescent moon hung high, surrounded by stars.

I blinked once again, and my mouth tasted of almonds mixed with flower petals. My tongue was numb. But the pain had subsided to a prickling dullness. My right arm was freshly bound. I tried rolling myself into a sitting position. My ribs stabbed into my side. but it was no longer the paralyzing pain as before.

I examined my body as best as I could. The fabric was torn from my shirt and wrapped around my stomach to serve as support. Some more fabric, along with the excess rope, held my right arm in a makeshift harness. My shoulder no longer protruded outward, but there was only a large red bruise now coupled with swelling.

My head spun, and I choked out a little laugh.

Why the fuck am I giggling?

My head was too heavy for my neck. My eyes rolled. I couldn't focus. I searched my surroundings. Purple flowers that smelled like ammonia greeted me. Neither Missy nor the griffes were in sight.

I giggled, but none of this was funny. I damn near couldn't feel my legs. Attempting to roll over to my knees, a hand clasped my left shoulder and pushed me backwards into the bed of flowers.

"Be still," a voice commanded. More footsteps trotted toward me.

"Who are you?" I grunted.

A face came into focus.

"Rwju?" I moaned.

"Yes," he squatted. "Fia, Sarue, Oneo and Twoa are here, too." Rwju checked my right arm.

"Fuck. Not the twins, anybody but the twins," I slurred.

"We are standing right here," Oneo said.

I ignored him.

"Why do I feel so...good?" I rubbed Rwju's bearded jawline. His hair was rough. My fingers wandered to his scar. Rwju grabbed my wrist, placing it at my side.

"You're high," he said, his brow set in a hard line.

"Why do you look so serious?" I giggled.

"Princess Bellamy, you're severely hurt. Out of all days, you have chosen the absolute worst day. We are all trapped within the tournament," Rwju said, checking my ribs.

"I doubt that."

I reached for his scar again. When I was this close to Rwju's face, I was obsessed with the details of his smooth brown skin, his black facial hair and how it curled at the ends. His scar made him deadly but beautiful.

"What you're feeling is a drug. We had to feed you opi, princess," Rwju said.

Twoa stomped over, his boot stopping right next to my ear. "Every time we moved you to treat you, you screamed like a banshee. If it were left to me, I would've put you out of your misery."

"I believe you. I know how easily you kill things. How did you find me, anyway?" I retorted.

"I–" A female voice spoke. "Felt we were getting close to the exit, but instead, we discovered you unconscious."

Sarue, her green locs piled on the top of her head, squatted beside Rwju. She gave me a knowing look, and I knew what she wanted to say was that she sensed I was close. But the real question was if she could sense if I was in trouble or not?

Sarue continued. "What you're feeling are some benefits of

the drug we gave you. Numbness of pain, euphoria, relief. It should last a while until we get you to camp." One of Sarue's green locs fell loose. I squinted. Her locs were moving like little green snakes. I reached for one, but the locs snapped at me. I yanked my left hand back.

"Your hair just tried to bite me!" I screamed.

"Disadvantages of opi, hallucinations," Rwju tapped my shoulders.

Sarue looked up at someone I couldn't see. "I told you we gave her too much."

Fia, voice low and deep, answered, "We had no choice. Had to act fast. We were losing her. She should be fine once we get her to the Life Doctor." Fia shifted, his boot crunching the flowers as he walked to the end of my feet. "Do you feel any pain?" he asked.

I shook my head.

Rwju pressed on my ribs. A stabbing pain struck my nerves. "How about now?"

"Well, of course, I feel pain now!" I punched his hands.

"We should move. We have little time." Fia lifted a makeshift bed of branches, grass, and fabric.

Twoa stomped. "I helped carry her last time. Oneo, you're up!" Sarue chimed in. "We haven't found a way out of this maze yet. And no one on our team has earth gifts, so we can't just cut our way out of here."

"Especially while carrying dead weight," Twoa replied.

"Hey," I winced. "I am very much alive weight! And you weren't saying that earlier when you asked me to join your team!" Twoa huffed.

Looks like someone is still bitter from rejection.

Fia turned to the twins. "Oneo, Twoa, could you use the stars to direct us to the correct path?"

"We tried that," Twoa spoke. "And you saw what happened."

"What happened?" I asked, dragging myself to a sitting position.

"Earth beast or some shit," Oneo answered. "Big, green, grass field earth beast with rocks for teeth." Oneo bared his teeth as he chopped down on the air.

"And the night just got better." I laughed. "Maybe if you sacrifice the twins, you'll be able to win the tournament," I said in quick breaths.

Twoa clicked his tongue. "Maybe since we've found you, we should feed you to it instead. Solve all our problems. Then we can finally win and get back to camp." Twoa kicked the purple flowers.

"Yes, sacrifice me. I think that is a brilliant idea," I said as I turned to Rwju. "You heard the man. Give me over to the beast." I laughed, this time uncontrollably.

"I don't know which is scarier: mad and angry Bellamy or high and happy Bellamy," one twin said, but at this point, voices were fading into white noise. My eyes rolled shut under heavy lids.

"I don't think she can make it," Oneo whispered. That snapped me out of my fading consciousness.

"I can make it. Don't worry about me. I can pull my weight." I climbed to my feet, using Rwju as support. My body protested. But failure would hurt worse and last longer. I swayed, Sarue and Rwju stabilizing me as I attempted to stop my head from trying to disconnect from my neck. I fell forward. Fia caught me in his arms, his body solid as a rock, but gentle. I snuggled into him like he was my personal pillow.

"We don't have a choice," Fia's voice rumbled. "There has to be a way out," he concluded.

"Yea, if that way out was forfeit!" Oneo sighed.

"No. We can't quit." Twoa shoved his twin.

Rwju cursed under his breath. "We've been out here since lunch. It's around 2100 hours now judging by the position of the moon. If we could find a way out, we would have by now."

"I guess the Earths are harder to defeat than you anticipated," I chuckled at the twins. The twins rolled their eyes exactly at the same time.

"We need to do something fast. We have the princess. She's unable to heal. We must get out of here, even if that means forfeit," Sarue added.

Oneo cut in, his voice annoyed, "How did you get in here?" He pointed at me.

I snuggled further into Fia. "When an earth pig and a griffe really love each other," I chuckled. "They use rope and red claws to fly away over the wall and live happily ever after."

The group went silent. "Did any of that make sense?" Fia patted my back. The group said, "*No,*" in unison.

"Where's Venus?" I asked Sarue.

"She couldn't participate." Sarue avoided eye contact with me.

Oneo cursed. "This makes no fucking sense. How about we retrace our steps? We have to be close to the exit. I mean, how else did Bee get in here?"

Twoa marched over, yanking me from Fia's grasp. "I need you to focus, princess. Look around. Do you remember the way you came?"

I stumbled.

Twoa straightened me. "Focus, look around."

I giggled, turning to the massive purple flowers. It all appeared the same. There weren't drag marks. It was as if I had landed here out of nowhere. Plus, it was pitch black. Through my haze, I could not make out anything other than more fields and earth walls. I turned back to Twoa. He split in two, then stitched himself back together. I shook my head until my eyes focused.

By the Spirits, don't let them be triplets.

Twoa snapped his fingers, regaining my attention. "Well, do you see anything? Notice anything?" I pointed to a boulder.

Twoa followed my finger. "What? What about the boulder? Is it a clue? A secret chamber? What?"

I pushed past Twoa, staggering to the boulder. My stomach flipped, acid forcing its way up my throat. Twoa shouted, "Is that the way out?"

I shook my head and vomited.

"Fuck!" Twoa yelled. "What the fuck are we doing?"

As I hurled, the background argument began. The group shouted at each other. I leaned on the boulder. The surface was cool. As I rested, the ground shifted. The flowers puffed up like a hill, then fell flat.

Was I hallucinating again?

I cocked my head, wiping my mouth. The ground rose, the purple flowers waving, as the earth fell flat. This time, much closer. I shut my eyes and then opened them. The ground shifted, hauling the flowers higher.

Okay, this is not a hallucination.

"Hey," I called out. The team ignored me and continued shouting. Twoa screamed at Rwju. Sarue attempted to calm everyone down. Fia held Oneo in a headlock.

"Hey, people! The—There's something out here," I said, pointing to the shifting ground. A mound of earth thrust into the air, then fell. I pushed off the boulder, hobbling to the squad.

My high was blown. My ribs cut into my side something fierce. The earth shifted, and I took off in a sprint.

"Everybody, shut the fuck up!" I said, panic streaming

through my nerves. All eyes turned to me. "There's something out there. Look!" I pointed toward the shifting earth.

"I don't see a damn thing," Oneo said, running his fingers through his short hair.

"Shhh! Just watch," I pleaded.

"You're hallucinating." Twoa turned to argue with Rwju.

Twelve-feet away, the earth shifted, the vibrations sending shock waves underneath our feet. The squad froze. Fia grabbed onto me.

Twoa whispered, "How the fuck does it keep finding us?"

The inside of my palm burned. "What keeps finding you?" The earth exploded. Purple flowers, soil, and rocks rained on us. A giant creature compacted with dirt and grass roared. Its teeth were sharpened rocks. Eyes were black holes. It slammed its fist on the ground, causing the earth to ricochet us backwards.

XXIV

"If you can't stand the heat. Get out of the kitchen."
Proverb 92:41 from the Book of Face, Mortem Era.

THE TWINS WERE THE FIRST to their feet. As the rest of us gathered, Oneo and Twoa stood at opposite ends of the group. In sync, they threw out their palms, creating a fine blue barrier over the squad. I've only ever witnessed their tracking skills, but this was my first time witnessing their intertwining abilities. While the earth monster hurled boulders at us, the debris bounced off the protective shield. The boulders came at high speed. When they connected to the shield, it created spiderweb cracks like breaking glass.

"I'm sick of fucking earth creatures." I held the side of my stomach as I pulled myself up to my feet.

Fai shouted, "Let's go!"

Fia, Sarue, and I sprinted in the opposite direction of the earth monster. The beast dove into the ground to chase us. Before we could get far, earth walls burst out of the soil, blocking us on three sides.

The twins said in unison, "We can't hold it back for much longer."

The shield was worn thin at this point. The beast burst through the earth, this time flinging carriage-sized boulders.

Where was it getting all these rocks from?

I wheezed, placing my left hand on my aching belly. It was wet. When I pulled my hand away, blood stained my palms.

The twins yelled, "We're almost at our max! Someone do something!"

It would only take a few more boulders, and the cracks that zigzagged through the shield would break.

Oneo shouted, "Rwju, open the ground, create a pool or something."

Rwju, concentrating, tried to form the earth into an ocean. "The earth won't yield. Whoever is controlling this thing is far more powerful than me."

An Earthborn more powerful than a Waterborn?

Twoa, his boots digging into the soil to get a better grip, shouted, "That's not what we need to hear right now, man."

Another boulder collided with the shield, almost knocking Twoa off his feet.

Rwju clasped his hands together and then separated them, aiming them at the sky. Thunder cracked in the distance. The air grew thick with humidity. Lightning flashed. The beast slammed its fist to the ground, rocking the soil underneath us.

There was no room for escape. It was fight or else. Personally, I didn't want to know what "or else" would be.

Here I was again, broken, weak, and a burden to the group. I couldn't even handle an earth-gifted pig. How in the hell was I to fight an earth creature that's stronger than the B.E.? How was I to survive this?

CRACK!

The twins' shield shattered louder than the thunder. Rwju clapped, his arms shaking as he held them high over his head. Clouds formed above the creature. Rwju clapped again and water poured onto the monster like a flood. The twins retreated to us as Rwju took the lead.

"We're tapped out," Oneo said, struggling to catch his breath. Sarue cut in. "I have some energy. What about you, Fia?"

Fia looked confused, as if he himself wasn't sure of the answer.

Rwju clapped again. Thunder and lightning rang out through the night. The stars disappeared behind dark clouds. More rain fell like a tsunami.

The earth creature fought to stay upright as it melted. An earthy, gritty stench filled my nose as water mixed with dirt. The beast turned to slush, but the rain wasn't enough. Fia and Sarue ran to Rwju's side to assist. Black shadows spilled from their palms. The shadows leaked toward the beast, wrapping around its legs until they encompassed the creature in a shadow sphere.

The last bit of rain fell from the clouds as the flash of white light faded. The creature's mouth dropped open, creating a large black hole of broken branches and mud.

As the shadows took it, Rwju dropped to his knees. Fia and

Sarue's arms shook, but they kept pressing the beast until it shrank. With one last push, Fia and Sarue condensed the creature into a black shadow box. The box dropped to the ground, jumping as the monster inside fought to get out. Sarue took off running to capture the box, but with one last jump, the box dug itself into the earth.

Fia and Sarue drop to their knees, their shadow easing back into them.

"We have to move now!" Sarue said dryly, attempting to pull herself to her feet.

Oneo bent over, using his knees to rest. "You think it's coming back?"

"This was the third time we fought the motherfucker. There's no telling if it's coming back," Twoa answered.

Rwju stood. "Sarue's right. Let's get going. We have to find safety. We're tapped out."

Twoa grabbed his brother, who was barely standing. "You don't have to tell us twice."

I clutched the side of my stomach. My vision blurred.

"You good?" Rwju asked while limping.

I nodded. "Yea. I will be as soon as we get out of here."

Rwju glanced at my stomach, his hand reaching out to my belly. I twisted from him. "Let's go," I said, biting back the pain.

THERE WAS COVER in the canopies in the nearby woods. We squeezed through trees pressed against each other to avoid the sharp needle-like bark. We finally made it to a piece of flat land, where we took time to reassess the situation.

As the group bickered, I pressed hard against my bleeding wound. If this was a maze, then there had to be patterns. Once we figured out the patterns, then we could figure out the maze.

"Hey," I called to the group, who had gone silent in frustration.

"Are you guys sure this is a maze?"

"Yea," Sarue answered.

"Well, every maze has an entrance and an exit."

"No shit," Twoa responded.

"What I'm saying is"—I tried not to curse at him—"like any maze, we simply have to block off the dead ends."

"We could if the landscape didn't change," Oneo chimed in.

"How often does the landscape change?" I asked, easing myself onto a tree stump.

Sarue glanced at Fia, to which he shook his head. "Everything is sporadic. It's like there isn't any rhythm or rhyme to what's happening. There isn't a set pattern."

"Then how do you know we're in a maze?" I asked again.

Twoa chimed in. "We use the reflections of the moon to get a bird's-eye view of the layout. We thought it was an easy win for us until we realized the boxes shifted randomly. Every exit became a dead end by the time we got to it. We're trapped."

"Well, mazes are my thing," I flinched. The sting in my shoulder was making itself known. "I grew up with access to one of the hardest mazes in the Seven Kingdoms. And I don't know about you all, but what you're describing to me is no maze. It sounds like a puzzle. Better yet, it sounds like an earth game I played when I was a kid called Reposition."

Fai spoke, "Reposition? I heard of that game but never played it."

"Yea, it's a game my sister and I played when she manifested. It was the only game she could beat me at because it requires earth gifts to win. There's a box." I picked up a stick and used the sharp end to draw in the dirt. "Within this box, there are dividers. This might be the reason you thought it was a maze. If you're looking at it from above, it can look like one." I pointed the stick to the boxes I drew. "What happens is, as you play, the ground shifts to block all exits."

Sarue kneeled beside me. "So, how do we beat the game?"

"Well," I said, picking up rocks. "Usually, you take one rock and sit it here at the start." I placed a rock at the edge of the border. "The goal is to get your rock from here to the opposite end without the rock falling into the cracks. The cracks are what you assume to be maze pathways." I tried not to look smugly at the twins, but I failed as my face morphed at the revelation. "When the earth shifts, an Earthborn would use their gifts to bounce the rock from one section of the map to the other side."

"What does any of that have to do with helping us now? None of us are Earth-gifted. So, like I said, we're trapped," Twoa said as he kicked the base of the tree.

I swear, if we were twelve, he would have stuck his tongue out at me. I would have definitely returned the gesture.

"Well, if this is a replica of Reposition, then we need to find the nearest earth shift and begin climbing. Assuming we are the rocks, it is up to us to stay above ground and jump as the board shifts, moving from the start to the opposite end. Thus, moving past these border walls. If we stay on top, the exit will eventually appear. I would assume you were looking for it within the cracks, when you should look for the exit up above."

Oneo dragged himself over to examine the box I drew. "If that's the case..." He snatched the stick from my hand and erased my picture. Oneo sat, staring at the moon for a few seconds. When he dropped his head back down, his eyes were completely white. He traced a new map layout on the ground without glancing downward. As his eyes turned from pure white back to deep brown, he marked the map with an X. "This would mean we are around here."

I studied the map.

Oneo continued, "We are almost at the edge. According to this game, we need to be here." Twoa drew a line from the right side toward the end of the box. "We aren't far."

"Nice. We have a chance!" Fia said, cracking his knuckles.

"And just in time because I'm maxed." Rwju rose to his feet. "The sooner we move out, the better."

We gathered ourselves for the trek to the nearest shift. As we dragged ourselves along, the ground rumbled underneath our feet.

Twoa stood next to his twin. "Please let this be a shift." They gave each other a look, then a familiar figure zig-zagged through the trees.

"Run!" Sarue shouted.

But she didn't need to. We all took off. My side throbbed, the front of my shirt was wet and heavy with blood. Low branches ripped through my hair and caught my clothes. Each step I took, a pinched nerve set my right leg on fire. I was quickly losing sight of the group as their backs disappeared through the thick woods. The stench of earthy musk mixed with wet mud, leaves, and rocks filled the air.

One moment I was running, then limping, and now I was on my knees heaving something ugly deep from the pits of my belly. This was what I hated. Even if I manifested, what was the point? I didn't know how to control or gain access to it. For months, I tried to call forth my manifestation, and it only seemed to show up when it felt like it. I was tired of being a burden. I no longer wanted to be left behind. I clung to my side.

I'm fucking useless; I'm weak. If it wasn't clear before, then it's clear now. I am not cut out for this.

I punched a bloody fist into the soil, and it caved instantly. I cocked my head, raising my fist from the dirt, staring at the hole.

My skin itched. My arms, my legs, my neck, my face, and inside my throat all itched insanely. I clawed at myself, digging my nails deep to aid in relief. My skin peeled from my arms, revealing dry, patchy skin. Whatever drug they gave me was wearing off. Every single fucking bone felt like an invisible hand was breaking them. I doubled over, holding myself tight. My insides were moving, snapping, reforming, and breaking again. I roared in pain. The earth cracked underneath. The loud stomping got closer.

You gotta get up. Get up. Run! Get up!

I dug my hand in the soil, blood mixing with earth.

Get up. Get the fuck up!

The ground shook. The waves were faster. I could hear heavy movements bursting through the forest. The trees snapped and broke. I climbed to shaky feet.

Keep moving.

One heavy step at a time, I commanded my legs forward. They obeyed begrudgingly, but they obeyed, nonetheless.

A figure burst through the trees. "Bellamy!" Rwju said, his hair wild. "Thought I lost you." He ran to me, giving me a look over. "What is wrong with you?" His mouth dropped open as he staggered away from me. His face was in utter shock.

I couldn't speak. My throat burned. I clawed my neck.

"Bellamy," Rwju continued to back away. "What are you?" His voice was barely above a whisper.

My mouth went dry. I wanted to scream. Not scream... I wanted to roar. The dry scales on my skin cracked and huge chunks fell to the ground. Rwju glanced around, searching the woods.

"Bellamy," he said. "I'm going to touch you now." He took a

hesitant step forward. He placed his hand on my arm, then quickly yanked it away, wincing. "Fucking hot. You're burning up," he said, burying smoky fingers between his thighs.

I didn't feel hot. Beads of sweat dripped from my forehead. But I was cold. So cold that I shivered.

The ground shifted, knocking Rwju and me on our asses. The earth creature broke from the ground, its melting face barely holding itself together. Pieces of it dripped off its body in chunks. The beast didn't get enough time to regenerate. But I don't think it cared.

The creature dragged his muddy body toward us.

The earth monster's hand launched towards Rwju, picking him up from the ground. Rwju struggled to break free, but the earth creature closed its fist tighter around Rwju's body. Rwju cried out as his bones snapped under the pressure.

You can stop this. A voice not my own whispered into my mind. *You can save him.*

Rwju broke a hand free, raising it above his head. The thunder rumbled, and the lightning flashed. Rwju summoned every ounce of his strength.

"Bellamy, run!" he said, as his entire body glowed white. It was his aura. It was like silver amongst the darkness. I called to the last of his energy, exchanging mine with his. My red-orange aura dove into his mouth and gathered the white aura in his chest.

That's it. The voice said. *Take it all.*

And I almost did. I rose to my feet, a new power flowed inside of me. Before Rwju's light flickered completely out, I let go.

Lightning blasted from the sky, hurling toward the earth. I could feel the air buzz with electricity, and I called forth on that energy too. Another bolt of lightning fell from the sky and engulfed me in its power.

The earth creature threw Rwju on the ground, realizing that he wasn't the one it should be worried about. I was. I summoned the lightning within and flicked it towards the earth monster. White light bounced inside of the earth creature's body. Zapping it, as the molecules shifted and re-shifted. The mud creature mis-configured, growing larger as it pulled from the surrounding soil.

The lightning died. The earth creature twitched and jerked toward me. Fire licked the ground as the mud creature's branches and leaves burst into flames.

You can put an end to this, the voice said.

The earth creature's body grew taller than the massive trees surrounding us. One stomp and it could be the end of Rwju, who lay crumpled at the monster's feet.

"Run," he said, blood spat from his lips. "Bellamy, run!"

I am not weak.

New power flowed through me, I ran. Not away, but towards the earth creature.

Save him, the voice whispered.

I will.

Adrenaline pulsed through my veins; flakes of my flesh fell to the ground.

I won't leave you, Rwju. I'll save you. I'll save us both.

The earth creature turned to me and roared.

And I roared back.

Burn!

Lightning burst through my back like wings as I leaped onto the earth creature. Its muddy body sucked me in like quicksand.

"Burn!" I screamed as the fire erupted around us.

Yes, come to me. Consume me, use me, burn for me, the voice said.

I called to the flames.

The growing fire from the lightning strike became a red-orange hurricane. It obeyed my will as I set the creature ablaze. Hollow earth eyes were the last thing I remembered as an inferno of fire wrapped us in its embrace.

XXV

"History whispers in a thousand voices, urging us to take action
while also providing consolation and caution."
Proverb 15:98 from the Book of Face, Mortem Era.

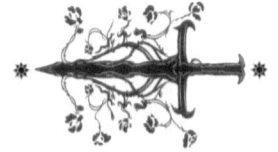

THE INFIRMARY REEKED of herbs and oils with a mix
of antiseptics and disinfectants. Seven days; that's how long I
laid in the infirmary. The first four days were a blur. A bunch
of flashing images, Silvia's face, glimpses of Quande and
Father. I remembered Rwju from time to time, but nothing of
substance. The last three days, however, I was held for close
observation under the Life Doctor's orders.

My head and arms were wrapped with white bandages. When Silvia finally took them off, my skin was clear, and smooth, with not one scaly patch in sight. I flexed my right arm, and it felt fine. Brand new even. The first thing I checked when I regained consciousness was the wound on my belly. According to the Life Doctor, there was never a wound there. They said my injuries were mild, but the shock of the night must have taken a toll on my body.

I lay in the infirmary bed, playing that night over and over again in my head. I was bleeding out, broken arm, ribs, and my skin was peeling away from my body. How could I just be... *fine?* I flexed my muscles, and I was energized, ready to face another foe, take on another challenge. I really felt...*fine.*

"I'm sending you home." The general paced the infirmary floor. I almost rolled out of bed, ripping the sheets off.

"What?" I searched his face. "You can't send me home. I'm just getting started!"

"You almost died, Bellamy."

"But I didn't. I'm fine." I leaped from the bed, rolling my shoulders. "Matter of fact, I'm better than fine. I feel...brand new."

"What were you thinking? Who gave you the permission to enter the tournament?"

"First, I didn't know I needed permission and second, I was kinda dragged across."

"How can you be so careless? Do you understand how important you are?"

"No, not really." I crossed my arms. *Ever since I could remember, I have always been told how unimportant I was, and what a disappointment I was.* But I didn't say that part out loud.

The general stopped pacing. He stroked his beard once before folding his arms across his chest. The infirmary was cleared in order to give us privacy.

"Must I remind you that you will be the next Queen of the Earth Kingdom? If something were to happen to you, what do you think would happen to your kingdom's future?"

That's a question I didn't need to think about. "Everest will gladly take my place. I'm sure that's what Mother truly wants, anyway," I mumbled, sitting on the edge of the bed.

"Your Mother isn't your enemy! She wants what's best for you."

"What if what's best for me is staying here at camp? Learning who I am and what I'm becoming? It's not like you or her are helping with that journey, instead you hide things from me and expect me to be a good little princess behind castle walls." I punched my fist into my open palm. "Besides, she hates me. The only thing keeping me in this family is the fact I have been cursed with emerald-green eyes. When we all know, I'm not fucking earth aligned."

The general went quiet. He stroked his beard, narrowing his eyes.

I quickly realized my mistake, but it was too late to take it back now.

The general took a step towards me. "Tell me what happened in the forest," he commanded, his voice deeper than usual.

I tried to remember the lie I forged. "Like I told you before, the earth monster chased us. Rwju summoned his gift, causing lightning to strike the creature. It set the thing on fire. Rwju then passed out."

The general nodded, "But that isn't true, is it, Beta?" He took another step forward.

"What do you mean? That was what happened." I focused on looking at my father in his onyx eyes. They began to suck me in, and I had to force myself to blink without looking suspicious.

263

"I spoke with Rwju. Aren't you the least bit curious about what he said?"

I shook my head. "I'm sure his story matched mine." I wasn't sure.

I had struggled to sleep the last few nights, panicking that he would tell. This makes four? Silvia, Sarue, Venus, and now Rwju. All holding my secret but for how long?

The general peered at me, waiting, watching, studying me. He never blinked or gave way to what he was thinking. He reached into his pockets and pulled out an obsidian patch. It had grooves like scales and it almost looked leathery. "Do you know what this is, Beta?" His voice was so calm that it made my heart speed faster.

"No."

He turned the leather patch in his hand. "There once was a man favored by the Spirits. This man had the ability to transform, reshape himself, become animal-like, and walk amongst the elements without harm. He became favored amongst his kin. He pleaded to the Spirits to allow him to have a wife and thus, the Spirits granted his plea. Soon, they welcomed in a son, who had the ability to shapeshift just like his father." The general balled the leather patch into his fist. "Do you know what happened to them?"

"No."

The general leaned down. I could almost see his shadow swirling in his eyes. "The council hunted down this family and murdered them all."

"Why?" I whispered.

The general leaned back, stuffing the patch into his pocket. "Whenever something new is born, it is a direct threat to something old. In order for those to remain in power, one must uphold the traditions. If not, something new will not only transform a generation but also lead to a shift in power. Thus, something new must die before it spreads."

"What does that have to do with me?"

"Beta." His voice changed. It was now smooth, almost tenor. "I am sure you've found out by now that you are something new. The first of your kind."

"My kind?" My eyes grew wide.

"The first to be half reaper and half earth to sit upon one of the most powerful thrones. Many see you as a threat."

My chest deflated. Of course, he was talking about my throne, my heritage.

"Then why push me to be queen if I'm such a threat?"

"A queen has protection, an army, a people, a kingdom. You, on your own, can't defeat those who rather see your death than your life."

"So, no matter what I want or how I try to make myself less of a threat, my life will always be in danger from those who uphold the old? Is this what you're telling me?"

The general stroked his beard. "Your Mother and I have done nothing but try to protect you. You and your sister."

"Is that why you—" I caught myself, my anger boiling to the surface of my skin. He was standing there acting as if he hadn't been erasing my memories for Spirits knew how long, preventing me from manifesting, sheltering me in the palace, and treating me like I was still a child.

The general squinted until his eyes became vertical lines swallowed by long thick eyelashes. "What, Beta? Say it. Tell me what you've been hiding," he hissed.

I wanted to say it. I wanted to blurt it out, confront him, but I knew that was exactly what he was waiting for. That standing this close to me, there was no way of me fighting him off before he pressed his thumb on my forehead and erased everything I knew. I had to say something. "The only secret I'm hiding is why my protective and loving Father is screwing Zef Coe."

His eyelids opened so wide, I could actually see the whites. I shook him.

"You have no idea about what you're speaking of."

I scoffed. "You stand here and counsel me about being different and hiding secrets and yet you can't even come to terms with sleeping with another right underneath Mother's nose?"

"Beta, your Mother and I—"

"What happened to she's not your enemy. Wouldn't she understand if you desired another? It's not like we live in some barbaric time where these things are taboo. The Water King has a wife and a husband. Many marry in multiples, and if Zef didn't want to marry, having the protection as your fer l'amor is the next best thing. So, why the sneaking around? No one would judge you," I said, folding my arms.

"There are certain things that I—that your Mother—we must—" I'd never heard my Father stutter or be unsure of what to say. For a moment, as he studied the infirmary floor, he seemed to age ten years yet remain a small boy. I'd never seen my father be anything other than The Great Agrim Tagore, the Reaper General.

"There're choices made in my past—" his voice cracked. Then his shoulders relaxed, his back straightened, his chin raised, and he looked at me with a fierce black gaze. "Enough of this. You're a child and should remain in your place until your Mother and I instruct you otherwise."

My skin prickled. I dropped my arms and balled my fist. I buried my nails into my palm. "See, that's the problem. I'm not a child any longer. I don't need you or her protecting me from some invisible foe that no one else sees. You're overbearing."

"Beta."

"Controlling!"

"Beta."

"You're smothering me and you don't even realize that you're killing me slowly. But I guess it's okay because instead of choking me with your own hands, you're using silky soft pillows with high thread counts." I didn't even realize I was yelling until I noticed my spit falling a few feet in front of me.

"Enough!" The general yelled back. "You're going home. Your Mother will know what to do next and we will go from there."

"I'm not going anywhere I don't want to be."

Before he spoke, he breathed deeply. "You just went through a traumatic experience, so I will forgive your little outburst. These months have been too hard on you."

I nervously laughed. "Yeah, so hard mopping floors and cleaning pig shit. Such laborious work." I slammed my fist in my palm. "These past few months haven't been hard enough! You said I wouldn't have special treatment. You were proud of me for standing up for myself. Am I not your daughter? Reaper is a part of me as it is you. I deserve to be here and to train alongside these soldiers." I held back the well of tears that tried to escape.

"These soldiers, Bellamy, have been training all of their lives! You being here was never meant for you to become a real soldier. Training for just a few months is a joke. Something to get the idea out of your system so you can take your rightful place on your throne without regret." The general paused. He fixed his mouth to say something else, but he pressed his lips together until they became thin lines.

"Oh, so all this was just a joke to you? To them?" I pointed towards the exit door.

"That's not what I meant."

"That's what you said."

"I think it would be a good idea if you—"

I cut him off. "This isn't a joke to me. I have been taking this seriously since I got here. I tried not to complain, did as I was told, and got stronger, faster, and more aware. Seeing every obstacle as an opportunity to learn and grow because I didn't want to be viewed as the pampered princess that didn't know shit from piss. I want to be seen as an equal. A warrior, someone who belongs in the Blood Elite!"

The general's voice was not the one that belonged to my father. It was brash, gruff, and cold. "You're not their equal. You're not a warrior. And you are not a member of the Blood Elite."

"Then what am I? Wait. Let me guess, *something new*."

"You're a fucking princess!" He grabbed the bridge of his nose, placing one hand on his hip.

I jerked back on the bed. Father might have yelled at me, but cursing at me? He had never.

"That's what you don't get, Bellamy. I finally admit that I've enabled you for far too long. Now you sit here thinking you are one of them!" He pointed outside. "You will never be one of them. You will be the next High Priestess of the Earth Kingdom and their rightful queen."

"I didn't ask to be born in this position," my voice quivered.

"No one asks to be born in any position, but here we are! Unlike them, the position you were born into matters. If something had happened to you out there, do you understand what this might mean for an entire kingdom?" His heavy boots stopped in front of me.

"I am sending you home."

"I won't go."

"This is not a negotiation; this is an order. I am sending you home. Pack your things. You have done all you can do here."

I tried not to bite the inside of my cheek. Instead, I

mustered up my courage and raised my chin. "If I'm not a soldier, like you say, then I don't need to take orders from a general. I am staying." I don't know what possessed me to speak back, but my heart was about to drop out of my ass. I knew I was playing with life or death.

"You defy me?" He stepped closer. I could feel the heat from his breath. Yet my back grew straighter, eyebrows creased.

"It is what you say. If I am to be queen, it is you who defies me."

Before I could blink, his backhand slapped across my face. The force shook me. I had to fight against gravity not to bring my hand to my stinging cheek. The tears welled up as I fought to keep them down. I would not cower away from him. I kept my resolve. Pushing off the table, I maneuvered around him. The general grabbed my shoulder. His face twisted in pain, as if he, too, was surprised. I dodged him and headed towards the exit.

"I'm not leaving. I will stay. I will train."

"Bellamy," his voice was just above a mumble. I exited the infirmary without another word.

A BLUR OF FACES whipped past as I rushed back to my cabin. When I entered, Silvia was there. She jumped from the bed, straightening out her dress.

"What happened?"

"My father slapped me!" I immediately confessed.

"He did what?"

"Exactly!"

Silvia rushed to my side; her hand cupped my face. She turned my cheek from left to right, her brown eyes assessing for any new marks.

"What provoked him?"

"Me, of course. He wanted to send me back home, and I told him no. I won't go."

"Why not?"

"What do you mean, why not?"

"I'm just saying, was there a reason for him to send you home? What did the doctor say?"

"The doctor said nothing to me. I'm fine. I feel fine. I'm completely healed."

Silvia stroked my three-month-old plaits. "Maybe going home isn't a bad idea."

"What?"

"I'm just saying. We haven't had time to stop and breathe. Maybe your Mother would be better at helping you."

I pushed Silvia's hand away. "How can you say that! Whose side are you on?"

"Yours, I"—Silvia's eyes darted from side to side —"I just want what's best for you."

"Then ask me instead of planning my entire life out."

Silvia reached to grab my hair. "Let's run you a bath, help you relax, and I will begin taking out your plaits."

I swerved out of her grasp, not wanting to be touched. I ran over to the dresser and opened the top drawer. Inside laid medical supplies along with shears. Grabbing them, I stood in front of the oval table mirror and chopped my plaits off at neck length.

Silvia gasped. My hair, even in plaits, reached past my butt. Now the roped strains were dead on the floor.

"Stop it!" Silvia pleaded.

I didn't notice that I was cutting the plaits unevenly. I just wanted to get rid of the palace, of my mother, of my duty to be something I didn't choose to be! Mother would never let me cut my hair. As the last plait dropped limply to the floor, I took the shears and smashed them into the mirror. The glass shattered on impact. It wasn't enough. I needed to take my anger out on something else. I tossed the dresser over and screamed.

I turned to Silvia, half expecting her to be cowering in a corner. She wasn't. She stood defiantly, her lips on full display, her fist balled.

"What! Afraid that I may attack you?" I mocked.

"I know you're upset, and I refused to engage with you while you're throwing your temper tantrum." Silvia headed to the door. I ran to block it.

"Move," she said.

"Make me."

Her lips disappeared into her mouth.

"You know." I tapped a finger to my chin. "You didn't seem all that surprised about Father wanting to send me home. Why is that?"

Her big brown eyes almost went blank.

"You're still *updating* Father about me, aren't you?"

"I have no choice. You know that."

"There's always a choice." I pushed off the door. "Make yours right here, right now."

Silvia backed away until she hit the end of the bed. "What are you asking me to do?"

"Choose me. I will be queen with the ability to fulfill your every need. Spy on my parents for me. Report to me."

Silvia's eyes went wide. "Your eyes." She fell back onto the bed. I was on top of her like prey.

"Choose me," I said, watching her aura shimmer to life. An explosion of beautiful violet.

"You're not Bellamy. You're—" Silvia bit her lips. "Her."

I cocked my head to the side. "I am just as much her as she is me." I bent over, holding on to Silvia's wrist, burying my face into her neck.

Blackberries.

271

"Bring Bellamy back," Silvia said.

"She's right here. Seeing what I see, feeling what I feel." I licked Silvia's neck before biting it, sucking the spot I knew made her melt. Her hips shifted underneath me. "Bellamy wants you right now. If I rip your clothes off and do as I please, she won't stop me."

"Then do it." Silvia spat. "Fuck me, right here, right now."

I cackled, a type of laugh foreign to myself. I had never made a sound like that before. "You think you can save her, don't you?"

Silvia's brown skin grew hot and her cheeks flushed.

"She's mine already, and you can be too." I kissed Silvia's lips, soft and supple. Her legs wrapped around my waist. Silvia bit hard on my lip and blood spilled into her mouth.

"Bitch," I said, gripping Silvia's wrist until she thrashed against the bedsheets. This made me wet with longing. I desired her more like this than I'd ever desired her before. "Why she persists in choosing you when you're not an equal, I'll never understand." I bent close to Silvia's ear. "But don't worry. I've found her another. One who will free us, her true companion."

"Bellamy!" Silvia screamed. "Come back, please!"

"I'm right here." I loosened my grip.

"She's right here." I tightened my grip.

I'm right here. I closed my eyes. The voice in my head echoed, *I'm right here.*

My grip loosened, rolling off Silvia onto my back. I was shivering. Silvia touched me and I moved away, her touch too icy to bear. She threw blankets on top of me.

"It's okay." She patted my thigh.

"I'm sorry," but my head was foggy. "I didn't mean to get so angry."

"It wasn't you," she said.

I studied Silvia. "I—" I searched for the right words to say. Defeated, I settled with, "I'm getting worse?"

Silvia nodded.

"Silvia," I rubbed a thumb alongside her jawline. "Leave me." She searched my face.

"Leave me before it's too late."

"You won't harm me."

"I will."

Silvia shimmied onto the floor. She picked up the dresser, careful to miss the glass. There was a comb she plucked out of a pile of spilled clothes, then she returned to bed, placing my head on top of her lap. Silently, she unraveled what was left of my plaits.

"Silvia?" I didn't mean for her name to come out as a question, but I had so many questions running rampant in my brain. *I was changing.* If I were something new, then why did I feel the power growing inside of me was something old? Ancient? Evil.

"Yes, Bee?" The soft rips of the comb separating my plaits were louder than her voice.

"I'm not returning home."

"Tomorrow?"

Her question hung in the air.

Never. I held that part in as a voice cackled within me.

Act VI

XXVI

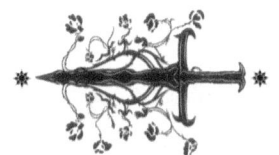

"Warning: Do not mistake lust with love. If you do, agony will
pursue. Be careful who you give your heart to."
Proverb 19:70 from the Book of Face, Mortem Era.

A SOFT KISS ON THE FOREHEAD awoke me from a
dreamless sleep. Stretching, I turned over to Silvia and smiled.
"Morning," I yawned.

"Morning." Silvia kissed me again. I wrapped her in my
arms. I loved to see her like this. Her hair packed into her
bonnet, fresh-faced, big brown eyes, and soft pink lips. She had
the cutest button nose I'd ever seen.

"I could get used to your new haircut."

She stroked the sides of my hair that were cut low in a tapered trim. On top, my hair was still thick and long enough to spill over both sides to hide the close-cut underneath. But Mother would not ignore my hair going from butt length to shoulder length. I never understood why she cared so much when she was bald-headed herself.

"I like it," I stretched. "It feels more like me." I surveyed the room. The glass was swept, along with the hair that I had lost. The dresser was back in order, except for the mirror that used to sit on top. The room looked normal, and I could almost pretend that what happened was just a bad dream, but I knew it was time to stop pretending.

"Silvia, we need to talk about the red woman."

Silvia tensed. Her light breathing cut short as if she was holding it in.

"How do you know when it's me and not her? Is it the eye change?"

Silvia shook her head. I could tell she didn't want to talk about it, as if doing so would conjure the other version of me up.

"It happens when you're having intense emotions." Silvia sat upright, pulling her knees to her chest. "My theory is that she feeds on your negative emotions. The greater they are, the more power she receives. Like an amplifier."

I pulled away the blankets and scooted closer to the wall to rest my back on it, but at the same time, giving Silvia space.

Silvia continued. "At first, I couldn't tell. The change was subtle, but after the argument with the prince and the confrontation in your Father's office, I now know what to look for. Do you not feel the switch?"

I ran my nails over my skin lightly, even though there was

no itch. Silvia rose from the bed, removed the cream from the closet, and proceeded to rub it into my skin. I welcomed it.

"I don't feel a switch. I feel like I'm the only one acting and doing things. I don't feel separated from her. Until recently, the voice in my head sounded like my own. When I first made contact with her, she was behind prison cells in my mind. I knew the key. It was like an eight-pointed star and with it, I unlocked the gate. Ever since, I've been feeling myself swell with power and change. But I don't know what I'm changing into." I swallowed hard.

Silvia closed the lid to the cream and tucked it away.

"What's so wrong with me that my father would rather suppress my gifts than show me how to work my manifestation? Yesterday, he told me a story about a man who was favored by the Spirits. He could transform or shapeshift, a trait that was passed down to his child. He said the council had the family killed because of it. My question is, why? The Blood Elite is filled with gifters who have rare manifestations or are strongly intertwined. Sarue and Venus can teleport together. The Moonborn twins can create a shield of protection when intertwined. My own Father and the queen of the Reaper Kingdom are blood gifted. What made *this* man and his family so much of a threat that death was much better than life?" I glanced at Silvia as if she had all the answers to my questions.

"We need to know what your parents know, and I think your Father gave you your first clue," Silvia said. Her bonnet was slipping off. I reached over and straightened it. She continued, holding my right hand to her cheek. "We need to investigate this man. I assume when your Father said council, he meant the Council of Amalgamation, correct?"

I dropped my hand and shrugged. "It could be."

"Well, let's start there. We'll have more resources once we go back home. There has to be some record of this man."

I wasn't going back home, but I didn't want to get into that conversation now. Instead, I said, "Not if the council wanted people to forget." I thought about that for a bit. If I were the council and had enough power to wipe out a family, then I would have made sure that deed never came to light. "There must be birth and death records," I said.

"Did your Father mention the man's kingdom?"

"No."

"Time, place, or anything?" I shook my head.

"How do you know if your Father was telling a real story or a fictional one?"

"He has never told me a story that was fictional. If he said it, it happened, and nine out of ten times, he was there."

"Can you ask him more?"

"I can ask, but that doesn't mean he would give me more."

My brain turned as I flipped through everyone I knew. "Fia. I could ask Fia, maybe even Rwju." I needed to speak with Rwju, anyway.

"Okay, sounds good. Now, our other issue." The strap of Silvia's sheer gown had slipped off her shoulder. She pulled it up. "We need to test your powers." She held her palms facing me. "Whatever you did to Sarue, do it to me."

"No," I almost yelled.

"You won't hurt me."

"What makes you so confident? Haven't I hurt you before? Sarue was damn near a corpse before I recovered her. What makes you think you're any different?"

"Because you love me."

"What?"

"You love me. I know that now. And she will not hurt anyone you love. Intimidate, yes. Possess, yes. Remember, she amplifies the emotions you already have. So, as long as you're feeding her the right emotions, she can't act outside of those emotions. We should be fine."

"And what's the right emotion? Should I reach deep inside and call out the power of love?" I rolled my eyes.

"No, I was thinking about something more..." Silvia snatched the bonnet from her head. She stood up on her knees and pulled off her gown and tossed it to the floor. "...primal."

I watched her breasts bounce, her nipples already hardening. My mouth watered as heat built in my stomach. My eyes drifted to a nice bush between her legs. Instantly, I wanted to pounce. My skin was tingling as the voice inside said *eat*.

"No." I forced myself to look away. "Too dangerous, not on you."

"Are you saying I can't take it?" Silvia grabbed my chin, turning my head back to her.

"Unless you like pain with your pleasure."

Silvia kissed me. "I'm really glad you cut your hair." She said, climbing on top of me. "It gives you an edge, makes you look dangerous."

"I am dangerous."

"Show me."

"Silvia." Her name left my lips like a prayer.

"Fuck me," she said as she bit my ear. My grip tightened on her ass.

"Which one of us do you truly want?" I asked, letting her pull my top over my head.

"Both of you."

She licked my neck and bit down hard.

I growled, gathering her into my arms and flipping her onto her back.

She looked up at me with doe-shaped eyes and a playful smile. "Can you feel your control slipping?" she asked, massaging her breast.

"Yes." I grabbed her inner thighs, separating them, licking my bottom lip.

"No!" She slapped my hands but kept her legs butterflied. "Gain control. Feel your power, your greed, your lust. Use your emotions to empower you, not control you."

I wanted her so badly that my body shook. We hadn't been physical for months due to the tension between us and now she was laid out before me like my own personal buffet and asking me not to eat. I looked away.

"Look at me, Bee."

She reached up and snatched my face so quickly that I lost balance and fell on top of her. "Never take your eyes off me again, do you understand!" she commanded.

"You don't command me," I slapped her hand away, gripping her wrist.

"You're mine, and there's nothing anyone can do about it," her voice almost sounded deadly.

This turned me on. My passion flared. Silvia's violet aura burst to life; her power called to me. Somehow, Silvia had grown. Her manifestation was like a field of opi flowers. Exhaling, I breathed her power in deep, so deep that I became lightheaded.

"You're mine!" I heard my voice scream when I released my breath.

Silvia's lips disappeared; her breath caught in her chest. "Your eyes are changing," she said, her body tensed. "Don't let her overtake you."

"I—" My skin itched so fiercely that I wanted to snatch it off.

"I trust you won't hurt me," Silvia said, her legs gripping my waist.

"Are you still afraid of me?" I asked, falling on top of her, pushing down the surge of power that was forcing its way to the surface.

"No," her voice was calm and gentle. "I love you, Bellamy. One day, when all this is past us, let's make it official."

My heart skipped. "Serious?"

"Deadly so."

I kissed her softly, removing my unders until my nakedness met hers. I gripped her thighs.

"You're mine." I tested the words on my tongue. A red-orange glow leaked from my mouth and into hers while her violet aura entered into me.

Silvia's energy radiated, and I knew I was strengthening her.

With one sudden movement, she flipped me onto my back, her aura cloaking her like rose petals. She kissed my neck, and my breast, trailing her kisses down my belly, until she was between my legs. Her touch allowed my entire body to relax like bathing in a hot tub enriched with chamomile and sage.

She split me open, and my eyes rolled back as her tongue slowly massaged my clit.

A voice in my mind stirred. *Enjoy it now while it lasts.*

XXVII

"Truth is a stone thrown and oftentimes dodged."
Proverb 4:11 from the Book of Face, Mortem Era.

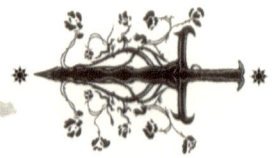

"YOU'RE SLUGGISH, BEE. Pick it up!" Oneo said, swapping a long stick underneath my feet. I jumped high, dodging the blow, only to land on my butt. Oneo stood over me. His strip of white hair fell over his eye. "What's gotten into you, Bee? Still need time to recover?"

"Fuck you," I said, pushing the stick from my face. I rolled away from him, picking myself off the ground and onto my feet. "I had a long night and an even longer morning. I'm drained."

"Excuses, excuses," Twoa shouted across the field as he dodged a hit from Fia. "You better be lucky the Earthborns had to reset the tournament, which means we get a second chance!"

Fia's shadow whipped out, grabbing Twoa's feet. Twoa tumbled to the ground. Fia cracked his neck. "Once you're inside the Earthborns' domain, you'll need to be much faster, quicker, and more focused than you are right now. Or you'll eliminate our entire team."

"You don't think I know that?"

I stood, dusting the dirt from my pants. I turned to observe my team. Sarue and Venus were practicing archery, while Fia and Twoa worked on offense and defense. Oneo twirled a stick, waiting for me to recover from my fall.

Then there was Rwju. He sat on the branches of a thick tree. His legs crossed, eyes closed, face pointed to the sky. Every so often, he would glance at me, and I at him, yet we hadn't said one word to each other.

A hard slap across my butt took me out of thought.

"What the fuck, Oneo!"

"Get your mind out of the clouds and into this combat. Or do you like to get your ass beat?"

That pissed me off. "The only person getting their ass beat today is you."

"Oh really? Do you honestly think you can defeat me?"

"I can show you better than I can tell you," I said, picking up the training stick. I spun it in my hand a few times, mapping out my defense and attack.

Oneo licked his lips, a playful grin setting in.

I enjoyed this being out in the woods fighting. The only thing missing was Quande. He was the best part of home. I shook my thoughts out of my head and charged at Oneo. I slammed my stick down as he used his to block. Our sticks collided with a clack as if they were about to snap. Oneo pushed me off, quickly turning to hit me in the ribs. I blocked and then used my legs to swipe his legs. In a matter of minutes, my strength and energy came back tenfold. My heart was pumping, my mind focused, and my limbs loved every second that they flexed.

Oneo and I danced to the rhythm of our own beat, lost in the fun and battle of it all. For a Moonborn, he was quick. His lean limbs were nimble as he dodged and returned blows. I adjusted, speeding up my reaction time. A smile on my lips, I switch from attack to defense. Sweat dripped from his forehead as he kicked our sparring into gear. His stick was the first to break. He quickly readjusted, creating two weapons instead of one. I took my stick, snapping it on my knee and doing the same. We were at each other's throats mere moments later, throwing a series of blows that had me in my element.

The singular thought in my mind was, *I will beat him.*

I hit him across the face with one of the broken sticks. When he turned, his eyes had gone full white like the moon. The first time today that he had used his abilities as a means to defeat me.

My skin burned and itched. My scalp was on fire. I needed to apply more pressure. I was fighting a fully charged Oneo. Let's see if he could track my movements now. I held my ground, hundreds of scenarios running rapidly through my mind. I went left. Oneo was already there. I went right; he cut me off in my tracks. He was reading me like a deck of cards. That's fine. Think less strategic, more sporadic, primal.

Oneo circled me, never blinking. Control, stay in control. Quande's and Silvia's warnings boomed in my ear. Oneo's aura flared to life. Pink, baby powder pink. I would have never guessed it. I called to it, trying to stay in control. *Just a little, just enough to beat him.*

Why stop there? A voice popped into my mind. *Yeah, why stop there? I can have him on his knees in seconds.*

Before I was about to strike, Rwju splashed me with a bucket worth of water, snapping me out of my blood lust.

"What the hell!" I shouted. "Seriously?" I brushed the water off my clothes. "What was that for?"

Rwju stared at me, his eyebrows netted together, his black hair pulled from his face. "We are supposed to be training, not killing each other," Rwju said, his gaze surveying me. A mixture of emotions ran across his face. Caution was what he eventually settled with.

That's when I noticed Venus, Sarue, the twins, and Fia stopped. Their full attention was directed at me. I brushed sweat from my forehead. "I'm not trying to kill anyone." I let my hair down from its ponytail so my scalp could breathe.

Venus stepped forward. "Are you sure you're Earthborn?" She said, not in a joking way, but there was a sheer curiosity in her long lashes and upturned eyes. She wore a leather shirt cut in an upside-down triangle with tight black leather pants with boots. Her long black hair spilled around her shoulders, framing her heart-shaped face. One sword was cupped in her hand.

I put two fingers to my temple, focusing as hard as I could on the ground, calling it to move. "Earth rise, move, come to me!" I eventually shrugged and gave up. "The jury is still out," I said, kicking the dirt.

"You move like a reaper," Venus said, stepping in front of Sarue. How long was she going to be on high alert around me?

I looked over at Rwju, who hadn't stopped gawking at me as if I were some sort of specimen.

"We saw you." Venus held up her sword. Sarue subtly touched Venus's wrist. The tension in Venus's shoulders relaxed, but only for a brief second.

"I don't know what you mean, Venus. Maybe being less vague would help?"

"It was like you were in my mind. I could feel you in trouble. I went looking for you over the tournament walls. You were like a beacon to me. I couldn't help myself." Venus's sword trembled in her grasp. Sarue placed her hand over Venus's knuckles, guiding her to lower her sword.

"What are you?" Venus sounded as if she were about to cry. Her hard mask crumbled right in front of me.

"I—I—" My nails dug into my itchy palm. I turned to Rwju, who had taken a step back. Oneo joined his twin and Fia watched the grounds, avoiding eye contact with everyone.

Rwju spoke, "Do you know the story of the first gifted?"

I clicked my teeth. "That's basic history that everyone knows."

"Yea, but what do *you* know?"

I recalled the story. "Six centuries ago, humanity went to war, almost causing our species to go extinct. At the last stand-off battle, a woman came between the two armies on the battleground and called out to the Earth Spirit for deliverance. The Earth Spirit answered and called upon the other guardians, thus ending the war and gifting humankind with manifestations. Yada, yada, yada," I said, forcing my eyes not to roll out of my eye sockets.

"Her name was Toka Freeman. Born pre-Mortem Era from a lineage of root workers that could be traced back to the beginning of humanity. It is important for you to remember her name," Rwju said.

Twoa added in his coins, "Especially since her blood runs through your family tree. She is your ancestor and yet you know nothing about her."

I immediately threw up my shields in defense.

"Unfortunately, I wasn't raised in the Earth Kingdom, nor

was I raised knowing their history. But what I do know is that Mother's line can be traced back to the first gifter, so don't you tell me what I do and do not know," I pointed out. "Why is any of this important?"

Rwju spoke. "It's all important. Knowing where you come from, the power you hold in your blood, the story behind your family line. You don't even know what you are."

I jerked my head toward Rwju. "Then be my guest. What am I? Huh?" I scanned the crowd. "I've been trying to figure that out since I got here."

Fia's lips sat tight on his face. The twins glanced at each other. Venus had yet to loosen her grip around the hilt of her sword. She stood in front of a concerned Sarue who bit down on her lower lip, her fingers running through her locs.

I continued, "Since you know me better than I know myself, tell me!"

Rwju turned to the twins, then to Sarue and Venus. Sarue shook her head. Rwju raised his bushy eyebrows, as if having a silent conversation that I needed the password to get into.

Twoa, doing what he does best, attempted to break the tension by joking. "Come on, team. We are supposed to be training, not giving history lessons. Let's get back to it."

Rwju stepped forward, then took two steps backwards before doing an about-face and walking away from the group. But I couldn't let it go. Or more so, I wouldn't let it go.

"What the fuck are you not telling me, Rwju?" He halted, his right foot paused midair.

I shouted, "I know you didn't tell my father what you saw that night. If you had, I wouldn't remember." I pointed my fingers to everyone. "None of you would remember. And we all know why." I glanced at Fia, who refused to meet my eyes. "So, I ask again, That night in the forest, what did you see? Tell me what you think I am." Rwju slowly placed his foot on the ground.

"We were all high off opi," Fia said. "We could have all been hallucinating. I think we should end this conversation." Fia grabbed my arm. I snatched it away, ignoring him, and marched toward Rwju. Before I could make it to Rwju, I stopped in front of Venus and Sarue. Venus completely covered Sarue, her knuckles going white as she twisted the sword in her fingers.

"Venus," I attempted to remain calm. "You have one more time to point that sword at me and I guarantee it will be your last."

Venus jumped at me. There were a few women I ever had to look up to and quite frankly, I hated I had to look up to her. A part of me wanted to force her to bow, remember her place. My skin prickled like tiny needles jabbing at my skin. I realized I was losing control.

Sarue stepped around Venus and answered, "We aren't trying to alarm you, princess Bellamy. We only want to help you." Sarue was patronizing. She gestured for me to calm down. "We both can feel your...energy somehow. We're just trying to make sense of it." She lowered her voice.

My arm was inflamed. I dug my nails deep into my skin to ease the itch. "It seems like to me everybody has been talking amongst themselves." I glanced at everyone. "What is it that you're not telling me? Huh? Anybody?" I shouted.

Venus gripped her sword but did not attempt to raise it. "Do you know what it means to be Fireborn?"

"What?" I gasped.

Sarue touched Venus's shoulders to shush her.

"You heard me. Do you know what a true gifted Fireborn looks like, how they manifest?"

I laughed. "Fireborns don't have manifestations. They are

cursed people. They have always been that way since the Mortem Era."

"Until now." Those two words leaving Venus's lips froze me.

"Enough."

The command came from Fia. When he spoke, Venus snapped out of her intense stare to glare at Fia.

Fia continued. "This is nonsense, and I no longer want to hear any more of this," he said, slamming a fist into his open palm.

"She needs to know," Rwju said as he stepped closer to the group.

I didn't know when he had migrated to the inner circle, but he was there now.

"She doesn't need to know anything that isn't true. We don't know what we saw that night. All of us were in the opi fields. We were affected," Fia said.

"Tell me Fia, what did you witness? Because this is my first time hearing about any of this."

Fia dodged his eyes. "I don't know what I saw."

Oneo jumped in. "Me too."

Twoa chimed, "Same."

Fia, still avoiding eye contact continued. "Exactly, no one saw shit. We went back to see where you and Rwju went. We saw Venus standing at the edge of the woods. When we caught up to her, we saw.... a hallucination of sorts," he confirmed.

I was not satisfied. "There's only one issue with that story, Fia. Venus wasn't in the opi fields."

Fia spoke, "Princess Bellamy—"

I cut him off. "With all due respect, Fia. Either tell me the truth or don't speak at all."

Twoa looked at his brother, shaking his head.

Rwju grunted. "Enough." He turned to me. "You were on

fire. Your irises were that of a predator, green cat-like slits, your skin scaled like that of the ancient one, a dragon. You were becoming a fire-breathing dragon, a sign that you are the Fire Spirit chosen vessel."

The woman in red, the voice in my head, the reason my parents would rather wipe my memory rather than allow me to manifest. If I were shifting into a dragon, I thought of the leather scale my father pulled from his pocket, then that would mean the Fire Spirit's seal had been broken. The steel bars with the eight-pointed star on the lock flashed in my memory.

"You're a monster," Venus said, her lips curling into a snarl. She took a half step forward. "You should have never been born."

Those words hit me with the force of one hundred reaper shadows. I whirled around, not knowing how to process the emotions that were unfolding within me. Anger, sadness, confusion, pain, betrayal, lies, secrets.

Venus had volunteered to be my target.

"And you're a rude bitch that deserves to be put in her place," I said through clenched teeth.

"And you think you can put me in my place?" Venus smirked.

The twins were at my side in no time, pulling me away.

"We haven't seen a Fireborn manifestation in centuries. None of us can be sure what we saw," Oneo said.

Fia interjected. "He's right. We were tired, depleted, and high that night. Venus could have somehow got caught up in the hysteria. She even said she didn't know how she arrived there that night." Fia turned to Rwju. "You need to go and get your head checked by the Life Doctor and forget these silly visions."

"I don't need to forget a damn thing. I saw what I saw. Bellamy is Fireborn," Rwju said.

"Shut up!" Fia shouted, quieting the entire group. "You're confused. You've already been tainted by the Fireborns and now you are trying to fill our princess's head with lies? This is bullshit. She's half reaper and half earth. What we saw could be"—Fia finally glanced up at me, his eyes filled with tears — "something new that we don't understand."

"Even if she isn't Fireborn. Will you still refuse to see what's right in front of you as if it didn't happen?" Rwju asked.

"All I see is some Fireborn sympathizer who is getting their rocks off to Fireborn conspiracies."

Rwju stepped toward Fia. "What the fuck you say?"

Fia moved closer to Rwju. "You heard me, you Fireborn fucker."

Rwju rubbed a finger alongside the scar on his face. "So, you're still blaming me? This is what this is really about?"

"No one has ever betrayed their own kind for a Fireborn, except you."

Rwju cursed. "I'm not doing this with you. This"—Rwju pointed around to the group— "isn't about you or about me."

"That's hard to tell, Rwju. Let me ask you a question. When you go to sleep at night, do you dream about your precious Fireborn? The way he snuck his way into our camp, then into your bed, corrupting your heart? Do you still crave for him, even after he ambushed us?"

"That wasn't him," Rwju mumbled.

I turned to the twins. Oneo slowly shook his head as a warning to not interfere.

"After seven of our men died, including my brother. You defend that Fireborn still?"

Rwju, spit flying from his mouth, his hand trembling, said, "This isn't about him!"

"He put lies in your head, Rwju. He curled his tail around you and brought you down into his snake pit. Admit it. You haven't been the same. Why the general didn't discharge you from the Blood Elite, I will never understand." Fia crept closer to Rwju. "Stop corrupting our team with your asinine Fireborn conspiracy theories. None of us know what we saw that night. And if I ever see you"—Fia crept closer, closing the distance between himself and Rwju— "fix your mouth to spread a rumor about our princess, I will make sure you will never mutter another sound again." Fia was so close to Rwju, their foreheads could easily touch.

Rwju's face flushed red, his scar pulling tight across his eye and cheek. He sneered at Fia. With one blink of an eye, Rwju clapped. Water seemed to drop out of nowhere as he aimed it all at Fia.

Fia, a shadow bursting out of his palm, snapped his shadow in place as a protective barrier. The water hit but was quickly absorbed by Fia. Fia stomped his feet, clapped his hands to his chest, his face contorted, his tongue on full display. His eyes were wild, and the amount of energy flowing from his body overwhelmed my senses.

I had never seen anyone use shadow like Fia. It was like he was dancing, stomping, shouting, the ground and air bending to his will. The bright forest became gloomy. It was like he was calling upon the Reaper Spirit. The grass underneath him fading from green to brown.

Rwju clapped again, but this time, the water did not come. Fia consumed all life, including water. Rwju dropped to his knees, grabbing his throat. Fia stomped again, beating at his chest, then slapping his thighs. "A Ka Mate! Ka Mate! Kaora! I die. I die," he chanted.

I was lightheaded, my eyes rolled back, my balance shifted. Rwju bent over, barely holding himself up. Venus jumped in front of Sarue, and the twins threw up a shield that flickered in and out. Rwju clapped again, calling down the water from the sky. But Fia wouldn't let that happen. Rwju was choking, clawing at his throat, the very moisture from his skin was being sucked from his pores.

Venus turned to the twins. "Throw the shield around Fia. Block him."

The twins tried again to summon their shield, but it flickered out. Fia was draining them all. Everyone except me. I could see Fia's aura cover him like a second man. It was all black shadow and the more Fia drained, the larger the shadow man grew. It licked out a long black tongue, almost guiding Fia's steps. We needed to contain him. The group was on the ground, calling out to Fia to stop, but I knew the look on Fia's face. It called for blood and only blood was going to satisfy him.

"Stop, Fia," Oneo heaved. "Stop!" he commanded.

I called Fia's energy towards me. As Fia continued to look at Rwju, who was passing out. Fia's shadow man turned its blank face toward me as if he could sense me.

"Come," I willed the shadow, angry black swirls jolted towards my mouth like a sword down my throat. It was overwhelming. My throat felt like it was being shredded into pieces. I drew my energy out to fight against it. Red-orange into Fia's shadow, but only a slither.

"Stop." I cut Fia's energy off and Fia immediately went limp.

Rwju gulped breaths as he choked guttural coughs.

Fia scanned the team, spotting everyone on the ground catching their breath. He pointed at Rwju to say something to him, his mouth forming the words, but no sounds came out.

He turned to the rest of us. "I'm sorry," he said, before rushing out of the clearing and heading back to the main camp.

XVIII

"A balled fist earns fear, not respect."
Proverb 23:5 from the Book of Face, Mortem Era.

WE WALKED TO THE MAIN CAMP in silence. Questions bounced in my mind. Some I knew the answers to, and others I didn't want to know. What the fuck was I? If I asked Father outright, would he tell me? Could he tell me? I found myself outside his door, about to knock. Quande threw open the door and rushed out. "Whoa" I said. "Where're you going?"

"Not now, Bee." His face was all hard lines. The dagger tattoo on the side of his temple was on full display.

"I just wanted to see my father. I mean, the General."

"He isn't in there. I'm going to him now." Quande walked away.

"Where? Did the letter come yet requesting his presence at the Council?"

"No, Bee." Quande stopped. "Shouldn't you be training?"

"You mean cleaning other people's shit? I don't think that counts for training," I jabbed at his shoulder. "Come on. I haven't seen you in forever. I miss you, Quande."

With that, his face lightened up just a little. "You're right." Quande glanced over his shoulder, then turned back to me. "Technically, I'm not supposed to be *training* you, but what if you want to meet for a little non training—definitely *not* sparring—fun, we can later."

"That sounds good. So, are you going to tell me where you're going?"

"Top secret."

"Top secret my ass. Did you find the Fireborns?"

Quande's eyebrow raised, his brown eyes went so dark, for a second, I thought I was looking into Father's eyes.

"Who told you about that?"

"I hear things around camp."

"Stop hearing things, okay? I'll let you know once we finish interrogating them what the next step will be."

"Interrogating *them*?"

Quande cursed. "Pretend you didn't hear that," he said as he marched away.

I rushed to his side. "So, is that where you're going?"

"Keep your voice down."

"Just tell me."

"No, nosy."

"Fine," I said, stopping in my tracks. Quande continued to walk on before throwing his head back and turning around.

"That's it?" he asked.

"Yep, that's it. Have fun at your secret interrogation meeting!" I shouted. Some B.E. stopped and looked between us.

"Childish," Quande shook his hand, and disappeared through the trees, almost blending into the shadows. *Almost.*

Learning from the best trackers on the team, I kept my distance, watched where I stepped, and kept cover. I trailed Quande as he passed the B.E. camp, into the mountains. Up ahead, there was a cave. If one wasn't looking, the entrance easily blended in like a thin layer of wallpaper. Quande slipped in.

I sat behind a large rock, debating if I should enter or not. I made it this far. What's the worst that could happen? My father erasing what I saw? No. I wouldn't let him do that. Never again.

I waited a little longer when I thought the coast was clear and darted into the entrance of the cave. Inside, it was pitch black. I could barely see my hands in front of me. I kept to the cave's walls, feeling alongside the jagged rocks. I stumbled a few times, but the walls did not echo my footsteps, nor the rocks being shoved around by my feet. *Odd.*

Up ahead, there was a faint orange light. I squinted until that glow became clearer. It was a torchlight. I rounded the corner and almost stopped dead in my tracks as illuminated in the soft orange glow was Quande, the general, Zef, and the Life Doctor, surrounded by a man in chains on his knees on the ground. I hid myself in the corners and watched.

"State your purpose, Fireborn," The general, fist behind his back, voice even, said as he leered at the man on his knees.

"Listen." The man spat blood onto the ground. "I mean no harm."

"Answer, wessie," Quande's hand tightened around the hilt of his dagger. His voice was as cool as a summer breeze, but as deadly as colliding tornados.

The man looked from Quande to the general. "I told you. I sent my men here to request help, not attack." He sat back on his knees, running his hand through his wavy blonde hair. "There is a war coming. I want my people to be on the right side."

My mouth dropped; I recognized his voice. The Fireborn from the dead end and the club.

"You want us to protect you while you and your people hide with tails between your legs?" Quande said, squatting with a blade out and ready. I looked at the general, whose face didn't betray his emotions. Neither did Zef's. The Life Doctor was the only one that looked like they didn't belong. They constantly rubbed the back of their neck and paced in one spot.

"You can call us cowards all you like, but that doesn't negate the fact that you're just as bad as the Fire King."

Quande lashed out, his blade slicing a thin line on the Fireborn's face. The man did not flinch. He stared Quande down with a ferocity that was all his own, while blood dripped from his wound.

Father lowered his hand, calling Quande back. "Your name," he commanded.

"My name—" the Fireborn coughed, finally wiping the blood from his cheek. "My name is Malakey Fireborn. But you knew that already, didn't you, General Agrim Tagore?"

To my left, I swear I heard Zef move closer to the general.

"As you know..." The Fireborn addressed the room. "I'm among the children of the Fire Spirit. I bear no gifts and have no manifestation. I have no weapons. I gave myself over to you voluntarily to protect my people. I'm completely at your mercy." He paused, turning to Quande, who held his blade.

He turned back to the general. "I'm here to help, not harm."

The general signaled Quande to place his dagger into its holder and step back then nodded at Malakey to continue.

"My group is called Redux. We are a cut-off people from the Fire Kingdom. We have renounced our rights and citizenship and fled. We are strangers, outsiders, with no alliances. The Redux acknowledges our past and what our ancestors have done. We want to do better and bring peace instead of harm. I know you don't believe me, and you don't have to." He turned to the general, his face a picture of sincerity. Malakey continued. "Listen, The Fire Kingdom is killing us one by one. They want to uphold the old ways and the old traditions. We need protection. We have women and children depending on us. They're starving. We're barely surviving. I'm doing all I can, but no kingdom will accept a camp of Fireborns. Every border is closing due to the protest. No one will accept them. Maybe if..." He trailed off, his eyes gazing at the ground. He refocused, running his fingers through his hair. "They can't go back to the Fire Kingdom. They are slaughtering hundreds of innocents because of the Fire Kingdom's decree, making the Redux and all Fireborn deserters enemies of the realm. I'm not a perfect man. I've done a lot of fucked up shit, and I'll be the first to admit that." He wiped blood from the corner of his mouth. "But I refuse to be a monster and turn away people who need me the most. In exchange for safety, even if temporary, I'm offering information that'll affect your kingdom too. That's all I offer."

The general posed a question, "What makes you so confident that we won't extract the information from you and kill you and your people after we get it?"

I winced at that question.

Malakey nodded slowly. "Because I've heard of the great Reaperborn General. One who protects, shields, and destroys all of those who seek to do others harm. It is not my confidence I'm leaning on. It's yours."

I sucked in my breath. My heart pounded in my chest.

The general continued, "How many of your people are with you?"

"A little over two hundred. Mostly women, children, and doyens. I've done all I can to keep them alive out here. Trust me, I wouldn't jeopardize them if I didn't think it was absolutely necessary."

The general was silent. He appraised the man carefully.

My palms itched. Rocks shifted underneath my weight. The general turned his head slightly, listening. I went still, holding my breath.

Malakey glanced my way, his blue eyes searching in the dark caves.

But in the end, it was Zef who spoke. "You can come out now, princess."

"Fuck." How long had they known? I eased out of the corner, glancing at Quande. He shook his head and turned away.

"You," Malakey pointed, a wide grin appearing. He pulled at his chains as if he was ready to get up and run to me. "Princess!" he said.

Heat rushed to the apples of my cheeks.

The general eyed me. Quande held the hilt of his dagger.

The Fireborn continued. "Fancy meeting you here. I guess questionable meeting places are our thing."

I wanted to slap my forehead. *Spirits, please be a shield.*

Zef moved so I could stand right in between him and my father. The Lifeborn Doctor chewed at their fingernails. Their red curls mimicking the color of the fire torch's glow.

The general cleared his throat. "You know him?"

"Of course, she knows me. I was there at the taphouse

E.A Noble

when those guys attacked her, and we beat their asses. Fun times!" He smiled with a busted lip. Now that I was closer to him, I saw how badly he was bruised. His shirt was torn revealing old and new scars. There was a tattoo over his chest that I could barely make out due to his shredded shirt.

The general spoke. "Is this true?"

The memory unfolded all at once. He looked different, smaller, like he had lost weight. There was little to no fat on his body. His face was covered in dirt, blood and sweat. His beard and hair had grown longer. The taphouse fight felt like years ago and judging by the looks of the Fireborn, it seemed years could have passed for him too.

"Yes. It was him who assisted me. He risked his life for me," I added.

Malakey beamed. "The way you threw those punches, I should have known you were in the Blood Elite. Your Father should be proud." Malakey looked from me to the general and back to me. "The general's daughter? Damn. She's a warrior. Honestly, she didn't need my help."

Quande flinched but remained quiet.

The general signaled to the Life Doctor. "Heal him."

The Life Doctor went to work. They rubbed their palms together, then held them out over Malakey's wounds. The soft golden glow stretched over his body, healing his cuts and bruises instantly.

Malakey licked his cracked lips. "Does this mean you will help us?"

The general glanced at Zef, to Quande, then to me. "For now," he answered.

"Do we have your bond that you will not harm us?"

"You have my bond," the general said as he crossed his hand over his chest. "I will send soldiers with you to go back and retrieve your camp. Once you return, we will have a place for you and yours, with precautions."

Malakey's shoulders went slack. "Thank you. Thank you so much," he said.

Later that evening, The Blood Elite moved with efficiency. Sarue, Venus, Fia, and a few other soldiers loaded up wagons of provisions and went with the Fireborn to his camp.

The general and I watched as they left. "What if there's an ambush? What if he's lying?" I asked.

General brought his thumb to his eyesight. "I did my due diligence." He dropped his hand, placing it behind his back. "I know we were at odds. I still want you to know that I am proud of you. But as your Father, I worry, and I am sorry for ever placing a hand on you."

I looked up at him; he had a large patch of grays in his beard that reminded me of Moonborns. But except for being stark white like the appearance of the moon, I could tell that this was old age.

"I want you to know that I can handle the truth," I said.

His black irises met my emerald greens.

"I know you want to protect me, but you cannot do so by hiding behind glass walls. Eventually it will break. I need to be ready, prepared. Do you trust I can handle hard things?"

The general reached out his hand, pulling my head into his chest. His thumb pressed against my forehead, and I tried hard not to jerk away. He swiped a piece of leaf that had fallen, then kissed my forehead. I relaxed, resting on him, but at the same time aware of his movements.

"I will tell you everything, I swear, Beta. But it must be after you pledge to the Earth Temple. If you can just be patient with me, your Mother, then you'll understand why we did what we did."

I wanted to ask more questions, but I knew this would be all I was going to get.

"Beta." He lifted my chin. "I'm only letting the Fireborns into our camp as a favor. He helped you and now you're helping him. Never owe anyone any debts. You hear me?"

I nodded.

"We have a lot of work to do." He placed his arms around my shoulders as we returned to camp.

XXIX

"Keep your allies at the table and your adversaries in bed."
Proverb 44:44 from the Book of Face, Mortem Era.

TWO WEEKS PASSED, and the camp was on edge. We received word that the Redux would arrive today. The general sent Rwju, the Moonborn twins, and me to be the greeters and caretakers of the crew. Honestly, no-one else volunteered for the job. We stood outside of the earth wall surrounding the camp. The sun was not yet high in the sky. The camp was silent. Many of the Blood Elite wanted nothing to do with the

Redux, but none would dare go against the general's orders. Zef and his Earthborn recruits not only repaired the training grounds, but they also made a separate camp from the Blood Elite in which the Redux could temporarily settle.

No longer doing chores, I trained day in and day out. Mostly to keep my mind from wandering about the growing shift happening in the camp and in my body. Rwju kept his distance, but whenever I looked over my shoulder, he was there. As if he was waiting for me to say something. With the Redux coming, I decided to halt any inquiries about the council or the shapeshifter until tensions eased.

I hadn't even told Silvia what Rwju had said. The mere implications were enough to be investigated by the council. But the mounting questions never ceased. As a matter of fact, they increased. Every day that I trained, I was swifter, stronger, and deadlier. I craved more power. I lusted for it, my mouth watered for it, and no matter how many training sessions I had with the Earthborns, Zef, or anyone else, it was never enough.

The unspoken conversations that refused to be addressed exhausted me. I needed to know the truth everybody was unwilling to give.

"Rwju, what happened between you and Fia?" I asked, staring at the rising sun.

Rwju squatted with a stick, drawing lines in the sand. "What do you mean?"

I clicked my teeth. "You know what I mean. What's the story between you two?"

Rwju threw the stick. He sighed as he stood. "It's not a story appropriate to tell right now," he said.

Twoa chimed in. "Ara Stone is what happened."

Oneo tagged teamed. "He came into our army like a sheep, when he really was a wolf."

Rwju rubbed the bridge of his nose. "Stop," he commanded.

"She asked, and she deserves to know..." Oneo said.

Twoa continued the sentence, "...who these people are and what damage they could do."

Oneo spoke, "It was twelve years ago. We weren't members of the Blood Elite yet, but we heard the story."

Twoa chimed, "A cautionary tale about two sworn enemies turned lovers. Rwju, a Waterborn and Ara Stone, a Fireborn."

Rwju shifted. I couldn't tell if his expression was anger or regret.

Twoa continued, "The Waterborn fell in love with the Fireborn."

Oneo stuffed his hands in his pocket. "And one day, the Fireborn was in trouble and came to his lover seeking protection and shelter. Of course, the Waterborn invited him into the inner circle of the most elite ranks, to which surprisingly..."

Twoa took over. "...the Blood Elite welcomed with open arms. This was the first time a Fireborn was ever invited into the army. As in the beginning of all budding relationships, it was good."

Oneo chimed in. "As all love stories are born."

"The Waterborn and Fireborn ate, drank, and—" Twoa danced over to Rwju like the trickster he was, in a voice loud enough for me to hear but soft enough to tease "—fucked." He laughed.

Rwju reached for the twin, but Twoa was back at his brother's side. Twoa smiled playfully at his twin as if he knew what he said annoyed him too.

Oneo rolled his eyes. "To make a long story short, it all ended in betrayal."

My eyes bounced to Twoa. "One night, the army was

called out to investigate a little town that claimed to be terrorized by the Fireborns. The general dispatched seven men. One of those men was Rangi, Fia's little brother."

"The other six were Jax, Daygun, Miyon, Fu, Rwju, and Ara Stone," Oneo said, watching Rwju. "When the troupe got there, the town was void of people. It was an ambush."

Rwju walked away from the twins telling the story.

I continued to listen as Twoa spoke. "More like a slaughter."

Oneo, his voice hushed, made me move closer to hear him. "Five out of the seven men died that day. Ara Stone, his lover, dealt the blow that left him with a scar going down his face."

We all paused, turning our heads to Rwju, who had walked several feet away.

Twoa concluded, "Ara left with the band of his people and to this day has never been seen again."

"Rwju has never been the same after that." There was a look on Oneo's face that I'd never witnessed before. It was a cross between longing and sympathy. His eyes glossed over as if tears were forming. Was he truly empathetic toward Rwju? After a couple of blinks, Oneo was himself again. Stern with a face of eternal annoyance while Twoa held an inane smirk.

What could I say? I wanted answers, but I didn't feel any better when I received them.

Oneo spoke with a low snarled tone, "I swear, if ever I come across that Fireborn, I will kill him."

He glared, not at Rwju, but more so at the thought of vengeance. Oneo didn't know the five fallen Blood Elite, but he knew Rwju and he knew Fia. And the heat pulsating off Oneo's body let me know that the requirement to kill had been met.

The very thought of spilled blood stirred the need to fight within me. I clenched my fist, my nails digging into my palms. Ashamed of my own thoughts, I snapped myself out of it as soon as a line of bodies dotted our view in the distance. Rwju quickly turned and headed back our way.

Rwju, the twins, and I waited in anticipation as the troupe of Redux made their way to us. When they arrived, I saw the sunken eyes, loose clothing, and dried dirt caked to their bodies like a second skin.

Fia, Sarue, Venus, and a few other Blood Elites came forward and filled us in on their journey. Malakey stepped out of the crowd, his shirt open, revealing years of muscle that had toiled rough terrains and the scars to show for it. On his right pec was an eight-pointed star.

"Thank you for accepting us, Warrior Princess," he bowed.

I had to force my gaze to stop looking at his chest and meet his eyes. The title he addressed me with made me arch a brow. No one, and I mean no one, had ever called me that. My chest swelled because I didn't hate it, so I didn't correct it.

"To all the Redux, we welcome you here." I paused, assessing the crowd. Their faces were plastered with fear, doubt, and worry. I examined others, and even though their outer appearance was in shambles, defiance was set in their jaws and they glared with distrust.

That's fine. Everyone was on the same page then, no matter which side.

"I know you don't want to be here, just like you know that some of us don't want you here. But I can assure you, regardless of how you feel right now, we promise to treat you with the utmost respect. I only ask that you treat us the same. We are inviting you to our house, and because of that, there will be house rules. We set these rules in place to protect everyone. Anyone that refuses to follow these rules should feel free to continue your journey in the desert. Do we all have an agreement?" I scanned the line. The Fireborns glanced at each other and then at Malakey for confirmation.

Malakey nodded and then his people followed him and did the same.

"We understand," Malakey bowed. His blonde highlighted hair fell into his face. The Fireborns behind him bowed too.

This was awkward. I cleared my throat and forced a smile.

"Alright, the first line of business. Rule number one, no weapons. Any current weapons you have will need to be surrendered to us before entering. Your weapons will be returned once it's time for you to pack up and leave camp." I turned to Rwju and the twins, signaling them forward. They snapped into action, assessing the people and breaking the line up into three sections. As the Redux were directed to their designated area for search, a man spoke out.

"Why should we trust you? What if you betray us? How can we defend ourselves? We have no gifts." I recognized the voice as Bunko from the trio of men I saw in the mountains.

"I know the world has not been kind to you. But I can promise you, you are under my care. I will not allow any harm to come to you or your people," I confirmed.

Fia spoke loudly, "Keep in mind that if any of you cause harm to any of our people, I will personally enjoy dismembering you all. Shipping your limbs piece by piece back to the hellscape you spawned from!"

I immediately wanted to slap my forehead in embarrassment, but I remained calm. The Fireborns murmured underneath their breaths. Women squeezed their children, men's faces hardened, and the wind picked up the cry of babies.

Malakey didn't flinch. "We understand fully," he said. He stood tall, his confidence soothing the crowd.

Bunko cursed under his breath. "Fuck this. We survived the fucking Fire Kingdom! We can survive the desert." Bunko looked around, but nobody met his eyes.

Minks stepped to Bunko, placing his hand on his shoulder. "Come on, Bunko, don't do this."

Bunko shrugged off Minks' hand. "We don't need them. This was a mistake."

"Then leave." Malakey didn't turn to face Bunko. "Pack your shit and leave if you don't want to be here."

Data went over to Bunko and Minks and whispered something inaudible. Whatever it was, Bunko wasn't trying to hear it.

Malakey finally turned around to address the Fireborns. "This goes for anyone. This is your chance to leave. I don't have to remind you where you come from or where you were when I finally found you. Go if you want to go," Malakey locked eyes with Bunko.

Bunko spit on the ground. "Fuck you Malakey, eksil pri." Bunko picked up a brown pack and slung it on his back. Minks and Data tried to calm him, but Bunko pushed through the line, setting off on his own.

"Anybody else?" Malakey shouted. "Now is the time." The remaining Fireborns shook their heads.

The rest of the search went smoothly as weapons were surrendered. After a thorough check, access was granted to enter the camp. The Earthborns created a tunnel in the earth wall and waited for the last person to enter so they could seal it shut.

Toward the end stood a woman with swollen feet and belly, worriedly looking at Malakey. He smiled, reassuring her she would be fine. The woman looked at me and I handed her an apple. The way her eyes rounded, I could tell she hadn't had one in a while.

"There's more behind the wall," I said.

The pregnant woman bit into the apple with one big bite.

Apple juice dripped from her bottom lip, and she happily started down the tunnel.

Malakey and I were the last ones standing on the barren side of the wall.

"Question," he said. A coy smile played on his lips. "We never got to finish what we started back at the taphouse."

I clicked my teeth. "That isn't a question, Fireborn."

"You're right," he said, jogging into the tunnel, a smile on his face.

XXX

"An enemy of my enemy is my friend."
Proverb 67:21 from the Book of Face, Mortem Era.

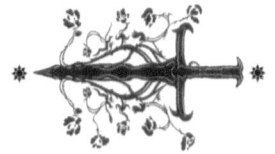

I STOOD IN THE MIDDLE OF THE NEW FIREBORN CAMP, watching as the Fireborns placed their belongings in front of the wood cabins they were to occupy. "Before you all settle in, I need to tell you rule number two," I said through a sound amplifier that carried my voice across the camp. The camp stopped shifting. Even the laughter of children faded with the footsteps. I pointed to the earth wall that separated their camp from the Blood Elite's main camp.

In between the earth wall was a pathway that guards monitored. "You are not allowed to cross into the main camp without permission. Rwju—" I pointed to him. "Oneo, Twoa, and I will be frequently visiting you. If you need anything, anything at all, let one of us know and we will get it for you. I know this journey has been a weary one. I hope you will use this time spent here to recharge yourself."

"You act as if you're our jailers!" a woman, tall, thick with short white hair the color of winter snow said.

"I assure you, prison wouldn't have the luxuries we are affording you." I sounded just like my damn Father. "In any case, I hope as we foster a relationship with one another, you won't see me, or any of my fellow soldiers, as cruel as jailers can be."

"And what about the watchers in the trees?" she said, her gaze fixed on the green pines surrounding the earth wall. I turned, scanning the trees. The leaves rustled in the wind. I squinted, readjusting my sight to see beyond the forest greens to a subtle sea of black. Their clothing appeared to be shadows in between branches.

"There should be only four guards on duty at the wall. If anyone disagrees, take it up with the general. Until then, please exit from your post and move back to your camp," I said, not waiting for a response. The branches shifted. One by one, the soldiers exited their hidden areas and made their way to their side of the camp. I faced the white-haired woman, with an eyebrow arched in a 'Are you happy now?' gesture.

She nodded.

"Okay, the remaining rules are simple. Treat the land, camp, and your neighbors with respect. Stay in your designated areas and keep clean. You can unpack now."

The white-haired woman lingered a bit, her eyes scanning her surroundings.

"That is X," Malakey said, his footsteps silent. "She is overly cautious. Before I found the group, she was the one who led them."

I turned to him. "So why did they feel as if you were better?"

He smiled. "Long story."

"Seems we will spend a lot of time together. Start now."

"Demanding, Warrior Princess."

"Demanding? More like sheer curiosity. Bunko, was that his name?"

"Yes."

"What did he mean by eksil pri?"

Malakey rubbed his fingers through his loose waves, pushing his hair from his face. "Just another derogatory term, like wessie."

"Hmmm. You would think the name-calling would exhaust your people."

"Some habits are hard to break."

I strolled, fist clenched behind my back. Malakey followed beside me. "I never got to thank you for helping with the fight. You really put your life on the line for me, and I won't easily forget that."

"Please, no need to thank me." He laughed. "Plus, you know what they say about us Fireborns. Fighting is in our blood."

I huffed. "I must be part Fireborn too. There's nothing like the rush of knuckles colliding with bone."

Malakey studied me. "You might just be," he said matter-of-factly.

I hadn't forgotten his touch or the night when I first met him. The electricity that ran through my body was the first taste of my manifestation. We fixed our sight on one another, but with so many watching, I think we both knew we had to be careful. I closed my eyes and the noise from the camp drained out. There were two steady rhythmic thumps and when I opened my eyes, I knew our heartbeats were synced.

If Malakey knew, he didn't show it. Instead, he broke the tension with a wide grin. "You know, I could tell you might be part Fireborn by the way you dealt that punch, knocking that coward clean on his ass! That was a turn-on."

He punched the air, his blue eyes flickering through long blonde lashes.

"Really?" We continued our stroll.

"Yeah, what man doesn't like a woman who can kick their ass?"

"Plenty, and they mostly live in the Earth Kingdom."

"Yeah, but aren't Earthborns pretentious know-it-alls?" Malakey paused. "Sorry, I didn't mean to overstep... hum... I just meant that they're kind of..."

"You had it right." I cut in with a grin. "Stuck up assholes. We are camping with a few. They believe women should be dainty, soft, delicate things, and that they should despise fighting of any kind. When the Earthborns came to camp, not one trainee was a woman."

"I think that's bullshit," Malakey said. "I'm glad you aren't letting that hold you back. There's something special about you. You're a fighter, a natural-born warrior, and I see you have gained some muscles since I saw you last." Malakey reached for my biceps and squeezed. "Yeah, nice. Flex for me."

I flexed.

He nodded like a Life Doctor as his fingers traced the hill of muscle I constructed.

"You're not intimidated by me, then?"

"In order for me to be intimidated by you, I must hold the belief that I'm lesser than you."

"And you, a Fireborn, don't believe you are lesser than an Earthborn Princess?"

Malakey smirked, letting go of my arm. "Roles, my warrior princess, can always be reversed."

"You believe you're on top of me?"

"Only if you want me to be."

Flashes of that night at the taphouse played behind the light of my eyes, the way he smelled, his touch, his kiss.

"You should watch your tongue, Fireborn. You don't want anyone to overhear such rebellious thoughts."

"Me, rebellious? Never."

"Bellamy!" Quande's voice called from over my shoulder. I whipped around to witness him running towards us.

"General wants to see you," he said, finally catching up. He looked from me to Malakey. "Bring him too." His held a firm grip on the hilt of the dagger.

I nodded to Malakey. "We better get going. Don't want to keep the general waiting."

Quande glared at Malakey for a long while before I broke the tension.

"This fine young gentleman is Quande, first lieutenant. He is also an overly cautious, brooding, pretty boy type."

"Trust me." Malakey rubbed the side of his healed cheek. "I will never forget him."

I grabbed Quande's arm. "Lead the way."

Quande flicked his wrist. "You first, wessie."

I kicked Quande's leg. "Malakey. His name is Malakey," I said. Quande ignored me. Malakey straightened his shoulders, rising to the full length of his height and began strutting toward the earth wall.

When Malakey was out of earshot, I nudged Quande. "Lighten up. I know this is tough for everyone, but at least show a sign of good faith by not calling them a derogatory name."

"It shouldn't be a problem. They call themselves that too. Why can't I?"

"Don't be pig shit, Quande. You know that's not okay. Let's obey our own rules and show a little respect. They're human too."

"Are they though?" Quande stopped abruptly. "I hope you don't think they're your friends now, because they're not. You need to keep that in mind. I don't give a fuck how innocent and pathetic they look. Do not drop your guard, Bee. They're nothing but trouble, all of them."

"I choose not to believe that. And I'm not dropping my guard."

"You sure? The Blood Elite trusted a Fireborn in their ranks before, and five men died because of it. I'll be damned if I let five more die on my watch." Quande took his dagger out of its case.

"May the Spirits rest. Put that away. No one is dying: not today, not tomorrow. Okay?"

"Be careful, Bee. That's all I'm saying."

"And I will. But as first lieutenant, I would think you would show diplomacy if human decency is too hard to muster."

Quande stopped, his eyebrows knitted together. "Who are you? Has Everest taken control of your body?"

I shook my head. "No, but she's not wrong."

"No, for real. Who the fuck are you right now?" Quande reached for my clothing, pulling at my shirt. "Where have you tucked Bee away? You have her face," he teased.

"Shut it." I said as I slapped his hand. "I guess I'm learning more than how to simply beat your ass out here. Is that so bad?"

"Not at all, Bee." Quande nudged me with his shoulder. "Let's see how you handle this meeting with the general. Put some of that newfound diplomacy to work. Oh, I've been meaning to tell you, I love the haircut. Come by my cabin and let me line you up, proper."

WE ENTERED THE GENERAL'S CABIN. The maps, letters, and other documents that were normally sprawled on his desk were all cleared. There was nothing out that gave away any information to wandering eyes. The general sat at the table in the middle of the room. Quande, Malakey, and I took our seats. Quande, of course, sat at the general's side. Not even seconds behind us, the cabin door opened. Zef glided in, his face serene as he held his chin high and glanced at the general.

The air became thick as two overpowering energies collided, as if causing the cabin to shrink. Quande shifted in his seat. I watched him take a gulp and swallow, his nails tapping at his dagger. Zef took the seat at the opposite end of the general. General's eyes lingered on Zef for just a breath, before he snatched them away, focusing instead on Malakey.

"How are you settling in?" the general asked, reaching for the pitcher of water which he filled a mug and passed to Malakey.

Malakey took the mug, peering inside before taking a sip. "Fine. Thank you for letting us in. On behalf of Redux, we're in your debt."

Malakey reached out his hand. General clasped his forearm and shook it.

"Let's call this even for now. Let's get down to the meat, shall we?" General reached underneath the table, revealing a single map which he spread out on the surface.

"Of course," Malakey said as he scanned the newly drawn map.

"You said there was a war coming. What war do you speak of?" The general gestured to locations on the map.

Malakey leaned in, "My inside sources state there will be attacks coming from here, here, and here." He pointed from the border of the Wind Kingdom as it curved northwards to villages lined along the coast and stopped at the Reaper Kingdom's border. "I don't know when these attacks are supposed to take place, but I know this will be the first of many attempts to expand the Fire Kingdom's military."

"Are you telling me the Fire Kingdom is planning to attack these villages and capture the people?"

"Yes, they will take the children and train them up to bolster their army. As for the parents, they plan to kill them."

"The Fire Kingdom has attempted similar attacks before, and I have led my army into battle to push them back into their lands. Never has the Fire Kingdom taken villages this close to the Reaper Kingdom."

"This time will be different, General."

"How different?"

"The Fire King, King Dricon, has developed technology that will enhance non-gifters to have temporary manifestations, so my sources say."

The general glanced at Zef, who was still as a painting, his eyes focusing only on him in return.

"And you know this for certain?" Zef asked, slightly turning his neck to Malakey.

"Yes. My sources are reliable."

"And who is your source?" Quande cut in.

Malakey looked at the map. His jaw clenched and unclenched.

"I'm unable to reveal that information at this time."

"And why not?" General asked.

"Doing so will jeopardize the Redux and myself."

General leaned into his seat and stroked his beard. "Tell

me, Fireborn. What is this technology that would give power to the powerless?"

"It's called booster. A red liquid fluid."

My mouth dropped. Was that the red tube wrapped in Mother's earthbox? If so, what was the blue liquid? Did my father already know this information, or was he trying to obtain it? And how did Malakey know what was in the earthbox? Why was he trying to steal it?

Malakey and the general locked eyes.

Quande spoke. "This booster, are we able to get our hands on some?" Quande thumbed the hilt of his dagger.

"Maybe," Malakey broke eye contact with the general to glance at Quande. "It depends on my source."

The room went silent. Quande's eyes twitched. I coughed, pulling the water container to me and pouring some into a mug

"Other than this booster, what of the rest of the plans for this coming battle?" General stroked his beard.

Malakey leaned in, his attention hovering over the map. The shimmers of blonde hair peeked through the brown every time he moved. "I cannot confirm this, but I believe King Dricon is working with someone on the inside of the Reaper Kingdom."

The general paused. "Do you understand what you are suggesting?"

Malakey straightened in his seat, "I do."

Zef spoke. "What is the basis of your accusation?"

"Enchainment," Malakey said.

Quande sucked his teeth. "You mean enslavement?"

Malakey's voice hitched. The taboo words hung in the air, making the tension so thick someone could cut it with a butter knife.

"The Fire Kingdom doesn't see it that way. They believe

321

everyone is given a choice and those that choose to work for the kingdom are there willingly."

Quande retorted, "If the choice is to die or live a life of bondage, it isn't much of a choice to choose from."

Malakey replied, "Be that as it may, the Fire Kingdom has been preparing for centuries. Experimenting on those they capture in order to create this booster. Many Fireborns truly believe they will rise again. Many of them will die to uphold that belief."

"You mean to uphold your people's beliefs?" Quande said. "Don't separate yourself from them as if you're not a part of it too."

Malakey leaned back in his chair. "If I were a part of the Fire Kingdom, I would be sitting at their table instead of yours."

Quande threw more fuel on the fire. "Who says you're still not? Maybe if you reveal your sources, then that would hush some doubt."

Malakey ran his fingers through his hair. "I can't do that."

"Then I do not believe you." Quande gripped his dagger.

Malakey chuckled, "You don't have to."

He turned to me, then to the general, "What I say is true. I don't know all the details, but I do know what King Dricon is planning. And it is something this new world has never seen."

Malakey looked directly at Quande. "You sit in your comfort thinking you're keeping the enemy at bay. They want you to believe that. They want you to think that these minor battles here and there for centuries are the best they can do. Your army has become bitter, and that bitterness will prevent them from seeing the truth right underneath their noses. Soon, the Fire Kingdom will rise again, and all gifted will be power-less to stop it."

Quande slammed his fist on the table, reaching for his

dagger. "This is blasphemous. What you're saying could have you facing the death penalty."

"For speaking a truth you don't want to hear?" Malakey let out one good laugh before his face turned vicious. "Clearly, you're past hearing. And that, Reaperborn, will be the reason for your death."

The dagger slipped from Quande's waist. Multiple emotions played across his face until he settled on one. "I won't have anything to do with them," he said, kicking his chair backwards and exiting the cabin.

Zef sat unphased, his attention on the general.

General stroked his beard as if in deep thought. If Quande took out his blade and killed Malakey where he sat, would they let it happen? Would I? All of this anger and fear, and for what? How was any of this productive?

I guzzled the mug of water, but my mouth was still dry,

"Malakey, are you able to reach out to your sources for more intel?"

He nodded.

"Good. We will need all the information we can get. What is your point of contact?"

"We have a meeting place. The next one will be this full moon."

"That's soon." I said.

"Yes."

I turned to the general. "We need to make a plan."

Zef chimed in. "Do we trust him to go alone?"

"We can send one of our own with him." the general said.

"With all due respect, General. Your men will blow my cover. The hatred they foster towards us is all too evident, I'm not willing to compromise my source."

"What about me?" I said.

The general stopped stroking his beard. "Too risky."

Being careful not to overstep, I continued. "General, the risk is greater if we sit and do nothing. Malakey is right. The men here are on edge. I volunteer for this mission and request the assistance of Sarue. I believe we're your best bet to be tasked with this mission on such short notice. The full moon is only a few days away."

General turned to Zef, who simply nodded in reassurance.

A slight smirk slid across the general's lips. "We will take your offer into consideration. Until then"—he turned to Malakey —"enjoy your stay."

His comment signaled the end of the meeting.

"Bellamy, show our guest back to his campground. Zef, you don't mind staying for a while longer?"

A twitch played at the corners of Zef's mouth. "Of course not."

I gave the general an accusatory look. To which he gathered up the maps on the table without giving me a second glance.

Malakey and I exited the cabin. The soldiers stopped and mean-mugged Malakey as if he was the Fire Spirit reborn. He remained straight, not glancing at the soldiers. He walked with a cool calmness as if reality itself bent to his will.

"How are you so...unbothered by this?"

"By what?" he said.

Another Blood Elite held a long sword in hand, pointing it at Malakey.

"Like that," I gestured to the soldier to stand down.

Malakey eyes stayed focused on the earth wall. "I wouldn't say I'm unbothered, just used to it."

"How can a person become used to being hated?"

"Well, when you're born with the cards stacked against you, you can either play your hand or fold."

"What's the point of playing a rigged game?"

"I assume you'd choose to fold?" He broke his attention and glanced over at me.

"I won't quit."

"Neither do I. We have that in common then."

We made our way to the earth wall. I signaled for the guards to let us pass. Soft crunches of leaves smashed underneath our feet as we entered the pathway.

"Malakey, do you truly believe we won't be able to stop the Fire Kingdom?"

We were halfway down the pathway when he stopped. "I believe in order to win, sometimes we must fight fire with fire."

"And the booster. How did you know what was in the earth box?"

Malakey looked back and then whispered. "Your Mother."

Act VII

XXXI

"To each one — teach one."
Proverb 6:6 from the Book of Face, Mortem Era.

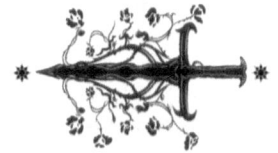

MY MOTHER. It was hard to wrap my mind around his answer. What did Mother have to do with this? I sat in the general's cabin as he nailed trade routes, financial budgets, and customs across the kingdoms into my head like packed dirt. He had decided it was time for me to learn politics and commerce. School taught me most of this stuff. At one point in his lesson, his mouth was moving, but my ears only heard static. The full moon was tomorrow, and I still needed to convince my Father to send me instead of one of his people.

"Are you paying attention, recruit?" The general's voice boomed. He gauged me with the weariness of a father, but shouted commands at me all day as if I was one of his soldiers.

Was I one of his soldiers? A true member of the Blood Elite?

He clapped his hands, popping me out of my thoughts. "Recruit. If you're here, what is the currency?" He pointed to a spot on the map on the borders of the Water Kingdom.

"The enny," I said.

"What is stronger, the enny or the coin?"

"Trick question, it's the trade. No matter if it's enny, coin, bucks, or yen, trade is triumphant."

The general studied me.

"What resources are the most valuable?"

"Food, water, steel. This is the reason why the Earth, Water, and Reaper Kingdom are also known as the big three."

"If you had to decide to feed—"

"Daddy!" I said, almost falling out of the chair. "We've been going at this for hours. Have you decided to send me?"

"Beta," He turned to the study board. "It's like asking me if you would trust an anaconda to babysit your newborn baby."

"Only, in this scenario, Malakey is a thinking, breathing, decision making human, and I'm not a newborn baby. You said you would give me more responsibility. Trust me more. Let me go. I can do this. I'll have Sarue."

The cabin door burst open. Quande stomped in. Black wisps of shadow disappeared into his hand. His face was splashes of red as he shouted, "And that's where you are wrong, Bee!" He turned to the general, "I came here to tell you: she broke her leg in training today. She won't be going anywhere for three days until the bone mends."

"Can't the Life Doctor heal her?"

"He's depleted for a while. He's currently recharging."

I sunk into my chair. This was not the news I wanted to hear.

Before Quande could further ruin my day, I answered, "I can still do this, with or without her."

Quande clicked his teeth. "I'm not allowing her to go with some Fireborn to an unsecured location."

"Allow me?"

I had to do a double-take to make sure what I heard was what I heard. "Last time I checked, you weren't the general. It's not up to you to say what I'm allowed to do." I was on my feet in a flash.

"You're not going." Quande pointed at me like I was his child.

"And you don't get to make those decisions." My voice rose an octave too high.

Quande continued speaking to the general. "The Fireborn has been in the camp for two seconds and we are trusting him with the next Earth Queen?"

The general, in all black, grinned as he stroked his beard. He raised his eyebrow at me as if he were waiting for my response.

I licked my lips. My mind raced with thoughts, sifting through information and facts I knew. "I know, General, that this might not be the best of circumstances. If under any other conditions, then I would agree with Quande. We must protect the future of the kingdom. As you have said before, if something were to happen to me, what would this mean for an entire people? I acknowledge Quande's concerns..."

Quande stood, his thumb hooked into his waistband.

I continued. "... but given the facts, the Blood Elite, as highly trained as they are, will blow this mission if sent. The Blood Elite motto is to protect at any cost, meaning it is in their nature to not sit still when someone is in need. And where we're going, it will be filled with those in need. This mission requires someone who observes. Not someone who is clearly hot-headed and thinking with nothing but their emotions."

Quande made a guttural noise, shifting on his feet.

"And since we don't have shadow assassins at our beck and call, I'll be your best shot."

Quande attempted to cut me off, but I spoke over him. "Also, Malakey risked his life to ask for our help. He wouldn't dare abandon his people or jeopardize putting them in harm's way. It is in his best interest to keep me safe because if something happens to me, then what'll happen to his people under the care of those that hate them?" I took a breath, hoping what I was saying wasn't turning into a rambling mess. "General, the Blood Elite is compromised. I'm not. This is something I can do." I marched over to the maps on the board. "I have committed these maps to memory. If something were to happen, I know how to escape to safety."

"And what about her eyes?" Quande said. "The moment they see her emerald-greens, they'll know she is Earthborn. According to what I've heard, Earthborns fetch a heavy bag of coins on the market."

"Easy. Colored lenses. I already have an extra pair."

The general stroked his beard, his eyes bouncing from me to Quande.

"Father. I mean, General. Trust me. I can do this," I pointed to my waist. "I stay strapped. Each dagger on my belt is ready for use. I have proven myself over these last four months. I'm ready." I was damn near pleading at this point.

Quande cracked his neck. "I don't agree with this plan."

"Do you not agree with the plan because you don't trust a Fireborn or because you don't trust me?" I said.

Quande opened his mouth to speak, then closed it. He paced for a moment. His hesitation made my heart skip.

"I don't trust him with you," he concluded.

"Well," I shrugged. "You might be the general's favorite, but right now, I wouldn't trust you to keep the level head you need to carry out this mission. Your emotions betray you." I strolled to my chair. "Tomorrow morning, I'll be leaving. Your approval, Quande, is not required."

Quande stopped pacing, giving one more ditch plea to the general. The general shrugged.

"I can't believe this," he said before giving up and exiting the cabin.

I released my breath, sliding down in my chair.

The general dragged a chair next to me. He flipped it, sitting on the chair backwards. "Making these types of decisions is difficult," he said.

"May I ask you a question?" I asked as I sat up straight.

"Sure."

"I notice whenever you're in a meeting, you say little. You just let things play out at the table. Why is that?"

"That's a good question, Beta." The general stroked his beard, "One thing I've learned over the years is this, when sitting at a table of power, no matter how great or small, the loudest one hears nothing while the observant one hears it all." He reached over, placing his hand gently on my shoulder. "In this line of work, Beta, it is important that you not only hear what is being said, but you also hear what is not being said." He patted me on top of my head. "Now recruit, recite every town that makes up the trade route between the Wind Kingdom and the Reaper Kingdom." I threw my head back with a sigh.

XXXII

"Observe the spark before the flame."
Proverb 69:4 from the Book of Face, Mortem Era.

THE SUN WAS SETTING in the south as I rode next to Malakey. "My mother?" Now that we were a day away from the camp, speaking freely should be safe.

"Yea?"

"Tell me what happened."

Malakey shifted on his horse. "I saw her in Reaper District Twenty."

"The outer district? What would she be doing out there? It's the slums."

Malakey flinched.

"Sorry, didn't mean it in that way."

"No, what you said is true. Slums, lowlifes, the ghettos. No one that's someone would risk going there. So, when I spotted the outcast Earth Princess. Or would it be an outcast queen?" Malakey creased his brow. "Anyway, when I saw her, I knew who she was immediately, even under the ash-dusted cloaks."

"What did you do?" Yemi neighed, and I brushed her mane.

"I followed her. That's what any good low life would do."

I clicked my teeth. "I'm not calling you a low life. Sorry if you got offended."

"I didn't."

There was a pause as the setting sun lit up the desert terrain and a soft glow. We needed to get to our location soon, or we needed to find somewhere safe to sleep for the night.

"Your Mother was visiting a doctor out there."

I immediately wanted to ask why when we had the best doctors at our beck and call. But I kept my mouth shut, waiting for him to continue.

"I hadn't seen this doctor before. In the Reaper Twenty, the most care physicians they have are high healers, but that's it. I snuck round back to see if I could get a glimpse inside. Call it a hunch." Malakey looked over, brushing his wavy blonde hair away from his face. "To my surprise, when the good old doctor pulled out tubes of booster and handed it to your Mother, I needed to know why? This stuff, as far as I knew, was strictly under wraps in the Fire Kingdom."

"What possessed you to follow my mother back to the Second District then break into our home and take it?"

Malakey went silent.

That was the last straw. I stopped Yemi.

"What?" he said, slowing down his horse.

"Listen, I'm tired of all the secrets. From my parents, from my friends, from the people that I love...." My voice trailed off. "Regardless, what I'm not going to do is continue to get cryptic messages from you or anyone else."

"I'm not being secretive."

"But you aren't forthcoming with information either, are you?"

"What do you want from me, princess?"

"I want the truth."

"Have you ever stopped for one second to think that the truth is hard to talk about?"

I searched Malakey's face. He had shaved his beard low, his hair was now neatly trimmed, and it hung loosely past his shoulders. His eyes were pinched and his mouth curled as if he just tasted something awful. I didn't know what to say, so I decided to say how I felt.

"No. I haven't. Not once." I tapped Yemi's side, motioning her forward.

"I'm sure you didn't tell your Father about our first encounter, right?"

I shook my head.

"Why not? You could have snitched on me. Your Father would probably have me tracked down and punished."

"Because, when I asked Father about what happened to the earth box, he proceeded to tell me it was being delivered to whatever lie he insisted upon. So, I decided then not to say anything." I pulled my coat from my pack and slipped it on. Now that the sun was gone, the cold was taking its place.

"Do you regret lying to your parents?"

"I do not."

"Do you think they regret lying to you?"

"Not sure," I sighed.

"I don't want to regret lying to you, Bellamy. Is it okay if I call you by your first name?"

I nodded.

Malakey grunted. He kept his face forward, aimed at the horizon. "I needed it."

My neck snapped to him in confusion.

He continued. "Like I said, booster is scarce. The red liquid is the ignitor, whereas the blue liquid is the extinguisher. Basically, once you get high, if you have nothing to bring you down, your body will burn from the inside out."

I was stunned. "Why would you put yourself through that?"

Malakey hung his head, his hand gripping the reins. "My fath—I mean, the man who raised me, made me take it since birth. My body built somewhat of an addiction to it. If I don't consume it, my body is covered in sores and blisters. I begin to deteriorate. It's like damned if I do and damned if I don't." Malakey lifted a necklace from his shirt. Inside the clear necklace were red and blue liquids separated in their own chambers. He tucked the necklace back into his shirt. "That night, when we met, I need you to know it was never my intention to fight you. My plan was to get in and get out. But, when we connected in the alley way, that raw power exchanged between the both of us, I knew without a doubt we were connected."

I thought about that night in the alley and in the taphouse. How raw electricity shot through me at his touch. How I craved more of him. "You said we were Intertwined. How do you know for sure?"

"You don't feel it?" Malakey stopped and dismounted. He held onto Yemi's reins, asking me to dismount too. I did, standing in front of him, his body meeting mine. He threaded his fingers through mine and I could instantly feel the buzz of electricity surging to my palm. He closed his eyes.

The power within me swelled. Not the one to give, but the one to take, to control, to own. He drew me in close. So close that the warmth of his body made me want to peel off my coat.

"I can take it," he said, staring down at me with beautiful dark blue eyes. "Do it."

I licked my lips, wanting to taste him, to drain him. My mind drifted as the voice stirred in my head. *Do it,* it said.

I yanked my hand from his, backing away. I was losing control. *The shift.* I saw it that time. I felt it course through me in a wave of deep desire and passion.

Malakey didn't move. When I looked up at him, his aura was bursting in a bright red-orange. I peeled my eyes away, shutting them tight until my heart stopped pounding and my skin quit tingling.

"It's okay, Bellamy. You don't have to hold back from me." I heard his feet shift in the sand. I drew back to the other side of Yemi, putting as much distance between us as possible.

"We can't be Intertwined. It's impossible," I said, trying to convince myself more than him.

"I wish we weren't, Bellamy. I really wish we weren't."

I lifted my head over Yemi to Malakey who hoisted himself back onto his horse.

"I won't lie to you. I'm not good, princess. And keeping your distance is probably the right move." Malakey tapped the horse and continued down the path.

Hours had passed. Malakey nor I had spoken a word. I was processing, as if processing was talking myself out of stopping these horses and calling to his aura that glowed the same red-orange as mine. I could still feel the pressure of his essence caressing me like an erotic massage.

"We are almost there." Malakey's voice was low and gruff. I

wasn't sure if he was mad that we didn't go further or something else. His jaw was set tight, and the reins were clenched in
his fist as if he was fighting something in himself too.

"Tell me about this town we are going to. Squablers Quarrel, right? I heard it is true to its name."

Malakey nodded. "It's not that bad once you get used to it."
He didn't look at me.

"How did this place start?" I glanced at him. Yemi drifted
closer to his horse and the surge of power between us was raw.
Malakey stiffened, his back straight, his skin blotchy red. I
moved Yemi about three arm lengths away. And the power
subsided a little bit.

Malakey spoke through gritted teeth. I could tell he *was*
fighting, maybe more than I was, to curb his desires. He spoke
as if he was losing breath. "It first started off as a pocket of land
between the Wind Kingdom and the Reaper Kingdom. When
the land was divided, neither kingdom thought it was worth
fighting for. So, that little pocket became freeman's land.
Which is a fancy way to say '*without government*'. It's kind of a
haven for a few."

Yemi neighed. I stroked the back of her mane, calming her.

Malakey continued, "Before it was established into its own
town, many people would go here to air out their grievances."

"You mean to fight?"

"Yes, exactly. Whenever someone had issues, they wanted
to settle outside of court, they would come to this pocket of land
to settle it on their own terms."

I adjusted myself in the saddle. "And they wouldn't get in
trouble?"

"Nope. How could they? Would it be a Reaper Kingdom's
problem or a Wind Kingdom's problem?"

"I would think it would be whatever the citizens are," I
suggested.

"But what if the two parties involved are Reaperborn and Windborn? As a matter of fact, what if they were Moonborn and Waterborn? Whose problem would it be, then? What if the person had renounced their kingdom? Then what?"

I glanced off. The stars made their appearance. I watched them as I pondered my response.

"As time went by," Malakey continued. "This town developed into what it is today, Squablers Quarrel. A place with their own set of rules and with their own forms of justice."

"Is it dangerous?"

"It could be. When I first left the Fire Kingdom, Squablers Quarrel became my home."

"How old were you?"

"Fourteen."

"How did you survive on your own?"

"It was hard at first. A lot of stealing, fighting, and trouble with the law. When I came to S.Q., I thought I would have to do ruthless things to put food in my belly. I remember my first night as if it were yesterday." Malakey went quiet. A few minutes passed, and he didn't speak.

I leaned in and gestured for him to talk. When he remained silent, I blurted out, "What's next? A flashback? How was your first night?" Many questions tumbled from my mouth.

Malakey's smile grew. The tension between us broke.

"What the hell are you smiling about? Are you going to finish the story or what?"

"Maybe later," he teased.

"What! You can't do that. You just can't start and stop a story."

"Why not?"

"Because!"

"Because what?"

"Just because that's not how storytelling works. I need to

know what happened on your first day. I'm going to be thinking about it the entire ride now!"

Yemi drifted nearer to Malakey. This time, there was no tension. Just ease. Malakey tossed his hair out of his face. The hair only stayed briefly before it fell back into place.

"You're criminal!" I grunted.

"Then punish me."

"Maybe I should."

"Well, we are in the perfect place. Warrior Princess, welcome to Squablers Quarrel."

Darkness flooded the sky. Torches of fire lit one by one, winding upwards around a massive sand mountain.

"Bellamy," Malakey stopped the horses and dismounted.

I followed his lead.

"Before we enter, we need to put in your lenses."

"Of course," I said, reaching into my bag. The desert was too dry to ride a full day with colored lenses. Even with a tunic that covered my nose and mouth, they were raw from the sand. I could only imagine how my eyes would be feeling right now if I had traveled the entire day with a foreign object lodged in them. Malakey took the lens box from my hand, assessing them.

"Come here," he said, stepping closer. The height difference wasn't a massive one, but I couldn't help but take notice of how his lips sat right at my forehead. He opened the box, carefully taking out one lens at a time and placing them into my eyes. They burned, and I had to fight the urge not to rub them immediately. Malakey tilted my chin up, took the liquid drops, and squeezed a little drizzle into each eye. "How is that?"

His breath smelled like the strawberries we ate on the journey here.

I blinked a few times before answering. "It feels fine. How do I look?" I lowered my chin.

Malakey studied me, his pupils bouncing from left to right.

341

"Different. As if I was first gazing upon a beautiful forest of lush trees, only to look up and behold the glory of a night sky."

He licked his full pink lips. I fought the urge to touch him. I quickly moved away before the energy thickened around us. Malakey shut the lens box and handed it to me. "Here."

I grabbed it, and our fingers brushed against each other. A jolt of electricity sparked at the touch.

"Ouch," I pulled my hand back.

"Careful," he said, handing me the reins of my horse. "We might not be able to hold back next time."

SQUABLERS QUARREL WAS A SIGHT OF PURE ORGANIZED CHAOS. What I assumed would be a tough and rough place was more like an opi's drug illusion. Our black clothing, made to cross the heavy sands, was bland compared to the local fashions. One man had on seven colorful thick jackets, a miniskirt, and bright orange boots with six-inch heels. Another person had what seemed to be a reaper dress with a puffy long black skirt, but it had bottle tops and crushed cans glued on the tail. For a hat, this person wore a purple umbrella. They wore sunglasses behind their head and were adorned with bulky silver chains around their neck and waist. Every person we passed was full of color, exaggerated fashions, or both.

The colorful buildings matched the people. I didn't realize I had stopped until Malakey threaded his arm into mine.

"I bet your mouth is wide open underneath that tunic," he whispered into my ear.

It was. I slammed my mouth shut. It fell back open at a person who stood six-foot-six with orange hair that grazed the ground. They had muscles on top of muscles on top of muscles, which had more muscles all fitted into a hot pink crop top and shorts.

"You grew up here?" I said as Malakey pulled me down the streets.

"Yep," Malakey said proudly. "Turns out, the most ruthless and lawless place on earth is one of the most creative and peaceful places a person can go."

"Why didn't you bring your people here instead?" I scanned Malakey's side profile. His lips tightened. He swallowed hard, and his Adam's apple bobbed.

"It's too dangerous for them."

We hooked a hard right down a sandy alleyway, arriving at a building with a sign that read "Bucket Inn." The place was lively. The inside was just as colorful as the outside. Glasses of beer clacked against each other. Shouting and screaming ensued when a topless bartees slid down a pole. I searched the back of the bar and lo and behold, a large sign read:

"Rules: Don't break our shit and don't touch our bartees!"

Even in the land of the lawless, the bartees was still the safest occupation.

Malakey led me to an attendee. "We need two beds, please."

The attendee, with large circle lollipops in her ponytails, didn't look up as she wrote in a book. "We out of rooms," she said, blowing a large pink gum bubble.

"Do you know if anyone has any beds open?"

"The other inns have shut down. We all ya got. Unless you go to the nearest kingdom." She flipped a page, popping her gum bubble.

"We can't go to another kingdom."

"Then I guess your best choice is a night on the street." The attendee finally looked up. Her eyes widened. "Key?" she exclaimed.

Malakey cocked his head. "Boom?"

"Key!" she screamed, leaping from her chair. She jumped across the counter, landing in between Malakey and I. She threw her arms around his neck and gave him the sloppiest kiss on the lips. "I didn't think I would ever see you again!"

Malakey chuckled nervously. "It's nice to see you too, but I'm just passing through." Malakey pointed his chin at me.

The attendee gave me a once-over. Her mouth twisted in a snarl as she smacked her gum. "Who's she?"

"Someone important to me."

"Like a lover or something?"

I waved my hands, about to say "No."

Malakey cut me off. "Yes. She is my lover, and we are passing through."

The attendee turned her back to me to face Malakey. "She doesn't look like much."

Excuse the fuck out of me. I don't know who this Boom thinks she is, but I could yank every piece of dirty, limp, sticky, candy filled hair from her lightbulb-shaped head.

Malakey must have read the thought on my face because he separated Boom from me by sliding her out of my grasp.

"Please, Boom. We need a room. Any room. I can pay you for your trouble."

Boom played with her split ends, twirling them around in her fingers. "Let me see what I can do," she said, slapping her palm on Malakey's chest. "Still hard as a rock." She slipped that same hand down his chest, below his waist, and grabbed between his legs.

Malakey coughed. His face went red, eyes squinted. He avoided eye contact with me as he faced the counter again.

Boom hopped over the counter. "Let's see, the only room

we got is a room a man died in four months ago. Nobody really wants it and the keepers stopped cleaning it a couple of weeks ago." Boom looked up from her book. "Ghost and all."

She turned her attention to the page. "I mean, if it's only for one night, I can let you have it. How does that sound?"

I leaned into Malakey. "Are you sure there isn't another place we can go?"

"A high breed? What's wrong wit' what we got?"

"High breed?" I mimicked. Was it *that* obvious?

Malakey interrupted. "We will take it. Thank you, Boom," he said, grabbing her hand, forcing Boom's attention to himself.

Boom batted her eyelashes, "You can have anything you want while you're here, Key." She leaned in, revealing the top of her breast. "Including me." She winked.

She was fucking lucky Malakey wasn't my lover because if he was, I would have jumped across the counter to beat her ass.

Boom reached under the counter and grabbed a key. "Here you go, sugar," she said, her gum tossing from one side of her cheek to the other.

Malakey took the key. "Thank you."

We climbed an old, janky stairwell until we found the correct hallway. Our room was at the end of the hall. A faint smell of piss and strong alcohol coated the carpets. With each step, the aroma smacked me in the nose. We finally arrived at our room and heard an enormous crash. We swiveled our heads behind us. A bottle broke in the room across from ours and a man called out, "Hit me harder, bitch!" Then another glass broke, then a thud.

"If we make it out of here, I'm going to kill you," I said.

"Understandable," Malakey replied. He slid the key into the lock and turned it.

When we entered, there was a single full-sized bed that had more dirt and dust on it than there was paint on the walls.

Malakey's blue eyes locked on my fake-colored ones. He dropped the bags on the floor and took off to the bed. I ran behind him, pulling at his tunic. Malakey threw himself on top of the bed, which released a balloon of dust.

Through coughs, Malakey said, "I call the bed."

"What!" I fanned the dust away. "You can't do that."

"And why not?" He lay on his side, propping his head up with his fist.

"Because..." I searched for the right words. "Because I'm a..."

"Woman?" Malakey finished my statement. "Don't you think that's sexist?"

"I wasn't going to say that. I was going to say it's because I'm a princess."

"So, you think the bed should be yours because you are nobility?"

"Royalty," I corrected him.

"You're pulling rank on me?"

"I'm just saying, do you not have one chivalrous bone in your body?"

Malakey glanced at the hardwood floor. Jagged wood chunks stuck up while nails bent at crooked angles throughout the room's layout. Malakey laid back on the bed, fluffing the pillow to his liking. "Not one." He crossed his legs and then closed his eyes as if he were falling asleep.

"Fucking Fireborn," I mumbled under my breath.

"At your service, princess," he retorted.

"I'm not the only one you're servicing." I crossed my arms. "I wonder what Boom might do if I tell her you're up here, all alone," I mocked.

Malakey slapped his forehead as he laggardly slid off the bed.

XXXIII

"Past ghosts linger in present dreams."
Proverb 73:47 from the Book of Face, Mortem Era.

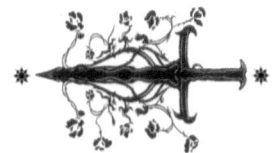

THE NIGHT RAPIDLY FADED as I lay in bed, tossing and turning. Malakey, on a pile of blankets and pillows, was so still that I thought he might be comfortable, better yet peaceful. The light of the moon shone through the window, resting on his face as his chest rose and fell. I almost felt bad making him give up the bed. Maybe we could have shared it? No. I couldn't have him sleep next to me. I didn't trust myself. Plus, this was the first night sleeping without the little snores of Silvia to lull me to sleep. My arm felt abandoned, and I didn't like that.

I turned my back to Malakey, facing the exit door. The cheers from the bar drifted up and down the halls, slipping into our room from the large crack underneath the door.

The plan was to sleep, rise early, meet his contact, and immediately return to the camp. The plan was simple; no way I could possibly fuck it up. Yet, my legs were restless, my arms itched like tiny ants were biting into them, and I could not shut my thoughts down for the life of me. Especially the ones of my mother.

Glancing over my shoulder, Malakey was as he was for the last three hours. According to my calculations, it was roughly 2200 hours. Hollering and shouts crescendoed from downstairs. I could tell the party was getting started. What would be the harm in peeking?

I promised myself I would only stay for an hour and be back in bed before Malakey even knew I was missing. I slid out of bed. The metal creaked loudly. Why was it that whenever I needed to be in stealth mode, that was when everything I touched became a siren?

I reached for my boots, coat, and checked the little dusty side table mirror for my reflection. My lenses were in. Dark brown irises gave my entire face a new construction. I wondered how my life would be if I had been born this way instead of with emerald-green eyes. The emerald hue had shaped my identity. They created paths for me, and allowed the door to open for my eventual rule. All because the Earth Spirit thought I was worthy enough to bear their resemblance and carry their gifts. Gifts that I'm not fully sure were even the Earth Spirit's. Even if they were, then why the emerald greens? What was the point of giving me these eyes?

I glanced over at Malakey for the last time. He hadn't

moved. How in the universe could he sleep so soundly on a pile of pillows and blankets on a jagged floor? I couldn't even manage to sleep on a worn-out mattress and dusty pillows.

Tiptoeing out of the room, I shut the rusty door with a click.

When I was finally outside, I let out a breath of relief.

Downstairs, the bar was packed like sardines. Barteeses held platters of beer above their heads as they navigated through the thick crowd. I jumped out of the way as a shirtless man with large breasts fell backwards onto the sticky floor. A bartees stepped over him as they sashayed to the nearest table. Strong ale filled the air and someone on the far end of the bar yelled, "Drisunki!"

Oh hell, nah. Not getting caught up in that again.

A song played as I moved to the exit and out into a smoke-filled night.

I learned quickly that this ungoverned town didn't have electricity connected throughout. Each building had several torches attached. I rubbed my eyes as the smoke pulled the moisture from them. I yanked the excess fabric of my tunic over my nose and mouth and drifted deeper into Squablers Quarrel.

I didn't know what to expect. During the day, it was a color-ful, extravagant explosion of an artist's brain matter, but at night the streets were eerie. I looked over my shoulder several times because I couldn't shake the feeling that someone was watching me right outside of my peripheral. I knew I should turn back if I didn't feel safe. That was what a smart person would have done. But my cockiness and the fact that I truly believed I could beat anybody's ass kept my feet moving forward.

A radiant blue-white light caught my attention. The closer I got, the beckoning strings of a violin sucked me in.

I cut through the last of the bushes until my boot touched

soft grass. No, not just grass, prairie grass and wildflowers. It was a tiny meadow surrounding a statue made of sand. The statue was crafted in the figure of a woman's top half and a man's bottom. Their arms extended toward the sky. At this angle, it appeared as if their index finger had poked the moon. The sand shifted continuously, giving the illusion the statue was running toward something I could not see. Something just out of their grasp, something so close if they would just extend their fingers just a bit more, all things would be theirs.

At this moment, tears escaped. My eyeballs burned, and I dug my palm into them until more tears wet my cheek.

You are a disappointment, Mother snarled.

A joke, something to just get out of your system, Father confirmed.

Pathetic, Everest spat.

I would never be good enough, never strong or smart enough.

You can't survive a day in court without me. I will be a better queen than you, Everest's voice echoed.

Everything I wanted was just out of my grasp. I could almost taste it. Going on missions under the command of the greatest General known throughout the kingdoms, adorning the Blood Elite's battle black, and having an army at my ready. Being the pride of my father and the glory of my mother. The protector of my sister and fighter alongside my fellow comrades.

I traced the fingertip of the sand statue as it poked the side of the moon.

I want my family to embrace me as I am. How I've always been. Deep down, I want to be good enough for them. To finally earn their approval. Their trust. But how can I begin to even think about trust when our relationship is a lie?

Secrets create distance. Even if I *could* pretend, how many times would I have to split myself into variations of who they want me to be before I became nothing but fallen sand?

"High breed," a familiar voice came from behind me. The moment I heard the baby squeak, I knew exactly who it was. I wiped my eyes again, covering my nose and mouth with my tunic.

"What you doin' out here by yourself? You ain't lost, is ya?" Boom said, kicking her way through the grass.

I moved toward the lit areas of the meadow. "No. Malakey is around here somewhere," I said.

"Oh, really? That's funny. I just seen him ask for ya." She pointed behind her.

"Yeah, we got split up. I got distracted by this art piece."

"Art piece? Is that what you high breeds call pure talent?"

I shrugged, her voice working my last nerve. "What else would you call it?"

Boom was a few feet away. "This"—she opened her arms wide—"this is creation!"

"Isn't that what all art is?" I said, monotone.

"No, no way. Art, as you high breeds call it, are lines on a piece of paper. It's a stale gallery of pompous pricks who go around with their fancy suits and fancy dresses..." Boom hopped on one leg and then the other, mimicking some sort of dance, I assumed. "... and eat your fancy cheese and drink your fancy wine."

"I get it," I interrupted.

"See, no, you don't." She yanked a lollipop from her hair and pointed at me. "Creation is living, moving, and changing. Art is stale and stagnant; it is what everyone else says it is..." She turned back to the sand statue, "Creation just is."

I rolled my eyes. "Sure. I guess that makes a ton of sense."

Boom abruptly turned around, her red lollipop tucked into the side of her cheek. "Are you one of them?"

"Pardon me?"

She smacked her lips. "Don't play stupid, high breed. Are you what Key is?"

"A Fireborn?"

"Do you think I'm stupid or something?" She popped her lollipop out of her mouth. "Can you do what Key can do?"

I tilted my head, utterly lost in this conversation. Recognition of my confusion dawned on her.

"You don't know, do you?" She skipped, popping her lollipop back into her mouth. She laughed a high-pitched squeal that made my head ache. "How can you be his lover when you don't even know what you're fucking?" She twirled.

"By the Spirits!" I turned to walk down the path I came from. There was rustling within the meadow as if Boom was running through it. I was right. The next second, Boom twisted me around by my shoulders, almost knocking me on my ass. If it weren't for my training, I would have lost my balance. Clearly, she was a lot stronger than her small frame let on.

"Fire fucker," she giggled. "Fire fucker, fire fucker, you better be careful, or you might get burned," she teased, raising up her shirt. Underneath her top was a patch of warped skin like shadows of a third-degree burn. She rolled her shirt down, popping her lollipop into her mouth. Her head cock to the side. She leaned into me, and I leaned backwards. Before I knew it, her hand was on my face. No, in one of my eyes. I grabbed her by her wrist and held it steady. My dark brown contact lodged between her fingernails.

"What the fuck!" I screamed.

"Key has been hiding the goods," she laughed, harder this time.

"Momma will be so pleased."

"Get the fuck away from me!" I let go of her wrist.

"Why are you mad at me? I just wanted to see which eye was true."

It hit me. One of my contacts must have fallen out earlier. "Fuck!"

Boom sang, "Fuck, fuck, fuck, Earthborn. High Earthborn at that! No wonder Key hasn't told you who he is"—she popped out the lollipop from her mouth—"or what he can do." She licked the lolly seductively.

"I know one thing, you put your hands on me again and I'll make sure you choke on that fucking sucker," I warned before stomping away.

Her squeal-like laugh echoed behind me.

XXXIV

"In the beginning there was a BOOM, and all creation came
to be."
Proverb 84:12 from the Book of Face, Mortem Era.

I ENTERED OUR ROOM, slamming the door behind me.
Malakey sat on the bed, his boots planted into the sheets.

"Eww," I said, marching over, knocking his feet off
the bed.

"Where were you?" he asked without glancing my way.

I responded, "Do you have no home training? Who puts
their whole disgusting shoe on someone's bed?"

"Where were you?" Malakey repeated. His voice was etched with annoyance, his face cast in shadow.

"I went walking."

"Walking where?"

"Just around. No big deal."

"You went by yourself."

"So, are you my keeper?"

Malakey bit his lower lip. "I'm exactly that. What if something would've happened to you?"

"You said this place was the most peaceful place in all the Seven Kingdoms."

"For me. Not for you."

"That makes little sense. But I'm starting to think that nothing makes sense here."

"Don't go out again without me."

"And who's going to stop me if I do?"

Malakey took his time easing from the bed, his hair pooling into his face. He threaded his fingers through the strands, pushing the blonde waves back. One boot at a time inched my way until he was in front of me. The only light trickling in was from the single open window on the far side wall. Malakey's blue eyes almost glowed in the darkness.

I stood my ground, pointing my chin in defiance. I couldn't see the smoke coming out of his nose, but I could feel the heat radiating from his body. My heart thudded against my chest. Could I take him if I needed to? How strong was he? What was he? The question popped into my mind as Boom's voice played in my head. *Who was he?*

Malakey glared at me without blinking. His jaw was all angles and sharp lines. He grabbed my chin. The old wood floor creaked under our weight.

"Where are your lenses?"

I cringed, shutting my eyes tight. "I lost them," I whispered.

"You what?"

"I can explain."

Malakey let go of my chin, sucking in his breath.

I rapidly tried to repeat tonight's events to him, but everything came out in jumbles. "I was walking and there was this art or creation sand piece thing and then Boom had the nerve to put her hands on me."

Malakey froze. "Boom was there?"

"Yeah."

"And she saw your natural eyes?"

"Yeah, are you not listening to me? She snatched out one of my lenses!"

Malakey swiftly grabbed our bags and stuffed our belongings in them.

"I almost beat her ass, I swear. I don't know how you slept with her."

Malakey glared as he threw my bag to me. I caught it, my mind registering that he was packing.

"What are you doing?"

"We're leaving."

"What? Where? Why?"

"I don't have time for your questions." Malakey ran to the open window, peering down. He pulled his pack onto his back. "Let's go!"

"I don't understand what's happening. Just tell me what you're thinking. What about the plan?"

"You fucked the plan up the moment you didn't keep your ass in this room."

I blinked rapidly, clutching my chest. "Who are you talking to?"

"Bellamy." Malakey took his time. One of his legs rested outside of the window. "I told you, high Earthborns are a rare

commodity. I need you to trust that I'm trying to keep us safe."
Malakey held out his hand. "Please, can we go?"

Damn, here I am again, fucking shit up.

I tossed my pack on my back and jogged to the window.

Malakey grabbed my hand, and I snatched it away, the electricity buzzing. "I got it," I said, scanning the ground below us.

Malakey went first. He shimmied to the right until he caught hold of a silver pipe that ran from the roof to the ground. He signaled me to come, and I carefully followed his movements. I slid down the silver pipe until my feet safely hit the ground.

"This way," Malakey said, pointing away from the entrance of the Bucket Inn. We rounded a dank alley with no torches for light or guidance. When we arrived at the end of the road, several men stood in a straight line. They were dressed in loud, colorful crop tops. Some wore shorts so short that they should have been unders. One man had heels on, carrying a spiked bat. The commonality was they were all shredded to the Spirits.

Boom squeezed her way through two men three times her size. "Going somewhere?" she said, twirling her fingers into her raggedy blonde ends.

I glanced at Malakey's profile. His jaw clenched tightly. "Listen, we're just passing through. Just let us pass into the night."

"Hmmm..." Boom huffed, pressing a finger to her thin lips. "You can go, Key." Boom reached out her hand. The man with heels holding the spiked bat placed the weapon in her palm. "But she"—she pointed the bat at me— "has to stay."

"You know I can't do that, Boom."

"And why not?" She pouted.

I could see several thoughts running across his face. "Boom, darling," Malakey said, his voice in a smooth bass tone. He slid his fingers through his hair, tossing it to one side. "What is it you desire? I can get it for you."

Boom hopped on one leg, squealing to the top of her lungs, "Really, really, really? Anything I want, I get?"

"Just say the word," Malakey confirmed.

Boom's facial features went from dewy-eyed schoolgirl to vicious villain. "I want the emerald-green eyes scooped out of that bitch's head!"

The men behind her took her signal and advanced.

A smile curled onto my face.

Malakey cracked his neck. "You're not supposed to be enjoying this," he said, bouncing on his toes.

I stretched, rotating my hips and shoulders. "Neither should you."

Malakey smirked, showing a little twinkle in his eye.

"This time," I said, "I'll take the big one."

Malakey bowed to me. "As you wish, princess."

He grabbed my hand. A surge of electricity from his touch re-energized me like my very own personal energy drink. Bloodlust stirred in me. Malakey grinned wickedly, and I took off running.

Bone on bone, skulls crushing against skulls. I was in my element. A Waterborn whipped a stream of rushing water toward me at the same time as a Reaperborn hurled his shadow. Light on my toes, I backflipped out of the way, allowing the two elements to collide. When I landed, my practiced fingers went to my waist, yanking out my daggers. I let them soar through the air as if I was wind-gifted. The daggers connected to both men's shoulders. They fell backwards with a loud thud, screaming like pathetic little children.

I caught a glimpse of candy-coated hair attached to a snarling Boom.

Yea, bitch. If you come for me, you better come correct. I smiled.

The rush of the fight fueled the blood coursing through my veins. I locked eyes on my next target. The only one standing between me and this fucking rot-mouth candy licker. I braced myself. He was the biggest one of them all.

Remember your training, Bellamy.

Rule One: Commit. There's no going back, only forward.

Rule Two: Assess. Don't zero in so much that I become blind to the surroundings.

Rule Three: Attack. I am here to dominate, kill, and destroy. I am of reaper blood, and this fight will not end until he begs for mercy.

The big fella pounded his fist into his palm and then vanished. I blinked several times before I felt a rush of wind barreling at my neck. I rolled out of the way as the big fella's fist crashed into the earth, shattering the ground.

By the Spirits, why didn't they make me Reaperborn? I would be faster, deadlier, and if they blessed me with blood gifts like my father, I would have stopped him in his tracks. My skin was on fire. I fought the urge not to rip off my clothes. *Pay attention! Focus!*

I stood, regaining my balance.

"You didn't think it would be that easy, Earthborn?" Big fella said, picking the dirt from his nails.

"No, I was hoping for a challenge." I surveyed the area. Malakey was taking on three smaller men at the same time. Blood dripped from his nose. The back of his tunic was split in half. Boom sat crossed-legged, sucking on a lollipop, completely in her own world as bodies flew past her.

"I ask that you surrender now. All we want are your eyes. We will let you go free."

My eyes aligned with big fella. "So basically, you'll let me walk out of here minus my eyes?"

"And minus your tongue; your mouth is so pretty. It's hard not to resist taking a little trophy of my own." He held out his pinky. "I promise. You'll be fine, eventually."

"And what if I win? Can I carve out your dick and balls?" Big fella gasped, placing both his hands on top of his private area.

"How dare you assume I have dick and balls!" He glowered.

"Sorry. I like pussy too; either is fine, really."

Big fella giggled. "Oh, I like you. Too bad after tonight, I'll never have the pleasure of hearing your lovely voice again."

"Damn, and I really thought we were bonding," I said, racking my brains for a way out.

Big fella vanished. I didn't wait for his attack. I kept moving sporadically. Zigzagging and curving in and out of the alleyway as wind-gifted punches barely missed me. He was toying with me. And that realization pissed me off the most.

My back hit a wall right as his fist punched through the building, sending me flying before I smacked into the ground.

I tumbled until arms wrapped across my waist, stopping me in my tracks. I looked up through a haze-filled vision to see Malakey bruised, bloodied, and panting hard over me.

"I thought you had the biggest one," he wheezed.

I grunted, bringing myself to a sitting position. "I tried. You're it." I patted him on the shoulders.

"Oh, no, no." He patted me back. "Finish what you started!" Malakey, and I helped each other to our feet.

Boom's squeaky voice cut in as her heels clicked against the broken concrete. "What's the matter? Are you giving up?"

The alleyway was full of unsettled dust. Every man was out except one. For two supposedly ungifted, that was a damn good job. But even I could admit, big fella's manifestation was far from depleted.

Malakey glanced over at me, and I shook my head.

Last rule: Every soldier must know when their final fight will be.

This was not my last fight. I refused to die in a dank-ass alley while Boom gloated.

"Until we get those pretty eyes, you won't be leaving here." Boom shrugged. "The price of one pair of those could set my family up for the next five years. You do understand, right?" She tilted her head with a grin.

Big fella punched his fist in his palm. The other men were stirring. *Whatever we do, we need to do it now.*

"I completely understand. And if I were you," I said, slowly backing away. "I would do the same thing. But here's the thing: I need my eyes. For at least the next... ummm..." I tripped over a large piece of overturned land; Malakey grabbed hold of me. "...for the next sixty years. How about we meet around that time, and I will gladly give you my eyes. How does that sound?"

Boom pulled out a lollipop from her hair, pondering my offer. She unwrapped it, popping the lolly into her mouth. She tossed the wrapper paper into the wind. "That does sound like an amazing offer, but I'm broke now, so... I'll have to pass." She snapped her fingers.

Malakey and I turned to run. Big fella was in front of us before we could get five steps in. He grabbed me by my neck, his grip crushing my windpipe.

"Can I take her tongue first?" he shouted to Boom.

"Sure, why not? We really should take all the high breed's ability to speak."

The most vicious smile unfurled on the big fella's face.

I kicked and clawed as he lifted me off my feet. His arms were longer than my arms, so I couldn't connect with his face. I reached to my side, plucking one blade from my waist and stabbing it into his forearm. Big fella didn't flinch. He just grinned a toothy, animalistic grin. Malakey acted but was quickly batted away.

I was losing consciousness fast. My body limp in his hand. I didn't even feel the itching on my skin. Everything was fading. Big fella reached into my mouth and with a last-ditch effort, I bit down like a starving beast. Blood squirted into the back of my throat. He loosened his grip from around my neck. I sucked in a few breaths.

Big fella dropped me to the ground as he pulled his fingers close to his chest.

"She gave me an owie!" He wagged his bloody nails at Boom.

"Well, be more careful. Hurry it up. I'm growing bored," she said.

Big fella reached for me again. I was far too tired to move. Every bone in my body was turning into liquid. In my peripheral, a blazing blue flame glowed brightly. I covered my eyes to block out the light. Boom shouted with joy behind me. Big fella's mouth widened into a rounded "O."

Malakey gathered up a ball of blue flames into the palm of his hand, then launched it full force at big fella. About the time big fella realized he was quick enough to dodge it, it was too late. The flame set him ablaze. He went screaming backwards, patting himself, dropping into the dirt, and rolling on the ground, but the flames refused to dissipate.

Malakey rushed to my side, picking me up by the waist and throwing my arm over his shoulder. Boom clapped her hands, bouncing with pure glee.

"Fire Fucker!" Boom screamed. "Fire fucker, fire fucker, fire fucker!" She chanted as we limped our way out of the alley.

XXXV

"Truth has many enemies..."
Proverb 92:05 from the Book of Face, Mortem Era.

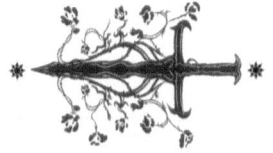

WE DIDN'T STOP RUNNING. Even when we grabbed our horses and took off into the night. We didn't turn back. Malakey doubled over, holding his stomach. My lower back was in so much pain that I thought one more twist and it would snap. A safe distance away, Malakey dismounted. His feet hit the sand and he crouched, letting out a low growl. I unhorsed, stabilizing myself on a sore ankle.

"Are you alright?" I limped over to him.

"No."

"How can I help you?"

Malakey straightened up, his face filled with sweat. His iris was the same blue blaze of flames.

"You can't," he said, directing his horse forward.

I grabbed Yemi's reins, but I did not follow him.

A few feet away, he paused. His shoulders stiffened, and then he doubled over to his knees. My mouth was dry from any spit I could muster, but I gulped hard, not sure what should come next or if I should follow.

"What are you?" I said hoarsely.

Malakey rose to his feet, his horse neighed as he leaned on the beast. "We don't have time for this. We need to get to safety."

"I'm not going anywhere until you talk."

Malakey turned to face me. Each step he took appeared painful. "I'll tell you everything you need to know once we get off the road. There..." he winced, almost collapsing to the ground. He swung his arm over the horse to hold himself straight. "There's a crevice not too far from here, carved into the sand mountain. There's a Life Doctor that can help us heal." His voice was breathy and detached.

I walked backwards. "That won't do. I will not go with you until I hear some explanations."

Malakey cursed. "I don't have much time, Bellamy. I can..." He screamed. The arm wrapped around the horse smoked. The horse revved back on its hind legs before speeding down the beaten path. Malakey fell to the ground.

Against my better judgment, I took off to him. He was lying on his side. I kneeled and rolled him over. The moment my hand touched his shoulder, there was a slight sting at my fingertips. I examined the padding as burned flesh quickly healed over.

"I need the extinguisher," he said through spats of coughs. "I cannot hold it much longer."

"Hold what? I don't understand. How do I help you, Malakey? Just tell me what to do."

"Get...away...from me." He pushed himself from the ground, pulling off his tunic. He yanked off his pants, stumbling toward the mountain area. Steam rose from his body like a boiling pot of water on the stove.

I dashed behind him, grabbing his shoulder once again. Blue flame burst onto the surface of his skin. I yanked my hand back as I watched the flame dance up my arm, setting my tunic on fire. I quickly snatched my tunic off, stomping it onto the ground. But the flames would not be tamed. It was like the blue blaze had a mind of its own as it leaped to my pants, crawling up my leg and onto my bare belly. I was prepared to burst out into screams just like the cries of big fella, but this fire did not burn. I placed my hand at my navel and the flame tucked itself into the palm of my hand. The heat felt like a heavily padded blanket on a winter's day.

The flame was peaceful to the touch. I closed my eyes and let it consume me, like the heat of a crackling campfire. Of warm soup and freshly baked bread. Of laughs and stories about a world lost to the gluttony of time. When I opened my eyes, the previously blue flames were now a blazing red.

Steps came from my left, and there was Malakey, a walking blue flame. He wrapped his arm around my waist and my arms went around his neck. And it felt right, safe, and so deliciously warm. Malakey's hands roamed over my body as my hands searched his face. Our flames intermingled and swirled, both our gazes examining the other. And I knew without a shadow of a doubt that we were Intertwined.

I drew him closer. I needed to consume his flame. Every muscle was urging me to suck every bit of his fire. I grabbed the back of his neck, pulling his head to me until his lips met mine. I kissed him deeply, the voice in my head screaming, *More! More! More!*

Malakey grabbed me by my wrist, allowing me to drain him. Our lips separated as I searched his aura, looking for the last of his power to drain from his body. There wasn't one. All of him was never-ending.

"I can take it," Malakey said, falling to his knees. "Consume." He held his head back, exposing his neck. My fire grew to a fury of lust and dominance. I wanted nothing more than this.

I fed until Malakey's arm went limp, the last bit of blue flame leaving his lips. He was weak and completely naked. He gawked up at me, my red flames flickering in his pupils.

He smiled up at me as if I were his God.

Worship me. A voice foreign to my own commanded me. *Worship me!*

The voice grew louder, the flames brighter. I stumbled backwards, clasping my palms over my ears. "No!" I screamed. "Get out of my head."

I chose you, the voice said. *You are my vessel. It is time for you to rise!*

I wrapped my arms around myself.

A loud noise rang out as Malakey screamed. Three men appeared; they were the same ones we fought in the alley. They must have followed us here. They were holding what looked like.... guns. Smoke whiffed from the nostril of the barrel. They took aim at me and my anger roared. My flames licked passed Malakey like fiery phoenixes. Two men dropped their weapons and took off running. One quickly tried to load his gun to take aim. But my flames were far too great. The fiery birds devoured the man holding the gun and the two men running. The three men turned to ash exactly where they stood, their screams feeding the increasing hunger inside me.

Malakey crawled over to me but collapsed before he could make it. I dug deep within myself, the shock of what I just did hammered into my heart.

They deserved it. The voice said. *Embrace who you are.*

This wasn't me. This was not what I wanted.

Stop fighting me.

"No!" I screamed. The fire rapidly died down around me. My foot stepped into a pool of blood leaking from Malakey's back.

See what they have done? Death was more mercy than they deserved.

I ignored the raging voice in my head. I yanked a tunic from the ground and placed the shirt over the hole in his back to stop the blood.

Let him die. I'll find you another, the voice laughed.

I threw the tunic away, placing my hand on top of the wound. "Please, please," I cried. My hands were soaked in his blood. The voice howled. The image of the red woman grew so great that it smashed against my temples. I calmed myself until I found another voice, a more familiar voice, one that drowned out the red woman.

> *Mother and daughter*
> *Wives and sons*
> *We find our way back home.*
> *No matter the fight*
> *No matter the trouble*
> *We find our way back home.*

I allowed Father's voice to calm the wave of panic in my soul and the flames slid down my body until they were isolated into my palms. Malakey's wound shifted as my heat poured into him. His aura faintly intertwined with mine until my flames faded completely away. There was something being rejected from inside of him, and I called it to the surface. A steel bullet revealed itself. As soon as I removed it from Malakey's wound, my heat sealed his wound shut. Malakey shifted just a little before completely going still. I checked his pulse. He was breathing.

No, the voice said. *You belong to me and only me.*

"I belong to no one," I hissed.

We will see about that. The voice vanished, leaving behind ringing in my ears.

I sat on my legs, checking Malakey's pulse again. I could not move my fingers from his wrist because I was too scared that the moment I let go, he would too. I wanted to cave on top of him, and allow sleep to take me as deep and as far away as it could, but I knew I had to push.

I gathered Malakey's pants and forced them onto him. His tunic became mine. It covered me right above my thighs. My horse was the only one I could find. I placed the guns into the self-installed storage on Yemi's side. Then I clicked the button for Yemi's chrome saddle to split in two. With the last bit of strength I had, I hoisted Malakey's limp body onto the back of Yemi, yanking myself up afterwards.

"There's a crevice not too far from here, carved into the sand mountain. There's a Life Doctor that can help us heal."

I kicked the side of the horse and held Malakey's body tight.

Too tired to think, to stop and to process any of tonight's events, I kept moving. Allowing the galloping of horse's hoofs to guide me forward.

XXXVI

"... and fear has many friends."
Proverb 92:05 from the Book of Face, Mortem Era.

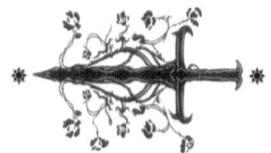

I HAD TO DOUBLE BACK a few times before I spotted the narrow opening of the sand mountain. Sliding off the horse, I wrapped Malakey's body securely with the reins. Yemi protested, but I rubbed her nose. Eventually, she calmed down, and we began our journey through the crack. Nothing but sand and jagged rocks crunched underneath my bare feet. At one point, I fell, and every ounce of energy drained from me. I was slipping, eyes closing, body numb, but Yemi nudged my head gently, blowing heated breaths on my cheek.

In the crevice, a gust of wind slapped me across the face as if someone poured cold water on me. I stumbled back to my feet, noticing blood at my heels.

Just a bit more, one foot before the other. We are almost there.

We walked for an hour or so. I didn't know. Time was an illusion to the tired mind. In the distance, a twinkle of starlight highlighted an exit.

I said a silent prayer. "Thank the Spirits."

We broke through the end to be greeted by a shimmering white glow. There was a meadow filled with prairie grass and wildflowers. A tiny home sat in the mist, along with sand figurines and statues. There was a double helix made of shifting sand and colorful petals that stood the length of the home. If this wasn't the Life Doctor's place, then it could have fooled me twice.

I led Yemi to the meadow. A man carrying an axe came from the side of the house. Another man swung the front door open with a crochet needle and a ball of yarn trailing him. A woman with skin as deep as the rare flower hellebore slipped out the door behind him.

I was too tired to fight or even defend. I dropped to my knees.

Tears poured from a well in me that I thought had long since run dry.

"Please," I said as the meadow spun. "Help us." I tumbled over, the wildflowers stretching their stems as if to say, "Rest now, sweet child."

Feet thudded against the soft grass, and my vision faded to black.

. . .

I AWOKE FROM a dreamless sleep with the sun spilling onto my face. The smell of maple syrup and honey biscuits filled the room, and my stomach rumbled. For a moment, I thought I was home. I turned to the right to catch a glimpse of a sleeping Silvia, only to be reminded I was not home and this was not my bed.

The walls were a burnt orange. Mother would have had a heart attack at the sight of this color. I sat up, and my shoulder stung. My right arm was wrapped in bandages. I threw the heavy blankets to the side, revealing dried blood on the cotton sheets.

I checked my bandages. Someone had freshly wrapped them all. I eased off the bed, the tip of my toes tapping the cold tile floor. The aroma of honey biscuits signaling to come and find them.

I stood, the aches in my back and hip surprisingly not as bothersome. I was dressed in a sheer silk gown that reached the top of my knees. I took a few steps until walking didn't feel foreign. Stabilized, I drifted into the hallway. As I searched, there were paintings on the wall depicting three bodies always intertwined. Rather, it was kissing, playing, or simply three abstract lines. I deduced that the three people I saw earlier had to be a trio.

Hushed voices and clanging dishes drifted from a room up ahead. I came to an entrance where the smell of bacon was the strongest and peered in. Two men and one beautifully dark-skinned woman sat around a table filled with biscuits, butter, syrup, pancakes, bacon, and eggs. I think my stomach dropped to my ass because I could not hold back any longer. I ran my tongue over cracked lips.

"Hey, Bellamy, right?" the woman said, her voice a lovely soprano. "I'm Doctor Evna and these are my partners, Julian and Rico." The men waved, soft smiles stretched across their handsome faces.

"Hi," I replied, using the wall to keep me from passing out. My eyes kept falling back to the food on the table. If I could just get a bite, I could think straight, reassess, butter and biscuits and bacon.

By the Spirits, focus for once in your life!

"Thank you for taking us in and fixing me." I raised my bandaged arm.

"Oh, it's no problem! We are here to help," Julian said, with deep dark hair and wide brown eyes attached to a round face and round body.

"Where is the man I came with? I want to know if he is okay."

"Key?" Rico laughed. "The moment he got a couple of hours of sleep, he was up and out the door."

"He left me!" I immediately cursed myself for not being strong enough to keep my eyes on him.

Rico waved my worries away. "Oh, he'll be back. Don't worry. He said he needed to go get someone."

I rested my head against the door frame and breathed out.

"Are you hungry, sweety?" Doctor Evna asked. I nodded, hoping to keep salivating to the bare minimum.

Julian pulled out a chair. "Come and sit."

I damn near started running. It took everything I had to look dignified. I sat in a wooden chair. Julian pushed me up to the edge. Rico grabbed a plate and piled food on top. Doctor Evna poured a cup of water and sat it in front of me.

"Thank you," I said.

"I know this isn't a palace, but I hope you enjoy our service all the same." Julian bowed.

I cringed. "Malakey told you who I was?"

"Yes, but don't worry. We aren't totally freaking out or

anything. This isn't our first time having royalty in our home, but an Earth Princess! Eating our food, sleeping in our bed. Oh, my goodness"—Julian clasped his red cheeks— "we should have put you in our bed. It's the biggest bed. We weren't thinking. Is this kitchen big enough for you? I told Rico we needed a bigger kitchen last year and did he listen?" Julian continued to ramble until Doctor Evna took his hand and kissed him on his forehead.

"What my darling partner is trying to say is... we welcome you here. Stay as long as you need." She winked.

Rico picked up a biscuit. At his belt, there was a black axe carved with an eight-pointed star on the handle. He bit into the biscuit. "Honestly, I was working on expanding the kitchen, but I had to finish the statue in town. But don't worry, Princess Bellamy, the next time you visit, I'll at least have..." Rico turned behind him. He scratched his head, then his butt. "Well," he said, shrugging. "We will all be surprised, won't we?" He chuckled.

Julian clicked his tongue. Doctor Evna laughed. My stomach was touching my spine.

"Is it okay if..." I pointed at the plate of food.

They all spoke, their voices drowning each other out. "Yes, of course. Go ahead. By all means, princess."

I raised the biscuit to my mouth to take a tiny taste, just like my mother and years of etiquette training tried to beat into me. Unfortunately, I failed those classes and ignored my mother in the process. Instead, I inhaled the entire thing. Then I ate another and another, the soft butter crisp dough melting into my mouth. I wasn't even swallowing. When I reached for a knife to slather an entire stick of butter on several rolls, the trio had stopped talking and was staring directly at me. Julian's wide eyes bounced from the bread to my mouth rapidly.

"Sorry," I said, with a tongue wrapped in food.

Rico and Julian instantly looked off as if they were admiring the pots on the wall.

"Your axe. Does that eight-pointed star mean something?" I stuffed another bacon into my mouth.

Rico unsheathed the axe and held it in his hand. It was beautiful. The blade had to be made of the most precious steel, the handle obsidian.

"It's a reminder that one day, the Spirits will remember us." He tossed the axe back and forth before returning it to his sheath.

A door opened and slammed in an adjacent room.

Doctor Evna clapped her hands and inhaled deeply. "Sounds like Key has returned."

MALAKEY ENTERED THE KITCHEN. My pulse quickened. The rush of yesterday's events, the fighting, the running, the fire. I didn't want to think about it. Acknowledgment made it real, made it tangible. And I wasn't ready to accept the impossible as my truth. I didn't want to talk about hard things, so when Malakey's gaze met mine, I bounced my eyes to the hooded figure next to him.

Doctor Evna threw her arms around the person. "It is so good to see you, Candia."

Candia dropped her hood and out spilled long blonde hair attached to a face very similar to Malakey's. They could have been twins; hard angular chins, high cheekbones, and large blue eyes.

Candia kissed the cheek of Doctor Evna.

"It has been too long," she said.

"How was your journey?" Julian grabbed another plate off the top shelf while Rico pulled an empty seat out across from me.

Candia untied her cloak. "The journey is getting more diffi-cult. With all the uproar from my kingdom, I cannot sneak away like I used to."

Doctor Evna took her coat and guided Candia to the table.

Rico tapped the back of the chair as Candia took her seat, "And how is King Dricon?" he asked, giving her a hug.

"Dangerous, per usual. Father is beside himself."

Malakey slid a bag from his shoulder and leaned against the wall behind Candia. Judging by the dust and rips of the bag, this was all he could recover from last night's spar.

"Your Father has always been dangerous. Nothing new, it seems," Malakey said, setting the bag at his feet.

Julian placed a loaded plate in front of Candia and greeted her before taking a seat next to me.

Candia scanned the food before her eyes rested on me. "Every year his son goes missing, he loses a bit more of his mind..." she said. "...Are you the one?" she asked, scanning my features. Her face was mostly neutral except for the growing crease in between her eyebrows.

Are you the one? The one of what? That question was loaded. I was a lot of things, but *the one?* I gulped down the food I was slowly chewing. Taking a napkin, I dabbed the corners of my mouth. "I'm Bellamy, and you are?"

"I am Candia Dricon."

The Princess of the Fire Kingdom?

Candia pointed to Malakey. "Key is my baby brother. Did he not tell you?" She tilted her head in curiosity or challenge. I could not tell.

Malakey, the prince? I attempted to suppress my anger by separating a biscuit into two, piling bacon and eggs in the middle and smashing the ingredients together to make a biscuit sandwich. "Apparently, your baby brother thinks I'm too incompetent to be privy to important information."

Malakey pushed himself off the wall. "I don't think that. I was going to tell you."

I brought the biscuit sandwich to my mouth before slamming it down onto my plate.

"Was that before or after you told everyone my identity, possibly blowing our mission?"

"Are you serious?" He ran his fingers through his hair.

"Deadly so" I bit into my sandwich.

"If I remember correctly, princess. You're the one who blew our mission. No assistance was necessary on my part."

Julian shifted in his seat beside me. Rico stopped pacing, and Doctor Evna pulled a chair out from the table that seemed to fill the awkward silence with a screech.

The food turned into ash on my tongue. "Yea, well, if you didn't sleep with a crazy woman, then maybe she wouldn't have reacted the way she did."

Malakey gave a low chuckle. "I've never and would never sleep with her. I-I can't help the fact that she's—" He paused, his mouth fumbling for the right word. "Obsessed."

"With you?" I scoffed.

Malakey looked taken aback. "What does that mean?"

Doctor Evna chimed in but was cut off by Julian. "Now dear," he whispered. "Let's just see where this goes. Let the lovers work it out a bit."

"We aren't lovers," Malakey and I said in unison.

"I have a girlfriend," I said as I pushed my plate away.

Malakey squinted his eyes. "You do? For how long?"

"I mean, we aren't official or anything. We haven't sorted out the details." I tucked my hair behind my ear. All eyes were on me.

Rico spoke. "Three lovers are always nice. It works for us."

Julian hushed him, "Quiet!"

Rico shrugged, "It's true, but to each their own."

I interrupted, "Okay, enough. We have more important matters at hand. Our love life is not one of them. Candia, do you have any information for us?"

She sat with a foxlike smirk on her lips.

Malakey pulled out a chair and plopped into it. He stared daggers at the side of my face. I ignored him, hyper-focusing on his older sister, *the Fire Princess.*

"Well," she said, crossing her legs, "What do you want to know? I'm an open book."

"Let's start with how the Fire Kingdom plans to gift the ungifted."

Rico lifted empty plates from the table. "Well, I'm gonna clean a bit. Julian, darling, your help, please." He dramatically raised his eyebrows.

Julian waved him off. "I'm okay. We are getting to the good parts." Julian placed his elbows on the table, ready for Candia's answer. Doctor Evna placed a gentle hand on Julian's shoulders, then began clearing the table, signaling him to help.

"Fine." Julian smacked his lips. "I never get to listen to the juicy stuff."

The trio cleaned at the opposite end of the kitchen, leaving Candia, Malakey, and me sitting at the table.

"To answer your question Bellamy, our Father—"

Malakey interrupted. "He's not my father," he hissed.

Candia straightened in her chair, flipping her blonde hair. "Fine, my father has developed a drug that can enhance powers that someone already has or give temporary power to those who aren't gifted. It's called a booster." Candia looked at Malakey.

"Is that why you can wield fire, Malakey?" I asked.

"Yes. As I told you before, the man who raised me forced me to take it ever since I was young. Fire is the power that calls to me. It is also our natural manifestation as Dricons."

I nodded, going over the notes in my head. "So, what I'm getting at here is, the red liquid is booster and the blue liquid?"

"It's called, extinguisher. It helps put out the gifts if your body begins to self-destruct."

"Great. A drug that's extremely unstable."

"But effective," Candia chimed in.

"Yesterday," I said, picking at my wrapped arm. "We were confronted by three men that looked to be holding...guns. I've never seen one before up close, but the way it shot. It sounded like the stories in our history books."

"Oh my." Candia clasped her jaw.

I couldn't tell if she was being sarcastic or if this was a real reaction.

"Yea, they shot Malakey."

Her fox face fell immediately.

"You didn't tell me this." She searched Malakey's face as he looked away.

"Apparently withholding information is what he does best," I mumbled.

"Key!" Candia grabbed his hand.

"I'm fine." But when he said that, he stared at me, not Candia.

Candia withdrew her hand from Malakey and crossed her legs.

"Is this weapon a part of the Fire Kingdom or is this something else the kingdoms should be worried about?"

"It's hard to say," Candia shrugged. "I'm not allowed to go in the rooms where he does his"—she glanced at Malakey—"experiments. And plays with his toys."

"Does a device that can kill someone that easily seem like a toy to you? Your brother could have died."

Candia's foot shook. "Well, he didn't. He's tough."

Yeah. I don't like her. And the anger building in the pit of my stomach also gave me confirmation.

"Does life mean so little to you?"

"I don't know. What happened to the three men?" Candia leaned in, ready for my answer. An answer I wasn't ready to face.

Malakey cleared his throat. "On the way here, my sister told me about the king's decree." Malakey nodded for Candia to continue.

"Oh, yes. He has sent a call to round up anyone from ages zero to thirteen for enchainment."

"You mean enslaved?"

"Tomato, tomato."

That was it.

"How can you casually sit here and think that what your Father is doing is okay?"

"I don't think it's okay." The crease in between her eyebrows grew deeper. "He's my father and I am his eldest daughter. We all have our roles to play, and I'm playing mine."

"And if the role requires the people you love to be enslaved and experimented on? Then what?"

Candia's nose flared, and her eyes darted to Malakey, to which he did not return a look.

"Why are you here, Candia?"

She flipped her hair. "Be specific, princess," her tone layered in annoyance.

A subtle itch pricked my forearm.

"If your loyalty is to your Father, then what is your reason for coming here? To give information about the war? To agree to help?"

She pushed her chair back, standing. "I just want to clarify that I wasn't aware that you would be here. Why did I come? I came for my brother, the only other blood relative I have. The reason I'm giving any information is so that Malakey will be safe and know how to direct my lost people. Not yours."

Malakey reached for her hand, but she slipped away. "Candia, sit," he pleaded.

Candia shook her head. "No, because it has to be said." She looked to the trio who had stopped in the middle of drying dishes and then turned back to me. "For centuries, your people have held our past over our heads, refusing to let it go. Punishing us for the maleficence of our forefathers. Is it not enough that the Spirits cursed us? Do you people ever stop and think about the harm your persistent judgements do to us? How we feel? How we are hunted every day by ghosts of the before?" She pointed to everyone in the room. Her voice cracked as tears bloomed.

Tiny prickles underneath my skin spread to my entire left side. "I'm going to say this once, and I will not say it again. You need to lower your tone when speaking to me..."

Candia scoffed.

".... second," I said, "I'm holding you accountable for what you are taking part in now. Your role in this matter. You play it instead of dismantling it entirely. You refused to use your role to put an end to those who wish to continue a legacy filled with bloody battlefields and chains. The past will be held over your head because people like you haven't learned from it. And now, there's another war coming and all you can offer is tears." I sneered. "And you have the nerve to sit across from me like you're the fucking victim. Like you're not sitting at the table with your Father as he plans to bring destruction upon us all. Snatching babies from their cradles and forcing them into a world where they are nothing but science experiments?" My entire body itched intensely as I spoke through clenched teeth. "Dry your fucking tears. They're not welcome here."

Candia turned to Malakey, who did not return her gaze.

She then held out her arms to Rico, who was at her side comforting her. I rolled my eyes, trying my best not to flip the table over.

"There, there." Rico patted her on her back. "I think we just need to breathe and restart."

I threw up my hands. "No, we need information. That's the point of us coming here." I stood up, one arm leaning on the table. "Candia, we know your Father is planning to attack local villages. When will these attacks occur?"

Through sobs, she said, "I don't know."

"Then why is your Father choosing to attack those particular villages? Is it something he's looking for? The Fire Kingdom has never attacked this close to the Reaper Kingdom."

"I don't know." She rubbed her palm into her eyes.

"Then what do you know?" Candia was silent.

My skin was burning. I dug my nails into my forearm.

Julian pulled out a bundle of sage and a matchbox. "I think we need to clear the energy in here."

I didn't want to clear the energy. I didn't want to reset. I didn't want to calm down, take a breath, or pause. I wanted answers, and I wanted them this instant.

Malakey whispered, "Princess, you're sweating."

"I don't give a damn. Talk to your sister. Get the answers we need."

"I'm not sure if she knows anything else."

A cackle bubbled in my throat. "Then what was the point of all of this? We almost got our asses handed to us, and for what?"

Julian lit a match. The fire flickered away. He lit the match again. The fire flicked away before the sage could take it.

Candia pulled away from Rico, drying her eyes. "You won't be able to stop it, so it doesn't matter, anyway. My father has teamed together with nobility in four of your kingdoms."

"What do you mean by that? Which kingdoms, what nobility?" I tugged at my right arm, which was bound, tension built underneath the bandages.

"Wind, Water, Life, and Reaper. Father has sleepers planted and they are simply waiting for his word to move forward."

"That's impossible. There were decrees sent to all the kingdoms wanting to ban the ungifted from their borders. Requesting the Counsel of Amalgamation to push laws passed, make it illegal to even be with a Fireborn. There's no way the nobles would be caught in between that." I ripped the bandages on my arm, shredding them with my nails.

Candia smirked. "I'm not worried. Neither is my father. The Fire Kingdom might not have a seat at the table, but you better believe there are those who will stand in our place."

Julian shouted with glee. "Finally, a flame!" He went to light the sage.

"You're lying." The itch shot through my entire body.

"You wish I was, but I'm not."

"The names?"

"I don't know."

"You don't know, or you don't want to know?"

Candia leaned in, saying each word with emphasis, "I... don't...know."

I slammed my hand on the table. A pressure was building in my head. All I wanted to do was let it out. Release myself from what seemed like... chains wrapped around my skin. I don't know why I said it or what compelled me, but before Julian shook the match dead, I called to the flame, and it answered.

All it took was a spark and fire burned through the bandages wrapped around my arms. Malakey leaped from his chair, his seat flying backwards. Red flames danced in Candia's wide blue eyes as her mouth dropped open.

I would get the information I wanted by any means necessary. With one hand, I tossed the table to the wall. Malakey jumped in between me and his sister.

"Bellamy!" he shouted, but all I saw was his mouth moving. The voice in my head was loud and clear.

Take power. Burn them all.

Malakey reached within his shirt, pulling out a red vial, and gulping it down. Rico pulled Candia and Julian out of the kitchen through another room. Ignoring Malakey, I swiveled past him, chasing the answers I knew lay within her.

"If she isn't willing to give me the answers, then I will make her."

Yes, that's it. Take it, the voice encouraged. *Take it all.*

Blue fire blazed, cutting me off from my target.

"Move," I commanded.

"No!" Malakey lunged at me, our flames tangled in a dance of fury, burning everything we touched. I called to his flames, but they resisted, which made me blaze higher.

"This isn't you!" he said, pinning me to the melting tile floor.

"This is me. This has always been me!" Before my orange flames could consume his blue ones, a cold burst of white liquid rained on top of us, burning my nose and mouth. Malakey and I coughed, rolling away from each other as our flames dissipated immediately. I wiped the freezing cold suds out of my eye to look up and see Doctor Evna, Julian, and Rico each holding a container. They sprayed until the last lick of flames died. My skin was cool to the touch. Itch gone, anger vanished, clothes completely burned away.

A quarter of the kitchen was blackened wood. The rest was filled with fading smoke.

Julian sighed. "Well, we said we wanted a bigger kitchen." He handed his container over to Rico.

"No, you wanted a larger kitchen. I was just fine." Rico followed him.

Malakey pulled me into his arms. "It's okay. We're okay."

No, no, it wasn't okay. None of this was okay. My teeth clattered together, my limbs shook. *I could trick myself into believing that yesterday was a dream. That I didn't burst into flames, that I didn't crave the power and control that it offered me, that the voice that slithered its way into my head wasn't my own.*

"What was this? What am I?" Fear was running along my spine. I pushed Malakey off me, but he wouldn't budge. He gripped tighter, wrapping his leg around my own.

"You're not alone. You're safe," he chanted, and I wasn't sure if it was more for himself or me.

"I can't go home like this. I can't face my family like this," I whimpered. Shame piling onto the fear. "I'm Earthborn. This cannot be. Tell me this isn't happening."

Doctor Evna squatted, her gentle touch easing my sobs. Malakey held me until I wasn't sure how to separate my body from his.

"You're safe," he repeated. "You're safe."

For now. A sinister voice faded into the darkest regions of my mind.

XXXVII

"If fire destroys, who destroys fire?"
Proverb 37:37 from the Book of Face, Mortem Era.

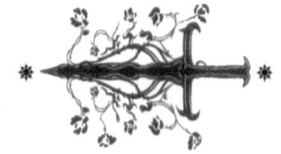

I WAS LOSING CONTROL. Fresh out of the shower, I could smell the fading scent of smoke in my hair. It was like it was a part of me now. White ink spilled on black paper. No matter how much I tried, I could never get rid of this stain. I avoided the mirror. How could I look at myself? How could I look at my father? My sister, mother, the people I love? Was it not enough for me to be different?

And now I'm some fire-flaming inhuman? Every time I

think I've figured it out, new information punches me in the gut. What do I do now?

A gentle knock at the bathroom door. "Princess Bellamy? This is Doctor Evna. I need to show you something whenever you're done."

"Okay, just give me a moment." I reached for the oversized black t-shirt and tan cargo pants off the sink. Sliding into them, I noticed the waist was loose, requiring a belt. Even my physical body was changing before my eyes. When I finally had the courage to glance at myself in the mirror, I did not know the reflection staring back. A once round face now had sunken cheeks. Hair that used to cascade down my back fell short at my shoulders, the sides completely shaved with a design that was supposed to mimic the flowing wave of water, but now those waves appeared to be lines of flames. My emerald green eyes...

What was I supposed to say? Something I despised since birth, the weight of a kingdom on my shoulders, a destiny carved out before I could consent, a plan to redeem a rule that I didn't ask for. Emerald green eyes, a linkage passed down from my mother and her mother, and her mother to the beginning of all Earthborns. A bloodline that I'd taken for granted only to find out I was the mistake, the error, the disappointment.

Other than my eyes, every other feature on my face was my father's. His nose, his mouth, even the slight cut in my eyebrows, he had the same. My hair and my rich brown skin were the exact shade of his, and his father, and his father before him.

If my mother was earth, and my father was reaper, then what was I? And why did it seem like I was the last to know?

I blinked back the mounting frustration at the slight itch that crept just beneath the surface of my skin. Slipping on black socks and boots, I opened the bathroom door and exited.

The answers to my questions were what I desired. Doctor Evna and Malakey were the start.

RICH EARTH TONES and a bright color pop of turquoise made up the walls of Doctor Evna's lab. Malakey was sitting on a table, his shirt removed. Scars on top of lean muscles were hooked to wires attached to monitors. The eight-pointed star over his heart was burned into his skin, not like a tattoo. Doctor Evna stood at Malakey's side withdrawing blood. A necklace hung loosely around his neck. The red and blue chambers were no bigger than fingers.

I'd seen Malakey naked twice, and yet as my eyes trailed the length of his torso, it was as if I was seeing him for the first time. A smile lit Malakey's face as Doctor Evna laughed. Candia stood next to him, a crease between her eyebrows, crow's feet at the corner of her eyes. When she caught a glimpse of me, those lips became thin pink lines.

I wasn't happy to see her either. Clearly, we had our differences, but on the account that I nearly burned her to a crisp, maybe I owed her an apology. The memory of the Reaper Queen's advice flickered into my thoughts. *"The first thing I learned as a young queen was once you make a decision, stick to it, and never apologize."* It must've been an uncursed day in the Fire Kingdom if the queen's advice was what I sought as justification for choosing to say nothing.

Candia flipped her hair as I crossed the room, then refocused her attention on something else that wasn't me.

The feeling is mutual, baby girl.

Malakey and Doctor Evna's chuckles silenced as I stood before them.

"Didn't mean to interrupt. I can come back." I pointed to the door behind me.

Doctor Evna rested vials of blood on a silver tray. "No, this is good timing. I need samples from you."

"Samples?"

"Yes, blood samples, skin samples, etc. I want to run some tests." I looked at Malakey, who gave me a nod.

I rubbed the back of my neck. "What would this prove?" I cursed myself silently because I knew what it would prove. That I really was an anomaly. That somehow, my parents were right to lock me away behind palace walls. That I was a danger to myself, and to others.

"It'll prove that you're Erba," Malakey popped the round monitors from his chest.

"Yea, right. Like the Fire Spirit would choose her." Candia rolled her eyes.

Malakey grabbed his shirt and hopped off the table.

Evna patted the surface, gesturing for me to sit. "There's only one way to find out."

Malakey and I switched places. I sat on the table. Malakey stood in front of me, sizing me up, analyzing me, his gaze lingering too long and too close. Blond lashes over blue eyes made me pull at my already baggy t-shirt. I shifted in my seat.

"What is Erba?" I asked, tying my best to hyper-focus on Doctor Evna and not the way Malakey licked his lips and leaned backwards on the object behind him.

Candia cut in. "It means a lot of things."

She began listing. "The select, the inherited, the grass that grows across the field."

"And what does that have to do with me?"

Doctor Evna prepped a new needle. "Initially, Erba is an old prophecy that was foretold about five hundred years ago. That the Fire Spirit would rise again through the Inherited One, or as we call it, Erba, the selected one."

Malakey spoke in a low tenor. "The prophecy said that The

Erba would be born to restore what was taken from us and what was lost. Fire will rule in glory."

"When you say 'us,' you mean Fireborns?"

Malakey nodded.

The doctor cleaned a section of my arm. "Might feel a little pinch..." she said, sticking in the needle.

I flinched slightly.

The doctor continued. "The Erba is supposed to ascend when blood meets the earth during a great war amongst the kingdoms."

"There have been wars and battles throughout the centuries. I don't understand why now and why me."

Candia huffed. "Exactly. Neither do I. Why not our bloodline, someone who is actually Fireborn?"

The doctor hooked sticky round monitors to my chest

"Because," she said, "gifts only work if the user already can manifest. The Fire Spirit cannot choose a body that is anti-manifestation. It simply wouldn't work."

Candia flipped her hair, her blonde ends almost catching me in the face. "Then what was the point of Malakey going through what he had to go through if the Fire Spirit was just going to choose someone that wasn't us? We are her patrons. It isn't fair. And giving the gift to an Earthborn of all people! That's a slap in all of our faces."

I rolled my entire neck because my eyes were not enough. "You have a problem with Earthborns now?"

"I have a problem with all of your kind." She leered at me, and I held her gaze with the same level of intensity.

A beep sounded steadily, then spiked quickly. My heartbeat pounded. The doctor tapped me on the shoulder. "Let's try not to burn down another room, please."

Malakey tugged at his sister's clothing, an action that made him seem so boyish. "Sister, give us the room."

"Why do *I* have to leave?" She snatched her gaze from me.

"Because you're not the one being tested. Unless you want the good doctor to poke you."

Candia gathered herself. "Ugh, no." She grabbed her items. "Don't waste your time too much, little brother. Remember, I leave in the morning." She nudged him with her shoulder.

I took a deep breath, holding every curse word I knew on my tongue out of respect for the doctor.

"Forgive her, princess. She means well," Malakey said.

"I can tell by your grin that even you don't believe that," I said.

The doctor stepped away, sorting the vials of blood on a nearby counter. She picked up a pad and pen, then pushed a chair next to me and took a seat.

"I need to confirm some information, princess."

"Just Bellamy," I corrected.

"Oh, my apologies." The doctor glanced at Malakey and then back to her notes. "Let's start with, when did you begin using extinguisher?"

"I've never used it. I didn't know what it was until recently." The doctor shared a glance with Malakey.

"What?" I bucked.

Malakey straightened. "We have to show you something," he said, walking over to a counter where a burned bag lay on top. Beside it was my skin cream. He strolled back to us, handing it to me. I took it. The container was damn near in perfect condition. I unscrewed the lid, the cream untouched.

"So?" I shrugged.

Doctor Evna flipped through her notes, her leg slightly tapping.

"Bellamy, how long have you been using this cream?"

I thought for a moment, "Since eleven, maybe twelve. I itched so badly that I scratched my arms until they bled. My mother took me somewhere to get tested and a few weeks later, it was determined I had a skin condition. I was told that it was worse when I was under extreme stress or when my blood pressure spiked and that I should rub this cream on daily in order to reduce the symptoms. I've been using it ever since."

The doctor scribbled in her notebook. "Do you remember the doctor you saw? Name, location, anything?"

"No. Why?"

"How do you receive your cream, Bellamy?"

"My mother. She monitors my usage. When it's getting low or if I'm itching more than usual, she shows up with a fresh container."

Doctor Evna leaned into her chair, clicking her pen. "Bellamy..."

"What? Just tell me, what's all this about?"

"The cream you're holding is not skin cream. I know this because I created it. Extinguishers can come in three different ways: powder, liquid..." She pointed to Malakey.

He raised his necklace from underneath his shirt and pointed to the blue tube.

The doctor continued, "... and this cream-like version. It works by the recipient rubbing it into their skin and allowing it to seep into your pores. Basically, your body absorbs this, causing any fire manifestations to well... extinguish."

The room went silent. But my breathing echoed in my ears. My grip tightened around the cream container as I peered into it and saw Mother. Memories of her rushing me into the night to see a doctor I didn't know. The way she looked at me afterwards as if I was her biggest regret. The way she prevented me from going anywhere outside of the Reaper Kingdom. How she never wanted to touch me, hold me, or love me as she did my baby sister Everest. The distance that grew between us, every word unsaid. At one point in my childhood, I couldn't even remember her being there. Or was that because my father erased it all?

"They knew. They both knew." Neither Malakey nor the doctor replied.

My jaw stiffened. I squeezed the cream container so tight that if it were glass, it would have shattered. The monitor beeps increased, and I ripped the wires from my chest to silence it. I hopped off the table. I threw the cream to the side, over- whelmed by this information. My skin shifted underneath, prickling as I stomped toward the exit. Malakey called my name, but I didn't turn back.

PACING RAPIDLY IN THE CENTER OF THE MEADOW, I screamed at the sun above. Malakey caught up with me, slightly out of breath, as he held the extinguisher in his hand.

"Keep that thing away from me!" I screamed.

"Princess, this is for your safety and for ours." He pointed to the side of the house where the walls were burned black.

I inhaled, stabbing my nails into my skin. I flopped to the ground and rested my face in my palms. "She lied to me all these years." Malakey sat next to me.

"She knew what I was and hated me for it, and I never understood why. Only to find out from a stranger."

"You can't jump to conclusions. There could be an expla- nation behind this."

"What explanation could there be that justifies lying to your child and forcing them into a role that you already knew they could never fulfill? What type of physical and emotional mind fuck is that?"

"Princess..."

I glared at him.

"Bellamy...." He pulled out the cream that wasn't cream. "Put this on. We don't know if you are able to"—he searched my body—"tame it."

I snatched the cream from his hands and threw it across the meadow. "Of course, I don't know how to tame it!"

"Oh-kay, but you forgot to put it on your skin first."

"I'm not in the laughing mood."

"I know. Trust me, I know. But that doesn't mean we shouldn't take precautions. Believe it or not, you need this until you're able to control it." Malakey pulled out another container and unscrewed the lid. "Here"—he leaned it toward me —"I figured you would throw the first, so I brought two."

I looked from the cream to him and back to the cream.

"You're really annoying."

"You too."

I dug my fingers into the cold, silky mixture. My very being wanted to do the opposite of what I was told. Logically, I understood he had a point. The doctor and her partners have already suffered because of me, and they've done nothing to deserve the chaos I caused. Yet a part of me wanted nothing more than to let it all burn.

I knew who I was really mad at. I couldn't stop imagining her face, her sneer, the look of pure disappointment and disgust that was on her face when she looked at me. I couldn't stop imagining flames that burned so hot that they seared away her upturned nose until she became nothing but a blackened canvas. I rubbed the cream into my skin, and the coolness instantly seeped into my pores as the itch went away.

Malakey closed the lid and sat the container on the ground. "We need to run more tests. I know we should head to camp today, but I think it's best to leave tomorrow morning instead."

"I don't want to go back." I plucked a petal from a flower and smoothed it out between my fingertips.

"You don't have a choice. If I don't come back with you, then I'll be wanted by two kingdoms. And something tells me your Father would be much harder to hide from."

"He knew too." I plucked another petal.

"How does that make you feel?"

I thought for a moment, gazing at the clear sky. "Abandoned, lost, maybe alone," I said. "Why couldn't they just tell me?"

Malakey shifted beside me. "I don't know. As Fireborn, if I had a daughter with natural Fireborn gifts, we would shout it to the world. You would be praised, honored, and men and women would lie at your feet. In our kingdom, if the king and queen's genes are good, they harvest their sperm and eggs and create as many offspring as possible."

I swiveled my head to Malakey.

"What?"

"You mean to tell me if I were Fireborn, they would harvest my eggs?" I sat up on my elbows.

"Yes, and pair them with the best genetics. And don't worry. You wouldn't have to carry them all. There would be surrogates for the queen. Women who would be honored to carry the heirs."

"Interesting. Not sure if that is creepy or genius." I laid back on the grass.

"The point is, if you were raised in our kingdom, you wouldn't be a secret. You'd be celebrated."

"But I wasn't. As far as I know, my mother is my mother and my father my father. And if they both knew I was...different. Then why put me on the Earth throne? Why make me take the pledge?"

"Maybe. If your doyens knew what you were, then they would never have passed the throne to you. There's power behind a throne."

"Then why haven't you taken your throne, prince?"

Malakey breathed heavily, "My f-fa-..." He choked on the words.

"...my sperm donor isn't Father of the ear either."

"What happened between you two?"

Malakey dug into his shirt. The dark red and blue liquid sloshed around in the tube. "You were chosen, Bellamy. I was created." He let the glass drop to his chest.

"How?"

"Because of a stupid belief called purebloods. He believes in our blood lies a remnant of the first fire manifestation."

"But I thought all ungifted Fireborns came from the first fire manifestation?"

"Yes, and no. Pre–Mortem Era, our ancestors were the first to call upon the Fire Spirit. Through their sacrifice, the manifestation was then given to all those who pledged to the Fire Spirit. In the end, when the world was almost destroyed and the Fire Spirit was sealed away, the descendants of those bloodlines believed that their blood held the key to unlock the manifestation again."

I shifted in the grass to get a better look at Malakey, who was staring at the sky. "So, how does this pertain to you?"

"The experiments..." He tucked one arm underneath his head. "Ever since I was strong enough to walk, I trained mercilessly. I was beaten, burned, and locked away for days in dark rooms because he was convinced that it would make me better. At six, I received my first injections. Each one was worse than the last. When I hit puberty at twelve, my skin wouldn't stop itching. It felt like I needed to rip myself away from myself. Like there was something underneath the surface that was fighting to be set free. Thing is, I couldn't ignite the flame on my own. I needed a catalyst." Malakey wrapped his fist around the necklace. "Doctor Evna made the first editions of the liquids. She warned him it could either kill me or help me manifest. She refused to administer the liquid to me because—" Malakey closed his eyes. "I never knew a Mother's love. She died at my birth. The doctor is the closest thing I have to that love."

Malakey opened his eyes, a tear formed at the corner. "When he found out that the doctor refused to risk my life, he punished her right in front of me. Ripped her clothes, revealing her bare back. He made me watch as the whip cut through her skin, and she blacked out in a pool of her own blood." Malakey dropped his arm to his side.

I threaded my fingers between his and squeezed. "If this is too hard, you don't have to go on," I said.

"No, you need to hear the truth." Malakey continued. "That day, he forced the liquid down my throat himself. Sometimes I can still feel him ripping my mouth open, and then closing it shut so I couldn't spit it out. I can feel the fear mixed with hatred and revenge for hurting someone I considered more than family. I wanted to kill him where he stood, but instead, I doubled over, convulsing, wishing that he would put an end to me. When I thought all hope was lost, blue flames burst into my hand." Malakey swallowed. "I couldn't control the flame. When he bent down to grab my arm, I burned the left side of his face. Truth is, if I could go back in time, I would have burned all of him. When Doctor Evna came to, she was able to put me out before I burned the entire building down." Blue flames danced in Malakey's irises.

"What did you do next?" I met his gaze.

Malakey pulled me into his arms. A gesture I wasn't expecting, but one I allowed. He buried his chin in my black waves.

"I fought not only for myself but for Doctor Evna, my sister, the people I loved and the rest of the Fireborns who wanted to rid themselves of the kingdom. I got stronger and learned how to control my gift. He wanted to use me as his weapon, the key to gain control over all the kingdoms. He experimented on more Fireborns, turning them into monsters. Their screams haunt me in my sleep..." Malakey paused, biting hard on his lip. "I knew I had to leave because staying would do nothing but harm more of the people I love. Once on the outside, I could help my people escape. Thus, the Redux was born." Malakey ran his fingers through my hair. "I met the doctor and her partners in Squablers Quarrel. She had been looking for me and just in time, too. I was a mess," he chuckled. "My skin was filled with boils and sores from the fire being trapped within me and no way to let it out. If I cannot trigger the release, the flames attack my body from the inside. It will eventually kill me until now. Until you."

"Why me?"

Malakey rolled on top of me, the ends of his hair brushing my cheek. "When we're together is the only time I feel healed. When we intertwine, you consume my flames, releasing me from the fire forever burning within. When our fingers touch" —Malakey laced his fingers into mine, holding my hands above my head, the electricity bouncing in our palms— "you free me. And I know no matter how brightly we burn, we could never burn each other. We could never hurt each other." Malakey lowered himself between my legs. I opened wide, wanting his hips to sit in the perfect place.

He kissed me and white crackles of electricity like thunder jolted between our lips when he pulled back. Blue flames lit his eyes and through their reflection, I saw red flames lighting mine. Warmth rushed over my body and between my legs. My mind went blank as I drowned in his red-orange energy.

He kissed my neck, then my shoulder blades and the top of my breast. "I will celebrate you, worship you, praise you." His hands slipped underneath my shirt. "Erba, let me be your servant." He clamped down on my nipples and sucked.

The voice roared in my mind. It was a laugh so loud. It brought me back to my senses.

The shift.

"No!" I pushed Malakey off, crawling backwards into the grass.

Malakey looked puzzled; his aura flamed around him. I closed my eyes tight before opening them again and I saw him normally.

"Did I hurt you?"

I shook my head. "No, it isn't that. I just..."

Malakey sat on his knees. "Your girlfriend?"

I nodded.

"Do you really think she could give you what I can?"

"She gives me enough. I love her."

"I don't mind sharing," he whispered.

"It's not about that. It's...the red woman."

"Another girlfriend? How many do you have?"

"No, Malakey. It's...you're going to think I'm crazy."

"Tell me."

"It's the voice in my head. It's like this entity is trying to overtake me. And somehow, she has chosen you to be my lover."

"You commune with the Fire Spirit?"

"What?" I crossed my legs, straightening my clothes.

"It is said that when you are chosen by the Spirits, they have the ability to dwell within you. Live through you. See through you."

"Are you saying the Fire Spirit, the one that was locked away, is trying to control my body?"

"No. Not control, guide. I don't think she can do anything you don't already want to."

"Like murder those three men? I didn't want to do that."

"A part of you might have."

"She wanted me to leave you dying after you got shot. She said she would find me another. Do you think a part of me wanted that too?"

Malakey was silent for a long while before he spoke. "I don't want to disappoint you."

"You don't want to disappoint me or the Fire Spirit?"

"You."

"Malakey, are you truly drawn to me or the power within me?"

"When I kissed you"—Malakey said, rising to his feet — "what excited you the most, my lips or my flames?"

Act VIII

XXXVIII

"You say, 'Friend or foe?' and I say, 'Stick or branch?'"
Proverb 28:02 from the Book of Face, Mortem Era.

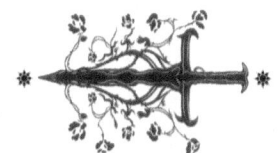

QUANDE GRIPPED HIS DAGGER as he stood beside the general sitting behind his desk and stroking his beard. The expansion of gray hairs grew the last three days I was away on mission.

Malakey and I sat on the opposite side of his desk, relaying our journey and what we had learned. We agreed to edit the parts about the alley fight and fire manifestation until I could sort it out in my mind. I desperately needed help, but turning to my parents and friends didn't seem like the best choice. Not when all of them loath the Fireborns or have been deliberately hiding vital information from me. Who could I trust when I couldn't trust the people close to me? I turned to Malakey, who looked calm, his necklace removed and tucked away, his hair tossed to the side. Could I trust a Fireborn? No, not just a Fireborn. Could I trust Key Dricon, the prince of the Fire Kingdom?

Malakey turned to me, a light smile on his lips.

I smiled in return and refocused on the general. When we arrived back at the camp only an hour after sundown, Malakey and I were rushed into the general's office before we could climb off our horses. The general and Quande had been tag-teaming us relentlessly about the information we had gained. The general's face did not give way to any emotion he was thinking. He stroked his beard while Quande glared daggers into Malakey.

"With all that being said, we still don't know when these attacks are going to occur. So much for your inside man," Quande flipped his dagger into his other palm.

The general leaned in. "My concern is the four kingdoms in cahoots with the Fire Kingdom. Malakey, is your informant able to get the list of sleepers?"

"I have already given them that task to complete, General."

"What's the timeframe?"

"Two full moons from today."

"That isn't all," I said, reaching into my bag. I pulled out the steel bullet and gun. "This is what was discovered by some bandits. We don't know the source of these but look closely at the bullet."

The general reached over, plucking the bullet off the desk. He twisted the bullet in his hand.

Quande leaned in. "This is reaper steel."

"Exactly."

The general and the first lieutenant looked at each other as if information was being passed telepathically. The general balled his fist around the bullet.

"Thank you for this information, Malakey. You're dismissed."

Malakey nodded. I rose from my chair.

"Not you," the general said. He opened his desk drawer and pulled out a pen and paper.

I gave an unsure smile at Malakey, who brushed his fingers alongside the back of my hand as he left. When the cabin door closed, the general licked the tip of the pen and began writing. Quande's shoulders relaxed, but not by much. He strapped his dagger onto his waist belt. He moved to the corner of the general's desk and sat on the edge.

The general dipped his pen in black ink. "The Fireborn," he said, returning the pen to the paper. "Did he display any suspicious activity?"

"No, General."

"Were you with him the entire time?"

If you minus the time I left the inn for a few hours or when I was knocked out because my body burst into flames, then yes.

"I was with him the entire time, General."

"Do you think we can trust the Fireborn's informant?"

I remembered Candia with her foxlike grin. "I questioned her myself. I believe what she told was the truth, but I also believe she wasn't telling everything she knew."

Quande cut in. "His informant is a woman?"

I closed my eyes. *Shit.* I might as well continue. "Yes, she works under King Dricon. Her and Malakey are..." I searched for the right word or phrase. "... close," I concluded.

"A servant girl willing to risk herself for a runaway? Must be some connection," Quande said.

I shifted in my seat. "You can say that."

"Last question, recruit." The general paused his pen. A smile cracked his steely exterior. "How was your first official Blood Elite Mission?" He placed the pen down next to the paper.

I mirrored his smile. "Enlightening." Terrifying and earth shattering, I wanted to add, but I forced my grin not to waver.

"Good, good. I'm proud of you, Beta."

The knife was already in my chest, and it just twisted. The sting from hearing him say words I longed for now felt false. Would he still be proud of me if he knew what secrets I was keeping from him?

Once the ink went dry on the paper, the general folded the letter in three, then sealed it shut. "I'll be leaving tomorrow. The C.O.A. will host a hearing for the expatriation of Fireborns. Zef will take the lead on your training first thing tomorrow morning. Do you have questions for me?"

I tapped my foot on the floor, shifting in my seat. "No."

"Good. Good," the general said with a small smirk on his lips. "Go get some food and rest up. You've had a long trip. Relax, Beta. Unwind." He passed the letter to Quande. Quande tucked the letter into his pocket in one fluid motion.

"Yes, sir." I rose to my feet and saluted. A slight itch crawled right underneath the surface of my palm. I stabbed my nails into the center, biting back the wave of shame burbling in my stomach. I exited the cabin. Before the door could close, Quande was at my heels.

"Hey," I said, walking toward the kitchens. "Do you need anything?"

Quande grabbed my arm, stopping me in my tracks. "Enlightening? Your first mission was enlightening?"

I shrugged. "Yea, I learned a lot of things."

"Name one." Quande folded his arms. His eyes locked on my face.

Fuck Quande, I don't have time for your suspicions. Just let me go.

"I learned how to keep a low cover." I fumbled through my thoughts.

"Really? Was that before or after you lost your lenses?"

Shit.

"What makes you think I've lost them? I could have put them away once we arrived."

"You could..." Quande stepped forward. "But you didn't, did you?"

I stepped back. "I lost them on the way here. The sun was too hot and the sand too dry. They were killing me."

"Uh-huh." Quande stroked his naked chin. If he had a beard, it would have been like watching a mini replica of my father.

I pushed past him, the itch tickling upwards from my palm. Quande moseyed along at my side. I felt his stare. It was as if my entire left side of my face was heated from his energy. I damn near wanted to run away from him. The itch made its way to my forearm. I forced my mind to focus on each step as I walked along.

Slow and steady.

If I hadn't, I would have run right into the arms of Malakey. The very thought of him cooled the itch from jolting to my upper arm.

We entered the kitchens. I went directly to the fridges, yanked open the door, and pulled out a jug of water. I popped the top and gulped damn near a half a gallon before I released the jug from my mouth.

I wiped the last droplets of water from my lips with the back of my hand. I turned and noticed Fia, Sarue, Venus, the twins, and Rwju had entered. Sarue limped toward me, throwing her hands around my neck. Venus clutched her palm around the handle of her sword.

I didn't hug Sarue in return. If Venus reacted this way over a suspicion, how would she react if I told her it was true? That I could call forth power from a cursed spirit that was supposed to have been sealed away centuries ago? I could see how her eyes narrowed, watching, waiting, speculating about every move I made.

I gazed around the kitchen. The only smiling face was Fia's. Guilt bit into the base of my throat. Every other face was neutral, as if they were expecting something. What that something was, I didn't know.

What I knew, without a doubt in my mind, was that I couldn't trust them, any of them.

Quande threw his arm around my neck and squeezed. "So, are you going to tell us what really happened, or are you going to stick with your lie?"

"Nothing happened, Quande." I pushed his arm from around me.

"The wessie didn't hurt you, did he?" Fia said. His fist was damn near bigger than my head.

"No, and his name is Malakey." My back hit against the fridges.

Twoa tapped Oneo. "Looks like we got another Rwju situation. Our princess has gotten too close to the sun. I hope the bed was warm." He giggled.

I froze. That was enough. Who did they think I was to joke so casually about what and who I did behind closed doors?

"Moonborns..." My voice was low. "I suggest you mind who you're speaking to when addressing me."

Twoa, a wide grin on his face. "I was just joking, geez."

Quande spoke. "Not okay, Moonborns. Plus, Bellamy knows better than to sleep with a wessie. Fucking scum."

The itch built into my palm. It exploded down the full length of my arm as if my blood vessels were carrying the itch to every major artery. I smacked the water jug on the counter and stomped out of the kitchen. My right shoulder collided with Twoa's left arm, knocking him backwards.

"Really!" he yelled.

The general was right. I wasn't one of them. I would never be one of them. Returning to camp, I thought it would give me the reassurance I needed that I'd be okay. That I could come out to those who love and support me. That maybe, just maybe, they would embrace me and not make me feel like a freak.

Quande called my name, and the sound of his voice made my skin crawl.

I SLAMMED THE cabin door behind me, pacing frantically. Silvia sat on the edge of the tub, wrapped in a towel. She smiled, her brown skin glowing in the candlelight.

"You're back!" she said, jumping to her feet.

I didn't realize how much I missed her until she was in my arms, her lips upon mine. I held her tight, refusing to let her go. Holding her, I buried my lips into the side of her neck. One wet curl escaped from her bonnet and hung loose on her shoulder. I kissed her where the curl coiled, breathing her in.

"Bee?" Her fingers traced alongside my spine.

My body shuttered.

"Bee?"

"Shhh..." I spoke. "Let me hold you."

And so she did until we found ourselves tumbled into the sheets. She called my name over and over again until her soft skin had raspberry marks in all my favorite places on her body.

Three days and two nights I had gone without her touch. I've never in my life craved anyone or anything this much.

Well almost.

Silvia held me in her arms. Her nipples hardened at my lips. Even though hours had passed, I took her nipples into my mouth. She quivered.

"Sensitive?" I asked.

"Yes, but I like it."

I nibbled, this time gentler, using the point of my tongue to tease.

Silvia grabbed my ass. I chuckled.

"What?" she asked.

"Do you like what you see back there?"

"Absolutely." She slapped a butt cheek. "You lost weight, but you didn't lose this ass and those thighs!" she said, clutching tightly.

"Oh, you liked when I was thicker?"

"I like you no matter your weight, but if you lose this ass, I might like you a little less."

"And here I thought you were a breast girl."

"You're the breast girl! Look what you've done to me." She pointed to her red areolas.

I flicked her nipple.

"Hey!" She covered her breast, turning her back to me.

I wrapped my arms around her waist, kissing the point of her shoulder. "You got to have a little pain with pleasure," I whispered.

She melted into me.

"How was your first mission?"

I closed my eyes tight. "Fine."

She wiggled, "Just fine? Really?"

"Why doesn't anyone believe me?"

"Because I was expecting you to return and talk my ear off.

I was prepared to have a sleepless night yesterday. But when you didn't arrive, I was a little worried." Silvia flipped over, tucking her hair into her crooked bonnet. "What happened?"

"Nothing really." I let her loose to lie on my back. I stared at the ceiling. Maybe I was being too protective. Too cautious. Maybe I could trust Silvia.

"Bee, you were out with a Fireborn for three days and two nights. They're like the worst of the worst. I woke up from a nightmare thinking that he had stolen you away and sold you to the Fire Kingdom or something."

I sighed deeply, pulling the blanket to cover my exposed body.

"He wasn't so bad."

"If he had hurt you, Bee, I don't know what I would've done." Silvia tucked herself underneath my arm.

"I'm surprised you care that much."

Silvia popped her head up. "Of course, I care. What do you mean by that?"

"I don't know." I shrugged.

Silvia pinched my arm.

"Ouch..." I shifted away from her. "What was that for?"

"For being so stubborn. I care for you, truly. No matter what paths we choose to take."

I took the same hand she pinched me with and brought it to my mouth with a kiss on her knuckles.

"Silvia?"

"Hmmm?"

"What if I were Fireborn, would you still... care?"

"But you're not Fireborn."

"What if I were?"

She paused, taking her hand and placing it on my cheek. "My mother once said, 'Never reach your hand into a fire pit and be surprised when it burns you. No matter how cautious

411

someone can be with fire, it'll eventually remind you of what it really is."

My arm fell loose to my side.

Silvia continued, "You're different, sure. Something unique, something powerful. Absolutely. But Fireborn?" Silvia pulled me close, her leg wrapped around my thighs. "It just doesn't make sense, does it?"

Doubt ran rampant through my mind. The weight of Silvia's body pressed against me wasn't enough to clench the emptiness creeping in. She never answered the question and my thoughts drifted to Malakey.

"Bee, are you okay?"

I almost didn't hear her. "I'm fine."

"Are you sure? Was there something that happened during the mission that I should know about?"

I felt the pressure of her big brown eyes staring at me. Before I turned my gaze from the ceiling, I slowed my fast-beating heart. I brushed a thumb over her chin.

"No, nothing. The mission was completely normal."

Her lips disappeared into her mouth.

"I promise to tell you all about it tomorrow. Just"—I raised the blanket to cover her— "let me hold you," I said, kissing her forehead.

As the night continued to fade, the candlelight grew brighter on the far side of the room. The flames danced and waved as if the fire itself were pointing at me, laughing at me, mocking me.

Calling me.

XXXIX

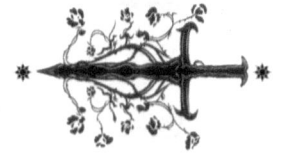

"It's hard to see the picture when living inside the frame."
Proverb 47:67 from the Book of Face, Mortem Era.

I WOKE WELL BEFORE Silvia, packed a few things and made my way to the communal showers. I washed, scrubbing my skin as if I could somehow wipe my manifestation clean. My deep brown skin went raw. I snapped the water off. I took the cream out of my pack, scooping out a large amount on my fingertips, then balled it into my fist. This entire time, since puberty, my mother had known. She made it seem like I was the failure, when all this time it was her! She did this to me. She had to.

The cream dripped into the shower. Before more was wasted, I slathered the thick paste on my skin. It left an ashy-white hue as residue, but I didn't care. I would not risk calling the flames forth again. Not until I had a solid plan.

First, I need to control my manifestation, find my triggers, and learn to control this curse. The only teacher I had was Malakey. The only other Fire user. According to Doctor Evna, there was a great chance that I could shapeshift. Well, that's what the legends say. Those who are favored by the Spirits, no matter the Spirit, have been always given a gift to manifest more abilities than just elemental. This meant that what Rwju saw that day in the forest very well could have come to pass. My manifestation was growing to the point that the cream would be ineffective soon. I had so many unanswered questions that it felt like I was drowning in them.

I slid on my black tactical pants, shirt, and black boots.

Silvia's words echoed in my mind, *"No matter how cautious someone can be with fire, it'll eventually remind you of what it really is."*

Was I Erba? Fireborn? A mistake so vile that even my own parents kept my true identity away from me? Hated by my sister who chose a psychopath over me? Surrounded by friends who hold grudges so deep and bitter that even the thought of the Fireborns in the camp had everyone on edge? My father—who used his gifts to erase my memories, to hide myself from myself, to make me forget—what would he do when I told him I knew? How would he react? Would he try and take away all that I know again?

Curiosity kills the cat. Should I just let it die?

What was I supposed to do next?

"Fight." Malakey's voice echoed in my ear. *"Fight."*

I tied my boots taut and exited the building. Afterwards, I grabbed a heavy axe and entered the woods. The sun wouldn't rise for another hour, so I used this time to sit at the base of a tall redwood tree. I dug my palm into the rich soil. The smell of slight ammonia and pine needles wafted to my nostrils as I split the earth apart. I shut my eyes, breathed deeply, and called the earth to answer my will.

I prayed to the Earth's Spirit. Why give me the mark of emerald green eyes if I was just going to be cursed with fire? Why send me on this path? What was I supposed to do? Who was I supposed to be? I needed answers!

Digging my palms deeper into the soil, the mud rose to my wrist. "Answer me!" I shouted into the crisp, cool wind. The only answer was the batting wings of birds taking flight.

Ripping my dirt-stained hands from the ground, I concluded the Earth Spirit's refusal to answer had to do with my years of not believing, not trusting, and not caring about being Earthborn. I glanced at my hands. The mud was so brown it damn near matched my skin tone. I leaned back into the tree, dusting my hands off. Then I took up my axe and rose to my feet.

I needed to release. I turned to face the tree. The redwood, too great, too wide, too overbearing, made me smaller than I already felt. Swirling the axe in my hand, with one swing, I swung with all my might, chopping into the tree. My little axe did little to no damage. I chopped anyway, until I hit the wood with so much force, it broke the neck of my axe. I kicked the tree, again, and again, and again. Sweat dripped from my forehead and into my eyes. My breathing was sporadic and labored. My arm ached from the swinging and my bottom lip busted from sinking my teeth into it.

I wanted to punish someone for this misfortune. I could not accept this fate. A life plan was already in place for me. So, what do I do next? Assume my role? My position? Sell myself into serving the kingdom? What about what *I* want? What I *need*? I wanted control over my body, my path, and my decisions.

"Princess Bellamy?"

I didn't hear the voice behind me. I continued to kick the tree and wood chips flew into my face. When the tap came at my shoulder, I whirled around, throwing my fist first and asking questions later. Zef dodged, redirecting the impact with a flick of his wrist. I stumbled forward, losing my balance and crashed to the ground.

Rolling over onto my back, I buried my face in my hands. Every time I inhaled my chest burned. I was ready to defend myself, come up with another lie, another excuse, another half-truth in order to convince this man I wasn't some crazy fool.

When I rose to my feet, Zef wasn't looking my way. Instead, he was examining the tree. He rubbed his hand across the choppy pieces and placed his forehead on the bark. He hummed, a nice low tone that made my skin prickle. Right before my eyes, the tree sewed itself back together. The wood pieces that were laying haphazardly on the ground, rose in the air and spun. Zef's eyes were closed. With one flick of his wrist, the wood chunks snapped into place like puzzle pieces.

The tree was as good as new. Zef stepped back and faced me. His emerald-green eyes had an intoxicating glow. If I looked closely, I could see specs of shimmery gold, like tiny explosions bursting into life. I blinked. And his eyes settled back into a deep forest green. Under his observance, I shifted on my feet, tucked my shirt into my pants, and straightened my hair that had fallen.

Zef remained silent.

"Are you just going to watch me or are you going to say something?" I rubbed the back of my neck.

"Should I?" He arched one eyebrow.

I dropped my arms to my side, shoulders slumped. "I don't know. Isn't that the reason you came?"

Zef glanced back at the tree. "I came because the redwood called for me."

"A tree called for you?"

Zef tucked his hands behind his back. He had this air about him, as if he had everything figured out. As if it were everyone else's responsibility to play catch up.

"And how does a tree speak?" Annoyance dripped from my tone.

"You're Earthborn. Shouldn't you know?"

"Okay," I chuckled. A deep throaty irksome chuckle. "Come on Zef, let's not play dumb. You know, just like I know, I'm nowhere near Earthborn."

I couldn't stop laughing. "I'll let you get back to hugging your tree." I bent over, scooping up my broken axe.

"Princess..." Zef said. "You still have a choice to manifest the gift of your liking."

I paused, slowly turning around. "What do you mean?"

"You must pledge to the Earth Temple and take on the responsibility as High Priestess."

"Your point?" I said, kicking dirt.

Zef continued, "Listen closely, Princess Bellamy. The High Priestess must take on the trials. Every Earth Queen before you has taken on those trials. This is the tradition of your bloodline. Specifically, your bloodline. You must uphold the tradition."

I studied Zef. His face hardened, his eyes still. "It's really hard for me to read between the lines, Zef. If you want to say something, now would be the perfect time."

Zef crossed his hand over his chest, a wave of pain flitted across his face before he straightened up. His face glossed over like a statue.

"You've been earth bonded?"

He nodded.

"By who, my mother?"

Zef didn't move.

"My doyens?"

Zef tilted his head toward the sky.

"The Spirits?" I chuckled in disbelief.

Zef slowly lowered his head; his eyes were swirls of emerald green. He spoke slowly. "Every queen before you has had to assume the throne and acknowledge the Earth Spirit. Do you know why it's so important to pledge to a temple and what that means?"

I paused, throwing my head back before answering. "When we pledge," I mumbled. "We are swearing our allegiance to the Earth Spirit. The Spirit's manifestation becoming ours, their strength becoming ours, their gifts becoming ours."

"There's a balance that must be restored. And it's up to your bloodline to restore it. Just like the others who have walked your path."

"And what about the prophecy?"

"How did you—" Zef doubled over, clutching his chest.

The itch reemerged underneath my skin. His aura burst from around him in a dark gold. My manifestation flared at the amount of power surging from within him.

"You...are...like me." Zef struggled to breathe, his hand going around his chest.

I ran to him just as he fell to his knees.

"Stop talking. You're hurting yourself." If Zef was really held to an earth bond, this would mean that just the mere thought of telling what he shouldn't, could kill him.

"I would die to protect you," he said, raising a shaking finger to his hair. "This is sacred magic, long forgotten by time. This is the only way." He snapped a long fine black strand of hair from his head. "Forgive us," he said, thrusting the hair into my mouth. Before I could shove his hand away, roots burst through the soil, grabbing my wrist and ankles, and pinned me to the ground. Leaves, pebbles, and small flakes of earth rose from the soil.

"What are you doing?" I screamed, fighting the roots. My body jerked and convulsed against its grip.

"Showing you what I can before it's too late." Zef's hand movements grew wider. Evergreens, more roots, and pine needles circled around us. The earth shifted, splitting open. Something underneath the ground clawed its way upward. I could hear it. Hundreds, no... thousands of fast-moving roots reached out to me. All connected, growing, and wrapping around my legs, planting me farther into the ground, my legs disappearing into the soil. I screamed.

Zef's voice cut through the overwhelming audio overload. "You must learn control, Princess Bellamy, or your rule will be the end of us all."

My eyes grew wide as vines snaked up my body. "Let me go!" I yelled. "Let me go!" The root wrapped around my mouth, muting me.

The crack in Zef's statue spider-webbed through his entire body, revealing a pain and fear that I'd never witnessed from his face. Tears rolled down his cheeks as he clung tightly to his chest. His eyes looked as if they were incandescent mixed with shimmering gold.

My throat went dry as something sprouted inside of my mouth. Hair, it was hair mixed with roots, forcing its way into my mouth, wrapping around my tongue, choking me as it shoved its way down my throat. I couldn't scream. I couldn't make a sound. My head went back as the surrounding trees all leaned in, watching me. I involuntarily swallowed and I could feel it slipping its way past my esophagus to my chest, wrapping around my heart, heading toward the pit of my belly.

"It's true..." he said.

I forced my eyes to look at Zef, to beg him to stop.

"I'm too late. It has already begun." He turned his fluorescent-like glare to me. His words came out in breathy puffs. "In order to change the future, we must first learn from our past. As it is above, so it is below." Zef flicked his wrist. The roots yanked me into the ground. I fought with every fiber of my being to be set free, but just like a seed planted in the earth, the soil swallowed me whole.

The roots cocooned around me until all I felt was cold.

XL

"Your future is today, and your today is your tomorrow."
Proverb 7:7 from the Book of Face, Mortem Era.

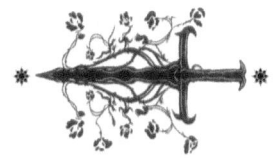

BLURRED IMAGES QUICKLY SWEPT my mind. At first, they were jumbled, as if several voices were speaking at once, but with concentration, the images evolved. Some images were louder than others, more demanding of my attention. I grabbed those. Expanding them into each corner of my psyche until the darkness faded. I could almost imagine sitting in the front row at a performance created just for me. I sunk into the velvety red seats as the images played before my mind.

The first one was of Zef. He was younger than he was now, skin smoother, face rounder. The innocence of youth shone in his eyes. He held my mother. She had hair, long, black and wavy, just like mine. This entire time I thought I had the hair of the Reaperborn, but seeing the waves fall into her face, I almost cringed at how much we looked alike. Her belly was swollen with child, tears dotted her cheeks, and Zef wiped them away. He kissed her on the lips and held her close to his chest. She accepted his embrace, her arms wrapped around his waist.

Father appeared, clean-shaven and dressed in his typical black. "We need to leave now," he said.

Zef covered Mother, "But it's too early. The baby will not make it across the trek," he warned.

Mother rubbed her belly. "He must."

He? Confusion played in my mind.

Shouts came from the distance, heavy boots on concrete, and torches lit the night sky.

"We need to leave now!" Father said, whisking Mother away.

Zef grabbed Father's arm. "Keep her safe. I will lead them in another direction."

Father embraced Zef. Their foreheads touched. Zef gripped Father's neck, and Father returned the embrace with intensity.

"I love you," Zef whispered into Father's ear.

Father returned his affection with a kiss on Zef's lips. "Don't get caught," Father said before letting go.

Zef nodded and dashed into the night. Father's shadow leaked from his hand, casting himself and Mother into blackness. The image melted, merging into another.

. . .

THE SCENE SHIFTED, they were older. Zef, unlike the calm demeanor I knew, was enraged. He yelled at Father. Zef's shirt was off, revealing heavy scars crisscrossing his torso. Blood trickled from his nose as his body arched backwards and froze.

Father held out his hand in a strangling gesture a few feet away. He was using the blood-control, stopping Zef where he stood. Mother rushed in front of Zef. Her hair was in braids. Her belly was flat, her emerald-green eyes glowed. She stomped her feet, causing the earth to rise, blocking Father's connection to Zef. Zef hit the ground. Mother threw her arms around him in protection. Father's shadow flowed from his palm, and he used it to leap across the earth wall, landing in front of the two.

"Move," Father said to Mother.

Mother's grip grew tighter. "No. I will not let you hurt him."

"He murdered our daughter!" Spit flew from Father's lips.

Zef's jaw flexed, but he remained silent, his fist burying into the ground.

Mother let Zef loose and rose to her feet. "I killed the creature!"

Father lost his footing as if she had knocked the wind out of his lungs. "You're lying to cover him."

"I do no such thing, Agrim. You know this to be true."

"No." Father stumbled backwards, "No, you couldn't."

"I could! And I did!" she shouted.

"Why!" Father roared, tears streaming from his eyes.

"You know why, Agrim. Or are you going to ignore the Moonborn prophecy?"

Father gripped his chest. "To hell with the prophecy! This was our first child, Oyame. No one knows the fate of a new life set in this world. We could have protected her; we could have kept her safe. And now the cries of my firstborn will never be heard again."

Mother placed the back of her right hand to her lips while using the left to cradle her stomach. "You don't think I know how you feel, Agrim, my love. My first child, stolen from me; the second murdered by my hand. Don't you think my heart aches every day from regret? Phantom cries plague me throughout the night, and I awaken to find the crib empty."

Father spun around, holding out his hand in choking form.

Mother's body froze, blood dripping from her nose.

"Then why did you do it!" Father shouted. "Why did you take my child from me!"

Zef leaped to his feet, running to Father's side. Zef cradled Father into his arms, "Let her go, Agrim."

Father bit his lower lip.

Zef forced Father's head to turn to him.

Tears welled in Father's eyes. "I have sacrificed everything for her."

"And you will sacrifice more..." Zef held Father's face. "Because you love her."

Father's hold on Mother loosened. "Why did you protect her, Zef? Why?" Father whimpered, finally releasing his hold. Mother dropped to the ground, catching her breath. Father threw his body into Zef's arms. "Why?" he cried.

Zef glanced over to Mother. "Because I love her."

MY HEART HURT as if someone had reached into my chest and squeezed it. What was I seeing? These memories? Was this the daughter born before me? How could she do such a vile thing? Because of some prophecy? What prophecy could have been foretold that she took it upon herself to murder her own child? Would she have done the same to me? Had she already tried?

I itched so deeply underneath my skin that I dug my nails into my arms until blood trickled from the open wound. Another memory formed before me.

ZEF, THE CORNER of his eyes now pinched with crow's feet, held Mother, whose hair was shaved clean from her head. Father entered the scene, cradling Mother from behind, with a new beard forming alongside his jawline. They were naked.

A dark-skinned woman with snow-white hair stood in front of them. She rubbed oil on Mother's forehead, between her eyes, her chin, her neck, in between her breasts, and lastly, her belly.

The woman spoke. "Your womb has been cursed from defying the Spirit's will. Your crown has been ripped from you as well as your home. The Spirit's wrath will remain upon your head unless you allow destiny to take its place." The old woman tossed a coin into the air, catching it when gravity took hold. "Just like a two-headed coin, your destiny can go one of two ways. Heads"—she placed the oil on Zef's forehead—"or tails." She moved her wrinkled finger and placed oil above my Father's brow. "This ritual assures the Spirit's will once and for all. If broken, it will be the three of you who will fall." The woman stepped away. The image was so dark I couldn't tell if they were in a forest, a dungeon, or a bedroom.

Zef leaned past Mother and kissed my Father. He returned his kiss with one just as passionate and deep. Then, one at a time, it was Mother's turn.

I shut my eyes tight, not wanting to know what happened next, until I heard the cries of a baby. I glanced up. Mother lay in bed surrounded by white sheets soaked in blood. Father was

425

on one side and Zef on the other. Mother held onto a green-eyed little girl, with lungs so strong, Father plugged his eardrums and laughed.

The same dark-skinned older woman waddled over to the bed. She took the screaming babe from Mother's arms.

"The Spirits have chosen the path." The elder rubbed oil on the baby's forehead and the screaming child went silent. She turned to Zef, whose face fell in sadness. Then she handed the baby to Father.

Mother pushed herself up. "What will this mean? Her future? Our future?"

The elder's eyes rolled back into her skull, revealing solid white irises. "When blood meets earth, the flames of fury will burn eternally, unlocking the dragon of fire." The elder slumped over. Zef caught her before she hit the ground. The elder pointed a wrinkled bony finger toward the baby. "She... she..." Her eyes grew wide as she clenched her chest. "...you all shall burn." The woman's body went limp, and her irises returned, but this time they were vacant of life.

Zef looked to Mother, and then they both looked toward Father, who held the baby tight in his arms. The child cried. Father hummed, "Beta, I will protect you from harm. I will protect you with my blood." Father rushed the child out of the room and the red curtains closed.

THAT CHILD WAS ME. Father knew; they all knew.

You all shall burn.

In our family, we do not speak about hard things. I leaned back into the seat that had crumbled underneath me. The stage melted, and the roots cocooned me. The soil being my amniotic fluid. I heard the pounding of my heartbeat as I balled into a fetal position.

I attempted to process what I'd witnessed. A past no one dared speak of.

They had all done this to me. They and their river of lies.

If only Mother had allowed her first daughter to live, to fulfill her destiny, then maybe I wouldn't be here!

Maybe I wouldn't have been here.

I do not want to be here.

XLI

*"To those who find it hard to get up, I feel you. You are valid.
Rest in the rain, love."*
Proverb 8:01 from the Book of Face, Mortem Era.

I EMERGED FROM THE GROUND, curled in a tight
ball, shaking. My clothes clung to me soaked with water and
earth. Globs of wetness splashed across my face. As the rain
fell, the drops reverberated as they thudded against the soil.
The sound amplified as if it were also drumming a story to be
told.

I needed no more noises. No more voices. I wanted to

forget. Go back to a time when beauty didn't look so ugly. Have Father take away my memories, to live a life never knowing the truth.

I snapped my palms over my ears and screamed. When my throat went raw, I did not move. If I could not still time, I would force my eyes shut and sleep it all away. Maybe then my story would end.

Act IX

XLII

"Safety is often found in obscurity."
Proverb 10:72 from the Book of Face, Mortem Era.

THE RAIN STOPPED and the sky was blanketed in shimmering starlight. My teeth clattered. I bit my tongue a few times, blood embedded in my taste buds.

A hand nudged my shoulder, and I pushed it away.

"Princess..." He cleared his throat. "...Bellamy. If you die on the Fireborn side of camp, that would not be good for us," said Malakey.

My heart skipped a beat upon hearing his voice. I rolled

over. I couldn't hold back the tears, nor could I hide them in the dried rain. Instead, I buried my face in his shoulder as he held me tight.

When I finally let go, a piece of me had also disappeared. It was that piece of childhood ignorance before life bitch-slapped me. I knew too much, had seen too much, and that piece of ignorant bliss floated in the waves of the wind like a white dove. No matter how much I called to it, I could not retrieve it. I could not call it home.

Malakey wrapped a blanket around my shoulders.

"Bellamy, you don't have to talk about it if you don't want to, but I'm here," he said, brushing my hair from my face. "Judging by your clothes, you've been out here for a while. You need to get back over to your side—"

"No!" I croaked like a frog, twisting his shirt into a knot. "No, I don't want to go there," I whispered.

"Okay. It's okay. You don't have to go. But you need to get out of these clothes." Malakey checked my forehead. "You're burning up as well."

Me burning up? That's funny. I just feel cold. Ice cold.

I wrapped the blanket tighter around my shoulders. Malakey helped me to my feet.

"Let's get you outta here," he said.

AT THE FIREBORN camp, Malakey took me to a cabin. It had a private shower attached to the back porch enclosed with curtains.

"This is the only cabin with somewhat of a private bath," he said, handing me a towel. "I'll be back with some food, okay?"

I nodded. Before Malakey could close the door good, I snatched off the wet fabric. After a hot shower, I wrapped the towel around myself and hung the damp clothes over the bar to dry.

Afterwards, I went back into the cabin. Malakey must have slipped in while I was occupied because there were clothes folded neatly on a tiny cot. The shirt and pants were hand-sewn. They were warm, oversized, and comfy, just like I liked them.

The cabin was bare. A dull candle barely lit the entire room. My heart rate went through the roof. I frantically patted myself from my head to my thighs, my eyes searching for the fire cream. When I finally registered that I was not in my room, I slinked into the cot. I crossed my legs, pulling the oversized t-shirt over my knees. I slowly inhaled, then exhaled, calming myself the best I could.

A light knock at the entrance door.

"Is it okay if I come in?" Malakey asked, the doorknob twisting slightly.

"Yeah."

He entered, bringing along with him two rowdy kids. One had a large bowl filled with bread. Her toothless smile was wide, her straight blonde hair plastered to her forehead. The other kid, all bones and height, held a large jar of water. Some spilled over the side as he tripped into the room. Malakey held the main course.

"You're in luck, Bellamy. Tonight's meal is tomato soup. Just what the patient needed!" Malakey spun over to me, bowing once he reached the end of the cot. "Princess, it's kinda hot. Can you grab it?"

"Oh," I said, shocked out of my stupor. I grabbed the bowl by the brim and brought it to my lap. The heat instantly warmed my thighs.

The children danced in a circle, giggling at one another as they mimicked Malakey's movements. They danced like nobles at court, stiff backed and dry. After the dance ended, they bowed. My cheeks flushed red.

"There's no need..." I said, quickly taking the bread and water jug and placing them on the floor.

The little girl spoke, her tongue sticking through her gap. "I've never met a princess before. Do you go to balls?"

Before I could answer, the dark-haired boy spoke. "Of course she goes to balls; that's what princesses do!" He shook his head. "The real question is, have you ever eaten your boogers and liked it?"

"Okay," Malakey said, turning to me. "You don't have to answer that." He rushed the kids to the door of the cabin.

The dark-haired boy fought to get around Malakey. "But Key, it's a legit question with whole new poss-se-billites," he said, his tongue tripping over letters.

Before Malakey closed the door completely, I called out, "Yes, and it wasn't so bad."

The boy gasped; the girl burst out laughing. The boy rushed more questions as his head floated behind the closing door.

"Enough, Diyo. Go, now!" Malakey said, eventually locking them out. "Kids, right?" he huffed, running his hand through his hair. His tunic was open. He leisurely strolled my way as his skin glowed under the candlelight. The liquid in his necklace swooshed. My eyes lingered on the red chamber.

"May I?" He pointed to the open spot on the cot.

"Sure."

Before he sat, he picked up the bowl of bread. I looked closely. They were thin cheese sandwiches. He picked one out and broke it in half, handing it to me.

"Thanks." I took it, taking a bite. I scooped a spoon full of tomato soup afterwards.

Malakey cocked his head. His mouth dropped open. "Are you a sociopath?"

"Excuse me?" I rolled my eyes.

"Who eats a grilled cheese sandwich without dipping it into the tomato soup?"

"First off, it's to-may-to, not to-mah-to, let's correct that. Second, literally no one."

Malakey smacked his lips, waving me off. "Maybe not in the high court, but around here, we dip." He snatched the half sandwich out of my hand, "And it's to-mah-to. Always been, forever will be!" He dipped my half into the soup and then held it to my lips.

"Do you expect me to eat that now? It's all soggy."

"I absolutely expect you to, and it wouldn't be soggy if you spent more time chewing instead of brewing."

"Are you serious?" I laughed.

"Deadly so," he mocked in his finest noble voice.

I sucked my teeth, then bit into the sandwich. The tomato juice rushed into my mouth with the mix of cheese and bread.

"Yeah, just like that. How you like it?" Malakey raised a brow.

"It's umm... wet," I said, attempting to cool the food with my tongue.

"Wet! It's fucking delicious. That's what it is." Malakey took the rest and stuffed it into his mouth. His cheeks poked out.

Under the rough and gruff, it was in these moments I saw the little boy in him. I took my thumb and swiped the tomato juice running to his chin.

He chewed slowly and gulped. He searched my face, his blue eyes staring deep into my emerald-green ones. The silly little boy had retreated. What sat next to me now was all man.

Lean muscles, sharp jawline, and a wave of energy radiating off him that made me ache to be in his arms.

I wrapped a blanket around my shoulders, feeling naked in more ways than one. Malakey did not look away, but I had to.

He leaned into me. The room's temperature turned hot. I heard the heaviness in my breaths, and I needed to distract myself with something, anything other than his skin on mine.

"I believe I have an older brother." I reached for the water jug.

Malakey rested his back on the wall while shifting his focus to his cheese sandwich.

"I don't know how old he is or where he is, but neither my parents nor my doyens have ever mentioned him." I took a sip of the water. It was refreshing, like a clear spring. "How can someone have a child and never mention them?"

Malakey bit into his sandwich.

"I mean, whoever this kid was or is," I continued. "He wasn't born of my father. Or maybe he was? I can't remember now. The images seem so clouded in my head."

"Images?"

"Yeah, these memories. It's a long story." I reported the morning events to him all the way to where he found me. Malakey's mouth was wide, chewed food on full display.

"Malakey," I said, pointing to the half-chewed food.

"Oh, sorry." He gulped. "I just...that's a lot of information to process. And you're learning this just now?"

"Yeah."

"The prophecy told to your parents, and the one told to us are different. Do you think they're connected? Oftentimes, Moonborn prophecies are."

"I don't know. Maybe they could be."

"Fuck, Bellamy. What other secrets are your parents hiding from you?"

"I don't know..." I said, placing the jug on the ground. "Father said he and Mother have always tried to protect me. But I don't feel protected. Malakey, I feel abandoned. I feel lied to. Stupid and a fool. All these years, were they ever going to tell me?"

Malakey shifted, moving closer. "Are you going to ask them?"

I guess that was the real question. How was I supposed to confront them when I didn't even want to look at them?

I turned to Malakey. "How did I even see those memories?"

"You said this Zef guy plucked out a piece of his hair, right?"

"Yeah."

"Some say hair carries fragments of memories, that judging by a follicle, a person could determine things like health, age, stress levels, and stuff like that. I mean, for all we know, it could be an ancient Earthborn practice. I know little about Earthborn traditions, but I do know they cover their hair all the time."

This was true. Even my sister and Silvia covered their hair. I knew my sister did it because she was told by Mother, but it was never explained. When I saw Silvia do it, I didn't ask why. I just assumed it was a part of Earthborn culture. I cared not to learn more than that.

A thought flickered. "You know, when I saw the images of my mother, it wasn't until the ritual that all her hair was shaved." I paused, rubbing my chin. "Do you think she did it to erase the memories of her past?"

"Could be," Malakey ran his fingers through his hair. When it got to the end, he plucked one long blonde strand. "Can you imagine a ritual so strong that it can unlock your deepest secrets with one fine string?" The blonde hair, barely noticeable, hung from the tips of his fingers. He passed the single strand over to me.

I took it. "What is this for?"

"Just in case you ever doubt me."

I clicked my teeth. "Should I give you one of mine now?"

Malakey half-smirked, "There aren't many people in this world I trust, but you... there isn't any doubt in my mind."

I examined the fine blond strand, then blew it out of my hand. "Same," I said.

Malakey's face lit up. "Well, Princess Bellamy..." He shuffled out of the cot. "You have two options. You can sit here in this cot, eat, sleep, do whatever you please and I will make sure nobody bothers you, orrr..." he sang, "...you can hang out with me and my people. It's still early and if we make it, we can sit and listen to Six Finger Jack tell tales around the campfire before he passes out." Malakey tucked his hands deep into his pockets.

I thought for a moment before answering, "Honestly, sitting here in this cot wallowing in pain and misery does sound very appealing. Almost a perfect way to end the night. But I got to say, tales from Six Finger Jack have caught my attention. I mean, does he really have six fingers?"

Malakey chuckled, "See, I keep telling him he needs to change his name because it's confusing. He actually has twelve fingers. An extra digit on each hand."

I slapped my thighs, scooting out of the cot. "Well, I am officially sold. I can bring my food, right?"

"Yea, of course."

"Nice." I passed the bread bowl and water jug to Malakey. "I will not be missing twelve-finger Jack's tales tonight."

As we prepared to leave, Malakey set the bowl and jug aside. He plucked my tomato soup from my hand and hugged me.

He smelled so fucking fresh that I dug my face into his chest.

"With me, you never have to be ashamed of who you are. You know that, right?" he said, his breath blowing slightly on my ear, which made bumps prickle onto my skin.

I pulled his body closer to mine until there were no gaps between us. His lips brushed against my neck as he gathered me into his muscular arms.

My hand slipped underneath his tunic; his skin was warm to the touch.

"Princess..." The word came out in breaths. His chin brushed the top of my forehead.

I slipped another hand under his shirt, rubbing gentle fingers across his belly button.

"Princess, you don't want this," he said without moving.

But I wanted this. Heat, pressure, skin-on-skin contact. I needed another way to forget. To feel an emotion other than sadness. I needed control over one thing I knew I could do and do well. As my fingers traced the length of his v-cut, a bulge expanded in his pants. Malakey quickly released me, putting distance between us.

The fire was immediately extinguished. I wrapped my arms around myself. Tears wet my cheeks. "I'm sorry," I sniffed. "I just wanted to..." Use him? When he has done nothing but help me.

"We can stay in the cabin if you like. It's your decision."

But it was too late. I saw the way he kept his distance. The pity in his eyes.

"No." I swiped the tears from my waterline. "I'm good," I said, opening the door.

"Princess..."

"I'm okay, Malakey. I'm fine." I exited without caring if he followed.

XLIII

"Life experiences are the mere difference between a moth and a butterfly."
Proverb 57:11 from the Book of Face, Mortem Era.

THE NIGHT AIR WAS a welcome friend. The aroma of garlic, parsley, along with a few other spices carried across the camp. It brought me memories from back home. From when I was a little girl behind palace walls, outside the kitchen doors waiting for the uma's to sneak me treats before dinner. As long as Glaydecee was nowhere to be found, I usually got my way.

I really am a brat. Selfish inconsiderate—

442

I cringed at all the names I called myself within thirty seconds of leaving the cabin. Why did I do that? What was I thinking? The moment replayed as I attempted to force it from my brain. What would Malakey think of me now?

"So, about you eating boogers..." The boney dark-hair kid was back, Diyo. The blonde-haired girl, with a gap-tooth smile, was at his side. "... when did you start? Like, at what age? And do you still eat them?"

"Umm..." I rocked on my heels, forcing my demeanor into a preppy one to not ruin the little boy's mood. "I think I was maybe three. I grew out of booger eating when I discovered bread and butter at maybe..." I thought hard, rubbing my chin. "Five."

The boy threw up his hands. "And I thought you were a cool Princess."

"She is cool! You're just the weird one." The blonde girl shoved the boy. "He just ate a booger while running over here. He's 8."

Diyo looked embarrassed, his pale cheeks turning pink. "No one asked you, Tika. You ruin everything." He stomped away.

"Not before you ruin it first!" she shouted after him, pulling at his t-shirt.

The pair reminded me so much of Quande and me at their age. We would fight over everything. And I, being stubborn in the worst possible way, would always argue until my face turned purple. At one point, Quande and I could only speak to each other in screams and shouts. It drove the uma's mad. They would attempt to separate us for days and weeks until we bumped into each other in the hallway, only to start again.

Allowing the memory to fade, I wandered away from the cabin to scope out the rest of the camp. Most of the Fireborns were out, meeting and drinking. A group of men were huddled together, sharing some obtuse joke. The women were surprisingly doing the same. Kids dashed from left and right, playing with handmade toys. Their faces were much rounder than before. I noticed their clothes went without holes, rips, or stains. The Fireborn's laughter rang like bells. How could they be so happy when at this very moment, the Counsel of Amalgamation was discussing their future fate?

Candia's words floated in my memory, *"The Fire Kingdom might not have a seat at the table, but better believe there are those who are willing to stand in our place."*

I paused, scanning the merry group. A boiling pot of doubt sat in the pit of my stomach.

How much did they truly know?

A voice called my name from over my shoulders, "Princess Bellamy!"

I spun around. Behind me, there was a dimly lit cabin with its door open. A woman sat at the head of the bed, wrapped in blankets. She coaxed me to come inside. Cautiously, I stepped into the cabin.

The inside smelled of apples, and I instantly remembered the woman's face. She was the same pregnant woman I gave an apple to when the Redux first crossed the barrier. She held a sleeping, freshly born babe in her arms. The flaky skin was peeling, which revealed a smooth, pink layer underneath.

"It's a girl," the woman said.

"She's so tiny and lovely. What did you name her?"

The dark-haired woman glanced down and smiled, "Her name is Tapestry."

"Oh, wow. Does it have meaning?" I said, stepping closer.

"Yes. She is my first child born without the weight of shackles. She will have a chance at threading her own life as she sees fit. Tapestry, may she weave an intricate life of color and beauty." The woman shifted the baby slightly, reaching under her blanket. She pulled out a beautiful, embroidered cloth mixed with various shades of reds, blues, and blacks. She handed the wool cloth over to me.

I opened it to get a full look at the design. A large eight-pointed star decorated the front.

"What does it mean?" I asked, rubbing the tips of my fingers along the mixed texture.

"Erba, the Inherited One."

My smile faltered. A gust of wind flew in, creating chill bumps running the length of my arm. The baby squirmed, her eyelids opening, revealing glossy black eyes. The woman plopped out her breast, feeding her nipple to the babe. Tapestry took it greedily.

I handed the fabric back to the woman.

She shook her head. "No," she said. "It's yours. I made it for you."

"I–I..." I couldn't find the right words.

There was a knock behind me. "Hey," Malakey said, standing in the doorway, legs crossed, leaning on the frame. "Six Fingered Jack is about to get started." He pointed over his shoulder.

I nodded, turning back to the woman. She gently rocked her baby to sleep.

The image of my Father cradling me right after my Mother gave birth flooded my mind.

He hummed, "Beta, I will protect you from harm. I will protect you with my blood."

I folded the blanket. "Thank you," I said, "It's perfect."

The woman gave an approving nod.

I followed Malakey out of the cabin. The air changed from spice to the heavy smoke of the campfire. A few people threw more logs into the flames. I stopped in my tracks.

I grabbed the cloth tight, pressing it against my chest and whispered, "I need my cream. I really need my cream."

The fire rose higher as if there was a forming giant in its midst. Every fresh log was a sacrifice to its greatness.

Malakey touched my elbow. I shifted away from him. A ping of hurt fluttered across his brow.

"You don't have to worry..." He placed his hands in his pocket.

I had plenty to worry about. My heart pounded and all I could do to keep from jumping out of my shoes was dig my nails into my arm. This action, repeated over the years, gave me more comfort than Malakey's words.

"Come on," He flicked his chin, leading me to an open wood log to sit. More Fireborns shuffled from their gathering spots and filled in the rest of the seats. I spread the cloth out on my lap, seeking solace in an added layer of fabric. With the help of the adults, the Fireborn kids passed out sticks, marsh-mallows, and chocolates. The adults passed down brown crackers.

The fire highlighted Malakey's face. "You have had s'mores before, right?"

"S'mores?" My brow furrowed.

"Oh, wow! It's a longstanding tradition in the Fire Kingdom. Our ancestors have passed it down since pre-Mortem Era. Let me show you." Malakey took his marsh-mallow and stuffed it on the stick. "See, once the marsh-mallow gets all nice and melted, you place it between the chocolate and the graham crackers." He slid the marsh-mallow off and onto the chocolate and crackers. White mixed with brown oozed out as he pressed the pieces together. He passed the treat over to me, and then licked his fingers.

I examined it. It looked delicious enough. I bit into it, and the burst of chocolaty goodness exploded on my tastebuds. "Oh, this is good!"

"See!" Malakey nudged my shoulder. "We have good things too," he said while blue flames twinkled in his irises.

"Okay, boys and girls. Theys and rainbows. Frogs and toads! I'm looking at you, Minks and Data."

Minks threw a middle finger. The children ooed and awed.

"You know it's true!" A tall, heavy man with a round belly stepped into view. He had a long white beard, deep olive skin as if he had spent most of his life toiling in the sun. While passing, he bent over and whispered loudly to me while pointing at Minks. "You got to be careful with that one. I heard he has three women pregnant in the camp already."

"Stop telling stories, old man!" Minks yelled. But I noticed three women giving each other the eye.

"I only tell what needs to be told, and boy, do I have a tale to tell you tonight!" He tucked his thumb in his suspenders and walked on. He didn't deviate from his path. He seemed like he would stroll directly into the campfire. Instead, he spun like a kite picked up by the wind and flew above the dancing flames. There, high in the sky, he crossed his legs and sat.

I dropped the s'more from my hand. Malakey caught it, a smile playing on his lips.

Minks called out, "Stop showing off in front of our guest, you old fart!"

The kids clapped and jumped as their parents attempted to return them to their seats.

"Only the best for todays honored guest!" The man's voice boomed as if he were speaking directly into a megaphone.

I turned to Malakey, "No one said there were Windborns here."

Malakey leaned in. "True, he is wind-gifted, but he is very much Fireborn. Four generations, I think."

"But, if he was wind gifted, he could have easily sought refuge amongst the Wind Kingdom."

Malakey, his lips mere inches from mine, "Sometimes, family isn't what you've been born into. It's what you create." His eyes bounced from one end of the camp to the other. "We are his family, and he is ours." He handed me back the s'more.

Malakey lingered.

Why does he linger?

I ripped my gaze from him and instead allowed the laughter from the Fireborns to fill the gap between us.

Minks had picked up a rock and threw it at the floating man, to which the floating man returned the rock with extreme speed. Minks took off running as the rock chased him, until he finally flipped over a water cooler, drenching himself from head to toe.

The camp roared with laughter. I even snickered at the spectacle.

"Now that the trash has taken itself out—" the old man cleared his throat. "—let me introduce myself to those who don't know me." He winked at me. "I am the legendary—"

Minks cut the man off. "Booo!" he yelled.

The old man flicked his chin. A rock lifted from the ground, soared past the camp, and clucked Minks upside his head. Minks officially went night-night.

"Is Minks going to be okay?" I whispered.

Malakey whispered back, "They go through this every night. To be honest, I think this is the only way Minks can get a good night's rest. He'll be out until the morning."

Data, with a few other men, marched over, lifted a sleeping Minks off the ground and toted him away.

The floating man clapped his hands. "As I was saying. I am the legendary Six Finger Jack and tonight, I have a story to tell..."

Jack grew a large wind ball filled with twigs and branches. His tongue poked out the side of his mouth as he formed the twigs into seven stick bodies. Six of them were large. The seventh was small, dressed in dirty reddish leaves.

"In the beginning..." Jack shifted the wind bubble. The inside went from pitch black to fire red, as he used the campfire to help tell the story.

"...the Great Consciousness, the one who binds us all, said let there be light. And thus, it was." The flames roared as the wind fanned the campfire. "The Great Consciousness chose seven guardians to watch over creation. Earth..." he said, lifting one stick figure, "Life, Reaper, Moon, Wind, Water and..." Jack raised the smallest stick figure wrapped in leaves. "Fire. Together, they were the protectors of humanity..." The scene inside the bubble shifted as the expansion of centuries formed throughout the years.

"... at first, the guardians helped mankind. Teaching them to sow seed, clean water, heal their wounds, read the stars, use the wind to soar across seas, create fire to keep warm, and when life is over, how to return to the one from which we came." Jack allowed the scene to unfold.

"One day, civilization no longer relied on guardians. They chose to lean into their own strength. Out of that strength rose great nations, kingdoms, and peoples. The seven guardians rested from their labors, allowing themselves to no longer take the form of flesh. Instead, they became the very elements themselves, morphing into the Seven Spirits. While the six of the Spirits slept, the seventh continued to look on." Jack laid the six Spirits to rest. The stick figure dressed in leaves was alone.

"The Fire Spirit never abandoned their duties, always reaching out when humanity needed them the most. Until one day, secret combinations clothed in greed and lust tricked the young Fire Spirit. This group trapped the Spirit with the sole desire to feed from their flames. Consuming this power, the organization used it to seize control over people, nations, and kingdoms. Chains and shackles were their legacy. But even that was not enough. Their hearts grew even colder with hatred. Their souls hungered to be gods!" Jack displayed the Fire Spirit caged while surrounded by figures that represented the voracious organization.

"This organization devised a plan to consume the life force of the Fire Spirit. In order to execute this power, a great sacrifice had to be made. The exchange of the souls of humanity for the rise to godhood. They wanted to remake the world in their own image. The Fire Spirit knew it had to be stopped. As the war grew thick with bloodshed and lives lost, the Fire Spirit was forced do the unthinkable."

Jack went quiet.

I leaned in, holding on to every word.

"The Fire Spirit had to consume the life force of all those who had fallen in order to break the cage which bound them. But the war and death were too great. As the Fire Spirit consumed, their sadness became rage, their flames licked the blue sky, causing the world to be cast into ash gray." The scene in the bubble went dark. When Jack moved again, a flicker of light shimmered.

"When humanity thought all was lost, an Erba rose from the ashes. She called forth help from the sleeping guardians. Through her blood, the remaining Six Spirits arose, saving humanity from the brink of extinction. The Six Spirits confronted the Fire Spirit, who was driven by temporary madness. Furious, the Six Spirits locked the Fire Spirit back into the same cage." Jack slammed a wooden lid on the Fire Spirit's cage.

"Imprisoned deep in the earth, never to be seen again—" Jack cast the Fire Spirit away. "—while cursing the bloodline of all those who willed the Fire Spirit's flames. Taking away their power for good."

The air bubble vanished. Remaining was a lone stick figure. The branches seemed to bend and twist as if the figure was dancing. "One day, a new Erba will rise and correct the wrongs of the past. Freeing the Fire Spirit from their cage and giving them a second chance in a world that does not believe in second chances."

The stick figure danced into the wind, then dropped into the fire. When it rose, the stick was in flames. Six Finger Jack held his hand out to me.

The camp was silent. All heads swiveled, their eyes like a six-ton weight, smashing me into the ground.

They couldn't know. No one should know. The pressure built within the pit of my belly. My legs shook, causing my entire body to vibrate. I dug my nails into my skin the moment a flicker of an itch rose to the surface.

Jack slowly descended, his feet touching the soil as light as a feather.

They were waiting for me. Listening, praying, and hoping that I was the Inherited One. I didn't even want to be the Queen of my own people, and now I must be some savior of theirs. *No!* Malakey rested a heavy hand on my bouncing leg, and I jumped.

"It's okay," he said. "We will protect you."

"No." I shook my head, "No, no, no, no..." I rose from my seat, yanking the blanket from my lap and throwing it onto Malakey. "I don't know what you think I am, but I am not this!" I said, pointing to the stick figure that had gone black from flames. The stick dropped into the fire. A wave of whispers launched at my ears.

"Princess Bellamy," Malakey reached for my arm. When

his touch met mine, electricity shot through both of us, causing me to snatch my hand away.

I retreated, damn near stumbling over the log. Their eyes were still on me, waiting, wondering, wishing.

"No," was all I could muster as I marched back to the cabin, wanting nothing more than to crawl into a ball on the tiny cot.

I was no one's savior, leader, or Queen. I was Bellamy, just Bellamy.

XLIV

"A tree bends until it breaks."
Proverb 42:42 from the Book of Face, Mortem Era.

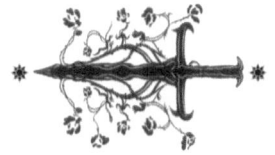

I TOSSED AND TURNED throughout the night. My mind and body were utterly exhausted. The sun's rays were peeking through the small cabin window. I sighed, getting dressed in my dried uniform to leave. When I opened the cabin door, Malakey stood, fist frozen in mid-knock. "What do you want?" I said, annoyed.

"I was coming to check on you. I thought you had left."

"I'm leaving now." I pushed past him.

Malakey ran behind me. "Princess."

"Prince." I whipped around to face him.

Malakey stepped back, running his hands through his hair. He let out an agitated laugh.

"You cannot run from your destiny."

"You ran from yours," I said, stomping to the earth wall.

Malakey ran in front of me, cutting off my path. "Bellamy, you are the Inherited One for a reason. The Spirits wouldn't have chosen you if they didn't think you could do it."

I kept walking, ignoring Malakey and the raging itch underneath my skin.

"There was an old saying, pre-Mortem Era, that went something like, 'The Spirits wouldn't give you more than you can bear.'" Malakey reached out and grabbed my arm, stopping me in my tracks. "You must bear this, Bellamy."

"I don't have to bear shit. Why don't you do it? What's wrong with you?" I shouted. The itch jolted from my arms to my legs. "Not everyone dreams of being a hero. If I could ask the Spirits to reconsider, I would. Give this curse to someone more deserving."

"What you have is not a curse. Don't you see that?"

"If anyone, and I mean anyone," I spoke through clenched teeth, "finds out, I will kill you." I pushed Malakey to the side, heading back to my side of camp.

"Not embracing who you are has already killed us."

I was done with everything. How could my family, friends, and all these people not see that asking a twenty-year-old to change the world was too much pressure? All my life, I've been told that I was nothing but a disappointment and now suddenly I was destined to become this Inherited One? My entire life has been built on one lie after another.

The Spirits, my parents, and people I barely knew supposedly knew what was best for me, what I should do, who I should be, and where I should go. But no one—no one!—had the decency to stop and ask me what I wanted. Malakey was wrong. This was too much to bear.

A massive amount of unanswered questions compiled in my head. Who was my brother? Was he still alive? What was this prophecy that killed the child before me? On top of that, there were threats of war from the Fire Kingdom, and laws that might affect all ungifted, Fireborn or not. Unrest built up around me. It was only a matter of time before it exploded. And then there was Everest. Engaged to a man that was worse than any Fire Kingdom leader. Just thinking about his stupid little face made me claw at my itching skin.

I couldn't breathe. My heart was pounding so hard that I could feel the beats right behind my eye. My head thudded. I squinted as the sun rose above. I reached my cabin, threw the door open, and froze.

Silvia was wrapped in Quande's arms. Her brown eyes were wide, she threw Quande's arms from around her and leaped out of bed, half-clothed.

"Bellamy, it's not what you think."

Quande, shirt off, pants unbuckled, hurried to toss on his shirt. I couldn't breathe.

"We just fell asleep here. I swear. Nothing happened."

I clenched my temples, my head pulsating. I stumbled backwards, my back hitting the cabin door.

Quande continued, "We were upset. We know you were out with the wessies the entire night. Hanging with them like they're your family. Do you know how that looks? You're going to be queen someday, and you're chumming it with the enemy?"

The air smelled like blackberries. *Blackberries.* I couldn't breathe.

The room was spinning, and my skin was exploding from

the inside out. I needed.... I needed air. I hurried outside. Extreme pressure, like hammers nailing both sides of my temples, intensified.

A hand grabbed hold of my shoulder, whipping me around.

"I'm sorry, Bee," Quande said. "You know how it is, right?"

I clenched my jaw. "No. Tell me how it is," I said, standing straighter.

Quande's eyes jolted from side to side. "Let's talk about this indoors. Not in front–"

"Tell me how it is!" I screamed. I could literally feel myself coming unhinged. It was like I was running right into a dead end with no desire to stop or correct course. I wanted to release it, her, me, *us,* the voice whispered into my mind. I needed to explode. I cocked my fist and slammed it right into Quande's nose. Quande staggered backwards. Silvia ran to his side. I balled my fist to throw another punch, but a wall of earth rose before me.

Zef, green eyes glowing.

A raspy laugh choked in my throat. Another soldier attempted to grab me from behind, instead. I twisted out of his grasp, yanked a dagger from his belt, and threw it right between Zef's eyes.

Zef stayed steady, a flick of his wrist. Another earth wall rose. The dagger planted perfectly where Zef's forehead should have been. The Blood Elite was too stunned. More soldiers spilled from their cabins. No one moved. They were waiting for orders.

When the earth wall gradually decreased, Zef's face hadn't changed, still as a statue.

Why did he show me those images? What was his point? It was his fault. I could have gone a lifetime never knowing.

"What else!" Tears dared to appear. "What else did they not tell me?" Another wave of hammering slammed my temples, and I winced. I steadied my stance as the world tilted.

Right as I reached for another dagger, the sirens blazed.

Soldiers jumped into action, flying past us as they marched to the source.

Quande, Silvia, and Zef were the only ones standing still amid blurred bodies.

A whisper, like the hiss of a snake, slithered in my mind.

These people were never your people.

A soldier sprinted to Zef. "It's the Fireborns, sir. We don't know how they got in, but we're surrounded." I took off running.

BARRELING THROUGH THE earth wall separating the Fireborn camp from ours, a few Fireborns stumbled their way to our side of the camp. Their faces were filled with dust, blood at their temples, clothes ripped, and nose bleeding. I stopped a woman.

"What's happening?"

She was dazed, her eyes barely focusing. "They came for us... they always come for us," was all she said.

"Go, get to safety," I said, releasing her to run through the earth wall. When I finally exited, a familiar voice flooded my ear.

"Well, well, well... that's the highborn I was telling you about, Daddy," Boom said, a lollipop in her hand.

They had the Fireborns in a circle on their knees. I searched the crowd for Malakey, but he was nowhere to be found.

"And look, Daddy. There are more Earthborns!" Boom pointed with her lolly. I looked to my right and there stood Zef with his students, emerald-green eyes blazing.

"We hit the jackpot, Daddy! Two, four, six, eight, ten green eyes! Along with a camp of wanted Fireborns. How much do you think we gon' get, Daddy? How much, how much, how much?" Boom cheered.

A man that stood at least six foot five with deep purple hair appeared. "You did a great job, my Boomy," he said, kissing her on the forehead. "Mother will be so proud. Let me handle it from here."

There were less than thirty-two Blood Elite. I quickly counted the group of mercenaries. There had to be about fifty.

Zef stepped forward, hands behind his back. "State your business."

"Hello," the man said, "I am Wallay Davient and this group standing before you are the Davient Mercenaries. But for you, handsome, you can call me daddy."

Boom giggled, popping the lolly into her mouth.

Zef remained calm. "Sir Wallay Davient. What is the meaning of your trespassing?"

Wallay clicked his teeth. "As you can see..." Wallay encouraged Zef to speak his name.

Zef remained silent.

"As you can see, handsome. We are here to collect the Fire Kingdom's possessions."

"On whose orders?"

"Oh," Wallay snapped, holding up his palm. Another mercenary slammed a rolled piece of paper into his hand. "On the orders of King Dricon, Fire Kingdom." Wallay unrolled the piece of paper, revealing a large red stamp of the Fire Kingdom's approval.

"Fire Kingdom has no right to collect those that have been permitted protection from the Reaper Kingdom."

Wallay rolled the paper and passed it to someone behind

him. "See, we beg to differ. It is absolutely our right to obtain stolen goods, regardless of who is protecting it."

"If we are speaking about objects and personal goods," Zef retorted, "then you are correct."

"These are personal goods. Under the Fire Kingdom's law, slaves are objects. Some are priced lower than cattle. It would be in your best judgment, Earthborn, to let us take what is rightfully the Fire Kingdom's or else."

Zef's fingers twitched. "Or else what?"

Wallay shrugged. "I hoped that a cute, intelligent face like yours would see reason, and we would not have to discuss it further." Wallay stepped forward. "I suggest you return the remaining Fireborns. Once we collect all that is due, we will get out of your hair."

"We decline your request. If the Fire Kingdom wants to protest our decision, they would need to obtain a hearing with the Counsel of Amalgamation. Until then, leave."

Wallay clicked his tongue. "No, no, no. See, we can't do that, boss man. That would be a slap in the face to the Fire Kingdom and a stain to our reputable name. See, we have never taken on a mission that wasn't completed, and we sure as hell won't start now." Wallay snapped his fingers. "Bring me the babe."

A mercenary clicked his boots and disappeared. He then reappeared with a screaming, dark-haired woman.

My heart dropped. *Tapestry.*

The mother's screams were blood curdling. The mercenary yanked the crying babe from her arms, handing the child over to Wallay.

Wallay grabbed the baby, allowing the blanket to fall away. He held the baby at her feet, dangling her into the air like a dead fish.

"Let's make a deal," he said. "Usually, the younger they are, the higher they cost, but since this was born on the outside of the contract, you can have it." Wallay swung the baby back and forth as if he was going to toss her into the air.

The baby's mother begged, snot and tears entwined as she groveled on her knees. Wallay danced in place like this was a game to him.

I bit my bottom lip. Blood squirted on my tongue. My fist clenched, my skin was ablaze, and my head was pounding. I ignored all of that.

If he hurts that child, I swear to the Spirits, he will fucking pay.

Wallay turned the screaming baby right side up, tucking her like a ball underneath his arms. "We have a deal?"

"Fuck your deal," I spat, unable to hold my tongue.

Wallay's mouth flew open. "Oh... and you must be Bellamy. My princess has told me all about you." He took his free arm and threw it around Boom. "She is gorgeous. Could be worth more whole than partial." Wallay examined me.

My blood boiled.

Zef cleared his throat, calling Wallay's attention back to him. "Unfortunately, you have no rights here. You broke into a private camp, harassed our guests under our protection, and threatened the life of our people. Leave now, before it is too late."

Wallay's smile dropped.

The dark-haired woman reached for her baby. Wallay backhanded her to the ground.

I was about to jump into action when a hand grabbed my shoulder, pinning it into place. Quande was at my side, dagger in hand. Fia, Rwju, the twins, as well as Sarue and Venus, all surrounded me. Their faces twisted in fury.

Wallay passed the babe to a mercenary, then wiped his hand clean with an extra piece of fabric wrapped around his waist.

"Listen," he said, holding his hand out. "We have started on the wrong foot. Don't you think? Let's just reel it back a little and think about what might happen here." Wallay pointed to the Fireborns, who were on their knees. The men were face down on the ground, mercenaries held their boots on their necks.

Wallay continued, "Are you really going to fight over wessies? Come on, they mean nothing to no one. They're pointless. Last chance, hand over all the wessies, and we will go about our business, there's no need for any bloodshed."

Boom stomped her feet. "What about her, Daddy?" She poked out her bottom lip.

"All things in time, sweety," Wallay said.

Zef turned over his shoulder to glance at me. I nodded.

He nodded back. Shimmers of gold sparkled in his irises.

Zef faced Wallay, "Then I guess, it's 'or else'..."

Wallay laughed, "And here I thought Earthborns were peaceful people. Not wanting to get into war and battles and such. Huh, I guess one learns something new every day." Wallay turned around. "Oh, by the way. A Fireborn... what was his name, princess?"

Boom popped the lolly out of her mouth, her squeaky voice shouted, "Bunko!"

"That's right. All wessies look alike. Sir Bunko sends his regards." Wallay grabbed Boom's hand. She took it, skipping behind him.

"Till next time!" she said, as she and Wallay disappeared into the mercenaries.

There was a loud explosion followed by an earth-shattering

shake. The trees rocked as if they were being yanked from their roots. A mass of griffes flew out of the trees, damn near blocking the sun.

Another explosion, the trees separated in the middle.

Then the sky went gray.

XLV

"Those who choose to rise will never fall."
Proverb 99:00 from the Book of Face, Mortem Era.

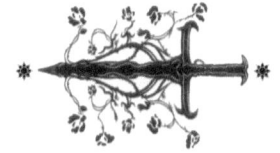

A FLEET OF METAL BEASTS BURST THROUGH THE PINES. Their wingspan exceeded that of the griffes by two times. They had hooked talons and black metal for eyes. Following the metal birds were massive Kodiak bears ripping through the ground. They were half-fur and the other half-mechanics. Rearing on its hind legs, it stood over ten feet tall.

More mercenaries flooded the camp. They were like spiders, crawling out of every hole. Their teeth were sharp razors, their faces painted white. One of the white faces jumped onto a nearby Fireborn who didn't think to look up as he ran. It took less than one second before the mercenaries' fangs bit into the neck of the Fireborn, blood spurting out onto the earth.

"Bellamy!" Quande shouted over the roar of the bears. He threw me an axe and a belt of daggers. "Get the unarmed to the other side of the camp!" Quande leaped onto a griffe and took off into the sky.

I snapped into motion. I grabbed a woman holding on to a child. The big metal bird attempted to swoop and pluck the child from the mother's arms. I took the axe, swinging it with the full force of my body. The axe connected to the metal leg with a clash. But the leg barely received any damage. Its claws scratched the child, down their spine, leaving a gaping wound. The kid hollered in pain. We did not have the time to pause. I snatched the child and placed them into my arms, shouting for the woman to follow.

The Blood Elite were enforcing the barrier wall. I handed the child to a soldier. The woman thanked me with tears in her eyes. I swallowed the "don't thank me yet" into my throat.

I yelled to a soldier, "Are we sure the other side will not be breached?"

"We can't be sure, princess. We are doing what we can. As of right now, getting people to the other side is the best plan."

I nodded, turning around to head to the eye of the camp.

A soldier shouted, "Princess, we need to get you to safety. This is far too dangerous."

My skin was inflamed. "Then I better get them before they get me." I sprinted toward the center of the camp to free Fireborns trapped under a fallen cabin.

A bear confronted me on all fours, stopping me in my tracks. I ran left, and the beast charged. I doubled back, hooking my fingers into its metal components and hurled myself onto its back. The bear bucked, rising on its hind legs.

This gave me the opportunity to examine the creature. The bear's mechanical parts weren't sophisticated. It was as if someone threw parts on an animal and expected it to function. I took out my axe and slammed the sharp end into the wires on its neck. It roared. The left side of its body completely shut off. The bear glitched, slamming face first into the ground.

The force of impact propelled me a few feet in front of the creature. The bear whimpered. It tried to stand, but its paws slid underneath itself. The mechanical parts were too heavy to lift without help from the hydraulics. I picked my axe up from the ground, limping over to the bear.

With one glossy black eye, the bear looked at me, then bowed its head. The gesture took me aback. The creature wanted to die. It was asking for it.

Loud screams and shouts filled the air. I needed to move. I lifted the axe and brought it over the bear's neck in one swift motion. The bear's eyes blinked off.

What type of people would do this? I stumbled away, trying to regain my composure. One after one, bodies fell, blood covering the earth like red paint on a brown canvas.

A mercenary sliced open a Fireborn's neck. The Fireborn gurgled, reaching for his throat as if his hands could somehow put the blood back into its proper place. As if it could stop his life force from spilling out of his body. The Fireborn dropped to his knees, his hands going limp at his side. The mercenary laughed, kicking the man over with his foot, like the life he took was nothing.

My hand gripped the axe handle, and I charged right into the insane bastard. The mercenary didn't even see me coming. When he looked up, a smile on his face, I removed his head from his shoulders. Even after his head tumbled to the ground, his smile remained.

They must all die. A voice whispered into my mind. *Burn them all!*

Quickening my pace, I dropped every mercenary my axe encountered. I freed the Fireborns from the cabin right as more mercenaries leaped from the trees and into the camp.

I readied my axe. Bones snapped, skulls crunched, my clothes drenched in fresh blood. I only had one goal, one plan. Even if it killed me, I was going to save them.

A caw-caw screeched above me. I rolled out of the way as a sharp claw barely missed my side. Another metal bird dove from behind me. I rolled again, the bird nearly catching me. Two birds flew in unison, circling around me like prey. One on my left and the other on my right. The creatures dove again, their claws clenching and unclenching.

A body was thrown into me, knocking my breath out of my chest, just as the two birds collided with each other. Entangled metal on metal created a deafening crash. The birds fought to separate, but to no avail. The creatures flew in tandem into the nearest trees, creating an explosion of flames. Above, some of the B.E. were hopping from the backs of griffes to the mechanical birds, severing the birds' necks, and leaping back onto the griffes. They had to be Windborns to move that fast. Their faces were nothing but a blur.

"You okay?" Malakey said, blood staining his face.

"Is that yours?" I said, my hands flying to his cheek.

"No. Someone else's. Come on," he said, pulling me to my feet.

White painted faces surrounded us. Their sharp teeth were drenched in blood. Malakey put his back to mine.

I winced. "You think you can handle them?"

"You think you can?" he retorted.

"If I know how to do anything, I know how to fuck and fight," I wheezed through heavy breaths.

"Even in the face of death, you somehow find a way to be cocky." I heard the smile through Malakey's words.

I twisted the axe in my hand and cracked my neck. "Let's go."

We sent the white painted faces flying. Intimidating, yes. An overwhelming number of them, also yes. But power level? Weak as a pinch on the arm.

Malakey and I spun circles around the group until they finally retreated, searching for easier prey. One hissed at me, its gums blackened like rot. It attempted to turn away, but my axe quickly connected to its skull. Its body hit the ground and I yanked my axe out of its forehead. The crunch from the bone was like nothing I've ever heard before.

There was no time to stop. Yet, I was constantly losing energy, as if I took a bunch of sugar and was crashing. My feet dragged into the wet mud. I slipped, my head pounding. Quande landed his griffe beside us and rushed to my side. Malakey was attempting to keep me on my feet as the world spun.

"You need to get out of here," Quande said. A painted white face leaped into the air. Quande whipped out a dagger, planting it right between the man's eyes like a red target.

Malakey grabbed me, throwing my arm over the back of his neck.

Quande tried to shake me off Malakey. "I got her. We don't need your help," he said through labored breaths.

Even amongst all this carnage, Quande saw the Redux as enemies?

I pushed Quande away. "No, we don't need your help," I said, trying not to pass out from blurred vision. A wave of hurt, anger, jealousy, maybe all three, flexed in Quande's features.

What would stop Quande from killing Malakey right here, right now? He would be another Fireborn, lost in a bloody attack.

Quande stepped toward Malakey, but I positioned my body to cover him.

"Quande, are you doing this right now? Look around you!" I said through clenched teeth.

Quande's jaw flexed, hand gripped around the handle of his dagger.

A painted white face shot out of the corner of Quande's eyes. Without even blinking, he shoved the dagger into the mercenary's neck and yanked it out. Blood spattered the side of Quande's face. "Get her out of here," he said to Malakey. He then grabbed hold to the side of a mechanical bear and yanked himself on its back.

Another invisible hammer slammed into my temples. I recoiled, almost losing my balance.

Malakey grabbed my waist. "We are almost there. Stay with me." A metal bird dove, yanking Malakey from my side. I hit the ground. My insides felt like millions of ants eating their way into my skin. I dug my nails deep into my arms. Another metal bird dove; its talons sunk deep into my thigh. It dragged me across the campground. I reached for my axe at my hip. The bird jerked, causing me to lose my grip on the handle. The beast slammed me into broken wood and collapsed cabins.

I couldn't tell if there was one bird or three. My vision was fading. The beast lifted me off the ground. It flew over a large red oak; the branches reached for the bird. Vines, leaves, more branches all wrapped around the metal bird's wings and body, halting it in midair. The bird screeched, the red oak snapping the wings off a little by little. Finally, the metal bird let go of my leg and I fell to the earth. The tree branches plucked me right out of the sky, embracing me like a newborn babe. It eased me to the ground to a patch of lush grass.

When I rolled over expecting to see Zef, I quickly realized it wasn't Zef, but one of his students. Blood dripped from his nose and mouth. His brown skin was pale, as if he was just holding on. He formed his lips to speak to me, but a spear went through his neck. Blood burbled from his mouth in chunks. Redder than the fallen leaves. I didn't even know his name.

The mercenary screamed out a war shout, pounding his fist to his chest. As he was aiming for me next, I heard a crunch before the painted white face crumbled to the ground. Emerging from behind him was Big Fella.

Big Fella's face was burned but healed. The skin warped around his nose and his mouth appeared charred with extra flaps of skin. He favored his left side; his right side appeared to be petrified. He dragged his right foot into the soil.

"Not happy to see me?" He dragged himself to me. "I'm happy to see you." His foot scraped against a pile of leaves. "Of course, I wanted to meet you again in my best condition, but as you can see, your friend did a number on me."

One step, drag. One step, drag. He spoke with the left side of his mouth, using his left hand for emphasis.

"See, the plan was... to hunt you down, kill everyone you love, and then bring you back to our home and do the unimaginable, one excruciating second at a time. But neither of us could predict that you were a part of the fearsome Blood Elite! If I knew I had a celebrity in the midst, I would have dressed better for the occasion." One step, drag. One step, drag.

I moved my hands across my waist, searching for any remaining weapons. There were none. I pushed myself up from the ground, a jolt of pain from my torn leg rocked every nerve in my system. The pain was like knives stabbing me along my spine.

Big Fella threw himself on top of me. His rubbery skin smashed against the side of my face. "I can still smell you," he whispered in my ear, burying his nose into my hair.

I grabbed a handful of dirt into my palms and flung it into his eyes. He yelped, giving me enough room to slam my fist into his nose. I flipped over onto my stomach, crawling away as swiftly as I could. Big Fella recovered, dropping his weight back on top of me, pinning me to the ground. The air shot out of my lungs as I strained to inhale. Big Fella shifted his weight, applying pressure to my torn leg. I screamed. His one good hand cupped my mouth.

"That's right. Scream for me, beautiful." He crunched my leg. I bit into my tongue. He added more pressure, twisting the wound on my leg like a wrung-out towel. He yelled, "Scream!"

I refused to give him the satisfaction.

A fist crashed into the back of my head. My head bounced on the earth until I saw a burst of stars. Big Fella grabbed a chunk of my hair, forcing me to focus.

We were hidden under the cover of the woods amongst falling branches and bushes. The entire camp was on fire. The Blood Elite had stopped helping the Fireborns to the other side of the camp and had officially closed the earth wall. Only a few of the Blood Elite remained. Quande, surrounded by dozens of mechanical Kodiak bears. Rwju, Fia, and the twins, their manifestation weakening. They had resorted to attacking with weapons implanted in fallen enemies and friends. Sarue and Venus, their hands wrapped around four Fireborns, their shadow spilling over the small group, and then they vanished.

More Fireborns were being ripped into pieces as mechanical birds and bears spilled in from the breach. Every cabin was on fire, including the forest behind it.

Rubbery skin slid alongside my ear. "We are winning." Big Fella straddled me, yanking my hair so tight that he could easily snap my neck. "See, I was supposed to bring you to Boom. Let her play with you. But I have other plans. I want you to watch while everything you love burns, just like I had to watch my face melt away!"

"You know..." I gurgled, "I wasn't the one who burned you."

Big Fella slammed my head into the ground.

"Oh, I know. Trust me. We already have plans for Key Dricon," Big Fella whispered into my ear. His hot spit sprayed my eardrums. "When we return him to his Father, he will never see the light of day again." Big Fella laughed, angling my head to watch bodies fall to the earth.

My blood boiled. I frantically searched for Malakey. Four mercenaries had him pinned on his knees. Malakey reached for the necklace, but before he could bring the liquid to his mouth, a mercenary sliced a blade across his chest. The necklace flew out of his hand as his body fell backwards.

No!

The mercenaries high-fived each other. Then divided into pairs. Two lifted Malakey's arms and the other two lifted his legs. Quande was nearby, slicing through the mechanical bears. As he turned to throw a dagger, a mercenary with a painted white face ran a sword through his stomach.

My eyes grew wide as Quande tumbled to his knees. Sarue and Venus appeared. Venus killed the white-faced mercenary where he stood. Sarue and Venus clasped their hands together, their shadow covering Quande as they all disappeared.

Sprinting toward the mercenaries carrying Malakey was Diyo. His small fist pounded at the legs of one mercenary that held Malakey by his feet. The mercenary backhanded Diyo to the ground and continued dragging Malakey.

Stay down, Diyo. Please! Stay down!

Diyo did not stay down. He picked up a sword that looked to weigh more than him. With all his might, Diyo slashed the back of the mercenary's leg. The man shouted, dropping Malakey's leg. The other mercenaries chuckled, releasing Malakey to the ground. Malakey did not move.

The mercenary that was slashed gripped the back of his leg. He turned around to face the boy.

Run, Diyo. Run!

All bones, and sharp edges, Diyo gripped the sword, standing his ground. The mercenary yanked a sword from his belt and charged at the boy. Diyo swung, but the mercenary flicked the sword out of his hand as if he swatted an annoying fly. With lightning speed, the mercenary ran his sword through the boy. The sword came out the other side of the kid as if it impaled him at the stake. The mercenary shook his sword, but the blade held deep into the young boy's ribs. The mercenary lashed out with his foot, kicking Diyo's lifeless body loose from his blade. Diyo's still body hit the earth.

I dug my hand into the soil and cried out in pain.

Big Fella held my head straight, slapping me across my face whenever I shut my eyes. There was so much innocent blood spilled onto the earth. They called for me. Their cries begged for justice, for vengeance. I could feel the earth pulsating underneath me as voices filled my head.

Big Fella slapped me across the face, bloodshot from my mouth.

"Watch!" He ripped my eyelids open.

Teka, little gap-tooth Teka, ran to Diyo's side. She cradled his head into her lap, her body racked by uncontrollable tears.

No, no, no, please Teka. Run!

Before the mercenaries picked up Malakey again, they nodded to the young girl. One man grabbed his belt and read-justed, flicking his chin. Two mercenaries, two grown-ass men, yanked Teka by her hair and grabbed onto her kicking legs.

Are you going to continue to sit and watch while evil wins?
A voice flooded my mind.

Call forth your power!

The men laughed while Teka bit and scratched. They dropped her. She hurriedly crawled back to Diyo's lifeless body. One mercenary snatched her back while another kicked Diyo's body a foot away from her.

You are not helpless, Bellamy! Call forth your power. Help your people! Help Teka.

My mind went completely silent. I could no longer hear the screams, the slicing, the fighting. The only thing I could hear was my heart pounding. I no longer felt pain or the weight of grief, but the spark of vengeance.

Show them who we are!

I held out my hand to Teka as a mercenary boot kicked her in the stomach.

"Flames!"

An inferno of orange and red barreled toward me in a hurricane of light and glory.

I didn't know when Big Fella rose from my back nor when he attempted to run away.

"Burn him," I commanded, and the flames obeyed.

Who are you? The voice of the red woman grew louder. *Who are you!*

My bones snapped then mended together as if being welded by the eye of a furnace. My flesh burned away, revealing dark scales with red zig zagged lines that ran the length of me. I arose from the ground, my clothes melting away while fire became my shield and protection. They covered me like a cloak of righteousness.

"I am the dragon, the chosen vessel of the Fire Spirit."

You are mine.

"I am yours." I stepped out of the forest like an exploding

volcano, scorching every beast and creature that dared to cross me. Every painted white face, every mercenary became ash. I didn't know if I flew or walked, nor did I care. I told the flames who I wanted, and they fetched the four mercenaries like fire hounds, biting into the side of their necks. They were dust before a drop of their blood fell to the earth.

Teka, sitting on her bottom, looked up at me in awe. Fire danced in her black pupils. She held out her hands to me as if she wanted me to pick her up. She was not afraid. I lifted her into my arms, red flames surrounding her small frame.

My chosen cannot be burned, the voice confirmed.

"Princess," Teka whispered. "You're so warm."

I held her close. When I turned, the camp was frozen. The remaining mercenaries had vanished, leaving nothing but the Blood Elite and Fireborns. I tightened my grip around Teka, whose breath was shallow but steady. The flames were dying as I made my way to the earth wall.

"Erba," the Fireborns called.

As I passed, they fell to their knees and bowed their faces to the ground. The Blood Elite watched with mouths open, weapons dropping from their hands. When I arrived at the earth wall, a section slid open. Zef waited on the other side. I deposited Teka in his arms, my body racked with shakes. My mind thinking of a bleeding Malakey face down in the soil.

"Help them," I said, before I collapsed to the earth.

XLVI

"Journeys in life are made by multiple beginnings, but only one ending."
Proverb 1:00 from the Book of Face, Mortem Era.

I AWOKE TO THE SMELL OF ANTISEPTICS. My vision was clear as I stared at the white ceiling. The only cabin in the entire camp that had a white ceiling was the infirmary. I pushed myself to a sitting position, but stab-like pressure from my belly forced me to lie back down.

"Don't rise too quickly," Doctor Axiom said. "You've been

out for a few days." Doctor Axiom flashed a small light into my eyes.

I squinted.

The doctor slid the light into their front pocket. "You suffered from head trauma, broken ribs, legs, and a dislocated arm. On top of that, you were on fire, which I'm sure didn't assist in your recovery time."

I cringed, dread overtaking my senses.

Doctor Axiom clicked a pen, then clicked it again. "Despite the literal fire your body has gone through, you're on track for a full recovery. I would contribute that much to myself." Click, click, click.

"But I cannot. Yes, I set the bone, cleaned the wounds, bound you all together, but before I could use my gift to heal you..." Click, click, click. "You had already begun to heal yourself." Click, click, click.

"Which is rather odd. Because the type of healing your body is doing threads together much like a Reaperborn, but there's a shimmer in your blood much like a Lifeborn..." Click, click, click.

"But there's something else strange about your healing capabilities. I've never seen anything like it before. I would have to do more tests, maybe some experiments..."

Click, click...

"You won't be doing any of that."

My neck almost snapped when I heard the voice entering the infirmary's door.

"Daddy." Tears welled in my eyes as he ran to me. Doctor Axiom moved out of the way to make room. Father threw his arms around me, pushing my tangled hair out of my face.

"I'm so sorry I wasn't there, Beta. I should have never left you."

I cried into my father's chest, ignoring the pain that rippled at my side anytime I moved. "I'm here now. Don't worry."

Click.

"Excuse me, General. Not to interrupt, but as you have now heard, I'm sure, this patient was on fire and did not burn."

"You mean my daughter?"

"Well, yes, of course. But she is still under my care, and I think I should run some tests on her to figure out what is the root of this manifestation."

"You will do no such thing."

"But, sir. Medically speaking, this patient...excuse me, your daughter, is an *abnormality*. If not clinically researched, there's no clear result as to what damage this type of gift can cause to the longevity of her system. Just by my examination, her body will not be able to maintain the stabilization of this manifestation. It's as if the gift, or gifts, I should add, are using the stored fats and nutrients to depletion."

Father laid my head onto the pillow.

"Then she will eat more," he said to the doctor while detangling the ends of my hair.

Click, click, click, click...

"It's just not enough for her to eat more, sir. It's vital that we begin the test we need in order to pinpoint the exact nutrient her manifestation is absorbing or else every time she uses her manifestation she will, in lack of better words, burn from the inside out. No one has ever witnessed a fire manifestation in the last 600 years. We need more tests."

Father's eyebrows wrinkled. I was too tired to process the gravity of Doctor Axiom's words. I wasn't sure if my brain was lagging or if Doctor Axiom was speaking at the speed of two times the normal sound. Father checked my arms, his calloused fingers running over the bandages. He raised my shirt to check my side, then the large wound on my thigh.

"She seems to heal fine. Quicker than..." Father paused, his deep brown eyes staring at the wound on my leg.

If I could concentrate, I could feel the fresh wound sewing itself together almost like a zipper.

"... she's healing quicker than a Reaperborn."

"Exactly." Doctor Axiom clicked their pin rapidly. "It is my hypothesis that the only reason this... fire manifestation hasn't burned her from the inside out is because she has other gifts or manifestations developing at the exact same time. One of them is healing. Only gifted to Lifeborns and Reaperborns. And even then, Reaperborn's self-healing gifts are mended together by their shadow. Whereas Lifeborns can only heal others by threads of light..." Click, click, click.

"... this..." Doctor Axiom shifted toward the bed, his pen pointed at my thigh. "This is something else entirely. Still, it behooves you, General, to allow me to proceed with my first round of testing as soon as possible. In the last three days she has been sleeping, she has already lost six pounds. If she drops any more weight, it can get deadly."

"Daddy?" My voice was small. I almost hated how I reverted to being a child whenever my father was around. Whenever things were too tough to handle or when I needed the weight off my shoulders, he had always come to my rescue. What should we do? How should we handle this? Questions collided together in my mind, but the only word I could summon was, "Daddy?"

As if reading my thoughts, Father leaned down and kissed my forehead. "Don't worry, Beta. I have you." He then rose to his feet to face the doctor. "As of right now, she needs to heal. Focus on giving her nutrients and calories—"

"But General. This is historical. Groundbreaking. We can't just—"

The infirmary door cracked open. In walked Quande and

Silvia. Father nodded to the pair, then took Doctor Axiom to the far side of the infirmary. Doctor Axiom pleaded their case until I could no longer hear their voices.

Quande, dagger in his hand, the sharp end pressing into one of his fingers, leaned against a nearby wall. He was in his usual army black, not a bandage or any damage could be seen.

"You were stabbed," I said, licking my tongue across my dry lips.

Quande shrugged. He lifted his shirt to reveal a large bandage taped on the side of his gut. He tucked his shirt back into his pants. "The cut was clean. My shadow did the rest."

Silvia reached for the pitcher of water sitting next to my bed. She poured the water into a cup and handed it to me. My fingers brushed alongside hers and she shot her arm back, her eyes flickering to Quande.

The soft smile I had when I first saw her faded into a hard line. She was dressed in white with a white hair wrap. She had a white line going from the top of her forehead to the base of her chin. A sign Earthborns wore when they were in deep fasting or mourning.

"Why are you here?" I rubbed my fingers together, blocking out the sensation of Silvia's skin.

"When were you going to tell me?" Quande asked, dagger twirling.

"Going to tell you what?" I sipped some water, resting the cup in my palm.

"That you're one of them."

I chuckled. "A Fireborn? Last time I checked, my father is the great Reaperborn General, Agrim Tagore, and my mother, Oyame Abiola, came from the high noble lineage of the first Earthborns. You tell me, when did I become one of them?"

Quande shifted, his dagger halted.

"Was it when I was born? When we grew up together in

the palace? When I hit my first blood? When exactly did I turn Fireborn because if you have that answer, I would love to know."

"I'm not judging you."

"Oh, it seems like you are."

"I'm just saying you could have told us. You didn't have to hide it."

"But could I really? I mean, with your hatred of Fireborns, you didn't make an environment for me to happily come out. So, what now? You know what I am and what I can do."

Quande stepped backwards, his fist grabbing tightly on the handle of his dagger.

Silvia glanced at Quande, then back to me, "Bellamy, we just feel—"

"We?" I sneered. "When did the two of you become, we? Was it when I caught the two of you in our bed, or has it been longer than that?" The smell of blackberries wafted to my nose. I should have put two and two together.

Silvia drew in her lips, glancing downwards.

"Don't yell at her, Bee," Quande stepped in. "It's not what you think. Nothing happened between us."

"Yet it seems like something is happening now." I chuckled. "It's wild because I really thought you loved me. Despite you spying on me, hiding things from me, I still thought we could really make things work. That you would one day be mine. I loved you, Silvia. Do you understand? I loved you." I whispered underneath my breath.

"Bee, don't be like that." Quande slipped his dagger into its holder at this waist.

"How else should I be? I'm fucking tired, Quande!"

The infirmary went quiet. I heard the faint click, click, click of a distant pen. Footsteps rushed toward me. A tiny itch grew in my palm, and I bit down on my lip.

The infirmary door cracked open again and the smell of forest greens flooded the room.

Zef.

Doctor Axiom pushed Quande and Silvia away from the bed as they hooked a monitor to my chest. As soon as the sticky round end touched my skin, the monitor went haywire. The line rose and fell, the beeping rapidly getting faster. I was crowded, cornered, and surrounded.

I needed to breathe.

Doctor Axiom's pen dropped from their fingers and onto the bed. The monitor went from beeping rapidly until it hit an inclining capacity of one continuous high-pitched sound. Everyone covered their ears, jumping back from the monitor.

Doctor Axiom turned to my father. "I-I... this hasn't happened before. I-I," they tried to explain.

Zef stepped forward, shifting the doctor to the side. Zef leaned in until his lips brushed the tip of my ear. He whispered a message, and my eyes went wide.

"Your brother is alive, and he needs you to survive. Your Mother knows where he's hidden." He yanked the wire from my chest, and the monitor fell silent.

Emerald-green eyes met mine as the water in my cup boiled over.

"General," I said, without turning my gaze from Zef. "It's time to go home."

About the Author

"Have the audacity to have faith in yourself. When no one else is willing to defend you, have the courage to stand. When silenced, have the determination to speak up. Write what no one else can with the conviction that you have within. Finally, rest. This is something your ancestors could only hope for.
Allow them to rest in you."

E.A. Noble

E.A. NOBLE is a dark fantasy and gothic lit writer. She was raised in Jackson, Mississippi, and was encouraged to dream by her grandmothers. They compelled her to read, write, and keep a journal. Poetry was E.A.'s first love since it gave her the freedom to express herself in a way that no other activity could.

Since then, E.A.'s pen has changed into her keyboard, and her journals into worlds without end. She is now listening to the advice of her ancestors as she dares—for the first time in her life—to share her talents with the world.
If you would like to keep in touch, follow her @authoreanoble

Link Tree: https://linktr.ee/eanoble
Website: theeajournal.me

Book Two of the Mortem Era Series is Coming Soon!

Until then, check out *Supersized Bubble*, a superhero fiction about fat women gaining superpowers by eating bubblegum while taking down a multimillion-dollar corporation. Found Family, Fat women heroes, protected, and fighting for the people they love.

Call To Action

Reviews are AMAZING!

Fanart is the way to my heart! Please tag me in all your fanart.
I wholeheartedly support libraries and the profound impact
they have on their communities. I kindly ask for your assistance
in getting "When Blood Meets Earth" on their shelves, so it can
be accessible to all.
Thank you.
E.A. Noble